Dom

ALLIANCE BOOK THREE

S. J. TILLY

Relatives are the people we're born with.
Family are the people we chose to keep around.

Prologue
VAL (AGE 9)

It seems strange that so many people, even when they aren't talking, can make so much noise.

Heels clicking on the polished wood floors. Whispered *excuse me*s. The swooshing of skirts.

My fingers tangle in my black skirt.

Mom said she bought it new for me, but I know she didn't. It had *that* smell, the one clothes have when they come from that big store filled with other people's old stuff. But I shook it out a bunch. And I think I got the smell out. Mostly, at least.

I squeeze the fabric tighter.

Most of the people here are adults, and I know they dress differently than kids, but I still feel... out of place. Like I don't belong here. But that's stupid because—

"Valentine," Mom hisses, keeping her voice quiet.

I glance down and realize I've accidentally pulled my skirt up over my knees. I can sense her movement before I see it and manage to jerk my arm away just in time to avoid one of her pinches.

I don't dare look up at her. I know she'll be narrowing her eyes at me in that way she does. So I quickly push my skirt back into place and sit up straighter, folding my hands in my lap.

The pew is hard underneath my butt, and I have to fight the urge to wiggle.

This is my first funeral.

The church is huge. Like so much bigger than any place I've ever been in. And it looks just like it does in movies. The super high ceiling and colorful windows. The people dressed all in black with their murmured voices. The fancy floral arrangements on either side of the shiny casket. And the giant portrait of Dad framed in swirly gold.

I'm old enough to understand what's going on, what death is. And it looks just like I imagined it would. Except I don't know why my mom and I are sitting way back here. Shouldn't we be up front? In the first row? Isn't that where family is supposed to sit? And even though Dad didn't live with us—because he was a busy businessman—we're still family. He always told me we were family.

My throat tightens, and I drop my eyes away from Dad's smiling face and stare at my hands. My knuckles turn a whitish color as I squeeze my fingers together.

I want to ask Mom if we can move up a few rows, but the spots are already full. And she's been extra mean lately, so asking her questions now seems like a bad idea.

I remember one of my teachers telling us that everyone deals with emotions in different ways. But I don't know that she's sad about Dad, because she hasn't cried at all.

Not like me.

I miss Dad. It's been months since I've seen him. And last time...

Something in my chest twists as I think of it.

Last time, when Mom was still asleep, he made me a peanut butter sandwich for breakfast. It was good. And he made one for himself and sat with me at the little table. And when we were halfway done, I asked Dad if I could live with him.

Mom would be mad if she heard me say it, so I whispered it.

It took all my courage. But Dad loved me. He always said so.

Except, when I asked him, the smile on his mouth slipped away.

The look on his face made my heart hurt. So I scooted my chair closer to his, and even more quietly, I said, "*Please.*"

A small whimper catches in my chest as I remember the way he shook his head.

I wanted him to say yes so badly.

I was sure if I found the time to ask him, he'd say yes.

Because he said he loved me.

But he didn't say yes.

He just shook his head.

Tears start to fill my eyes all over again, and I'm too busy blinking them away to notice the next pinch aimed at the soft spot on the back of my arm.

I jump and press my lips together *hard,* trapping in the cry that wants to escape.

I will the stinging ache to go away and stare straight ahead, looking at Dad's photo.

We have the same hair color. His had gray in it, but he always told me mine was just like his when he was younger. The different shades of brown. The way it's thick and straight. He even brought me a picture of himself from when he was in high school. I'm not that old yet, but he was right. Our hair is the same.

I wonder if I can keep that big photo. I know it's printed that size just for the funeral, but the frame looks really nice, and I'd like to have it.

There's a loud thud as someone shuts the heavy church doors behind us, and a man dressed in long robes walks up to the front of the room.

I swallow.

Mom explained to me that Dad's heart stopped working. That it was over in an instant, and he was just alive one moment and dead the next. But I can't decide if that's good or bad. Is it really better to just be gone? I'm happy he wasn't hurt. I wouldn't want that. But wouldn't it have been better to know? Maybe if he'd known, he could have come home one last time. Maybe he'd have let me stay with him, for just a little while.

The man in the robe gestures with his hands as he starts to talk. He must have a microphone on him since the words are loud in the room. And I'm glad, because we're so far away but I still want to hear him.

He starts by greeting everyone and talking about being called home. I don't really understand all of it, but then he says something that's wrong.

"He is survived by his wife, Barbara, and their two children, King and Aspen." His voice fills the church as he gestures to a trio of people in the front row.

That's wrong.

Dad didn't...

We're his family.

I'm his child.

I look up at Mom, but her eyes are staring straight ahead, her jaw twitching as she bites her teeth together.

The room is still filling with the man's words, but I can't understand them.

I sit up straighter, stretching my neck, straining to see the people the man is talking about.

There's been a mistake.

But then I see it. The back of a man's head who is sitting in the front row. He's taller than those around him, and his hair is the exact same shade as mine.

The exact same shade as my dad's.

How?

I lean forward, trying to see the other person, the girl, but my mom's hand lands on my leg. Her fingertips dig into my thigh, a silent and painful message to sit still.

Wife? Dad has a wife?

But what does that mean?

I chance another look up at Mom. This time she's glaring down at me, daring me to make a noise.

I don't.

I don't say a thing.

I just wrap my arms around myself, trying to hold my heart inside my body.

What is going on?

My eyes are looking forward, but I'm stuck somewhere else. The look on Dad's face when I asked if I could live with him. The way he shook his head. How he would only come by every few months.

I blink, finally taking in the number of people here.

He lived here.

My dad had to have lived here, in the cities.

It only took us twenty minutes to drive here today.

He was this close the whole time.

He was this close and only visited every few months.

My throat starts to burn.

He would call me his little Valentine. His perfect girl. He would tell me he loved me.

And I loved him so much.

But he lied.

He tricked me.

Tears roll down my cheeks. And I don't know if I'm crying for Dad or for myself.

Why would he lie to me?

Mom lied to me, too. But that thought comes and goes, hardly leaving an impact. She's always been a liar, always been mean. She was always nicest when Dad was around. But he won't be around anymore. Not ever again.

I wipe my nose on my sleeve.

Mom can pinch me all she wants for doing it. I don't have any Kleenex.

The man up front says something, and everyone stands.

I've seen this in movies, too.

I stand and sit and kneel and stay silent when everyone chants things they've all memorized but that I don't know. And I do it all with tears on my cheeks.

This morning, I asked Mom if I could use her makeup. She snapped at me, saying no.

I wanted to look my best for Dad, but now I'm glad she wouldn't let me. I'd have ruined it. At least this way, the sleeves of my plain black long-sleeve shirt—that's too tight since I grew another two inches this year—are only damp, not stained with makeup.

We stand a final time, and the man in the robe tells us to *go with god*, and if my face wasn't so numb, I'd wrinkle my nose.

Didn't he say earlier that Dad was with god now? So isn't telling us to go with god kinda like telling us all to die?

A sharp finger in my side makes me focus, and I see that everyone is starting to leave, so I turn and face the aisle, waiting for our turn to go.

The front rows are excused first, and my throat tightens as a woman with a black veil covering her hair walks down the aisle toward the big doors that have been swung back open.

She must be Dad's wife.

I think the words, and a second later, her eyes snap over to meet mine.

I step back. I recognize the look on her face. It's one I've seen at home.

She hates me.

There's a girl, a woman, behind her. I don't know how old she is, but she looks like she might be my neighbor's age, and she finished high school a few years ago. The girl—did the man say her name was Aspen?—has her thick brown hair pulled back into a bun.

She doesn't look at me. Maybe she doesn't know I'm here.

But I think...

I think she's my sister.

I have a sister.

Just as she's about to pass, she flicks a glance at me. Or was that above me? At my mom? Whichever one of us she's looking at, she has the same expression on her face that her mom did.

The other one is next. But I don't dare think of him as my brother. And I drop my eyes before he can look at me. Because I don't think I can take it. I don't think I can take one more person looking at me in disgust.

My dad is a liar.

My mom is a liar.

I think I have siblings. But I think they hate me.

And I don't want to be hated.

I just want to be loved.

CHAPTER 1

Val

MY FINGERS FUMBLE WITH THE PAPER WRAPPING JUST as a firm body slams into my side.

"Watch it!" a deep voice booms in my ear.

My feet try to shuffle with the impact, but my balance tips just as I lose my grip on my cookie, dropping it to the ground. At the same time, the weight that was hanging off my left shoulder drops away, ending any hope I have of not falling.

An embarrassing squeak bursts from my lips, and I splay my arms, desperately trying to catch myself.

I wish my eyes would shut, but they're stuck wide open, watching all the people who are watching me and hoping to witness the klutzy girl wipe out in the airport terminal.

Except I don't fall.

What has to be a freakishly strong arm encircles my waist and pulls me back against a hard body.

"I got you." The same masculine voice from before speaks into my ear, only this time it's quiet. A whisper. A growl. A *something*.

Swallowing, I let my arms drop and force my body to relax. The need for bracing no longer there.

"Thanks," I breathe out before I notice that his big hand is splayed across my stomach.

A stranger is touching my stomach. My soft, squishy stomach.

I can only pray that he's not as attractive as he sounds.

"Don't be thanking me, Angel." His hand slides across my tummy to my waist as he moves from behind me to next to me. "If that asshole hadn't bumped into me, I wouldn't have knocked into you."

"Oh, it's okay. I..." I start to say more, but then my eyes flick up to the tall man beside me, and my ability to form words vanishes.

Holy fuck-me eyes.

I blink.

Scratch that. Holy fuck-me everything.

His piercing blue irises are only the beginning.

A man in a suit, with closely buzzed dark hair, a matching trimmed beard, and shoulders wide enough to sit on, is smiling down at me like he's truly happy to be inconvenienced by crashing into me.

His lips move.

They're a shade darker, a shade pinker than his tanned skin.

His lips moved.

"Sorry?" My cheeks heat as I admit I didn't hear him, even though we're standing face-to-face.

His smile widens. "Did I hurt you?"

My brain is straight-up short-circuiting because my mind dives headfirst into the gutter, picturing him asking me that when we're both sweaty and naked—in bed.

"No," I croak. *Jesus, Val. Get it together.* "Did I hurt you?"

Did I hurt you?

I want to slap a hand over my mouth. Or crawl under the nearest bench and pretend I'm dead.

The man's mouth tips into a smirk. "Don't think a little thing like you could, even if you tried."

Little?

Is it hot in here?

It's really hot in here.

The pressure on my back shifts, and I realize his big palm is still there, holding me in place.

He lowers his face.

Is he going to kiss me?

My eyes start to close before they snap back open.

He's not going to kiss me. This isn't a Hallmark movie. Or a porno.

He keeps lowering, though, bending down, and my eyes drop to the floor.

Oh, right, my backpack.

And my cookie.

My face heats even more.

Seriously, my brain cannot pick a lane.

I'm blushing over his closeness. Flustered over him calling me *little.* Self-conscious about how his hand was touching my stomach. Feeling fat over being caught eating a cookie. And just over-freaking-heated over him.

The hand that was resting against my back brushes over my butt as he drops into a crouch at my feet.

And that accidental touch is enough to frazzle me even more.

It's been way too long if an innocent graze of fingers against my butt cheek is enough to have my core tightening.

I force myself to snap out of my trance and squat down next to him.

"I got it," I say, but I don't even reach for the bag. Because I'm too busy staring at his tattooed fingers.

Tattooed. Fingers.

I almost mewl. But thank god I don't. That's a level of mortification I don't think I could recover from.

I love tattoos. There's something about them that's just so... hot. So brave.

I've always wanted them, but I've been too chicken to get one. Afraid the pain will be too much and I'll cry the whole way through. Or worse, bail after two minutes and end up with half a design.

But this man...

I press my lips together as I watch him pick up my broken chocolate chip cookie and wrap the pieces in the tiny brown paper bag it came in. And I really just can't stop staring.

His whole hand is tattooed. Fingers, the back of the hand, all of it. And when he reaches for the napkin I also dropped, the bright white cuff of his sleeve pulls back, exposing an expensive watch and more tattoos.

I sway.

"Steady, Shorty." The hand not holding the cookie grips my elbow.

His fingers against my bare skin are somehow grounding, but the use of a second endearment throws me right off balance again.

I didn't miss the way he called me Angel before. I just couldn't process it.

No one has ever called me anything other than Val. No one even uses my full name anymore.

"You okay?" The man's voice is softer now. Less amusement, more concern.

And it's all too damn much.

Crouched next to each other, we're closer to the same height. But even like this, he's taller than me. Wider than me. Bigger than me. And I need to flee. If I spend another moment in his presence, I'm going to melt into a goopy puddle of hormones on the floor. And nobody wants to witness that.

"Th-thank you." I try to reach for my bag, but he beats me to it. Using the same hand that's holding the cookie, he hooks the bag with just one finger and easily lifts it.

"You're welcome." His gaze flicks to my exposed knees, and I yank at my skirt, pulling it down to cover the extra skin.

He clears his throat. It shouldn't be sexy, but it is.

I'm tempted to yank my skirt back up, but then the man starts to stand. And his grip on my elbow brings me up with him.

4

"How much time until your flight?"

"Um, I think I have thirty minutes or so before boarding."

He dips his chin. "Perfect. Me, too."

"Perfect?" I ask, but he's already moving me along with him, his hand on the small of my back again.

"I owe you a cookie and a backpack. Thirty minutes should be just enough time." His voice is so deep and rumbly it nearly distracts me from his words.

"Backpack?" I'm just repeating words as I let him guide me down the main hallway of the airport.

I'm used to being around tall men. My half brother, King, is practically a giant, and he's probably only an inch taller than this man. But even with his much longer legs, this man is walking at my pace.

It's great because I don't have to jog to keep up, but I still wish I'd left my cute wedges on rather than switching into my tennis shoes before going through security. Because I glance down and—yep—his shoes match the rest of his expensive outfit. Meaning no tennis shoes for him.

"It was a casualty of war." He replies to the question I already forgot I asked, holding my backpack in front of him.

My mouth opens into an O as I see why it fell off my shoulder. The strap is broken below where the buckle is sewn into the nylon strip, the thick fabric torn straight through.

I blow out a breath. "I've been waiting for that to happen."

"You've been waiting for a clumsy oaf to crash into you and break your things?"

I glance up at him and find him looking down at me. My cheeks are still red from the first time I locked eyes with him, so I don't bother worrying about how much more red they can get. "I've had that bag forever. It was bound to fail me sooner or later."

"Hmm." He nods, then steers me to turn to the right. "Well, as the party responsible for its demise, I insist on replacing it."

I take in the name of the store he's trying to take me to and put on the brakes. "No."

5

"Yes."

"This place is too expensive," I try to tell him, but his hand doesn't let up, and he half pushes me ahead of him.

I've never even looked at the prices inside this store, but I know a backpack from this place would be literally ten times more expensive than what I paid for my old bag.

Losing the battle, I step into the store and am not surprised to find no one else in here. Because no one else is willing to pay the stupidly high price for the rather plain-looking luggage.

"Afternoon." The lady behind the counter greets us. "Can I help you find something?"

"No," I say, just as the man next to me holds up my grungy bag.

"We need a new backpack. Preferably the same size. Maybe with reinforced straps."

At the last sentence, he cuts his eyes down to mine.

I bite down on a smile, secretly enjoying that he's teasing me. "I can't let you do this."

"You can and you will, Angel."

I blink up at him.

My thick hair is a little longer than shoulder length, and I have it pulled back into a plain high ponytail. My makeup is probably half melted off my face. And my bright yellow wrap dress is just shy of indecent with how much cleavage the low neckline shows.

There's nothing angelic about my appearance.

Taking my silence as acceptance, he turns his attention to the display the salesperson has pointed out.

"What color?" the man asks, holding my bag up, showing that there isn't one the same shade of green.

I sigh. "Black is fine."

"Gold or silver?" He's asking about the metal accents, but I'm distracted, noticing that he's no longer carrying my broken cookie.

Did he throw it away? How did he do that without me noticing?

"Gold." He answers his own question as his hand slides up my back.

He drags a finger across the thin gold chain clasped around my neck and the tiny heart charm dangling just below my throat.

Goose bumps cover my arms. And they only get worse when he lifts his hand higher, his thumb brushing over my matching tiny gold heart earrings.

When I feel like I'm about half a second away from an over-stimulated heart attack, his tattooed hand leaves my body.

He doesn't even ask more, doesn't check with me. He just picks up the black bag with shiny gold hardware and carries it to the register.

Knowing I've lost, that this bag is getting purchased, I chase after him.

If I can get my card out of my broken bag, maybe I can quickly swipe it through the reader and pay whatever ungodly amount myself before he can buy it.

I really can't let a stranger pay for this.

He's already at the counter when I catch up. And it's like he knows what I'm planning, because when I reach for the front zipper pocket, where my wallet is stored, he lifts his arm and hugs the bag to his chest.

The lady scans the tag, displaying the total on the little screen.

"Oh my god!" I classlessly exclaim before I start to tug on the man's arm, making a point to ignore the silky-soft suit jacket under my fingers. "Please let me pay for that." I swallow, thinking of the total. "Or, better yet, just let me keep the broken one. It's fine."

It's not that I can't spend that amount. It's just that I'm... frugal.

The man's dark eyebrow is quirked when he looks over his shoulder at me. "You always this stubborn, Valentine?"

Hearing him say my name, my full name, stuns me long enough for him to hand a card to the cashier.

7

"How do you...?" Then I look at my backpack that's hugged to his chest.

Ah, yes. My bright yellow name tag, with Valentine Gandy written in careful letters, is right in front of his face.

A fresh wave of embarrassment floods my system. Something about this man tells me he doesn't write his name on his luggage. He probably just narrows his eyes at his suitcase, daring it to get lost.

While he finishes the transaction, I stand back and really take him in. His black leather shoes and dark navy suit. The swirling black tattoos peeking out above his collar and crawling up to his hairline on the back of his neck. The way his shoulder muscles round underneath the blue fabric. How I feel so small next to him. But small in a feminine way, not an insignificant way.

Crinkling pulls my attention back to the counter.

The salesperson has removed the bundle of paper stuffed inside the new bag, used to keep its shape. And before I can worry about the man trying to move all my stuff into the new bag, he sets my broken backpack next to the new one on the counter and takes a step back.

"Thank you." His deep voice says the words at the same time I do, causing him to smile.

Again. And he's just as startlingly handsome as the first time.

I give my head a little shake. "Why are you thanking me?"

"Because." He nods his head toward the pair of backpacks. "My mother would kill me if she knew I broke some pretty lady's bag in the airport and didn't replace it." I think my lips move as I silently repeat the words *pretty lady*, but he doesn't pause. "She'd also kill me for going through your things, so I'll let you do the honors."

I glance back and forth between him and the bags on the counter. "I don't suppose there's any way to convince you to return that."

He shakes his head. "All purchases are final."

My eyes move to the salesperson, but she's pretending not to listen. So I don't know if he's telling the truth or lying.

I roll my lips together before sighing. "You're kinda bossy, aren't you?"

The man laughs, loud and throaty, and I feel it in my bones.

"I'm not sure anyone has ever called me bossy before, but I suppose you're not incorrect."

I purse my lips, believing him.

Pretending he's not watching, I quickly move everything into the new backpack. Silently enjoying all the compartments and zippers and the quality of the material. It's still a ridiculous price, but at least it's nice.

Last, I remove the name tag from the old bag and tuck it into an interior pocket. If I'm going to be using this new *grown-up* bag, I'm going to adopt new *grown-up* habits.

I pull the final zipper closed and hoist the new backpack onto my shoulder, then turn to face the man. Or rather, face his chest.

I tip my head back. "Thank you again. It was completely unnecessary, but I still appreciate it."

"Anytime, Valentine."

I bite my bottom lip. "My friends call me Val."

The corner of his mouth pulls up as he reaches out and takes the backpack off my shoulder, swinging it up onto his.

I'm so mentally off balance by this whole encounter that I don't question him carrying my bag. And when he holds his hand out for me to shake, I place my palm against his.

"Dominic Gonzalez." He closes his fingers around mine. "But my friends call me Dom."

CHAPTER 2

Val

THE NAME SUITS HIM PERFECTLY. STRONG. MEMORABLE. And he says it like there's no chance he'd be anyone else.

"Dom," I say quietly, like I'm testing the taste of it.

He rubs his thumb across my knuckles. "It's nice to officially meet you, Val."

"You, too."

God, his eyes are so stunning.

"What time did you say your flight starts boarding?"

I have to focus, remember where we are. "6:05."

Dominic glances at his watch. "Fifteen minutes." I briefly wonder if there will be time to grab a snack before I board, since the cookie I dropped was going to be my dinner. "And where's your gate?"

"Um, twenty-four, I think. Just down the hall."

The tip of his tongue peeks out between his lips as he licks across his incisor. "Tell me you're going to Minneapolis."

I swear my heart stutters in my chest.

"I'm going to Minneapolis," I practically whisper.

"With luck like this, I'm tempted to switch our tickets and fly to Vegas. You can be my lucky charm. Win me a fortune."

My laugh is a bit strangled. "Maybe if you hadn't spent all

your money buying me a new bag, you wouldn't need to gamble for your retirement."

"You wound me." He presses a big, tattooed hand to his chest. "I might be forty-one, but I'm not quite ready to retire."

"Oh, I didn't mean..." I trail off as my brain starts to do the math.

Forty-one to my twenty-five. A sixteen-year age gap isn't too much, is it?

It's not like I have any parents to object.

Oh my god, it's also not like I'm actually going to date him, so this is the dumbest thing to think about.

"I'm teasing you, Shorty." He lets go of my hand, and I vaguely realize that we never actually shook. We just stood here holding hands. "Now, come on." He places his palm between my shoulders, turning me out of the store. "We have just enough time before we board."

I feel a bit like a lost puppy as I let this stranger guide me back into the main hallway of the terminal. But as fleeting as his attention might be, I'm soaking it in. For better or worse, I'm going to absorb every moment of it.

"Wait," I say. "Time for what?"

He doesn't reply. Instead, he leads me into the little bakery a few doors down, back the way I came from.

Another wave of embarrassment flushes through me. *Oh my god, he's going to replace my cookie.*

"No." I wave my hands in front of us. "I really don't need one. I shouldn't have gotten it in the first place."

Self-deprecation is an instinct at this point. A product of growing up with a mother whose skinniness was a result of poor nutrition and drug use. Growing up in a society that has only just started to appreciate bodies of all sizes. Growing up feeling *less than* because I always had to dig to the back of the clothing rack to find something that fit.

"Nonsense." Dom blows off my comment as we stop behind

the one other person in line. "Every flight should start with a cookie."

I mean, I agree. Which is why I bought one for myself. But he doesn't exactly look like the type of person who indulges in desserts. Unless he spends every morning in the gym.

I glance at his chest, trying to tell if I can see hints of more tattoos through his white shirt or if I'm imagining it.

The person ahead of us takes their purchase and moves away so Dom can step forward.

"Three chocolate chip cookies, please." He looks back at me. "Need a drink?"

I shake my head, not even bothering to protest at this point.

I'll just let the man buy me a cookie, and then I'll put it in my bag and wait until I can eat it in private, huddled against the window on the plane.

But then I consider the possibility of getting chocolate on the interior of my brand-new backpack, and it makes me want to gag.

Dom accepts the paper bag from the cashier, three cookies inside, and I sidestep around him, making way for the next person in line, before walking out of the tiny bakery.

I can feel his presence at my side before he holds out one of the cookies for me.

When I hesitate, he lifts it an inch higher. "Indulge my bossiness this one last time."

"I was always warned about taking candy from strangers," I murmur, even as I take it.

"Good thing it's not candy," Dom replies.

I can't help my eye roll.

"Shall we?" He gestures toward our gate with the remaining two cookies, which are stacked bottom to bottom.

Before I answer, I look at the backpack still slung over one of his shoulders. "Will you let me carry my bag?"

"Nope." Dom shakes his head once, then takes a giant bite of his double-decker cookie.

"I feel like I should probably argue with you one of these times."

"Why?" Dom takes another bite.

"Because."

His lips quirk as he drapes a heavy arm over my shoulders and starts us down the hall. "Life is too short not to *lean in*, my Valentine."

My Valentine. Jesus.

I follow his direction literally and lean into his side.

His body is firm and warm and... I inhale and almost groan.

He smells like sex appeal.

Like someone took every secret desire I've ever had and bottled it up into an exclusive cologne that only my soulmate could wear and get away with.

"And really, we're both getting something out of this," he continues, and I force myself to focus. "Probably me more than you."

"I got a new backpack that cost several hundred dollars and a fresh new cookie." I glance up at him. "What do you get?"

His arm is heavy around my shoulders as he speaks. "Something interesting to break up my day. The company of a beautiful woman." He lifts his other hand. "Cookies."

My eyes move to his half-eaten stack of cookies as I try to figure out if this is real or if I fell and cracked my head on the floor and am hallucinating the whole thing.

"Make me happy, Angel." I glance back up, finding his blue eyes locked on mine. "Let me feed you. Eat your treat."

My breath catches, my mind sprinting to images of me on my knees, one of his hands in my hair...

Don't go there, Val.

Tentatively, I take a bite of my cookie. When I do, I can feel his hum of appreciation where my body is pressed against his.

I think I hear him say something. Something like *that's my girl*, but that can't be right.

In silence that should be uncomfortable, I walk through the

busy airport terminal, eating a cookie, with a handsome-as-hell man at my side. His arm is still over my shoulder, and my backpack is on his back, like we're a happy couple on vacation, not a pair of total strangers who literally ran into each other.

But what's the harm in pretending?

Lean in.

My eyes flutter closed for two steps as I let myself lean into him. Lean into the feeling. Lean into the make-believe world where this is my life. Where this man is really here with me. Where I'm happy. Loved.

A tightness wraps around my throat, and I blink my eyes open, shoving another bite of cookie into my mouth.

Make-believe, indeed.

At least side by side he can't watch me eat, so I hurry and finish the rest of my cookie. Because this is the real world. And he's just being nice.

He's probably someone who travels a lot. Probably a little bored. And sure, I'm cute enough. I'm chubby, but I think I carry it okay and my face is nice. But in my tennis shoes and bright yellow dress, I'm no match for him.

He's probably the VP of something. Someone who owns more than one vehicle. Someone with self-esteem and a mom who loves him.

A pang hits deep in my chest.

This is only a moment. I will be happy in another moment.

I repeat the words my therapist has told me time and time again.

Then I repeat the words Dom said only a few moments ago.

Lean in.

I fill my lungs with a deep breath and decide to pretend this is my life.

I'll be happy in this moment.

A big hand plucks the empty napkin from my hand, and he balls it up with his own and drops them into a trash can as we walk past.

"So." I force my courage to the surface. "Do you live in Minnesota?"

There's a light pressure on my far shoulder as he tightens his grip on me, just the smallest bit.

"No, just passing through on my way to Chicago." His tone sounds almost apologetic, and I try not to feel disappointed.

It's for the best, I tell myself.

He's just being nice, I tell myself.

"I'm surprised they didn't have a direct flight," I say to make conversation, thinking there has to be one from where we are in Denver.

"Already trying to get rid of me?" Dom is clearly teasing me.

So I try to tease back. "You are a little clingy."

His laugh startles me, and this time he curls his fingers around my shoulder, holding me in place. "Valentine, you are a fucking delight."

Delight.

The blush on my cheeks is basically permanent now. "Thanks."

Thanks?

God, why am I so weird?

Usually, I'm outgoing. I've been called *bubbly* by coworkers, and it's fairly accurate.

It often takes a lot of effort, but I try my hardest to be nice, kind, and accommodating.

My therapist says it's a defense mechanism. That I do it because I want people to like me and I'm overcompensating for my fear of rejection. My fear of not being liked. Not being wanted.

Stay in this moment, I remind myself. There will be plenty of time for pity parties later.

Our steps slow as we reach the gate, which is overflowing with travelers waiting for permission to board.

When we come to a stop, Dom's arm slips away, and I have to fight off a shiver as cool air fills the space where his arm was.

"I suppose it's too much to ask what seat you're in."

His comment reminds me that I need to go up to the desk. "I don't actually know yet. My boarding pass says to get my seat assignment at the gate. Not sure why."

"They probably flagged you for being so unruly on your last flight."

I don't fight my grin as I look up at him. "Heard about that?"

He winks. "I hear about everything."

I let him see my eye roll. "I'm sure you do." Then I sigh, assuming this is it. "Well, I better go get that seat assignment."

Without arguing, Dom slides my new backpack down his arm before holding it out to me.

I grab my phone out of the front pocket, then hoist it onto my back, sliding both arms through the straps this time.

"Thank you for the backpack and the cookie and being..." I lift a shoulder.

I was going to say *nice*, but that sounds stupid. Even a little pathetic. Thanking someone just for being nice to me.

"I always try to *be*." Dom dips his chin, then steps away.

And I wonder if he's the most sincere person I'll ever meet.

CHAPTER 3

Val

THE SOAP DISPENSER IS EMPTY, SO I HAVE TO SCOOT over to the next sink to fill my palm with the foam.

First class.

Lathering up my hands, I think about Dominic's Vegas idea. He might be onto something since my luck seems to be miraculously good today. First, crashing into a hot guy who is way too nice to me. Then, going up to the desk and being told they overbooked the flight and I've been bumped up to first class.

Okay, so it's only two things if I don't count the material gifts, but I can't help but hope that maybe Dom flies first class, too.

With his fancy suit and nothing but whatever was in his pockets, he looks like an experienced traveler.

But when I turned around after being given my new seat assignment, I couldn't find him.

I move over to the air dryer.

Maybe he lied about being on the same flight?

No, that would be dumb. He's the one who asked if I was flying to Minneapolis, and he walked us right to the correct gate. He probably just had to go to the bathroom, same as me.

The line to the ladies' room was long, so by the time I hurry back to my gate, they're already boarding. And the digital sign shows that I missed the special boarding for the priority passengers. Whatever, I'll still enjoy the experience. Time to *lean in* to an evening of luxury.

I shuffle forward with the line as it moves.

Maybe it's unhealthy to adopt a phrase so quickly from a stranger. But it's a good sentiment. And it's along the lines of my *this moment* mantra. So, I don't really see the harm. And it's not like I'm going to scratch Dominic's name into my bedroom wall when I get home.

Dominic. Even his name is hot.

I scan my ticket, and the woman at the gate tells me to have a good flight.

Then, for the eighteenth time, I confirm where I'm sitting. Row three, by the window.

I find the window preferable because I like to prop my head against the wall and nap. But I bet the aisle person is already sitting down, so I'll have to ask them to get up. Which I don't want to do. But it's not like it's the end of the world.

I make my way down the Jetway, closer to the plane, wondering if I'll see Dominic. Wondering if I should say hi if and when I do. Wondering if I'll ever just be normal and figure out how to play it cool.

"Good evening." One of the airline attendants greets me as I step over the little gap and onto the plane.

"Hello." I smile back.

There's a large man ahead of me, so I can't see beyond the row I'm next to.

I try to make my glances look casual as I check the passengers, but none of them are him.

None of them have those broad shoulders. None of them have that short dark hair I want to run my hands over so I can feel the ends tickle against my palms. None of them have those blue eyes that sparkle with secrets.

Dominic said he's forty-one. But he feels older. Not older in an old man way, but in an experience way. In a *he's lived a full life* kind of way.

But maybe that's just the tattoos.

And damn, those tattoos.

I resist fanning myself but just barely.

The man ahead of me moves forward, and I look at row three.

At my row.

And at Dominic.

The edge of his mouth lifts. "Tell me you're sitting next to me."

I do my best to keep a neutral expression on my face. "I'm sitting next to you."

Dom slowly stands, keeping his eyes on me.

He has to duck to avoid the overhead storage, then he sidles into the aisle and straightens.

We stay like that for a beat. Chest to chest. And I watch his nostrils flare, as if he's holding something back and it's costing him. Then he swallows and moves out of the way, allowing me to scoot into our row.

My skirt catches on the armrest, flashing a bit of thigh, and I reach down to free myself.

When I make it to the window seat, I slip my backpack off and shift it so it's on my lap when I sit down.

"Want that up here?" Dom asks.

I look up and see he's still standing in the aisle. But now his hands are up, resting on the overhead bin.

The position flares his unbuttoned suit jacket out and stretches his white shirt across his torso. And *sweet baby Jesus,* those are definitely tattoos covering his body.

Lord, help me. This is going to be the best and worst flight ever.

It'll be like sitting in front of a giant cheesecake but knowing you aren't allowed to take a bite.

"Angel."

My eyes snap up to meet his, and the blush that had finally

faded from my cheeks comes roaring back to life. Because he just caught me ogling him.

I bite my lip, but it doesn't stop the guilty look on my face.

Dom lifts an eyebrow, and I lift a shoulder.

It's not like he doesn't know he's attractive.

In retaliation, he slowly lowers his eyes from my face, down my neck, over my ample cleavage, and down my body to where my skirt is riding up above my knees.

When his eyes move back up to meet mine, it's my turn to lift a brow. Copying me copying him, Dom lifts a shoulder before dropping his arms back to his sides.

Finally, I remember the question he asked me about putting my bag up.

"You can sit down. I'll put it under the seat. Wouldn't want someone to try and steal my new fancy bag." To punctuate my statement, I shove it to the floor and use my toes to push it forward.

But I'm not used to these spacious first-class seats. And my legs don't reach far enough to push the bag all the way under the seat in front of me.

Dom lowers himself into his seat with a chuckle, then leans into my space, reaching down between my still-extended feet and pushing my backpack the rest of the way forward.

"Shorty," he murmurs as he leans back. But he doesn't lean straight back. Doesn't take the shortest path. He stays leaned my way, the back of his hand brushing against my bare knee.

I still haven't acknowledged this particular nickname, but I'm too busy trying to breathe to think of a comeback.

And even breathing is hard, because he's so close my lungs are filling with his warm cologne scent, and it's reviving every hormone I've ever had.

Finally, Dom settles back against his seat and reaches down to buckle his seat belt.

With his attention elsewhere, I quickly reach for my belt and pull it to the longest length, hoping he doesn't notice.

Sometimes the seat belts on a plane are a struggle. Sometimes there is more than enough length, and I have to tighten it several inches, and sometimes they seem to be made for only slender bodies—or even men with beer guts who somehow have tiny waists—but not made for wide-hipped, thicker women.

The panic of impending shame edges into my mind, but then the belt clicks, and I realize first class is built differently because the belt is sagging across my lap.

I let out a breath of relief, though I'm not sure why. It's not like Dom can't see my body with his own eyes. But the thought of having to ask for a seat belt extender in front of him makes me want to peel off my skin.

Even if you had to, it wouldn't matter. It's just a body.

I take another breath. It's amazing how quickly shit you thought you dealt with can come flying back at you when you're confronted with a new situation. Such as the attention of an overly attractive man who happens to be your type in every way possible.

A hand I'm becoming familiar with appears in my line of sight, and Dom grips the little tab at the end of the seat belt and pulls it, tightening the belt until it's secure across my lap.

"Thank you, sir." A female voice sounds from the aisle, and I see one of the attendants smiling down at us. "Gotta keep your wife safe."

My mouth pops open to correct her, but before I can think of the right thing to say, Dom sets his hand on my thigh. "Someone has to."

All I can do is gape.

"Would you like a headset?" the attendant keeps smiling as she asks us.

"We'll share one," Dom answers.

The woman hands him a small package, and through the clear plastic, I can see the white coil of cord with two earbuds attached.

Dominic slides those bright blue eyes my way.

"Is this you leaning in?" I whisper.

He smirks. "You're getting it now, Mama."

Mama.

Jesus. Fucking. Christ.

The fingers on my leg flex, causing the fabric of my wrap dress to shift so the edge of the top layer slides down between my thighs. I'm still covered, but now the fabric is outlining the shape of my thighs and riding just a little higher.

Dom clears his throat and lifts his hand away.

I think he presses his palm to his lap.

I think he might be adjusting... *himself.*

But I'm too much of a coward to look.

I busy myself, checking out the tiny water bottle in my seat pocket. I use my fingertip to see if there's anything behind the safety pamphlet also in the pocket. Basically, I do anything *but* look at Dom as the last people take their seats. And since I didn't take anything out of my backpack, I don't have anything to hold my attention. So I fiddle.

Dom doesn't fiddle. He doesn't do anything. He doesn't even take out his phone. He just sits there, fingers laced together, hands in his lap.

If I look at him, I'd know where his eyes are focused, if they're on me or on something else. But I don't look. I just imagine them half-lowered, as close to rest as a man like him might get in public.

I have no idea what type of man he really is, but he seems like the type that doesn't easily trust others. The type that doesn't cut loose, no matter how much he *leans in* to a situation.

The speakers crackle, and the pilot tells the crew to prepare the cabin for takeoff.

I fiddle more.

Smoothing my skirt. Crossing my ankles one way, then the other. Lifting the little flap in the armrest that hides the lap tray, then lowering it.

When I adjust the little napkin sitting on the flat space of the armrest between us, an inked hand settles over mine, and my fingers still.

"Nervous?" Dom's voice is low, making sure I'm the only one who hears him.

"No," I answer too quickly. Then I let out a breath and try to relax my shoulders. "A little."

"Why?" He doesn't sound judgmental. He sounds like he really wants to know.

There's another announcement, and the plane starts to roll away from the gate.

"No good reason," I tell him truthfully. "But the sky kinda seems like the ocean to me."

"How so?"

I think I can hear a smile in his voice, so I glance up at his face. But the smile isn't on his mouth, it's in his eyes.

I hold his gaze. "Humans aren't made for either."

He's quiet for a moment, and I appreciate that he's thinking about my answer. Or at least he's acting like he is.

Then he nods once as he says, "Self-preservation is a good trait to have."

"It's gotten me this far." I try to joke, but the pain in the truth of it scratches against my throat.

I've lived too many days so focused on self-preservation that it's bored into my marrow. That I don't know any other way to live.

I look away from Dom.

For so long, it's been just me looking out for me.

Most days, it still feels like that.

Sure, King has a security guy drive me around. But I think that's just to make him feel better. So he can sleep next to Savannah at night and confidently tell her he's keeping me safe.

Savannah, my half brother's wife, is the only Vass I don't share blood with, but I think she might be the only one who really loves me. The only family I have that feels true affection toward me, not just obligation.

But her first loyalty will always be to King. And that's why I still feel so alone.

Fingers that I forgot were wrapped around mine shift. I think he's letting go when his palm leaves the back of my hand, but instead, Dom slides his hand under mine so we're palm to palm.

I have to swallow.

Savannah's casual hugs are the only real human touch I get anymore.

And *oh my fucking god*, I need to stop feeling so damn sorry for myself.

"Sorry," I whisper, hoping like crazy he thinks I'm just upset over flying and not picking up on the fact that we went from harmless flirting to me flaying my insides open.

"Never apologize." His stern tone has me looking back up.

I take in his face, take in his seriousness. "Never?"

"Never," he repeats.

"You don't ever apologize?"

"Not ever."

I roll my lips together, considering this. "Why not?"

"Because I mean everything I do."

"Everything?" I don't know why I ask. There's nothing about Dominic that doesn't scream confidence.

"Yeah, Valentine. And when you do things with purpose, you have nothing to apologize for."

The plane straightens out on the runway, then picks up speed.

I let the velocity press my head against the back of the seat, my neck still turned to look at Dom. "Then I'm not sorry."

I don't even remember what I was apologizing for anymore, but I know it's the right response when Dom nods his head once before mirroring my position. "Good."

The plane tips up, and we leave the ground.

My fingers tighten around Dom's.

"Sor—" I start when I notice that I'm squeezing his hand, but I stop myself.

And Dom's expression is pure approval.

I loosen my grip but don't let go as I tell him, "I usually fly alone."

"Usually?" he asks.

I let out a little laugh when I think about it. "I always fly alone. I'm not used to having someone to..."—*comfort*—"distract me."

"I'm happy to be your distraction."

His tone is back to teasing, and I vow to myself that I'll stay there with him.

"How very generous of you."

He huffs out a little laugh. "So, why do you always fly alone? Work?"

"Yeah. I design websites. And you'd be surprised how many people want you to come to them in person to show them how stuff works." I shake my head. "Ninety percent of the time, I could do this by sharing my screen from my living room. But everyone learns differently, I guess."

"Living room," he repeats. "Do you work for a company or yourself?"

"A company. It's actually based in Chicago." Dom makes an interested hum at the mention of his city, and I don't act weird over the fact that we're still holding hands. Not at all. "I did free-lance for myself for a while, but I didn't love it. I mean, I enjoy my work, but I do it for the paycheck, ya know? It's not like my life's passion. And running your own business is a lot of freaking work."

Dom nods like he understands, and I should've expected his next question, but it still catches me off guard. "What is your passion?"

I open my mouth, but the space inside me that should be filled with passion is just... empty. A blank space filled with dead childhood dreams that faded to dust long before I hit adulthood.

Stay positive. Stay flirty. You can't tell him that you have nothing in your life to be excited about. Nothing to hope for.

"Family," I kinda choke out.

"I'm close with my family, too." Dom takes my answer the wrong way, but I decide to run with it.

I meant that I would love to have a family of my own, but this is a much better, much less depressing path.

"Does your family live in Chicago?" I ask, happy to turn the conversation toward him.

Dom snorts. "The whole fucking lot of them."

That makes me smile. "Big family, then?"

He nods. "Too many to even keep straight."

"That sounds nice."

"You haven't met them," he jokes.

I tip my smile up toward him. "If they're anything like you, I'm sure they're lovely."

Dom's face contorts into a look of disgust. "Lovely? Clearly I'm giving you the wrong impression if you think I'm lovely."

"Oh?" I lift my brows. "And what impression should I have?"

He lowers his voice an octave. "That I'm manly."

The laugh bursts out of me before I can stop it.

Dom feigns a hurt expression, but I know he said it that way to be funny, so I stop myself from saying *sorry*.

"Anything else?" I grin.

He lifts his free hand, ticking off fingers. "Hilarious. Handsome. Great head of hair."

I make a show of looking up at his close-cropped hair.

Dom taps his temple. "This is by choice, not necessity."

I flex my fingers in his. "Can I touch it?"

Dom drops his eyes to his lap, and I squeak. "The hair!" Then I make another sound and add, "The hair on your head. Obviously. Oh my god."

The deep laugh Dom lets out loosens his grip on my fingers, so I take the opportunity to slip free and slap my hands over my face.

"Angel." He's still chuckling.

I shake my head. "Nope. I'm not here anymore. Go talk to someone else."

He laughs some more, even as he gently grips my wrist.

I resist him pulling my hand away from my face until I feel the puff of breath across my bare forearm.

Peeking between my fingers, I find him with his head dipped down, leaning into the space between us.

"Give me a feel, Shorty."

"I'm not that short," I grumble.

"Sure you aren't." He tips his head closer. "Go on."

Give me a feel.

I exhale and gently place my fingertips at the base of his skull, right where his hairline starts on the back of his neck.

Dominic stills beneath my touch—turns to stone. But I don't stop. I lean in.

As I slide my fingers up, the short bristles tickle the sensitive underside of my fingers.

His hair is surprisingly soft. And I don't stop. I don't stop when his hair brushes against my palm. I don't stop at the back of his head. I let my hand slide up toward the top.

Once there, I let my hand settle a little more, flattening the short hairs between my hand and his scalp as I slide my hand back down, then back up. And I definitely don't stop when he tips his head farther toward me.

"Jesus," he groans. "That feels good."

I catch myself before I agree, even though it does. It does feel good.

And then, because I like the way it feels when I do it to myself, I curl my fingers until the nails are just touching his scalp and drag my hand back down to the base of his skull, giving him a light scratch the whole way.

When I reach his neck, his shoulders hunch before he lowers them with a shudder.

And because I'm feeling bold, I drag my nails down the length of his neck, letting my fingers pass over the swirling design there until they reach his shirt collar.

Wanting to do more but not sure if I should, my boldness fades, and I drop my hand back into my lap.

Still bent over, Dom turns his head to face me. "I'm gonna need you to do that a hundred more times."

"I can agree to that," I whisper.

Why am I whispering?

Those eyes that look like they see too much roam across my face. From one eye to the other, down the slope of my nose, settling on my lips. The tip of his tongue wets his lips.

My chest rises and falls.

By the way one look from him affects me, I don't know if I want to experience more. Because more might kill me.

Without warning, Dominic leans down, putting his face nearly in my lap, and reaches under the seat in front of me to drag my backpack out.

My mouth opens to ask what he's doing, but he's already pulling open the front zipper and taking my phone out, proving he was paying attention when I switched everything over earlier.

Sitting back up, Dom turns the phone toward me. Not handing it to me, just letting the facial recognition unlock it.

I fight against the embarrassment of him seeing the generic background I have on my screen.

I thought the beach scene was pretty, and I didn't have a photo of my own that was better, so I stuck with it.

Dominic doesn't pause, though, unbothered by my choice of background.

I crane my neck to see what he's doing, but he turns the phone away from me, tapping away at the screen.

It doesn't take an expert to guess what he's doing, and he confirms it when he sets my phone in his lap and removes his own from his pocket. He just glances at it, checking to make sure the message went through, then he puts it back in his pocket and hands me my own back.

I open my texts, and sure enough, at the top of the thread is an outgoing one from me to Big Guy.

I raise my brows, but Dom just plucks the phone from my

hand and once again invades my space to return it to my backpack and push the bag back where it was.

"Well," he says, settling back into his seat. "If you'd've given me a nickname to work with, I would've used it. But it appears that only one of us is feeling the endearments. And, wife"—he cuts me a look—"if you're Shorty, then I'm Big Guy."

Wife? Gah.

I'm saved from responding when the flight attendant rolls a cart to a stop at Dominic's elbow, asking what we'd like to drink before dinner.

Being new to this whole first-class thing, I do my best to act unsurprised at the free Jack and Coke that Dom orders for both of us.

Keeping up the act of being together, Dom waits until the attendant moves on before asking me if I'm driving myself home from the airport.

Not going into detail—because explaining I have a family member who is into some bad stuff and therefore feels the need to have me escorted by an armed guard isn't really something I can share—I just shake my head.

"Good. Me neither." Dom lifts his glass, and I clink mine to his.

I take a sip. Then a second, letting the cold beverage warm me from the inside out.

I normally wouldn't enjoy someone ordering for me, but I'm new to this free-drink thing, and I'm happy for the little bit of liquid courage.

"Okay." Dom reaches up and turns on the screen on the back of the seat in front of him. "What movie should we watch?"

A wave of relief settles on my chest as I appreciate what he's doing.

It's not that I don't want to talk to him, but several hours of talking to someone you just met, who happens to turn you on with everything they do, is kind of a lot.

I reach for my screen, but his big paw shoves my hand away.

"What?" I laugh.

"My screen, Valentine."

I bite my lip before I mutter, "Bossy."

"Better than *lovely*." He says the word like it's an insult as he selects the list of movie genres. "Action, thriller, war reenactment."

I scrunch my nose. "Those are the options?"

"Uh-huh," he says with a straight face.

"How about Disney?" I suggest it to be a pest.

"Absolutely not."

I scoff. "What's wrong with Disney?"

"Nothing. But my little asshole nieces and nephews make me watch animated movies every time I see them. And this is adult time, so I want an adult movie."

"You probably shouldn't call them assholes." I try to keep a straight expression.

Dom tips his face down to mine. "Like I said, you haven't met them."

"Fine." I sigh dramatically. "If those are my choices, then I choose thriller."

"Interesting..." He drags the word out and starts to scroll through the list of options.

Dom pauses to look from his screen to mine, then to me, and back to his screen again.

"What?"

His big shoulders lift, then fall. "We'll need to use yours."

My eyes follow the same path his just did. "Why?"

Dom unfurls the headset he got from the flight attendant. "Because, Shorty, one of us is gonna need to lean over a bit to make this work. And I think it will be more comfortable for me to do it."

I widen my eyes at him. "Because you're such a big guy?"

He narrows his eyes. "Keep teasin' me, see where it gets you."

Pretty please, let it be pinned to his bed.

I banish that thought and turn my screen on so I can search the thriller titles.

I've only just started to look when our dinner trays arrive, and we eat in silence while I scroll through the titles—the chicken and couscous with a side salad and bread roll way better, and way more, than I expected.

By the time we finish eating, I've decided on a movie. When Dom is distracted by the trays being taken away, I hit play and then pause it after the title screen so it'll be a surprise for him.

Dom hums, seeing what I've done. "Sneaky girl."

Having finished my drink with my meal, I'm feeling more than a little flushed, and his voice is affecting me more than it did before.

Instead of handing me the earbuds, Dom stretches across me, bringing his masculine scent back into my space.

He slides the metal tip into place under the screen.

And I don't even question why, but that action makes me press my thighs together.

Uncoiling the cord, Dom hands me one of the little plastic earbuds.

I slide it into the ear closest to him, and he does the same. With his face so close to mine, he asks, "Are you ready?"

The question has my breath catching. And he doesn't wait for an answer, just hits play.

The movie starts, and all my attention is on Dominic Gonzalez as he gets comfortable next to me.

His elbow goes to the armrest between us, and he puts his chin in his palm, propping his head up. But since he's not a shorty, he has to hunch over. And it puts him in my space.

His exhales skitter across my skin, and my arms break out into another round of goose bumps.

Just act normal. This isn't a big deal.

Sure, we could just watch our own movies. Or agree to watch the same one at the same time. But this giant sexy man wants to share a screen, so that's what we're gonna do.

31

I'm trying to remain calm when one big, inked finger reaches out and pauses the movie.

I look at him, but he just holds up that same finger in a *one sec* gesture.

And then I watch him take his clothes off.

Okay, so it's just his suit jacket, but he might as well be getting naked with the way my panties are soaking themselves.

"Here." Dom holds out his jacket.

"What?" My voice is so breathy it sounds like I'm panting.

"You're cold." Dom glances down, and at first, I think he's referring to my nipples that are surely trying to break free of my bra, but then I remember the goose bumps on my arms.

"Thank you." I accept it. Because if anyone thinks I would skip the opportunity to be wrapped in his warmth and scent, they'd be wrong. They'd be so goddamn wrong.

Plus, I shoved my jacket into my checked luggage when I got to the airport because I hate having extra things to carry.

I drape the material, still heated from Dom's body, across my front, covering myself from my shoulders to the middle of my thighs.

Dom restarts the movie, and we watch the opening scene. I can tell he recognizes it almost immediately, and his murmur of appreciation fills me with satisfaction.

I haven't watched this movie in forever, but who doesn't love a classic Harrison Ford and Tommy Lee Jones film? Plus, it's the perfect level of excitement without a bunch of sexy-time scenes that would make it uncomfortable to watch on a plane.

As time passes, I relax into my seat.

And as more time passes, Dom lowers, his head sinking until he's resting his temple against my shoulder.

And after a few more minutes, his head gets heavier—with sleep.

Because this big, beautiful man just fell asleep against me.

CHAPTER 4

Val

THE MOVIE CONTINUES TO PLAY, BUT I'M TOO LOST IN the feeling of Dominic resting against my shoulder.

His breaths are heavy. Slow. Like he's all the way in the deepest part of where dreams live. And I don't want to miss a moment of it.

I saw the way the flight attendant looked at him a few moments ago, and I get it. Even if he really was my husband, I wouldn't fault her for that look. In slumber, he changes from someone intimidating to someone adorable.

A small sound, like a moan of contentment, reaches my ear, and Dom's far hand, the one that had been draped across the armrest, shifts, sliding forward until it's on my knee.

My bare knee.

It takes everything in me to stay still. To not flinch. To not grab his hand and shove it away. Or drag it farther between my legs.

He shifts again, and his fingers curl around the inside of my knee, like he's holding me to him.

I expect him to wake up, but he doesn't. And his breathing doesn't change.

I take a deep, slow inhale, and I make my muscles relax.

Just lean in, Val.

Taking Dom's words literally, I tip my head to the side.

My cheek meets the top of his head, the short length tickling my skin.

The feeling is so nice, so pleasant, that I nuzzle against him.

I rub my cheek back and forth, and it feels just as good as I knew it would.

Dominic lets out another tiny moan, and I freeze, keeping my cheek where it is against his head.

But that's all he does. So I stay there, just like that, resting against a man I met at the airport who is asleep against my shoulder.

And I feel...

My chest tightens as emotions swarm my senses.

I feel kinda happy.

No, that's not even right. I feel *happy*. Like a real level of happy.

But then my throat squeezes, and my eyes sting. Because this is fleeting. I know it's fleeting. And if I focus on it, it'll disappear right in front of me.

Out of nowhere, I'm reminded of a video I saw once. It was of a raccoon with a handful of cotton candy. He looked so happy to have it, but then he put it into a puddle, because raccoons sometimes wash their food, and it dissolved. And the look on his face...

I sniff.

Fuck.

He looked so sad and so confused, and just thinking about that stupid video is sending me over the edge. Because I'm that raccoon. And Dominic is my cotton candy. And if I pretend like he's mine, if I act like I can keep him, then when that reality dissolves, it's going to ruin me.

I let my eyes close.

I won't fall asleep. I'm too aware of where I am, who I'm with, to do that.

Plus, I don't want to miss a moment of this feeling. No matter how fleeting.

THE CREDITS ARE ROLLING WHEN DOMINIC STARTS TO stir. My eyes have been closed, but feeling him shift, I slide them open.

I'm grateful he stayed asleep for so long. Grateful I had time to get my raging emotions under control. And in that time, I was able to remind myself that we exchanged numbers. Or, more specifically, Dominic took my phone and entered his number after sending himself mine.

I'm not under any delusions that we're going to date. But maybe, just maybe, we'll see each other again.

And that has to be enough.

The warm fingers gripping my thigh flex, and Dom makes a deeper humming sound before his scratchy, sleepy voice speaks. "Well, this is a nice surprise."

My hands are hidden under his suit jacket that I've continued to use as a blanket, but I flex them in my lap in response.

"Guess I should add human pillow to my resume," I joke.

The weight against my shoulder increases before Dom lifts his head. "I'd hire you."

A small chuckle builds in my throat, but it gets caught when Dom moves his fingers a half inch higher before sliding his hand back toward himself, dragging a line of heat across the top of my knee.

Thank you, earlier self, for deciding to shave your legs this morning. Also, extra thank you for using that awesome anti-rub cream on your inner thighs today rather than the usual hideous bike shorts.

Not that Dom is going to see my underwear, but at least I

don't have to worry about unattractive shorts peeking out from under my dress.

I swallow and force my eyes up. "Guess you were tired."

"Guess so." He drags a hand down his face before narrowing one eye at me. "Or maybe you drugged me."

I snort. "You've found me out. I'm not really a web designer. I'm actually a drug lord."

He huffs out a laugh, one side of his mouth pulling up. "Drug lord? Do they still call them that?"

My lips part, then I shrug. "I didn't say I was good at it."

The other side of his mouth lifts until he's smiling at me. "I like you, Valentine Gandy."

I dip my chin, putting my nose against the collar of the jacket in my lap.

That hand moves back across the armrest until his palm is on my knee again. "Don't leave me hanging, Shorty."

I tip my head to the side so he can see my exasperated expression. "I guess I like you, too, Big Guy."

"That's more like it." Dom rolls his neck one way, then the next. "How much longer in this sardine can?"

"I'm not sure, but..." I wince in apology. "Can you let me out? I need to go to the bathroom."

"I think I can manage that," Dom says as he unbuckles his seat belt.

I brace myself for the chill before pulling the borrowed jacket away from my body and following him out of the row.

Dom moves back just enough for me to get past him. And call me a coward, but I keep my gaze averted as I slip past.

Thankfully the little restroom is empty, since I forgot to check that little light above the door to see if it was occupied. And while I do my business, I, of course, think of Dom. And I think of all the movies and books that talk about the mile-high club. And as I struggle to bend down far enough to reach my undies to pull them back up, I wonder how in the hell anyone actually has sex in one of these tiny bathrooms.

Maybe they used to be larger? Or maybe it's just fiction at its best.

I shake off the image of trying to fit in here with another body and busy myself washing my hands, taking my time as the cold water helps cool my heated blood.

I use two paper towels to dry my hands, then unlock and open the accordion door.

And, just like that, my blood is right back to simmering, because standing in front of me is Dominic. He's still not wearing his jacket. And now...

Heavenly Harrison.

Now he's rolled up his sleeves, and he's undone his top two buttons.

My tongue wets my bottom lip.

This is too much.

"You comin' out?" he asks me with a smirk in his tone.

My eyes stay on the exposed part of his chest, on the new set of tattoos he's made visible.

"Angel."

I nod. "What? Yeah. Yes."

A deep rumble leaves his chest before he reaches out and presses a finger under my chin, bringing my gaze up to meet his. "Go to your seat."

His fingertip feels like fire against my skin. "Yes, Dom."

I don't know why I say it. No idea why I say it like that. But the look that crosses his face tells me he liked it. That he liked it a lot.

"Now, Shorty."

My eyes move back to his neck and that exposed piece of chest as I step out of the bathroom. But he still doesn't move. He doesn't give me a single extra inch to get by. So, with my front pressed to his, I slide past him. My soft breasts press against his solid body, our height difference putting them against his stomach. A stomach that's flexed. And hard. And... my stomach, which is just as soft as my breasts, slides against...

I pull in a breath.

He's hard there, too. Maybe not all the way. But I can feel him. I can feel his length.

Dom's exhale ruffles my hair, and I hurry the last shuffle step.

I don't make eye contact with anyone as I quickly move to our row. And I don't waste any time side-stepping into our row and dropping into my seat.

Positive he won't take long, I straighten my skirt, buckle up, and pick up and drape his suit jacket back over myself.

My fingers curl into the material from the underside, and I bring it up to my mouth, letting the smooth texture rub against my lips.

When the bathroom door opens, I lower the jacket since I don't want it to look like I'm kissing it. *That would be crazy.*

As soon as I see Dom from the corner of my eye, his belt right at eye level, I make sure to look really busy—staring at the screen that's turned black.

When he's seated, I think I hear him inhale, like he's about to say something. But the seat belt warning dings a second before the overhead speakers crackle and we're told we're about to start our final descent.

The flight attendant walks down the aisle, collecting garbage, and Dom hands her our empty water bottles.

A weird sort of dread settles on my shoulders. Almost like grief. Which is absurd. We exchanged numbers. There's still a possibility I'll talk to Dominic again, maybe even see him. But knowing we're about to land makes me worry that I might not ever hear from him again.

"So, um, how long is your layover?" I ask. And as soon as the question is out of my mouth, I snap my jaw shut.

Oh god, I hope that didn't sound like I was inviting him over.

I mean, it's not like I wouldn't invite him over.

Maybe if he has a really long layover, I should invite him over...

Noticing he hasn't answered, I peek up at him and see those amused crinkles next to his eyes.

I roll my eyes. "You know I didn't mean it like that."

"I know. And that's a shame." He doesn't say it like he's upset with me. The way he says it brings an even deeper blush to my cheeks. "It's not a long layover, but I'm in no rush."

"That's nice," I reply quietly.

Maybe he'll want to walk with me toward baggage claim? Maybe not, but either way, I want to find out which way he's going so we don't say goodbye as we exit the plane and then walk awkwardly three feet away from each other while going in the same direction.

The plane around us shakes as we pass through whatever causes turbulence, and my heart hops into my throat.

Landing is always the worst part.

"I got you." Dom's voice draws my eyes to his mouth, and then movement lower brings them down to his hand, palm up, fingers spread, on the armrest between us.

We've held hands. We've leaned against each other. We've brushed our bodies past each other. But it's always been him reaching for me, him pulling me in.

I've never gone to him.

But I want to.

I slip my arm out from under his jacket and slowly, gently, set my palm against his.

I twist my hand until my outstretched fingers are lined up with Dom's. His hand is so much larger, his palm bigger than mine on all sides. His fingers are so much longer that when he flexes the top knuckle, his fingertips curl over mine.

They're strong hands.

They're warm. And I can feel the rough calluses that run along the base of his fingers. A contrast to my soft hands.

The plane dips with a rattle.

I twist my palm, and when I start to curl my fingers between his, he does the same.

And it's the best thing I've felt in a while.

With nothing else to say, I relax against the backrest and focus on Dominic's thumb as it rubs small circles on the back of my hand. Turbulence forgotten.

THE SEAT BELT LIGHT CHIMES OFF AND IS FOLLOWED BY the mass clicking of everyone on the plane unbuckling.

Following suit, I undo my belt and scoot forward on my seat until I can reach down and pick up my bag.

Dom has respected my need for quiet between us but breaks that truce when he grabs hold of my backpack strap.

I put up a minor fight, but he uses his free hand to pry my fingers off the strap. "I'll carry it."

I smooth my hands over his jacket that's resting in my lap. "Pretty sure security will have a problem with you walking all the way down to baggage claim."

Dom angles toward me to give himself space, then slings my bag over his shoulder. "Then I'll carry it until our paths part."

The crew opens the main door, and the first row of people starts to exit the plane.

Until our paths part.

When the aisle clears, Dom stands and shifts out of our row. Then he gestures for me to go ahead of him.

I do my best to look graceful as I shuffle out, and he manages to snag his jacket out of my hands so I'm left carrying nothing.

When I turn my back to Dom, standing at my full height, fingers brush against my ponytail, and he chuckles, "Shorty."

Teasing.

Stick with the teasing so you can keep smiling when your paths part.

I say thank you to the attendants, then take that last step off the plane and onto the Jetway.

It's evening, and the end-of-September air breezes up through the small gap, cooling my overheated nerves.

The trees will start to change in a few weeks, and I can't help but picture going on a fall-themed date with Dom. Complete with apple cider and scarves and curling up in front of a fireplace.

I blink.

Stay in the present, Val.

Dom walks behind me until we get to the top of the ramp and step into the Minneapolis airport. Then he moves to my side and matches his steps to mine.

The movement of his hands draws my attention, and my brows knit together when I look down at what he's doing.

Dom has rolled up his fancy suit jacket inside out so the blue silk interior is the only part showing. And he's shaped it like... like a giant burrito.

Dom tucks the bundle into the crook of his arm and presses his free hand against my lower back. "This way."

I look at the jacket and gape because it looks like he's holding a baby.

Sweet Mariah Carey. Could you imagine?

And then I look up at what's in front of us. What he's steering us toward.

I glance back down at the fake baby bundle, then up at the bright white free-standing lactation room situated along the wall in the main hallway.

"Dominic," I sort of hiss.

"We'll go in here, Mama." Dom doesn't keep his voice down. And the way he says "Mama" sounds different this time. Like he's saying it as a title, not a pet name.

As if he timed it, the door to the pod swings open, and a woman with a baby strapped to her chest steps out.

Dominic stretches his free arm out, catching the door and holding it open for her so she can get her luggage out.

"Thank you." She beams up at Dom, not even sparing a look at his *infant.*

And because my lust is stronger than my decency, I let Dom nod me forward into the lactation pod.

I let him hold the door as I go inside.

I let him step in behind me—with our fake baby in his arms.

I let him lock the door.

There's a small mirror on the wall directly in front of me, and the dim lighting above allows me to see the expression on Dom's face.

It's hunger.

Need.

Desire.

Dominic tosses his jacket onto the bench seat on our left, my backpack following it.

Then he steps closer.

His height puts his head above mine, and I watch his eyes as he looks at me in the reflection.

"What..." I trail off.

I don't really need to ask what we're doing in here. But he answers me anyway.

"I need a taste of you, Angel. A taste of whatever you'll give me."

My eyes immediately jump to the abstract drawing of a pair of boobs on the wall.

Dom groans. "Fuck, Valentine, I'd kill for just a kiss. But I'll taste those too if you let me."

My gaze snaps back to meet his in the mirror.

Those...? He wants to taste my breasts?

He gently—so gently—ghosts his hands up my hips to my waist.

"I'd let you," I whisper.

At my words, his hands clamp on to me.

The span of his fingers is so wide his thumbs press into my back on either side of my spine while his fingers dig into my soft, squishy parts.

A section of my brain tries to be embarrassed over how much his fingers press in, but the look in his eyes overrides that embarrassment.

42

He clearly likes what he feels.

He slides his hands around to my front, spanning over my stomach, pulling me back tightly against his body. *All* of his body.

That length that was half-hard when I brushed past him on the plane is... It's not half-hard. It's not half anything. And the steel of it presses into my lower back.

Lean in.

I fill my lungs, then twist in Dom's grip. He loosens his arms just enough to let me spin to face him, and I waste no time throwing my arms around his neck.

He leans down.

I stretch up.

My eyes close.

And our lips meet.

They come together in a frenzy. There is no closed-mouth peck. No sweet kisses to start. None of that.

Our mouths open the moment they connect.

Dom's tongue sweeps into my mouth, *tasting* me.

And it's been so long. It's been so damn long since I've kissed someone. But my body doesn't need any reminders.

My tongue lashes against his, and I tighten my grip around his neck, pulling him closer.

A sound rumbles from Dominic's chest into my own, and then he's dipping.

He grips my ass, then slides his hands lower. He presses my flowy yellow skirt into the crevice where my ass meets my legs, and then he lifts me.

The groan he lets out has nothing to do with hoisting me into the air and everything to do with me automatically wrapping my legs around his waist.

My mouth never leaves his. And as he grips me closer, I scrape my fingers up the back of his head. So much rougher than I was when I first touched him on the plane.

Dom takes a step, then one more, before he spins us in a partial circle.

"Legs," he pants into my mouth.

I don't know what he means until he starts to sit. Then I unhook my legs and bend them so I'm kneeling on either side of his lap when he sits on the bench opposite the backpack and jacket.

It doesn't occur to me to try and hold myself up. I like the feeling of him under me too much, so I let my weight settle on his thighs. But he's still palming my ass, and Dom must agree that I'm too far away because he pulls me closer.

Against him.

I moan when he drags me up over the bulge in his pants. A large bulge that rubs against my seam. The layers of fabric between us are hardly enough to dull the sensation.

One hand slides up. And up. Between my shoulder blades. Up my neck. And then he grabs hold of my hair, grips the base of my ponytail, and tugs.

My head tips back, finally breaking our kiss, and I slide my eyes open.

"You're gonna have to stay real quiet." Dom's lids are half-lowered as he tells me.

And I can't help myself. I roll my hips, my heat pressing into his length.

His jaw flexes, and I revel in the low sound he makes.

"We're both gonna have to stay quiet," he corrects.

"I can do that," I whisper, hardly believing what's about to happen.

"Can you?" Dom releases my hair but never lifts his hand from my body as he drags it back down to the base of my neck, then around until his hot palm covers my throat. "Can you swallow it down?" He tightens his fingers the smallest amount. "Can you swallow those pretty sounds for me?"

I nod, the movement frantic.

"What will you let me do?" his voice rumbles.

"Do?" I blink as his hand, still firmly against me, slides lower.

Dom's palm is covering my cleavage now. "What do you want me to do to you?"

I squirm.

I know what I want.

I'm sure he wants it, too.

So I lower my hands from around his neck and reach for the tie at my side that holds my dress together.

It's double knotted, but I've done this so many times it only takes me a second.

And as I pull the sides of my wrap dress apart, exposing my plain but cute white underwear set, I say it just how I would say it in my fantasies. "I want you to fuck me."

Dom makes a choking sound, and then he lets go of his hold on me so he can dedicate both hands to opening the shiny gold clasp between my breasts, popping my bra open.

"Christ, Mama, I'm gonna fuck you, alright." He cups my breast, and his other hand lands in the middle of my spine, preventing me from falling backward when he leans down and sucks my nipple into his mouth.

"Oh my god!" The sudden pressure sends electricity shooting through my body, zapping down to my toes before it comes back up to pool between my legs.

My back arches.

I can feel the slickness building at my core, and it makes me squirm.

I've always been self-conscious of how turned on I get. How wet I get.

The kiss alone was enough to ready my body for him. And this...

Dom slides his tongue over my hardened nipple.

This has me dripping.

"Your tits are perfect." Dominic moves to the other breast, proving he means it by sucking on the peak like it's giving him life.

I start tugging at Dom's shirt. "I wanna see them." I try to get to his shirt buttons, but he's bent over too far. "Please, Dom." I keep my voice quiet, but I keep pulling at the shirt. "Can I see them?"

He lifts his head. "See what?"

He pinches my nipple, and I gasp. "Tattoos. I wanna see your tattoos."

But I don't wait for him to reply, because now that he's sitting up, I'm already undoing his shirt.

Each button reveals another strip of skin, another strip of hard muscles and black ink.

Another button, and a skull stares up at me from Dom's rising and falling chest.

Another button, and his defined stomach is revealed.

My fingers hurry through the last few, then I spread the material and press my hands against his tensed torso.

I knew he had muscles. You can see it when he's fully clothed. But he's exactly the type of man I dream of. Strong. Built. Big enough to make me feel small.

Bare hands grip my sides, and I realize he's moved his hands inside my dress. "So soft." He tightens his fingers, flexing, feeling. "So goddamn soft. So warm."

I'm breathing so heavily, feeling sexier than I ever have.

Because he's making me feel sexy.

"I need to get you ready, Angel." Dom holds my gaze as he whispers to me in that deep voice. "I need you wet."

But I'm shaking my head before he finishes.

"I'm so wet." I breathe out the confession.

Fingers wrap around my nipple and squeeze.

My mouth drops open.

"I'm gonna check." Dom lowers his hand from my breast, rotating his wrist so his fingers are pointed down when he cups my mound.

That contact is enough to send another spasm through my body. And Jesus, I'm ready.

Dominic traces the edge of my panties, moving along the crease of my thigh.

When his fingers are beside my entrance, he hooks them around the elastic and pulls the strip of fabric to the side.

That motion alone is enough for his knuckles to drag across my slit, covering him with my readiness.

He drops his face forward and presses his open mouth against my shoulder to muffle the sound. But I think it was the word *fuck*.

"I t-told you."

Dom's teeth scrape over my skin as he pulls his mouth back. "Take my cock out, Valentine. You're fucking drenched and ready for it."

A wave of pleasure rolls through my body.

I like hearing him talk like this.

I guess I like dirty talk.

My hands shake as I reach down toward his belt.

Dom strokes one finger up the length of my slit but doesn't push in.

"I can't wait to be inside you." His finger slides the length again.

I pull his belt free from the buckle.

"I'm so tempted..." The first inch of his finger presses inside me. But he pulls it back out.

I whimper while I undo the button on his pants.

"But if I start now, you'll be coming on my hand." He traces his finger back up toward my clit.

I pull his zipper down.

"And I want you coming on my cock."

I pull down the top of his boxers, and his dick pops free.

It's so big and thick that it audibly slaps up against his hard stomach.

Dom slides his other hand down my back, down the crease of my ass, and keeps going until his fingertips touch below me. One hand in front and one behind.

"Hold my cock steady," Dom demands as he lifts me.

He lifts me up and off his lap.

47

His thighs are so thick, and I'm so much shorter, that even on my knees, I can't get the height I need to get his dick inside me.

So he's lifting me. By the vagina. One hand on either side of my entrance, holding me open.

I keep one hand on the back of Dom's neck, and with my other hand, I wrap my fingers around his rock-hard length.

It's so smooth. So... appealing that I want to put it in my mouth.

As easily as if I were made of feathers, Dom moves my lifted body forward.

We both hold our breaths as we near. And we both suck in a breath when his tip bumps against my clit.

"Get me wet," Dom demands.

I do as he says and rub the head of his cock along my slit, coating him with my wetness.

"I'm ready," I tell him, begging him with my eyes to hurry.

"You're ready," he says back to me, his blue eyes looking extra bright in this little room.

And then he's lowering me. And I'm spreading around him, stretching around him.

And it's good.

Oh fuck, it's so good.

Dominic's cock jumps inside me, and jolts of pleasure race between us.

It's so—

Dom drops me the last several inches, impaling me onto his lap.

At the same time, a hand flies up and presses into the back of my head, shoving my face into the space between his shoulder and neck, letting the collar of his shirt muffle my cry.

Dominic does the same, only his open mouth is against my skin again. His hot exhale makes me shiver.

Then he moves. Just a shift of his hips. And his cock pushes in a little more.

I groan into his body and rock my hips with his. My shifting thigh muscles squeeze my insides around him.

Fingers move between us, and the hand I'd forgotten about—when my focus moved to the hot length inside me—strums against my clit.

I close my eyes. All the background noise is gone now, and I'm only focused on what's happening between us, what's happening to me.

Dominic's motions get more deliberate, his lifting hips more forceful.

And I wish we had a bed we could fall back onto.

I wish I could see him completely naked.

I wish I could make this last forever.

But we're in the middle of an airport. And naked or not, I'm currently having sex with the hottest man I've ever talked to. And I've lost track of time, but I'm so close to what is going to be a screaming orgasm that I press my mouth harder against his shirt.

"I need you to come now, Angel." Dom turns his head toward my ear, enough for me to hear him. "It's been a long time, and this sweet-as-candy pussy is about to suck the cum right out of me. So I need you to come, Valentine. I need you to be a good little girl and come first."

He applies more pressure with his fingers and moves faster against my clit.

"Dominic," I say directly into his shoulder as I hug him to me with both arms.

My legs start to shake.

I've been in a state of arousal since I first saw Dom's face. And I can't hold it off much longer.

"That's it. Flutter that pussy around my cock." His words are ragged. Breathless. And he presses his fingers firmly against my bud as the tip of his dick strokes against that spot inside me, and I implode.

Dom doesn't let up.

His hips don't stop.

His fingers keep rolling.

And I keep coming.

Every muscle I have clenches, and I bite into his collar to keep from crying out.

Dominic bites down on my shoulder, pulling me down onto him as deep as he can go. His fingers finally leave my clit, and that arm bands around my back as the giant body below me flexes with release.

I can feel everything.

I can feel the seed pumping out from his tip.

I can feel his dick thickening as he pulses the final few times.

I can feel how full he's making me.

And it sends another jolt of pleasure through me, making my eyes water at the intensity.

His groan is so low it vibrates from my collarbones to my hipbones, and my core tightens around him one last time.

Dom's muscles finally relax at the same time as mine, and it feels like we melt even farther into each other.

Our heavy breaths echo around the tiny space, and I finally remember where we are.

A tiny laugh jumps up my throat, and still hugging Dominic, I slap a hand over my mouth.

"Something funny, Shorty?" Dom's lips brush my skin with every word.

"I can't believe we did that. In here." I press my lips together, keeping the larger laugh inside.

He shifts his weight from side to side. "Me either. This bench is hard."

I smile against him. "Well, my seat was perfect."

Dom nuzzles into my neck as he slides his hands down to grab my ass. "So fucking perfect." He moves his hands around to my hips, and he groans. "If we stay like this any longer, I'm going to want to do this again. And it won't be nearly as quick."

Quick? I almost moan again, not thinking that was very quick at all. And wondering what *not quick* would be like with Dom.

"I also won't be able to stay quiet for a second round." His hands flex. "And I'm pretty sure the good people of the airport will eventually take issue when we rock this pod away from the wall."

I grin as I raise my head. "Yeah, I'm not really into the whole *getting caught* thing."

His smirk makes me feel like he wants to say something but decides not to.

Then his face turns serious. "I will be buried in this sweet pussy again, Angel. This isn't the only time." His words swell inside my chest. "Tell me you believe me."

I wet my lips, my mouth feeling suddenly dry. "I believe you."

"Good." Dom leans in and presses his lips to mine in the gentle kiss we didn't start with.

And while his mouth is moving against mine, I don't notice him sliding me back on his thighs until his cock slips free.

Dom slides my underwear back in place, just in time, because with my legs still spread over him, I can feel his release leaking out.

He runs a finger between my legs, pressing the damp fabric against my swollen flesh, soaking my panties further.

Which is when I realize we never talked about condoms or birth control and certainly didn't use anything.

I inwardly cringe.

I'm on the pill, and I take it religiously, but I've never had sex without a condom. Not ever. And it was foolish and stupid and... hot. So fucking hot. But also messy.

"I know you need to clean this up." Dom traces my seam one more time. "But I'm going to be hard for the rest of the night thinking about you wearing these dirty panties all the way home."

Another pulse runs through me at his filthy mouth, causing my insides to clench, and I can feel more of him being pushed out.

Dom grips my waist with a sigh and lifts me off him, setting me on my feet in the center of the pod.

My eyes want to take in his bared chest, want to trace every inked line, but I need to focus on straightening my own clothes so I'm ready when he is.

I clip my bra—not looking up while I adjust my boobs into the push-up cups—and then rewrap the fabric of my dress before tying it off.

I glance in the mirror as I tighten my ponytail and see flushed cheeks, lips pinker than normal, and what might be a bite mark on the top of my shoulder.

Dominic, buttoned and righted, reaches past me for his jacket, which he quickly wraps back up, silk lining out, until it looks like a little baby bundle again.

"Pull the fake baby trick often?" I can't help but ask as I absently put my arms through my backpack straps.

"This is a first." Dom smirks as he hands me the bundle.

I hum and decide to trust he's telling me the truth.

And before I can overthink how we're going to coordinate this, I'm stepping out of the little lactation room, pretend baby in my arms, with my pretend husband stepping out behind me.

The door clicks shut after Dom, and he drapes his arm around my shoulder, keeping us moving.

I keep my gaze down when I notice a few people looking our way. The anxious part of me assumes that they know what we just did. But then I think about my reaction the first time I saw Dom and figure there's a good chance they're just looking at him.

"Yeah, go ahead and change him," Dom says like it's a response to a question I never asked.

Then I flick my gaze up and see the ladies' room right in front of us.

Still walking, Dom holds me to his side as he lowers his voice. "It was nice to meet you, Valentine."

He presses his lips against my temple, and then he's gone.

Moving down the hall.

Like he's headed toward the men's room, but I know the truth.

He won't be here when I come out.

CHAPTER 5

Val

"Sorry!" I lift my hand in a waving apology to Bo.

My driver, a.k.a. security guard, shakes his head and grabs the handle of my luggage next to the empty baggage carousel.

When I was in the bathroom *cleaning up*, I noticed my bag vibrating and dragged my phone out just in time to miss Bo's call. And to see the five other calls I missed.

I texted him immediately, telling him I was sorry for being late but that I had a stomach issue and would be a few more minutes.

I wasn't more specific than that. But I knew I wouldn't have to be, because Bo is good at his job and good at not asking me more questions than strictly necessary.

I feel a little bad about him having to wait for me, but then I remember he gets paid by the hour, and I don't feel so bad anymore.

We walk in silence out to the big SUV that's illegally parked in the pickup lane—but somehow not being ticketed—and Bo walks my suitcase around to the rear of the vehicle while I climb into the back seat and set my backpack next to my feet.

The moving air from the back door slamming shut wafts the perfume I sprayed on myself before I left the bathroom, since I was paranoid about smelling like sex.

My mind spins as Bo pulls away from the curb and we join the traffic leaving the airport.

And I can't help but wonder if I'll really see Dominic again.

And I wonder if he meant for me to keep his jacket, the bundle currently shoved into the top of my bag.

And I'm wondering how long I'm going to stress about this when my phone vibrates from inside my bag.

I take it out, and my chest fills with a soft, light feeling.

> Big Guy: Let me know when you make it home safely, Valentine.

I clutch the phone in both hands and smile out the window. Because that feeling is hope.

I'VE UNPACKED MY LUGGAGE, PREPPED MY LAUNDRY SO I can start it tomorrow—carefully tucking my dirty underwear into the middle of the pile, even though there's no one else to see it— showered, and put on my pajamas. And now, there is not a single thing to stop me from texting Dominic back.

With only the bedside lamp on, I crawl onto my bed and sit cross-legged against the pillows.

My hands are only shaking a little as I unlock my phone, the screen automatically opening to the text from Big Guy because I've looked at it a hundred times since Bo dropped me off at my apartment.

I lock the screen and set the phone on my bright white comforter.

Quit being a baby. He texted you. If he didn't want you to text him back, he would've just said have a good night *or* it's been fun *or something like that. He specifically told you to text him back.*

I pick the phone back up and unlock it again.

"Just send a normal text back."

I stare at the keyboard.

Then I stare at the text Dominic sent me.

And then I start to feel guilty because he was kind enough to text right away, and he asked me to let him know when I got home. And I've been home for a while now.

But there's about an hour of flying time between here and Chicago, so maybe this delay is perfect to catch him when he's back on the ground.

"I can be normal." My lips purse as I blow out a breath. "Think chill."

I don't know why the first person who pops into my brain when I say that is Aspen, my half sister, because she might be cool, collected, and proper when she has to be, but she's not chill. She's the opposite of chill.

My fingers tap against the letters, and I type out *hi*, then delete it.

Me: Hey.

Delete.

Me: Good evening, Dominic.

Oh my god. Delete.

I close my eyes.

I was acting like me, more or less, the whole time we were together. So I should keep acting like me.

> Me: I'm home! Sorry I didn't text sooner. I figured you'd be in the air, and I wanted to get all my crap unpacked before bed. And there was this guy today who bought me a new backpack, so I had to take the proper time to appreciate it because I was a little flustered when I got it. Hope your flight was smooth! And I'd love for you to return the favor.

Send.
Oh, wait! No!

> Me: Sorry! I meant for you to return the favor of letting me know when you get home safely.

Send.
I groan.

> Me: Not like return the favor "return the favor" because that was already very much returned.

Send.

> Me: Not that you'd have to do that every time. It's not expected or anything.

Send.
Oh my god, what is wrong with me!?

> Me: Please delete these and block my number without showing your friends. That's all I'll ask of you.

My face is on fire.
It's melted off.
I have no face anymore.

Which will make witness protection easy. Because clearly, I need to change my name and disappear.

I flip my phone over and put it back on the bed. Then I lay my hand over the top and press it into the mattress. Because maybe if I press hard enough, I'll be able to push it into another dimension, and this will have never happened.

The phone vibrates, startling me.

And it keeps vibrating. Not with texts. With an incoming call.

He wouldn't.

I pick my phone up, and sure enough, Big Guy is calling.

I almost don't answer. Almost hit decline. But he knows I'm near my phone. I just sent him five text messages in a row.

I shut my eyes as I hit answer. Maybe it will help if I can't see.

"Hello?" My voice comes out high pitched.

"Angel." I can hear the smile in Dominic's voice. "Just to be clear, you should absolutely expect me to *return the favor* when we're together."

His voice is pitched extra low, and the texture of it rattles in my chest.

"Oh," I barely whisper.

"And, if I were a gentleman, I'd make sure you get at least two favors to every one of mine."

I swallow.

"But also, if I were a gentleman, I wouldn't have fucked you in a breastfeeding room, sucking on those big, beautiful titties while you bounced around on my lap."

I choke on the air leaving my lungs.

"So, guess I'm not always a gentleman. But I can still promise that you'll always get your favors." Dominic pauses while my heart beats wildly out of control. "But save your favors for me. Alright, Mama?"

"I..." *Holy orgasms, I'm about to come just from his words.* "My favors are for you."

"Good. Now get some sleep, Valentine." Dominic slows his

speech on my name, stretching it out for a fraction of a second longer, then he ends the call.

Boneless, I drop sideways onto the bed.

I hope we can see each other again soon.

CHAPTER 6
Val

My hand flies down to my phone the second it vibrates with a text.

Disappointment flares when I see Savannah's name on the screen. Which I immediately feel bad about because I like Savannah. I like her a lot. She's only been my sister-in-law for a couple of months, but she's already my favorite family member. I just happen to be waiting for a text from someone else.

Or maybe he's waiting for me to text first?

But since we both witnessed my texting disaster two nights ago, I think it's safe to say that no one is expecting me to know proper texting etiquette.

I reply to Savannah, telling her that I'd love to come over for dinner next weekend.

It'll be nice to see her, and I'll need a break from sitting in my empty apartment fantasizing about Dominic.

Savannah texts back, confirming the time, and I add in the obligatory *what should I bring?* even though they have a cook that lives on their property. You know, like people do.

My desktop computer signals the arrival of the email I've been waiting for, so I turn back to my screen.

I'm reading through the email when my phone buzzes with Savannah's reply.

My hands go to my keyboard to type up the reply, but then I remember the text and glance down.

> Big Guy: Did you have a nice day, Shorty?

Not Savannah.
My cheeks are hot.
Why are my cheeks hot?

> Me: Pretty normal. How about you?

Send.

> Big Guy: Mine was pretty normal, too. But I couldn't stop thinking about this knockout I met at the airport this week.

Knockout?
Swoon.

> Me: Oh yeah? I bet she was super funny and brilliant.

Send.
I groan.
Why am I so weird?

> Big Guy: You think I would settle for anything less?

Gah, he's so perfect.

> Me: Of course not. I've seen your face.

Send.

I groan again.

I've seen your face?

> Me: I don't mean that in a serial killer way.

Send.

> Me: I meant that I've seen how handsome your face is.

Send.

> Me: And that obviously you wouldn't have to settle since you look the way you do.

Send.

> Me: Reimplementing the blocking request. See text from two days ago.

Send.

I turn my head to my second computer monitor, which is currently off, and stare at my reflection on the black surface.

This is why you're single.

My phone buzzes.

> Big Guy: I deeply regret not texting you yesterday. Clearly, you're the cure for changing a normal day into a good day.

How many times can a person swoon in one text conversation?

> Me: If you message me again tomorrow, I'll do my best to make your normal day good.

Send.

Wow, that sounded stupid.

I set the phone down and sit on my hands.

He knows what I mean. I don't need to clarify.

> Big Guy: I'm going to hold you to that. Until tomorrow, Angel.

I pick my phone back up and stare at the screen, wondering if it would be strange to kiss it.

Yes, it would.

> Me: Bye, Dom.

Send.

24 HOURS LATER

> Big Guy: Evening, Angel. Did you use your backpack today?

> Me: I did not. But it's sitting in the middle of my living room, so I saw it.

> Big Guy: Close enough. I have to jump on a call but wanted some Valentine goodness first.

> Me: Goodnight, Mr. Workaholic. I'm already in my pajamas.

> Big Guy: Goodnight, sleepy girl.

My half brother's chef clears away the dinner plates, and no matter how many times I eat here, it's still a little strange to be waited on like we're in a restaurant.

Brother. I'm trying to remember to just call King and Aspen my brother and sister and drop the half, even if I'm only saying it in my head. I don't want to have that divide between us forever.

King's housekeeper steps into the room, helping the chef with the dishes, and I'm reminded that nothing is ever normal around here—in this giant mansion with guard dogs, a manned gate, and round-the-clock armed security. But since King is some sort of mafia person, I suppose normal is relative.

Is The Alliance mafia?

I honestly don't know the difference between *the mafia* and regular organized crime. If there even is a difference. And it's not like I can just google it. Well, I could. But I know enough about the whole *Alliance thing* to know that King has some major computer skills. And I don't really want to be detained by his men for googling "what is the mafia."

It doesn't really matter anyway. Except for the driver that King makes me use, *for my own safety*, I'm not involved. I doubt the Vass siblings would have told me about it if they could have gotten away with it. And I don't really know what, if anything, Aspen does for The Alliance, but I know she knows more than me.

Either way, giving me a bodyguard is probably a sign that they actually like me and it hasn't just been some act. If they didn't care about me, they wouldn't mind if I got abducted by some enemy.

My mouth pulls into a frown as I remember the man who tried to kill Savannah not that long ago. In this very house.

"You okay?" Savannah asks me from her spot across the table.

I realize something must have shown on my face, so I quickly smile. "Yeah, good! Sorry, just zoned out there."

"Probably working too much. Seems to run in the family." She snorts.

King shakes his head as he stands from his seat next to her. "Quit spreading lies, Honey. You work more than I do."

Savannah just grins as she pushes her chair back.

Aspen got up to take a call a few minutes ago.

News recently broke that her husband, Leland, passed away while on a work trip overseas. Their sources are saying it was a previously unknown heart condition, one that runs in his family. But being a stubborn man, Leland never went to the doctor to get checked for it. Even though his wife constantly begged him to.

When the story first came across my newsfeed online, I nearly spit out my coffee.

I knew the family would have to pronounce Leland dead eventually, and I'm positive the whole string of information was carefully crafted by Aspen before it was released. Still, the whole concerned wife angle was too much for me not to react to. Since, in reality, Leland had been cheating on Aspen, and Aspen was the one who asked King to kill him.

But sure, *heart attack* it is.

God, I wish I had someone I could talk to about this!

And it's not because I'm scared of Aspen or King; I'm not. As far as I'm concerned, fuck Leland—he earned what he got. But it's just such good gossip. And I want to get drunk with someone and laugh about it.

But there's no one for me to do that with.

I take my phone out of my pocket, and my chest heats when I see a text notification.

> Big Guy: Hope you're having a good dinner. My family is over, and I'm about to kick a nine-year-old's ass in Mario Kart.

I grin.

It's been almost two weeks since our flight together, and other than the day right after, we've texted every day since.

We don't message a lot at once, but it is every day. And it's been so... nice. Like just *so* nice.

> Me: Sounds like a great achievement. I'm
> about to sit outside around a fire and eat
> dessert with a bunch of adults.

Send.

While I wait for his reply, I daydream about being able to tell him everything about my family. He's told me about his big family a few times, but with murder, crime, and intrigue, I'd definitely win the *my family is crazier* debate.

> Big Guy: I can think of a dessert I'd like to eat
> by the fire.

"Damn!" Savannah exclaims from behind me, and I smash my phone against my chest to hide the screen.

"Oh my god! Nosy much?" I'm too embarrassed to sound mad.

Savannah starts laughing. "I wasn't even trying to look."

I push back from the table and get up, keeping the phone against my chest. "Sure you weren't."

"I wasn't!" she insists. "I was going to try and startle you." Savannah snickers. "But I startled myself instead."

I lift a hand to cover my mouth in a vain attempt to hide my stupid grin. "That wasn't the response I was expecting either."

"So..." Savannah waggles her eyebrows at me. "Who is *Big Guy*?"

I slide my hand up to cover my eyes. "Just some guy," I groan. "It's new, and I don't want to jinx it, but I really like him."

"Hmm." I drop my hand to see Savannah narrowing her eyes at me. "So, where did you meet Mr. No Name?"

I was tempted to change his name in my phone the other night, but now I'm glad I didn't. Savannah and King share everything, and even if Savannah mentioned it casually, King would probably end up going into crazy overprotective mode and run a background check on him. Maybe even show up in Chicago to question him in person. And that would be bad. Like epic bad. And it would definitely kill this thing between Dom and me before it even started.

"At the airport," I admit as my phone vibrates against my cleavage.

Because I have no willpower when it comes to him, I pull my phone back to check the message.

> **Big Guy:** I really shouldn't let you distract me with your dirty talk. Now I'm going to lose my next race and it's going to be all your fault.

I press my lips together.

How is he so cute?

"What does he look like?" Savannah asks as she leans closer, arching her neck to try and look over the top of my phone.

I press the phone back against my chest. "Hot."

Savannah snickers at my answer. "That's a good start."

I sigh. "He's tall and handsome and has these beautiful eyes and..." I trail off when I see Savannah's wide-eyed expression. "What?"

"You really like him, don't you?"

My shoulders lift. "Yeah, but it's long distance. And it just happened, and I don't even know if we're, like, actually dating or just, like, talking every day." I lift my shoulders again. "But he makes me smile."

Her expression softens. "Well, whatever it is, I'm happy for you."

Warmer emotions push the embarrassment out of my cheeks. "Thanks."

It wasn't too long ago that Savannah and I got a little tipsy and shared our dream wedding ideas. Mine was ridiculous because it's been forever since I've even had a boyfriend, so no real chance of a wedding anytime soon. And Savannah's was ridiculous because she was already married. And her wedding was... unconventional.

"Come on." Savannah grabs my arm and pulls me toward the kitchen, where patio doors lead into the backyard.

I let her lead me and wait until I'm seated in one of the big wooden chairs before I check my phone screen again.

> Me: My sister-in-law saw your text about "dessert," and now I'm dying of embarrassment, so I kind of hope your nephew kicks your ass.

Send.

> Me: But I also don't want to date a loser, so you better win.

Send.
Crap.

> Me: Not that we're dating.

Send.

> Me: I mean, I'm not seeing anyone else, but we didn't make any commitments or anything.

Send.
Why am I even allowed to have a phone anymore?

> Me: If you can send one of your relatives to come push me off the Rainbow Bridge so I can plummet into the abyss and disappear from this world, that would be great.

Send.

"Who're you texting?" King's voice sounds from right beside me.

I jump so hard that the chair starts to tip over.

King places his elbow on the back corner of my chair, pressing it back to the ground.

Savannah laughs from the other side of the fire. "She's all jumpy because she's talking to a boy."

"Savannah!" I chastise.

When the man at my side doesn't move, I dart my eyes up to King.

And sure enough, he's staring down at me with a very serious look. "Who is he?"

I'm not even surprised by his question.

"No one," I squeak, then clear my throat. "He's not from here."

"Where's he from?" King hardly even lets me finish my sentence.

I hold up a hand. "We were seated next to each other on my flight back from Denver and exchanged numbers. I promise I'll tell you guys if it turns into anything, and then you can ask me all the questions you want. But since we've only met the one time, I don't want to make it into a whole thing. Okay?"

King tilts his head. "Is he the reason you were late getting your luggage?"

My mouth drops open.

My intimidating brother inclines his head. "That's what I thought."

"Wait, what are you talking about?" Savannah is leaning over her armrest to try and see us around the flames.

"Nothing," I try to say, but King talks over me. "Bo reported that she was thirty minutes late getting down to baggage claim after that flight."

Savannah grins. "Way to go, Val!"

I press my hands to my cheeks and stare at Savannah, refusing to look up at King. "Can we please talk about literally anything else?"

He doesn't move right away, and I'm worried he's going to

demand more, but then Aspen comes out of the house carrying a tray with our dessert.

"Warm apple crisp with ice cream," she tells us as she approaches. "Cici's really leaning into the fall theme," she says, referring to the cook.

Savannah comments on how crazy it is that it's already October, and I have to agree. But I also feel like these couple weeks of texting with Dom have made time fly by even faster.

King takes a pair of dishes for himself and Savannah while Aspen hands me the last bowl before she takes the chair between Savannah and me. Aspen jumps into asking Savannah something about the next charity auction they're hosting, and I thank the powers that be that I dodged that bullet.

It's not that I'm worried they won't like Dominic. And I'm not worried they'll find some shady past and try to tell me not to date him. I'm just not ready to pull Dom into this messed-up crime-family bullshit. Not yet. Not until we know each other better. Because letting people in on *all this* is probably more husband territory than fling territory.

My phone vibrates, and I remember the string of messages I just sent Dominic.

With everyone else distracted, I peek at his reply and smile around a mouthful of spiced apples.

Big Guy: Every day, you make my day.

Big Guy: Tell me to have a good day.

Me: Have a good day, Big Guy.

Big Guy: What are you having for dinner?

Me: Spaghetti.

Big Guy: Homemade?

Me: If adding stuff to jarred sauce counts, then yes.

Big Guy: Send me a pic.

Umm...

I debate for a moment, then hold the phone up, check the lighting, and snap the photo.

Me: *sends selfie*

Oh, shit! Did he mean the spaghetti?

Big Guy: Damn, Angel. You need to warn a man.

Uhh... what does that mean?

Big Guy: I was expecting carbs, not your pretty face.

Big Guy: For the record, this is way better than a plate pic.

He called me pretty.

Me: *sends photo of my half-eaten plate of spaghetti*

Big Guy: Valentine, tell me you're in town this
week.

I LOOK AT THE CALENDAR ON MY WALL, LIKE
confirming it's still Monday will change my answer.

Me: Dominic, tell me you're joking.

My phone vibrates with a call.

"Hello," I answer, and my voice sounds breathy with nerves.

We've been texting daily for the whole month of October, but we don't talk on the phone that often. So knowing I'm about to hear his voice has my heart thudding.

"Hey, Mama."

Since I'm sitting in bed, where no one can see me, I let my eyes roll back and mouth, *oh my god*.

Seriously, why is that so hot?

"Tell me you're in town this week," he demands.

I groan. "I can't. I leave tomorrow and then fly home Saturday."

"Of fucking course." Dominic sounds resigned.

"Should I even ask?" I bite my lip.

"Only if you want to feel crushing disappointment," he grumbles.

"Let me guess. You're going to be visiting my lovely state the exact dates I'm going to be gone."

"That's the gist of it." I hear the sound of an elevator's doors dinging open on Dom's end of the line. "Well, shit. Where are you going?"

"Hawaii." I sigh. Like going to Hawaii is anything less than amazing.

Dom chuckles at my tone. "Poor darling. Is this for work or fun?"

"Fun. Though staying home is sounding like a lot of fun, too."

Dominic lets out a full laugh. "Did you just compare me to a tropic vacation?"

I smirk into my empty room. "I didn't say I was canceling my ticket."

He laughs again. "Angel, you wound me."

"Uh-huh." I flop onto my back, the mattress making me bounce a little. "But even if I wanted to, it's a family thing, so I can't really reschedule."

I press my lips together. That sounded like a bit much. We've only met once, and even fake offering to reschedule a vacation is crazy.

Way to speed right to clinger territory, Val.

"Family thing could be fun."

Okay, so he's not acting like that was weird.

"My half—" I stop and correct myself. "My brother is renewing his vows with his wife. So it's basically a wedding, but not exactly."

Should I be saying this?

What if he asks about their first wedding?

Or how they met? Because I can't really tell him any of that since King literally kidnapped his wife and blackmailed her into marrying him.

"Ah." He makes a noise of understanding. "I've been to more than one vow renewal, so say no more. Nice place for it, at least."

I nod, glad he didn't ask any of the questions I just had a minor heart attack panicking over. "It is. My brother rented out a group of those over-the-water bungalow things. Which is great, because apparently, my new thing is to let men buy me expensive things."

"You better just be referring to me and that little backpack," Dominic says flatly.

I snort. "Who else is buying me things?"

"Good answer." Dominic exhales. "I gotta go. Tell me to have a good night and send me a picture when you get to Hawaii."

"Have a good night, Dominic."

"Night, Angel."

Me: *sends photo of myself standing on the deck of my bungalow*

MY LUNGS FILL WITH THE WARM MORNING AIR.

With the ocean underneath and all around, and with the sun just barely rising, the place feels magical.

Otherworldly.

I take another deep breath.

And quiet.

I'm ready early. I'm always ready early. So I'm the only one standing out here, but I know King is two bungalows down. His best friend, Nero, and his wife are in the one between us, and Aspen is on the far side of King.

And...

The breeze flutters my bright pink skirt around my knees.

And even with them all so close, I feel lonely.

So goddamn lonely.

I press my lips together.

This isn't about me. I'm here for King and Savannah.

I exhale.

And Aspen is here alone, too. So it's not like it's just me and a bunch of couples. But...

I do another set of inhales and exhales.

But Aspen and I aren't close.

She's not mean to me. And she's not indifferent to me like she used to be. I can't even begin to imagine the mind-fuck stuff she's dealt with recently. But still...

I've tried.

I've tried really hard to be her sister. Just as hard as I've tried with King. And they're both nice to me. It's just...

I close my eyes.

I'm happy King found Savannah. They're good for each other. And I'm happy he's doing this for her—surprising her with this sunrise ceremony. And I'm going to have fun today. I will.

I just need to quit hoping for things that are never going to happen.

I open my eyes and look around at the walkways connecting the buildings.

And I need someone else to come out of their fucking bungalow so I'm not standing here like I'm the only person left in the world, in possibly the most romantic setting in the world.

It's annoying.

I lift my phone the second I feel Dominic text me back.

Big Guy: You look beautiful.

Each word resonates between my ribs, meaning so much more than he could imagine.

Me: I wish I'd stayed home with you.

Delete.

Me: I wish you were here with me.

Delete.

Me: Thank you.

Send.

74

> Big Guy: *sends photo of empty first-class seat*

> Big Guy: I'm already annoyed at whoever is going to make me get up so they can sit here because I know it won't be you.

I SHIELD MY EYES FROM THE SUN AND SMILE AT THE phone.

> Me: Just remember, The Fugitive is off-limits.

Send.

> Big Guy: Obviously. That's our movie.

"You smiling over your mystery man?" Aspen says, surprising me.

I tip my head to the side, laid back in my lounge chair, to look at her.

She's in the same position as me, a few feet away, our faces shaded by the big umbrella.

"Yes," I admit.

Aspen purses her lips. "The longer you try to keep his identity a secret, the more curious everyone is gonna get. And a curious King can be an extremely obnoxious thing."

She's speaking the truth.

"I just want to meet him in person one more time." Everyone knows that we met in the airport and had a flight together. And everyone speculates about why I was late to get my luggage. "If we still hit it off after that, then I'll take a photo of his driver's license and give it to King."

I don't even bother complaining about Bo tattling on me.

Aspen leans her head back, closing her eyes. "I still say you should let King run the guy now. Can never be too careful."

I make a humming sound, understanding her point but having nothing to add.

Unlike Aspen and King, I'm not wealthy. I'm not powerful. I'm just a normal no one.

So there's no one out there targeting me for some sort of marriage of benefit. If a man marries me, he inherits an Ikea living room set, an expensive blender I've used twice, and a savings account that could buy a decent used car, but not a luxury one.

My lids slide closed.

Dom's not after me for my money or anything else. And when I get home tomorrow, I'm going to make seeing him in person a priority.

> Me: *sends photo of my feet between two other sets of feet on the plane*
>
> Me: Guess who forgot to make her seat selection and ended up sitting bitch in row twenty-seven?

SEND.

> Big Guy: My poor Valentine.

> Big Guy: Happy Halloween, Shorty. Tell me, are you dressing up as an angel?
>
> Me: Well, it's 8 p.m. and I've already got my costume on.

SEND.

Me: *sends photo of myself on the couch in a hoodie with a headband holding my hair away from the green clay mask on my face*

Big Guy: Terrifying.

Me: It's keeping all the kids away. Guess I'll just eat this bowl of candy myself.

Me: I'm having a sad day.

DELETE.

Me: Hope your flight to Arizona was good.

Send.

Big Guy: Some asshole bumped into me in the airport and didn't even buy me a cookie.

Big Guy: It's been a week, Angel. Tell me something good.

Me: Jury's still out if this is good or not, but I'm about to board a plane.

SEND.

Big Guy: That vacation a couple weeks ago already wearing off?

Me: Ha! I wish I was going back to Hawaii.

Send.

> Big Guy: Where are you going?

> Me: Vegas. I got invited to a last-minute bachelorette party by one of my coworkers. We're getting there tonight, staying two nights, and then coming back Sunday.

Send.

> Me: Make my weekend better and tell me you happen to be in Vegas right now.

Send.

> Big Guy: I'm in Vegas right now.

CHAPTER 7

Dom

MY CHEST EXPANDS AS I STAND FROM MY COUCH.

"Call Vance," I call out to Rob, my second in command, who's sitting at the kitchen island. "Tell him to get to the airfield. I want wheels up in thirty."

I stride toward the stairs on the other side of my penthouse. I need to pack a bag.

"City for the flight plan?" Rob asks my retreating form.

"Vegas."

CHAPTER 8
Val

MY MOUTH DROPS OPEN.

I blink at the phone screen.

Did he... Is Dominic really in Vegas right now?

My heart starts to beat faster.

Dom is in Vegas.

Holy crap. Dom is in Vegas.

My palms start to sweat.

I'm going to see Dominic again. Tonight.

I TAKE AN UBER TO THE RESORT WE'RE ALL STAYING AT and hurry through check-in so I can freshen up in my room.

I wasn't packing for a weekend with Dom. I was packing for a weekend with some of the women I work with. So I'm forced to pick the sexier of the two outfits I brought and hope it's good enough for whatever we end up doing.

I smooth my hands down the black silk tank top I have tucked into my high-waisted, wide-legged black pants that are long enough to cover my three-inch wedges.

The elevator doors open in front of me, and I get in, selecting the main floor.

Our group agreed to meet in the lobby in—I check my phone —one minute. Then we were going to walk across the street for dinner.

Except I'm about to tell them that I'm bailing.

Because Dominic is picking me up in sixteen minutes so that I can have dinner with him.

The elevator stops, and I step out, spotting my group immediately.

"Hey, Val!" one of the ladies calls out to me.

We all work in different cities, so we normally only see each other on web calls, but everyone still greets me with a hug.

It makes me feel bad about ditching because they're all so nice. But I don't feel so bad that I'll skip this opportunity to see Dominic.

I tell Bri, the newly engaged woman from our Chicago branch, congratulations on her upcoming wedding. Then I decide to dive right in before anyone can start a conversation.

"Okay, so, please don't hate me, but I just found out this guy I've been, um, talking to is in Vegas right now. And I'm going to go have dinner with him." I start talking faster as I go, feeling guilty and nervous. "I'm really sorry. I didn't know he was gonna be here until I was practically on the plane. And I really want to see him. And he's so damn good looking."

The girl from Dallas holds up her hands to stop me. "Val, trust me, we get it. Good dick is hard to come by."

My cheeks flame.

"You have met him, though, right?" Bri asks. "This isn't like an online thing, and he *just so happens* to be in Vegas."

I press my hands against my cheeks to cool them down. "I promise we've met before."

The first girl snickers. "Yeah, you have."

I flip my hands over, hoping the backs of my hands will be

cooler. "I can try to find you guys later." I give the half-hearted offer.

"No way." Bri shakes her head. "The schedule for the weekend is in our emails. You go do you. If you want to meet up, you know where to find us. But if you end up spending the whole weekend banging this guy, just check in and let us know you're alive."

I lift my hands away and use them to fan my face. My little wristlet purse flaps with the motion.

"Deal." I blow out a breath. "I don't know why I'm so nervous."

The girl from St. Louis pats my shoulder. "Because dating is terrifying."

I laugh. "It kinda is, isn't it?"

She nods, and we all turn, starting toward the main entrance.

They'll head down the strip a block, and I'll just wait outside the doors for Dom.

We're halfway across the lobby when Bri curses under her breath. "Fuck me."

My eyes snap up to the doors.

And standing there, a few yards away, on the other side of the glass, is Dominic.

My Dominic.

My Big Guy.

And damn... I forgot just how big he is. Tall and wide and filling out the black material of his suit like it's his job.

His eyes are locked on mine. The blue is so clear, even at this distance, that it makes me want to run to him. To throw myself into his arms.

But I don't do that.

I just keep walking.

And staring.

Because he's walking, too.

The automatic door slides open as he approaches the other side, and he doesn't break his stride, his trajectory obvious.

"Holy shit, is that your guy?" Dallas hisses.

I try to bite down on my smile, but it doesn't work because there's no stopping the way he makes me feel.

And he's so close.

Close enough that I can see the tattoos on his chest, since his black shirt has the top two buttons undone.

Close enough that we all hear him when he replies, "Yeah, I'm her guy."

"I want to switch itineraries with Val," St. Louis grumbles.

"Ladies." Dom nods to my friends before he turns all his attention to me. "Valentine."

He says my name a little deeper, with a little more gravel in his tone.

I think one of the girls groans.

"Hi, Dominic." My voice is surprisingly steady.

He holds his hand out, and I step forward to place my palm against his.

Dom lowers his face to press a kiss against the corner of my mouth. "My little Angel, all dressed in black. How delicious."

Okay, so I shouldn't have even bothered with underwear.

Dominic straightens and nods once more to my little group of coworkers before he pulls me along, back toward the entrance.

After a few steps, I glance back over my shoulder to see four stunned faces staring after me.

Dallas lifts her brows and mouths *holy fuck.*

I grin back at her.

Because yeah. *Holy fuck.*

CHAPTER 9

Val

DOM LEADS ME TO A BLACKED-OUT SUV THAT REMINDS me of the one Bo drives and pulls the rear passenger door open.

As I climb in, Dominic skims his hand over my hip, the thin material of my pants letting me feel the heat of his touch.

"Buckle in," Dom tells me, then shuts the door.

While he walks around the back of the vehicle, I do as he says and avoid looking at the driver, feeling too flustered to think about the money he must've spent to hire a driver for the night.

I hope it wasn't too expensive.

Dom pulls open his door, and the neon lights behind him seem to glow extra bright against the night sky. As he climbs into his seat and pulls the door shut, a glint of light reflects off his watch, and I remind myself that Dominic isn't hurting for money.

I don't know exactly what he does. He said something about property management and shipping—which I pretended to understand—but if he wants to spend his money on a driver in Vegas, that's on him.

"Ready, Boss?" the driver asks.

I'm watching Dom's profile, so I see him narrow his eyes at the driver through the rearview mirror.

"Uh, I mean, Mr. Gonzalez." The driver corrects himself.

Maybe Dominic doesn't like being called Boss.

"Yes." Dom's expression clears, and the driver pulls ahead.

My fingers twitch in my lap as anxiety bounces through my body.

This is what I've been dreaming of for over a month. Why can't I just be calm?

There's movement on the seat next to me. "Angel, don't be nervous."

I glance down, seeing Dom's hand palm up between us.

"I'm not nervous," I lie, even as I set my trembling hand in his.

"It's just me." His voice is soothing as he wraps his fingers around mine.

"I know." I take a fortifying breath, then look up to meet his eyes. "I'm just having a hard time believing this is really happening." Dom smirks, and my mouth pulls into a little smile. "I didn't mean *that*." I'm thankful for the dark interior of the car. Hopefully I can get this damn blush under control before we get to the restaurant. "I just mean... It feels like we met so long ago. I was starting to think we might be cursed."

His smirk stays in place. "Real life Montague and Capulet."

More of my stress slips away. "I believe they were considered star-crossed, not cursed."

Dominic dips his chin. "Fair. Plus, our ending will be better."

My stomach flips when he says *our ending*, like a future between us is inevitable. "It will?"

"I plan to die a very old man."

I purse my lips. "So, in like ten years?"

The driver coughs, and I think it's to cover a laugh, but I'll never know because before I can blink, Dominic is there.

Against me.

His hand is behind my neck, pulling me closer, making my body turn toward his.

He keeps our fingers in his other hand entwined but lifts them, pinning them to the seat next to my head.

It all happens in a flash.

One breath. And then warm lips press against mine.

I missed his lips.

The hand on my neck tightens, holding me up while all my bones turn to mush.

"Let me in," Dominic whispers against my lips. "Now, Valentine."

My mouth opens.

I have no other choice.

He slides his tongue across my lip. I try to pull it into my mouth, but his tongue retreats and his teeth close on my lower lip.

"You've been teasing me with this fucking mouth for over a month." He slowly slides the hand on the back of my neck around to the front.

"Teasing?" I'm already breathing heavily.

"With your sassy little selfies." He closes his mouth over mine again.

Sassy?

I inhale through my nose as Dom ravages my mouth, and I'm assaulted by his scent. With that warm, masculine cologne he wears. And it wraps around me like a blanket. Like I'm home.

Before the weekend is over, I'm finding out what he wears and buying some to spray on his suit jacket I still have.

The one currently draped over the armchair in the corner of my bedroom, making it look like he left it there, like he's been over and left it after stripping down to nothing.

Building heat gathers in my core.

I grip the front of Dom's shirt with my free hand, my nails scraping across his chest.

His muscles tense at the contact, and I feel his groan in my fingertips.

"Dominic," I whisper.

The fingers around mine squeeze a tiny bit. They tighten just that little bit, and I want more.

But Dom pulls back.

His eyes are inches from mine, the blue sparking with life. "I promised you dinner, so that's what we're doing. But you're coming to my hotel after."

I nod.

"Your friends okay with you staying out?"

I nod again. "They just want proof of life, if..." I trail off, but Dom raises a brow, prompting me to finish. "If we spend all weekend *banging*."

Dom grins. "I like your friends."

"Me, too." I debate telling him that I don't know them really well and that I was happy to leave them for him, but our vehicle slows to a stop.

Dom slides back across the seat to his side.

"You're supposed to wear your seat belt," I chastise him.

"I figured you were worth the danger." Dom opens his door, and his gaze turns serious. "Wait for me."

Dom slams the door after he gets out, and I glance up to catch the driver watching me through the mirror, but then his eyes immediately dart away.

I'm unbuckled and ready, so when Dom opens the door, I take his offered hand and climb down.

We stand there, chest to chest, for a moment.

Dom slides his tongue along his teeth. "You're not as short, Shorty."

I slide a foot to the side and pull up on my pant leg, the material rising to show the tall shoes hidden beneath.

"You're gonna twist an ankle in those."

"I'll have you know," I tell him, releasing the material and recovering my shoe, "I can move at an almost jog in these things."

Dom holds his elbow out away from his side, and I slide my hand through the V it makes.

"An almost jog. I retract my statement. Clearly, you're a pro."

We start across the sidewalk together. "For the record." He looks down at me. "I like you short."

I look up at him. "I like you big."

My eyes widen at the same time Dom lets out a bark of laughter. And, *Jesus fuck me*, the man just gets hotter.

I'm too distracted by his presence to catch the name of the restaurant before we step through the front door.

"Welcome." The host steps out from behind the front desk, two menus in hand. "Right this way."

Dominic doesn't lower his arm, so I don't drop my hold on his elbow as we walk through the large, dramatically lit dining room.

It's sexy. Blacks and reds and dark wood tones. With bright green plants hanging from the walls and ceilings and interesting wicker chandeliers.

Most of the tables are filled. And most people are busy in their own conversations, but lots of faces still turn our way.

I keep my shoulders back and my grip on Dominic's arm light. *I belong here. At his side. In this restaurant.*

We walk past a woman who gives Dom, then me, a once over, and I realize that without even trying, we've dressed like we planned it. Wearing black from head to toe.

His little Angel, all dressed in black.

The host stops before a table in the back corner. It's a four-seater, but it's already set just for two, the selected seats next to each other, both angled out to face the rest of the dining room.

"Here you are, miss." The host pulls a chair out for me.

I slide into the space between the chair and table, but before he can push my chair in, Dom crowds into the space, forcing the host to step back.

I bite down on the urge to laugh and let Dom push my chair in as I sit, forgetting about the fact that Dominic never checked in or even said his name when we got here.

Dom is lowering himself into his chair when a server reaches our table.

"I'll give you a moment with the menu," she says as she fills our water glasses. "But if you'd like to start with a drink, let me know."

She has trouble looking at Dom and instead bounces her gaze between me and the table.

Taking pity on her, because I get it, he's too hot to look at, I decide a drink is the perfect thing. "Can I have a margarita on the rocks, please?"

She nods. "Of course. Do you have a tequila preference?"

"Oh. Um..." I look to Dom.

It's not like I've never bought tequila or ordered a specific one, but this place seems a little fancier than what I'm used to. And I don't want to ask for something stupid.

Understanding my hesitation, Dominic requests one that starts with an *r* and ends with my panties disintegrating. He pronounces it like he's speaking another language, and I wonder if he's bilingual.

And I'm too distracted staring at his mouth to even hear what he orders for himself.

"That okay?" Dominic asks, his attention back on me.

I bite my lip as I nod, then blurt out, "Do you speak Spanish?"

"To my grandfather's complete sadness, I'm sure, I do not." He shakes his head with a self-deprecating huff. "Just enough to get by."

"Like ordering drinks?"

Dom tips his head. "Like that."

"So your grandfather..." I trail off, unsure if I should be asking this. And unsure if I really want to open the discussion of family because there's only so much I want to share about my own.

But Dom doesn't look offended or upset at my question. He looks pleased. "I don't remember him much. He passed away when I was little. But my grandmother, his wife, was around a lot longer, and based on the stories she told me, I think he would've liked you."

"Me?" My brows shoot up.

Dominic has never shied away from saying whatever he feels, but this feels extra... personal. Something you might say when your significant other finally meets your family.

"Yeah, Shorty. You."

"Why?" I can't help asking.

"Because you're sweet. And just the right amount of feisty."

"Your grandfather would like me because I'm feisty?" I laugh.

Dom nods. "A good woman can change your life. Or so he used to say."

I feel the warmth of that statement in my chest. "He must've really loved your grandmother."

"He did." Dom lets out a deep breath. "He grew up in Colombia, in a little town. But he came here, to Chicago, when he was twenty-two. It was supposed to be a short visit. Two weeks. But then he met a woman. A nice girl from the suburbs, from a respectable family, and the rest, as they say, is history."

"He just stayed?"

"He stayed." Dom's blue eyes don't waver. "Because a good woman can change your life."

I swallow. "I like that story."

"Me, too." The edges of his eyes crinkle with a smile. "So did my grandmother. Which is why she told it about a thousand times."

"Can't blame her." I think about our past conversations. "So that big family you have, did your grandfather's relatives move here too?"

Dominic shakes his head. "They disowned him."

I gasp. "What? Why?"

"They viewed it as betrayal. Abandoning his history and some other bullshit. But my grandfather stood by the fact that love is stronger than obligation. So, to make up for the lack of family on his side, they decided to have a fuck ton of kids."

I snort at his description. "What's a *fuck ton* of kids?"

"Nine."

I grimace at the thought of giving birth nine times. "Okay, yeah. That's a lot."

"My father was the oldest, and I was the first grandchild. But with eight sets of uncles and aunts just on that side, and with all of them having a minimum of three kids, with the exception of my parents who only had me"—he shakes his head—"there's still a fuck ton."

"Is your dad...?" I hate to ask, but since we're talking about family.

"Passed away about twenty years back."

"I'm so sorry," I tell him, feeling bad about asking and tempted to tell him that mine died about that long ago, too, but my family story is much more depressing, and I don't really want to go there.

"Basically, a lifetime ago. But pretty sure he'd like your feistiness, too."

I bite my lip, trying to picture what one of Dom's big, happy family gatherings might look like when the server returns with our drinks.

Realizing I haven't even looked at the menu, I quickly pick it up and skim over the items. But the second I spot pad Thai as an option, I set my menu back down.

"That mean you know what you want, Angel?" Dom is giving me that small smile, the one that means he finds something funny.

I lift a brow, daring him to laugh. "It does."

"Ladies first." Dom gestures for me to start.

I order my chicken pad Thai, and Dom asks for spring rolls and then a different noodle dish for himself.

Finally noticing the margarita the server set down, I pull the glass closer and am tempted to take out my phone just so I can take a photo of it. The rim is perfectly salted, and floating on top next to the paper-thin slice of lime is a trio of edible flowers. And they're so pretty.

A tattooed hand holding a short glass filled with some sort of amber liquid lifts into my view. "A toast."

I pick up my drink and tap it against Dom's.

"To good women." His voice is low.

"To leaning in," I reply.

Those full, tempting lips quirk as he presses his glass against them.

CHAPTER 10

Val

THE MARGARITA IS PERFECT.

The spring rolls are perfect.

Conversation with Dominic is perfect.

We talk about his cousin, who drives race cars. We talk about his aunt, who sews wedding dresses.

And I don't get at all flustered talking to Dom about weddings.

And I press my fingertips to my cheeks to cool down because the drink is making me warm, not the topic.

My next margarita is perfect.

My noodles are perfect.

We talk more. We share more.

I tell him about Hawaii.

I tell him how I missed him.

I tell him that I wished he'd been there with me.

I smile when he looks at me.

I drink the water he hands me.

I TAKE DOM'S HAND AS HE STANDS.

My vision swirls as I let him walk me to the bathroom.

I sway to the music as I close my stall door. Feeling... good. A little dizzy but good.

I struggle with the double clasp on my pants but get them open.

I struggle a little more putting them back on but manage.

The soap is extra slippery.

The water feels good, and I let the cool liquid flow over my wrists.

The door to the bathroom opens behind me, and it's him.

My Dominic.

His blue eyes lock on to mine through the mirror, and it feels like a dream. Like a really good dream.

"Come with me, Mama."

He's behind me now, holding out a paper towel.

"You shouldn't be here." I can't tell if I whisper it or if I shout it.

Dom wraps his arms around me from behind and dries my hands for me. "For once, we disagree." I start to close my eyes at his voice. "This is where I need to be."

Lips press against my temple.

"I really like you." I make sure I whisper it this time.

Those lips press against my temple once more. "I'm going to remind you that you said that."

THE LIGHTS KEEP CHANGING.

Darker to brighter. Blue to pink. Close to far.

"This way, Shorty."

My feet shuffle forward. And my hand squeezes around a set of fingers.

Dom's fingers.

Because we're together.

"Let's go in here." His voice is so far above me.

I follow.

I'm tired, sleepy, but I still feel good.

And I don't want to leave him.

Until our paths part.

"I don't want our paths to part." I think I say it out loud.

The hand in mine squeezes me back.

"I'm not leaving you," Dominic reassures me.

I glance up, wanting to see where we're going, but I can't read the name. I see the letter *t*.

"Step up for me, Valentine."

I step up. And the lights are brighter.

I have to squint.

Dominic lets go of my hand, and I let out a little whine, missing the contact.

I hear someone chuckle. But it isn't Dom, because his hand is now around my shoulder, pulling me into his side, and he feels solid. Still. Not vibrating.

My eyes slide shut all the way as I lean into him.

Lean in.

I think that phrase over and over.

Lean into the warmth.

A shiver runs down my arm.

"Stand still, Shorty," Dom whispers, then his body moves away.

My mouth opens, wanting him to come back. But then I'm being wrapped in warm silk.

I sigh into the feeling.

Someone is talking.

But I can't pry my eyes open.

Not yet. Not with Dominic's scent and warmth surrounding me.

"Say I do, Valentine."

I smile, sliding my eyes open enough to look up at the man against my side. "Say I do, Big Guy."

He lifts one hand and brushes the backs of his fingers over my cheek. "To good women."

His eyes look sad.

I don't like it.

I don't want him sad.

I reach up and grab hold of his forearm. "I'll make you happy."

Dom lowers his eyelids as the hand against my cheek slides around to the back of my neck. "You are."

My eyes are closing again as his lips press against mine. Soft. Slow.

Something nudges against my hip.

"Wrap your legs around me."

I don't know what he's talking about, but then he pulls me forward, out of the back seat of the black SUV, and I automatically do as he says.

He smells amazing.

I press my nose into his neck.

His steps rock me against him.

I tighten my hold on his neck.

I think I'm wearing his suit jacket, but I can't get enough of him.

I can't get enough Dom.

My hips flex, trying to reach. Trying to feel what I know is there.

We're in a building. I can feel the change in the air.

My fingers scrape up the back of his head, my nails against his scalp.

Dominic groans, hugging me tighter to his front.

His steps stop, and I open my mouth against his neck.

His skin feels so nice against my lips.

A bell rings. And then Dom's walking again.

Then he stops.

"You take the next one."

I blink my eyes open, wondering what he's talking about.

Then I blink again because, over Dominic's shoulder, I can see two men behind us. They're dressed all in black, too.

But they stop.

And the elevator doors slide shut. And we start to rise.

Dom turns and presses my back against the elevator wall.

"Do that again, Angel."

I scrape my nails from the top of his head down to his neck.

The sound he lets out rolls through my core.

And I want him.

I want him so badly.

My hips roll. "I want you."

"Fuck," Dom growls. "You're making this hard."

I roll my hips again. "Prove it."

The arms holding me in place shift until he's gripping my hips. And then he lowers me. Sliding me down his body just a few inches. And...

My fingers dig into his shoulders when I feel it, and I let out a loud moan. "Dominic."

"Christ."

One hand slides around my ass, down between my legs, and he cups me there.

He uses his new hold on me to press me harder against him.

Another bell.

I squeeze my eyes shut and cling to Dom tighter.

Each step makes my head spin.

Each rock of his hips makes my core clench.

A door.

Another door.

97

And Dominic.

His hands.

His mouth.

I fall, but only for a second, onto something soft.

I lift my arms when Dom tugs my shirt up.

I gasp when my pants are yanked off.

I try to help him as my panties are pulled away.

My eyes slide open when I feel the cool air between my legs.

And I groan when fingers slip between my folds.

Dom is over me.

Above me. Pressing his forehead to mine. "So fucking wet for me, Valentine."

Pleasure swirls.

"Most nights," I tell him.

"Jesus," he groans. "Do you touch yourself, Angel?"

His fingers strum against me.

I nod.

"Do you think about me while you do it?"

His touch is getting more insistent.

"Always."

Sensations overwhelm.

Dom has me so close.

I can't focus.

He asks me something.

"Dominic," I whine, too needy to concentrate.

There's a wet slap against my pussy, and I nearly explode.

"Tell me, and I'll let you come."

"Four," I pant, arching my back. "There's been four."

Another slap, but then his palm presses into me harder and a finger slips inside me.

My body shakes.

Colors explode behind my eyes.

I cry out. Trembling. Tensing.

"Fuck," Dominic curses, and then something warm splashes against my stomach.

A forehead drops against my shoulder.
And I smile into the dark.
I like Dominic a lot.

CHAPTER 11
Val

My blankets shift, warm air escaping, and I moan.

"Go back to sleep," a voice tells me from beside my ear.

I do.

"Take these, Shorty."

I blink. And awareness floods my brain in the form of a headache.

"Drink at least half of this bottle, then you can go back to sleep."

My vision clears, and Dom's hand is in front of my face.

I'm face down, how I usually sleep, so I shift up onto my elbows and grab the pair of white pills out of his palm with my right hand.

I pop them into my mouth, then take the open water bottle and swallow down half.

Dominic looks tired.

"What time is it?" My voice is quiet, and I can feel that I haven't used it in a while.

"Eleven," Dom answers as he takes the water bottle back.

My eyes widen, then close, that small amount of brightness from around the blackout curtains enough to make the pain in my head spike.

Dom screws the cap back on the bottle, then sets it on the nightstand. "We were up late. Go back to sleep."

"You joining me?"

Dom nods. "In a minute."

"Alright." I drop my weight back to the mattress, then lift my head to look down at what I'm wearing.

I'm in a white T-shirt that has to belong to Dom, and I wiggle my hips to feel what must be a pair of his boxers.

I don't remember changing.

Or going to bed.

But it hurts too much to think, so I lower my head back to the pillow.

My hand reaches out, missing what I'm trying to grab... And my eyes snap open.

The dream fades, and the room slowly comes into focus, the color of the light surrounding the curtains now a dark gold.

Dominic's room.

Or rather, Dominic's suite.

A few hours ago, I shuffled through the room to use the bathroom. So I know it's nice. More than nice, it's extravagant. And I think there's a separate living room on the other side of the double doors, because I heard Dom on the phone once. But I haven't looked. I've just slept.

And slept.

I try to roll over but finally notice the heavy weight pressed into my back.

I'm still sprawled face down across the king-size mattress, and apparently, Dom sleeps the same way I do. Only he's on top of me, his body covering about half of mine.

It's cute.

But it would be cuter if I didn't have to pee and if he wasn't so heavy.

I squirm to free myself.

Dominic groans. "Stay still."

Groggy Dom is adorable.

"I have to get up."

"Not yet." He leans into me.

"Stop." My laugh is smothered. "I need to go to the bathroom."

Dom sighs but lifts his weight enough for me to slide out of the bed.

I try to keep my eyes half-closed as I shut myself in the bathroom and find the switch that turns on just the lights behind the mirror. My headache is mostly gone now, but I don't want to chance it with bright lights.

I run my tongue across my teeth and grimace.

Standing on the tile floor, I realize how gross I feel all over. I haven't showered since yesterday morning, and I think it's probably close to sunset. A day and a half without showering is too long when you're sharing a bed with a sexy-as-hell man.

I turn on the shower, letting the stall fill with steam while I quickly use the toilet.

I didn't think we drank that much last night. But maybe I had more margaritas than I think I did. Or maybe we stopped for more drinks on our way back here.

After shuffling over to the sink, I'm rinsing off the hand soap when I realize what I'm looking at.

My toothbrush.

In Dominic's bathroom.

How did...

I use the mirror to glance around the spacious bathroom, and my brain finally registers what it jumped over before. My little roller suitcase is sitting in front of the tub.

Did we go get my stuff last night? I feel like I would've remembered that.

I spot my phone on the bathroom counter, having left that in here, too.

Picking it up, I see a text from the group of girls I came here with saying *have fun*.

Thankfully, I apparently texted them to let them know I'd be staying with Dom.

Conscious that the shower has now been running for too long, I let my eyes drift closed while I hurry through brushing my teeth. And then I open them just enough to zombie my way through a shower.

Since I didn't feel like digging my toiletries out of my suitcase, I use Dom's stuff. And the hotel's hair conditioner, because apparently, Dom's haircut doesn't need conditioner.

The bodywash smells like him, and I lather myself in it twice, but I still need to hunt down that cologne.

Just thinking about his cologne triggers a scent memory from last night. Him holding me while I ground against him, inhaling against his neck.

Heat blooms low in my belly.

I remember his hand between my legs. I remember his mouth on mine.

I reach out and turn off the water.

We didn't have sex last night. We've had sex before, so I know what I feel like *down there* afterward. I feel sore. Swollen. But I don't feel any of that right now, so I definitely didn't have Dominic's dick inside me last night.

I appreciate that we didn't do it while we were both completely wasted. But if Dom's also feeling better, then we're gonna change that.

I reach out with my left hand to open the glass shower door.

But instead of connecting with the metal handle silently, my hand connects with a clink.

I jerk my hand back and look at my palm.

The lights are low in here, but there's no missing the thick gold band visible on the underside of my ring finger.

I stare at it.

For three breaths, I stare at the bottom of the ring.

The ring on my wedding ring finger.

My next breath is choppy as I slowly rotate my hand.

The next breath stops altogether.

A giant round-cut diamond stares back at me.

It's...

I choke on my next breath.

It's so pretty.

Stunning. Beautiful.

A row of diamonds is inlaid into the wide band, highlighting the large stone.

"Oh my god," I whisper.

I reach up with my right hand to touch the diamond.

"Oh my god!" I say louder this time.

Because I'm married.

I'm married to Dominic.

CHAPTER 12
Val

DRESSED IN NOTHING BUT THE BLACK BUTTON-DOWN I found hanging in the bathroom, I swing the door open, my towel-dried hair already soaking through the cotton shirt.

Dom is still in the bed, but he's on his back now, lounging against a pile of pillows with his hands behind his head, blanket around his hips, and his naked torso on display.

My mouth opens and closes.

How is this man real?

Dom's stomach muscles bunch as though my gaze is affecting him like a touch, and I force my eyes up his body.

I open my mouth again, but I don't know what to say.

There are tiny bits, just seconds, here and there, of memories.

I remember standing somewhere with Dom.

Remember leaning into him. But did we really...?

Dom raises his brows and lifts one of his arms. His left arm. Which he holds in front of him, showing me the thick gold band circling his ring finger.

I shakily raise my hand, diamond facing him.

"We got married," I squeak.

"We got married." Dominic, calm as ever, nods his head at my hand. "At least we did it with style."

I turn my hand back over so I can see the sparkly side. "I..." A laugh bubbles out of me. "Did we seriously do this?"

"We seriously did."

My eyes bounce back and forth between my diamond and my... husband. My newly wedded husband who seems way too calm.

I drop my hand. "How did this happen?"

"If memory serves, there's a chapel just a few doors down from the Thai place we were at." He lifts a shoulder. "I'm guessing drinks, talking about family and good women, may have caused us to be a bit rash."

"A bit?!" Panic threads through my words. "Dominic, we got *married.*"

He smirks. "Yeah, we did. Now get over here, wife."

"Dominic, I need you to be serious."

"I'm deadly serious, Angel. Now get the fuck over here so we can talk face-to-face." Dom flips back the blanket so he can sit up. And my mouth goes dry.

He's wearing boxers. Only boxers. But they've ridden up.

And sweet Jesus... His thighs.

I knew they'd be strong and thick with muscles, but seeing them is different from sitting on them. Because they're also tattooed.

His juicy thighs are fucking tattooed.

I've wondered how far down Dominic's tattoos went. And now I know.

They go all the way down.

More symbols and designs trail from under his boxers, circling his legs down to his ankles.

Dominic pats my empty spot on the mattress, breaking my stare.

The bed hardly feels like safe territory, especially with him looking like that, but my legs are getting cold. And I might be a little insane, but I'm not dead.

I glance at my ring once more, then cross the distance to the bed.

I'm careful as I situate myself, keeping the front of his shirt down as I sit cross-legged facing him. The length is enough to cover the fact that I'm not wearing underwear.

Dom turns so we're facing each other. "Valentine, remember what I told you about apologizing?"

His question isn't what I'm expecting, so it takes a moment for me to reply. "You said you never do it."

Dom nods. "I also don't lie. And I won't start doing either now and pretend I'm sorry we did it." He settles his hand over mine, his thumb nudging the big diamond.

"But..." *Why can't I think of a single argument for why this is crazy?* "But we don't even know each other."

He shakes his head. "Don't do that. We might have rushed the process. Or skipped most of the process altogether. But we know each other. Tell me we don't."

My eyes bounce back and forth between his, and I can see how serious he is.

I reach out with my right hand, setting it over his left.

My pointer finger feels the realness of the ring he's wearing.

"We know each other," I admit quietly, because it's true. "I've told you more than I've told anyone in... a long time." The month plus of daily texting is more of a relationship than I think I've ever had.

"I know. And I talk to you more than I talk to anyone in my family."

I keep my eyes on his ring because the next thought I have is one I can't voice. One I won't.

Because *what about love?*

My heart squeezes.

I just want love.

Real love.

I want to get married *because* of love.

I bite my lip.

Just because we don't have it right at this moment doesn't mean we won't be able to find it together.

He's a good man.

Dom is a good man. And his relationships with his family prove he's capable of love.

And if he doesn't want to fight this, why should I?

I raise my eyes. "So what do we do?"

He slides his hand onto my bare knee. "First, we consummate."

I raise my brows as my cheeks warm. "Consummate? Do people really still call it that?"

He moves his other hand from below mine to my bare thigh. "I'm traditional when it comes to marriage."

"How so?" I breathe out as he slides his hands higher.

"A marriage isn't real until consummation."

His thumbs brush under the edge of his shirt.

"What else?"

"A marriage makes you family."

My poor lonely heart squeezes so hard it almost pops.

"I like that," I whisper.

Dom gives my legs a little squeeze, then he slides his grip higher, not stopping until his thumbs press into that soft crease at the top of my thighs. "I believe in loyalty. And trust. And living together."

My eyes were sliding closed until that last part. "Living together?"

"Living together." He yanks me forward as he shifts onto his knees.

I let out a sound of surprise, which gets knocked out of my lungs when Dom uses a hand on my chest to shove me back onto the mattress.

He braces himself over me. "I'm not marrying a wife this fucking sexy and then letting her live six hours away."

My legs automatically widen, allowing room for his hips. "You want me to move to Chicago?"

Dominic lowers his face until it's just above mine. "I'm afraid I'm going to demand it."

"But what if..." I press my hands against his bare chest.

"What if what, Shorty? What if we don't get along? We do." He drops his hips, and I groan. "What if we don't fit?" He presses his weight into me. "We fit together perfectly. And if you need space, my place is big. You can have your space."

He makes it sound so easy. So possible.

Dom is making me believe we can make this work. That we can make this crazy drunken *we've only known each other for a month and a half* thing work.

And goddammit, I want it.

I want him.

I want a chance to build the future I've barely dared to dream of.

Dom shifts, brushing his lips against my ear. "But most importantly, Valentine, when you move in with me, you'll spend every night in my bed."

Heat washes through me, a blend of desire and need as I arch into him.

"Okay," I pant.

"Okay?"

I grip his sides. "Yes. I'll move to Chicago."

"And?" Dom inhales against my cheek.

"And I'll sleep with you." Dominic chuckles, and I correct myself. "I'll share your bed."

He shifts his weight to one elbow, the other hand working to unbutton his shirt that I'm wearing. "Our bed."

"Our bed," I repeat, and emotion clogs my throat.

His fingers free the last button, and he parts the fabric, revealing my nakedness.

"My Angel." Dom skims his fingers down between my breasts, down my belly, and into my curls. I have a second to wonder if he'll want me to shave it off, but then he groans. And I know he likes me how I am.

"Dom." I lift my hips against him.

He lowers his face to my throat, breathing me in. "I love that you smell like me."

"Dom," I plead.

"I wonder if you smell like me everywhere."

"Please!" I cry, no longer able to take his teasing.

"Please what?"

"Please do more."

"You want more, Mama? You want me to give you more?" My hips lift just as Dom slides his hands lower. His fingers glide against me, my body ready for his. "Always so fucking wet for me."

I am. I always am.

Then he's lifting off me. All the way off the bed.

"Where are you..." Dominic shoves his boxers off, and my words fade into a moan.

That. I want that.

I've felt it. I've had it inside me. But seeing his cock like this makes my mouth water.

"I was gonna go slow with you. Spend some time with my tongue in your pussy. But now you have to wait for that." He kneels on the end of the bed. "Because you begging me for more is my breaking point. And I want to bury my cock in this sweet little pussy right now."

My pulse is going so wild I can't reply. I just hold my arms up, welcoming him into my embrace.

He drops down on top of me. His big body over mine is instantly comforting.

We've never been like this. This open. This naked. This together.

I slide my hands up to grip the back of his neck, digging my nails into his skin when the blunt head of his cock presses against my entrance.

I pull him toward me.

"What do you need?" he asks, his voice deeper than I've ever heard.

"I need you to kiss me."

He does.

Dominic lowers his mouth to mine, and the soft caress of his lips is exactly what I wanted.

His mouth moves against mine, just a little, and he pushes his hips forward. Just a little.

He moves so slow. Just one more inch.

His lips part against mine.

One more inch.

I lick into his mouth.

He groans, but he doesn't move quicker.

Our mouths seal together.

Another inch.

And my body is ready to take all of him.

I need all of him.

I need us to consummate.

I scrape my fingers up the back of his head. "Husband, please."

His whole body shudders, and he tips his head back into my hand.

"Wife," he growls, then presses his lips back against mine.

And he presses his hips forward.

Inches blur together until I'm full. Full and moaning and clawing to hold him closer.

He moves, his length sliding in and out of me, his chest heaving above me, my hands everywhere they can reach.

He slides his hand between us. His fingers circle my bundle of nerves, his slippery fingers working me over.

His mouth leaves mine and presses against my ear. "Come for me." His hips rock forward. "Come on this cock. Show me what a good little wife you can be. Show me how I make you feel."

I'm so lost to the sensations, so lost to him, that it just takes one more pass. One more circle of his fingers, and I'm coming apart, just like he asked.

CHAPTER 13
Val

"So." I dip my fry in the little ramekin of ketchup. "How, um, do you see this going?"

We've moved to the couch in the living room part of Dom's suite to eat room service burgers while the TV quietly plays a sitcom I'm not familiar with.

"Well." Dom leans back, his plate balanced on his lap. "Figure the easiest way is for me to change my flight so I'm heading home with you. And since I remember you telling me that you drive a little Honda, we'll get an SUV or truck or whatever you need to fit your stuff and then drive down to Chicago."

I watch him while I take a sip of my root beer. "You make it sound so easy."

He smirks. "It is easy."

"What about my apartment?"

Dom lifts a shoulder. "What about it? You rent, right?"

My nod is slow as I think about it.

It's currently the second week of November; my lease runs out at the end of the year, and I have until the end of next week to let them know if I'm renewing my lease or leaving. So it really isn't that big of a deal to pay for December, even if I'm not living there.

Dom misunderstands my silence. "I can buy out the remainder of your lease."

I shake my head. "It's not that. I only have it until the end of the year. It's..." I lean forward and set my plate on the coffee table so I can turn to face the handsome-as-fuck man next to me.

After our *consummation*, Dom took a shower, and I dressed in leggings and a sweater from my luggage, which Dom somehow arranged to be delivered.

But even after sleeping all day, I'm still exhausted, and I'm having a hard time believing this is real.

"Shorty, what's worrying that brain of yours?" Dom puts the last bite of burger into his mouth, then places his plate on the coffee table next to mine.

Loyalty and trust.

"It was hard to find an apartment I liked in Minneapolis. And if things don't work out and I have to move back, I won't have anywhere to go."

Dominic turns to face me, bending his leg onto the couch until his knee touches mine.

He takes his time before he answers. "Valentine, I enjoy being around you. I enjoy talking to you. And being in close proximity isn't going to change that." He reaches out to grip my thigh. "But if a time comes that we aren't able to make things work, I won't ever leave you to fend for yourself. This is a partnership, and whether you love me or hate me, I'll always protect you."

My lungs catch on the word *love*, and I can hardly breathe.

I'll always protect you.

I place my hand over his.

Protect might be a weird thing to say, but King uses that word all the time when he's talking about family. So maybe it's just an alpha-male thing.

Only, when King offers me protection, it's out of familial obligation. This... This is different.

"I can't imagine ever hating you," I admit.

Dom tightens his hold on my leg. "Good."

I roll my eyes. And then it hits me. *Protection.* Guess we're having this talk now. "Okay, so, there are two things about this plan of yours."

Dom raises his brows. "Only two?"

"Well, two to start with." I take a deep breath. "One, there's going to be a man waiting for me at the airport."

Dom leans toward me. "Excuse me?"

I press a hand to his chest, the soft T-shirt a contrast to what I normally see him in. "Hold your horses. It's not *a man* like that. He's a driver. Kind of a bodyguard."

"You have a bodyguard," he repeats.

"Yeah, so..." I groan and tip my head back. "My half—my brother is kind of a big deal. Like he's super rich. And he's over-protective to a fault, which has recently extended to me. So now I have a guy named Bo driving me everywhere. I don't even remember the last time I started my car."

"What's Bo's last name?"

Dom's question has me tipping my head back up to look at him. "I... I don't actually know."

"I'll find out," he states like there's nothing off about me having a bodyguard. "And that might actually work out. You can get a ride home with him and start packing while I find a good car to rent."

I slowly nod.

That's actually a brilliant idea. Because there's no way Bo will just step aside if I tell him I have a new husband to drive me home. And if Dom tried to ride with us, Bo would definitely call King, and I'd rather control the when and how of that conversation.

"What's number two?"

"Two?" Then I remember. "Well, it's my brother."

"The rich one?"

"Yeah." I blow out a breath. "So, he knows that I've been talking to someone. It was his wife who saw our texts that one time. They've been a little relentless in asking about you. But I didn't want to tell them your name until things got, well, more serious." I hold up my hand, the big diamond sparkling between us. "But now I think we're there."

Dom lifts his left hand, clicking his ring against mine. "I think you're right."

"It's just that he's a little unpredictable sometimes, and I think it would be better to break the news in person. If I call or text him, he's just gonna flip and demand to meet you anyway."

Dom nods. "My family would be the same way. How about we stop over there after we pack up your apartment? Get it all done in one go."

I bite my lip. "So we're doing this?"

Dominic hooks one of his hands around the back of my neck, pulling me in and pressing his lips to mine. "We're doing this." Then he releases me and grabs his phone off the coffee table. "I'm gonna change my ticket. And you can email your work to tell them you need to change your address on file."

My eyes widen. "I hadn't even thought about that."

"Work?" He looks up at me.

I smile. "Our main office is in Chicago. I'll still work from home. Er, remotely," I correct, wondering if it's weird to call Dom's place home when I haven't even seen it. "But I can go into the office for meetings and stuff. And the girl whose bachelorette party I came here for is based there, and she's cool, so it'd be fun to see her."

"Downtown driving can be a lot, so just let me know when you want to go to the office, and I'll have someone take you."

"Okay!" Excitement fills me as I reach for my phone to email my boss, too giddy to think twice about Dom getting me a driver.

We're really doing this.

CHAPTER 14

Val

THE COOL PLASTIC OF MY ICED LATTE DOES NOTHING to calm my nerves, or my palms, as we near King's estate.

"Not a bad location," Dominic comments as he drives our rented SUV alongside Darling Lake.

"It's really pretty out here." I look at bare tree branches as we drive past, wishing we'd had a chance to do that fall date.

"Valentine." Dom puts his hand on the center console for me.

I wipe the condensation off my palm onto my jeans, then place my hand in his. "Sorry, I don't know why I'm so nervous."

He squeezes my fingers. "Don't apologize. You can feel however you want."

"Right, sorry." I huff. "Not sorry."

Dom chuckles. "You'll get the hang of it."

"Turn here." I put my coffee in the cup holder, then wipe that palm on my pant leg.

Dominic follows my directions, and after just another minute, I can see the edge of King's property. The tall fence and looming gate, complete with armed guards, get closer by the second.

"It's that one there." I point.

Dom starts to slow, and I can see at least three men on the other side of the gate step closer.

Guilt and panic slam into my chest.

"Dominic." My hand is trembling in his. "There's something else about my brother..."

But then we're there. And one of the men, who stepped through a secure side entrance, is approaching Dom's window, gun visible at his side.

Dom lowers his tinted window, setting his left hand palm up on the sill.

A strangled sound catches in my throat when the guard pulls his gun from its holster.

"Afternoon," Dom greets the guard way too calmly. "We're here to see King."

When Dom says *we*, the guard steps to the side so he can see past my husband's big frame into the passenger seat.

I recognize him at the same time he recognizes me.

"Hi." I wave at him with my far hand.

The guard, whose name I can't remember, steps closer to Dom's window. I can tell there's movement at the gate, but I keep my eyes on the guard.

"Val, are you okay?" The guard narrows his eyes, and I follow his line of sight to where Dom is still holding my hand.

"Yep." I try to keep the stress out of my voice. "Is King home? I texted him earlier and let him know I was going to stop by." As I say it, I don't remember if I've ever used King's name in front of Dom before. But he just asked for King by name, so I must have.

The guard takes a step forward, and the hand Dom has on the windowsill balls into a fist. "That's close enough."

"Fuck you," the guard snaps at Dom, and my mouth drops open.

"You're not my type," Dom replies. "Now let us in."

The guard spins away, gesturing to the men inside the property to open the gate.

"I can't believe how rude he was," I whisper, because Dom's window is still open.

Dom shrugs. "He's just doing his job."

All the security men have their hands on the butts of their guns as we pass through the gate.

I've never seen them so on edge.

I take a slow breath as we make our way up the driveway.

"Dominic, my brother..."

Why is this so hard?

My brother is one of the leaders of a criminal organization called The Alliance, and they do a lot of bad things. But he's a good guy. Most of the time. Except marrying me means you'll never get to be rid of me. And now you're going to be a part of this life, too.

"Shorty." Dom lifts our joined hands and brushes a kiss across my knuckles. "I can handle your brother."

I stare at his profile as he parks in front of the massive house.

His perfectly cut jaw outlined with dark facial hair. His tattoos highlighted by the bright white button-down shirt he's wearing, the sleeves rolled up from when he carried the majority of my worldly goods out of my apartment and stuffed them into the back of this vehicle—proving his muscles aren't just for display.

And from looking at him, I think he might be right. One-on-one, I bet he could hold his own against King. But it's everything else about King that worries me. Because you'd need an army to go against The Alliance. And I doubt a businessman from Chicago has one on hand.

Dom turns my hand over and presses a kiss against my wrist. "Come on, Angel. Let's go say hi to your brother. Then I'll show you your new home."

My heartbeat doubles, and I don't know if it's from nerves or excitement. So I just nod my head.

Dominic turns off the engine, and I'm still working to undo my seat belt when he walks around the SUV and opens my door.

He keeps a hand on me as I climb down. And keeps his hand on the back of my neck as we walk up the sidewalk.

I don't know why I can't just calm down. It's not like King had someone else in mind for me to marry. We aren't an *arranged marriage* type of family, so this isn't going to be a big deal. He might be disappointed in my decisions, but they're my decisions.

I reach out with the hand closest to Dominic and hook my fingers into his pants pocket, needing the extra contact.

"It's going to be fine," Dom whispers before pressing a kiss to the top of my head.

Then, before I can delay any more, Dom pounds his fist against the front door of King's house.

CHAPTER 15

Val

NEARLY A MINUTE PASSES BEFORE THE DOOR SWINGS open.

But it's not King; it's his housekeeper.

"Hey, Val," Ginger greets me before she does a double take of Dom. "Come on in. King'll be just a second."

"Thank you," I try to say normally as we move into the grand entryway.

Ginger smiles, then heads up the grand staircase to the second story to continue with whatever she was doing.

The entryway is large and echoey, and from here, the house goes off in a few directions. It's an absurd home, but it proves that I wasn't lying when I said King was really rich.

I turn to face Dominic, wondering if there's something I should say to prepare him, but movement down the hall behind him tells me we're out of time.

Because King is walking toward us.

"Val?" King's voice fills the space.

Dom closes his fingers around my wrist as I step around him so his bulk isn't blocking King's view of me.

"Uh, hi." I put on my brightest smile.

King smiles back at me. "What's—"

Then Dominic turns so we're standing side by side, still holding my wrist, and King's smile disappears.

Oh god, he's not gonna take this well.

"King." I hold up my free hand. "This is—"

"What the fuck are you doing in my house?" King's voice booms through the space.

I start to stumble back a step. I've never heard King so loud before. But Dom slides his grip up my arm to steady me.

"I'm sorry," I whisper, not understanding why he's so angry. And not sure who I'm apologizing to.

But neither man hears me.

"Don't raise your voice around my wife." Dominic's tone is cold. Ice to King's fire.

King stops walking just a few steps away. "What did you just say?"

"King." I try again. *This is spiraling out of control.* "Please don't be mad."

"Mad?" He takes another step closer. "You bring Dom Fucking Gonzalez, the head of the Chicago mafia, into *my home*, and you don't want me to be mad?"

"I..." My breaths are coming fast now. "What?"

I look up at Dominic.

He's still standing next to me. Still holding my arm. But there's an expression on his face I don't recognize.

"Dominic?" I blink up at him.

That can't be true.

Dom can't be that.

They can't know each other.

King's furious gaze holds me in place as he points a finger at my husband. "Tell me he's lying. Tell me you didn't marry this piece of shit."

Head of the Chicago mafia.

With Dominic still gripping my upper arm, I bend my elbow and bring my left hand before me, the beautiful ring glinting in the light.

Dom makes a clicking sound with his tongue. "Is that any way to welcome me into The Alliance?"

Everything slows.

In one awful, horrible second, everything slows.

The Alliance.

Dom knows about The Alliance.

He knows King.

He's in the mafia.

Something tightens around my throat.

It's a coincidence.

It's some terrible coincidence.

"Dominic?" My voice is weak, but I know he hears me, because his fingers flex around my arm. "What's going on?"

Please, let this be some sort of mistake.

But he doesn't look at me. His eyes are still locked on King.

King takes another step closer until he's within arm's reach.

"What do you want?" King grits out the question, squaring off with Dominic, waiting for his answer.

Me.

Please say you want me.

"To join The Alliance."

My knees weaken.

No. No, no, no, no.

This can't be happening.

I thought...

Dom's grip on my arm tightens, and I realize I've sagged against him.

I thought he...

I try to jerk away from Dominic, but his hold doesn't budge.

"Not a chance," King growls. "Did you seriously think you could pull a stunt like this and—"

Dom cuts him off, taking a step forward and bringing me with him. "There is no stunt. This little sister of yours has been wedded and bedded. That makes me family, and if you have any honor at all, King Vass, you know that means I'm a part of The Alliance now."

Sorrow, like I've never felt before, blankets over me. And those last tiny pieces of hope, the little broken shards I've been carrying since I was nine, finally crumble into sand.

I was so close.

Tears form and fall in the space of a heartbeat.

I was so goddamn close to having what I've always wanted.

And it was all a fucking lie.

I have to tell my lungs to fill. Have to force them to suck in air.

It was all a setup.

A trick.

More tears roll down my cheeks.

I thought I could make him love me.

A strange sound comes out of my throat, but no one hears it.

No one is paying attention to me.

I thought someone finally cared.

But Dom never cared about me.

He did this for The Alliance.

He married me for The Alliance.

King darts his hand out and grips the front of Dom's shirt. But Dom does the same back to King, not backing down from King's fury.

I don't want to be this close.

I don't want to be this close to these dangerous men.

I try to shrink away, but Dom won't let me go.

"Tricking Val into your bed doesn't mean shit," King snaps.

And his words slice between my ribs.

Tricking Val.

It's exactly what Dominic did, so why does hearing King say it hurt so much?

And what does he mean *doesn't mean shit*? What part doesn't mean shit? The sex part?

Or the *me* part?

Dread hits me.

What if Dom did all this, only to find out I'm not family enough?

What if his plan doesn't work?

What will happen to me then?

I reach up with my right hand and press it over my heart.

I'm already a nobody.

"You owe me. Remember?" Dom says slowly. "A wife for a wife, King. Val is mine now."

Val.

I don't think he's ever called me that. It was always Valentine. Or Angel. Or Shorty. Or...

When he called me Mama at the airport.

My eyes squeeze shut.

When I followed him into that little room. When I had sex with him.

Numbness starts to wash through me. Starting at my toes. Up to my ankles.

I'm such a fool.

It's at my knees.

Such a sad, pathetic, love-starved fool.

My hips.

So desperate for love, I believed that the hot man on the airplane was desperate to be with me.

My belly button.

So goddamn broken, I believed every compliment.

I clung to every nice thing he said.

My rib cage.

So fucking lonely, I drunkenly married him and...

A fresh layer of sadness sinks into my chest, and I look up at Dominic Gonzalez.

"Were you even drunk?" I ask the thought out loud.

I have to blink to see through the tears, but I know the answer in my heart.

And the blank expression on Dom's face as he looks down at me is all the confirmation I need.

So I nod.

He wasn't drunk. Just me. Because he needed me to be. Because he needed me to marry him.

It was never about me.

The numbness rises to my shoulders, the horrible ache in my heart finally dulling as I let the disassociation win.

He'll never love me.

No one ever has.

King lets go of Dom's shirt with a shove. "Get out of my fucking house."

I don't look up to see if he's talking to just Dom or to both of us.

Because it doesn't really matter, does it?

I don't belong here either.

I don't belong anywhere.

CHAPTER 16

Dom

VAL COMES WITH ME WILLINGLY.

She walks at my side, not flinching away from my hold on her arm. Not shoving me away when I put my hand on her back. Not protesting when I help her up into the vehicle. She doesn't so much as look at me when I reach across her to buckle her in.

She doesn't react to any of it.

But she never stops crying.

Silent tears continuously roll down her cheeks. And they make me feel...

They make me feel.

Not trusting King not to shoot me in the back, I reach into the glove box and take out my pistol.

Val's pretty brown eyes are staring right at it, but I'm not sure she sees it. Not sure if she realizes now that this is my vehicle. Just like the one in Vegas. Just like the driver in Vegas. Just like the witnesses at our wedding.

I've been building this world out of smoke and mirrors. Carefully. Meticulously. All for this. For what just happened.

Because I had to.

Because I need this.

And I won't apologize for it.

"VALENTINE." SHE FLINCHES A LITTLE AT MY VOICE BUT doesn't reply.

We're two hours into the six-hour drive to Chicago, and she hasn't said a thing. She hasn't adjusted the air. Hasn't asked me to play music. Hasn't said anything.

I knew she'd be upset.

I have enough sense to know that this was all going to blow up in my face, and I braced myself for it.

Figured she'd yell and scream and probably try to hit me. Thought I'd have to carry her out of King's house, kicking and screaming, while fending her brother off as he tried to wrestle her back.

But none of that happened.

She just shut down. And King... Fucking King just let me take her.

The outcome is exactly what I needed, because I need Valentine in order to leverage King's, and therefore Nero's, cooperation.

But King just let me take her. He let me walk his sister out of the house.

Val was standing there, fucking crying, and he did nothing.

But I guess there isn't much he could do, because King knows I'm right. He knows that he owes me one. Because when his wife ran away, straight into the path of a human trafficker, I stepped in and protected her.

Val's body trembles with a shiver, so I adjust the temperature.

"Do you want your seat warmer on?"

She doesn't answer. Of course she doesn't.

Val trembles again, so I press the button to warm the leather seats anyway. She can turn it off if she wants.

Still no reaction.

I let out a sigh, then turn my own seat on low. Lounging in

bed all day yesterday, followed by flying commercial today, is making my back tight.

The day we met, I joked with Val about not being that old. But I've lived hard. I've fought for my life more than once. Killed way more times than that. And taken more hits to my person than I could ever count. And today, my body is reminding me.

Movement in the passenger seat pulls my attention to Val.

She's lifted her left hand from where it's been frozen in her lap and is staring at her ring.

A twinge of something nips at the edge of my conscience.

But I won't say I'm sorry.

Because I'm not. I'm not sorry for what I've done.

It had to happen, and once Val understands why, she'll forgive me.

I know her.

She might not believe that right now, but I do. And I know she'll eventually understand.

Her breathing changes, and little puffs of breath fill the car.

"Hey." I glance over at her. "What's wrong?"

It's a stupid question to ask right now, but seriously, I don't know what's going on with her.

I've never seen someone so catatonic, and now she's starting to breathe heavily.

I reach for her. "Angel."

"Don't call me that!" Her sudden shout fills the vehicle.

Only through a lifetime of not showing weakness do I manage not to react to her outburst.

I slowly lower my hand to rest between us. "Alright."

"This is what I've always wanted." Her voice drops to a whisper.

Keeping my eyes on the road, I sneak another glance, seeing she's still staring at the ring.

"I don't know how you knew." She sounds... lost.

I press my lips together.

Val touches the diamond with the tip of her finger. "You brought this with you, didn't you? To Vegas."

I don't answer. Because we both know that answer is yes.

"You offered me everything I've ever wanted," she says quietly as she pulls the ring off her finger, holding it up to the afternoon sun. "But you can't hold on to mirages."

Before I can stop her, she lowers her window, and the wind rushes through the opening as she throws her ring out onto the freeway.

It disappears from view long before it hits the concrete below us, gone forever.

And when her window is back up and she's settled once more into her seat, I smile.

CHAPTER 17
Val

BEHIND MY EYELIDS, UNWANTED MEMORIES OF MY mother flitter past.

"Valentine, you need to give men something to look at, or else they'll just use you and drop you."

My twelve-year-old self looks down at the baggy T-shirt that nearly hides the jean shorts underneath. "But I don't want men looking at me."

"You will," Mom scoffs. "And if you don't start taking care of yourself now, then you'll end up with some piece of garbage who just wants to use you."

I pull down the hem of my shirt, hiding the shorts completely as I try to cover my exposed thighs.

Four years later, my mom says basically the same thing to me. Only this time it's because my dress is too revealing. Because my breasts have grown bigger than hers, and she hates to see them.

And then, three years later, when the last words she ever spoke to me were punctuated by a slamming door. "You're a selfish, greedy bitch, and you'll eventually get what's coming to you."

I pry my eyes open.

I don't really want to be in the present, but it's better than the past.

Anything is better than the past.

I blink.

What would she think now? My mother.

Would she laugh, gleeful in the knowledge that I've finally been used by a man the way she always warned me I'd be? Or would she be jealous that I ended up married to a rich, powerful man?

My vision starts to clear.

The setting sun casts a glow through the SUV, and I vaguely remember Dom grabbing something out of the glove box when we left King's house.

He didn't rent this vehicle.

I glance around at the interior, thinking it's exactly like the one we took to dinner in Vegas.

What did the driver call him when we were leaving my hotel? Boss?

Another level of deceit.

Ringing fills the interior of Dom's SUV, and KV is displayed on the dashboard.

Dom presses a button on his steering wheel to answer but doesn't say anything.

It's quiet for a beat before King's voice fills the car. "Bring her back."

I stare at the letters on the screen, not sure how to feel.

Dominic lets out an acidic laugh. "Only took you three and a half hours to decide you want her."

His words are true. And that's why they hurt so much.

I turn my gaze out the window, willing that coldness to fill me again.

"I've been trying to call her," King growls at Dom. "She's not answering her phone."

My lips tremble, and I hate that I don't know whether he's telling the truth.

"Is she with you?" King's voice is different now. Worried?

I can feel Dom looking at me, but I don't reply. Not to either of them.

"Dom—" King starts.

"You don't deserve her." Dominic ends the call.

No one deserves me.

Just like no one wants me around.

As silence once again fills the vehicle, I focus on breathing.

Inhale.

Exhale.

But the breathing doesn't work. It doesn't push away the awful feelings inside me.

Squeezing my hands together in my lap, I walk through the steps my therapist taught me to get back into the present.

Three things I see. *Tree. Exit sign. Red pickup truck.*

Three things I hear. *The tires on the road. The rumble of the engine. Dominic's exhales.*

I take another slow breath.

Three body parts. *I wiggle my toes. I straighten my fingers. I lift my shoulders, then let them drop.*

It's all still there. All the badness. But some of the numbness is there, too.

Staring down at my lap, I ask a question I already hate myself for. But I need to ask it all the same. "Did King have anything to do with this? With you and me?"

Dom doesn't answer for a long heartbeat, and the first tendrils of betrayal flicker in my vision.

But then he replies. "No. It was just me."

Dom clears his throat, and then something is being set on my thigh.

My phone.

"If you wanted to check." He moves his hand back to the steering wheel. "See if he's telling the truth."

I don't know when he took my phone, but I slowly pick it up and see the settings have been changed to do not disturb.

I wait for one painful moment as I turn off the setting, and the screen fills with notifications.

Calls from King.

Texts from King.

He's been trying to call me since we left.

Gross guilt fills my stomach for thinking he might be a part of this. I open the texts and scroll through them with shaking hands.

King: Come back.

King: Are you okay?

King: Why were you crying?

King: Answer your phone.

King: I'm sorry if I was harsh.

King: Val, answer me.

King: Please reply to me.

King: I'm going to tell Savannah.

King: Don't make me tell her.

King: I'm sorry I didn't stop him.

King: Just tell me you're okay.

New tears, real tears, start to fall from my eyes.

Because King wasn't lying.

But none of it scrapes away the ugly doubt clinging to my ribs. Because King is an honorable man. And he's probably reacting this way because of familial obligation.

And I'm so fucking sick of being an obligation. A burden. The relative who doesn't fit. The one who gets a chair at the table out of pity. Because she has nowhere else to go.

I sniff, the tears still falling.

And that's not fair.

It's not fair to King or Savannah or Aspen. Because maybe they are trying. But it doesn't change the facts. And it doesn't change history.

I wipe at my cheeks.

It's nice that King called me.

But I'll get myself out of this situation. Just like I've gotten myself out of all the ones before it.

I type a reply to King.

> Me: Sorry, my—

Delete.

> Me: My phone was off. I'll call you later. I'm okay—

Delete.

> Me: My phone was off. I'll be okay.

Send.

I won't be anyone's burden anymore.

CHAPTER 18

Dom

I'M TRYING TO KEEP MY ATTENTION ON THE ROAD SO I don't kill us, but I can't stop looking at Valentine.

Did King have anything to do with this? With you and me?

Why the fuck would she ask something like that?

Were we not standing in front of the same King just a few hours ago? That man was ready to rip my fucking head off. His anger today rivaled his anger from those months ago when he thought I was being shady with his wife.

I don't know why Val would be doubting him, but based on the amount of scrolling she did on her phone, I think King was telling the truth about trying to reach her.

But she doesn't call him back. And after she sends a text, I glance over and see her turning her phone off.

What the hell?

I tap my fingers on the steering wheel.

I really felt like I had a good idea of who Valentine was, but her reaction to all of this has me second-guessing some things.

Deciding we could both use a little air, I flip on my blinker and move across the scattered traffic to take the next exit. The car behind us follows.

Val doesn't say anything as I take a series of turns toward a large, well-lit gas station, but that's not a surprise.

I pull up in front of an open pump and turn off the vehicle.

Val holds her phone out toward me.

"You want me to hold that for you?" I ask.

For the first time since standing in King's entryway, Valentine raises her eyes to meet mine. They're red rimmed and dull and have me gritting my teeth.

She looks between me and the phone still in her hand, then slowly lowers it. "You aren't going to take it from me?"

I turn in my seat to look at her better. "I'm not taking away your phone."

"Oh." She sounds confused, then looks out the windshield. "Can I use the bathroom?"

What?

"Yeah, Valentine. You can use the bathroom." My confusion matches her own. "You're not a prisoner."

She sets the phone back on her lap. "Can I go home, then?"

There it is.

I shake my head. "You have a new home now."

"But I don't want to go with you anymore."

Her words shouldn't sting. Obviously, she doesn't want to go with me anymore. I can't blame her. But I still don't like to hear it.

"That's too bad, Shorty." I purposefully use one of my nicknames for her just to piss her off. "You already emailed your boss and told him you were moving to Chicago. It probably wouldn't look good if you changed your mind on such a big decision twenty-four hours later."

Anger blooms in her cheeks, and it's so much better than the despair.

"I have my own income," she argues. "I can get my own place. I won't even tell King. You can still keep your precious *deal*."

"That's not how this works."

Seeing one of my men at the back of my SUV, I hit the button under the steering wheel to unlock the little door over the gas tank.

The click is audible, and Val's eyes dart to the side mirror.

She's fascinating to watch as her eyes narrow while she takes in the details.

When she leans forward to get a better look in the mirror, I know when she sees it.

Val spins around in the seat to look out the back window. "Is that my car?"

"Uh-huh." I unbuckle myself, then reach over to unbuckle Val.

She jerks back from me so violently she hits the back of her head on the window.

"Jesus, Val."

She makes a sound of pain as she hunches her shoulders.

And then I get it.

And then I get mad.

"I wasn't gonna fucking hit you," I growl, and it sounds like more of a threat than a promise.

"Well, I don't know!" Val's voice is high pitched as she reaches up to rub at the spot on her head.

"I'm never going to hurt you." I work to steady my tone.

But Val replies with a broken laugh. "Oh, won't you?"

She's aiming for sarcasm, but it just comes off sad. So damn sad.

This isn't going well.

"Have I ever been violent around you?" I try to use reason, wanting her to understand.

Val drops her hand from her head to stare me right in the eyes. "I've never even *met* you."

I'VE NEVER EVEN MET YOU.

Her words have rolled around in my head for the last hour and a half of our silent drive.

She's wrong.

And as I pull into the parking garage below my building, I decide it's time to set her straight.

CHAPTER 19

Val

DOM TURNS THE ENGINE OFF, AND QUIET DESCENDS around us.

I didn't bother trying to figure out what part of downtown Dom lives in. I'm not familiar enough with the city for it to matter. And I'm guessing he has a pretentious penthouse, so I'm sure I'll be able to look out the windows and figure out where I am.

I may still be ignorant about what exactly being the *head of the Chicago mafia* entails, but I'm assuming it involves massive amounts of money.

Dom climbs out of the SUV, and I want to slap myself in the face.

It seems so obvious now.

That's why he didn't bat an eye at the armed guards outside King's gate.

Probably also why that guard pulled his freaking gun out. He must've recognized Dom.

Love that I'm apparently the only person who doesn't know who Dominic is.

My door gets yanked open, startling a yelp out of me.

An angry-looking Dom leans into the open doorway, crowding me as he reaches across to unbuckle me.

This time I don't flinch. I just freeze.

His scent has been filling the car this whole time, but his leaning across me brings it right to my senses. No avoiding it.

As Dom starts to pull away, he grips my knees and spins me on the seat.

I should protest. Slap him. Something. But I'm too surprised to react.

Hands still on my knees, Dom drags me forward until my butt is ready to slide off the seat.

Geez, someone is in a hurry.

But instead of letting me slide out to the ground, Dom moves his hands to my hips and yanks me to him, lifting me out of the vehicle.

My body reacts on its own. Arms wrapping around his neck. Legs circling his waist.

Unwanted heat spears through my body as he digs his fingers into my sides. And he takes two steps to the side before shoving my back against the vehicle.

"Put me down," I try to snap, but it comes out weakly.

"No."

I unhook my arms and push at his chest.

Dom presses me harder into the side of the SUV as he lets go of me with one hand so that he can catch both of my wrists and press them to my chest.

My cleavage heaves against his knuckles as I try to catch my breath.

"Just hold still," he demands, but my focus locks on his hands. Those big, strong hands, covered in ink.

It never even crossed my mind that he was a gangster. But knowing what I know now, I don't know how I didn't see it. His eyes, the ones I thought were full of so much history, really are. But it's a darker history than I imagined. His calloused palms. The skull permanently drawn into the middle of his chest. The confidence.

How did I miss so much?

"I don't know how much you know about your brother's life, but mine is much the same. You'll have a driver everywhere you go. And a bodyguard who will accompany you when you leave the car."

"What?" *Someone escorting me, too?* "No."

He shakes my hands a little. "Yes."

"I can't have a bodyguard come with me to work."

"He'll wait in the lobby."

"You can't—"

"I can." Dom leans closer. "You're in my city now, remember? I can do whatever the fuck I want."

"You..."

Dom shifts his body, and I can feel him.

I can feel him pressing between my legs.

My body doesn't know that we don't like him anymore.

I try to close my legs, but his hips are still between them, so I just end up tightening my thighs around him.

"Put me down," I whisper.

"Not yet." Dom brings his lips just inches from mine. "If I give you another ring, will you wear it? Or will you throw it out another window?"

I look down at the hand he's using to hold my wrists and see the plain gold band on his finger.

He left it on.

And it fits him perfectly.

And he brought the rings with him.

Because he planned this.

I remember the look on his face earlier when I asked him if he was drunk, too, for our wedding night.

"Answer me, Val."

An awful suspicion sneaks into my brain.

I meet his eye. "Did you drug me?"

He doesn't so much as blink. "Will you wear the ring?"

Anger finally breaks through the hurt inside me.

"Did you fucking drug me?" I snap.

Dom stares back at me. "Yes." Then his mouth cracks into a smile. "Will you throw the ring out a window?"

"Yes." I bite my teeth together to keep from screaming.

The man just admitted to drugging me like it's nothing.

"Alright, then." Dom slides my body down his. "Let's go upstairs."

CHAPTER 20

Val

I'M NOT EVEN SURPRISED BY THE PRIVATE ELEVATOR with only one button for the PH level. *Figures.*

The car ascends rapidly before opening into a small hallway on the top floor of the building. There's only one door. But there is a second elevator, which must have access to another part of the building.

With little choice, I stand beside Dominic, who has my backpack slung over his shoulder, while he presses his whole hand to a black screen next to the door.

I briefly wonder if he uses Nero's company for his security system when a heavy *thunk* announces the door unlocking.

I try to keep my expression unimpressed when we enter Dominic's condo, but it's hard.

The space is huge. Industrial looking, with concrete floors so dark they look black and exposed metal on ceilings that have to be thirty feet high. All of which is overshadowed by the wall of floor-to-ceiling windows on my left, running the length of the space.

On the far side of the great room is a hallway that runs along the wall of windows and disappears out of view. And next to that hallway is an exposed flight of stairs leading up to another hallway on the second level.

Night has fallen, and the city skyline beyond the glass is breathtaking. But I refuse to move closer to admire it.

I'm still staring, though, when a shadow moves on the other side of the glass, making me jump.

"Just one of my men," Dom explains, seeing where I'm looking.

And I realize there's a door hidden in the windows, meaning there's some sort of outdoor patio space here at the tippy top of the building. Just the thought of being out there, that high up, makes me want to hurl.

When I tear my eyes away from the glass, I notice that we're not alone in here either.

A man is sitting on one of the couches between us and the windows, and another man is standing in the kitchen directly in front of us. He's on the other side of the large marble island, but I can still make out the gun on his hip.

It's almost funny—the black shirts, black pants, and matching serious expressions... But this is my life, for now, so that makes it less amusing.

"So we share our home with your army?" I ask, making my tone as bland as possible.

"No one sleeps here but us," Dom answers. "What would you like for dinner?"

The question is so bizarre I don't answer right away.

"Valentine," Dom prompts.

"I want to go to bed."

"You need to eat."

I fist my hands at my sides. "You need to let me go to bed."

Dom moves closer, his chest nearly touching mine. "Or what?"

"Or... Or I'll steal one of those guns off one of your guys and shoot you."

I don't think I could actually get a gun off someone, but if I did, I'd definitely shoot him.

The edge of his mouth pulls up. "Where would you shoot me, Shorty?"

I narrow my eyes. "Your shin."

Dominic barks out a laugh.

And it pisses me off.

"You wouldn't be laughing with a bullet in your shinbone," I snap and stomp toward the set of stairs, assuming the bedrooms are on the upper level.

Dom's chuckle follows me. "I'll give you that."

I'll give you that. I mouth the sentence before catching the movement of the guy outside again.

Whatever. It shouldn't be a surprise to his men that I'm not happy to be here. At least some of them were clearly in on the plot.

Since Dom doesn't do anything to direct me elsewhere, I start up the stairs, keeping my hand on the black iron railing.

When I reach the top, I pause. The hallway is much longer than I expected.

Dom stops beside me. "Would you like a tour?"

I shake my head. The full gravity of my situation is finally starting to sink in.

This fancy penthouse... This city that isn't mine... This is my life.

At least until I can figure a way out of it. But since I don't want to get locked in like the prisoner he claims I'm not, I'll play along. Better a gilded cage than a real one.

"Door at the end." Dom lifts a hand to point at the wide partially open door at the very end of the hall.

"That's my room?" I clarify.

"That's where you sleep," he responds.

I let out a sigh at his cryptic answer, positive it's his room and that he still expects us to share a bed. "I think I can find it from here."

I expect Dom to argue, but he doesn't. He just holds my backpack out in front of me.

The sight of it shouldn't hurt my heart so much. But it does.

I take it.

But neither of us moves.

"The airport?" My question is a whisper as I stare at the bag Dominic bought me.

I don't know what I think I'll get out of having every last shred of our history destroyed.

I shouldn't have asked.

Dom's fingers brush lightly over my ponytail. "Go to bed, Valentine."

My feet comply, and I stride forward without sparing him another look.

I pass three rooms, then reach the door at the end of the hall.

Keeping my hand on the edge of the door, I push it open enough to step inside, then let it shut behind me.

The room is obviously large. And as I stare at the platform bed, nicely made in dark gray bedding and facing yet another wall of windows, I have no doubt that this is the master bedroom. Dom's bedroom.

I will anger to fully overtake the pain that hasn't left my chest since King revealed Dom's identity.

I don't want to hurt anymore.

Not tonight.

I carry my backpack to the open doorway on this side of the headboard and find a luxurious bathroom that runs the length of the room. Oversized double vanity. Huge glassed-in shower stall with marbled walls. A separate room with a toilet. And a deep soaking tub in front of another large window.

Does no one worry about people with binoculars around here?

When I turn around to shut the bathroom door, I find a giant walk-in closet hidden behind the door.

Sure, I'm being paranoid, but not wanting a peeping tom to catch sight of me on my first night here, I take my backpack into the little toilet room and change into my pajamas.

While I wash my face, I don't think about how I packed my

bag this afternoon while blissfully thinking I was about to start my happily ever after with my new husband.

While I dab on my under-eye cream, I don't think about how Dom encouraged me to pack an overnight bag with a day's worth of essentials because *it might be hard to sort through your stuff when we get home.*

While I redo my ponytail with more force than necessary, I don't think about how Dom drove so calmly to King's house, knowing my world was about to crumble.

"He's an asshole," I tell my reflection. "A total fucking asshole."

The burning sensation behind my eyes lessens, just the smallest bit.

"He's a slimy piece of shit. A total fucking jerk." I forcefully put toothpaste on the end of my toothbrush. "I hate him."

I hold on to my anger as best I can while I practically scrub the enamel off my teeth.

I spit into the sink. "He's a... a... prick." I slam my toothbrush down on the edge of the sink and leave it there. Just like I leave my dirty clothes on the floor. And my backpack open on the edge of the tub.

They are small acts of defiance in his pristine living space, but they make me feel better.

I found my phone tucked into the side pocket of my bag, not sure when Dom stuck it there, but I carry it with me to bed.

A band of recessed lights built into the crown molding surrounding the room gives a nice soft glow. But even without it, there's enough ambient light from the city beyond the windows to light my path. Not that there's much to dodge in this room. The bed looks bigger than a normal king-size mattress with a large padded leather headboard. Matching—simple but, I'm sure, expensive—nightstands flank either side of the bed.

As I walk around the foot of the bed, circling to the far side, I untuck the blankets. I don't know what sort of person sleeps with their feet trapped like that, but it's not me.

With nothing left to do, I climb into the bed and sit with my legs under the blankets.

It's not even that late, but with winter almost here, it's already dark outside. And emotional exhaustion is real and upon me.

But before I lie down, I have one more thing to do.

Letting out a breath, I turn my phone back on.

I owe King more of an explanation.

The screen is just lighting up when it changes to show an incoming call.

Savannah.

I groan.

I'm tempted to turn my phone right back off, but I sort of doubt this is the first time she's tried calling.

Dragging the walls up around my heart, I hit answer. "Hey, Savannah."

There's a pause, followed by a noisy exhale. "Dammit, Val. I've been trying to get a hold of you forever."

"Sorry." I wince, feeling guilty all over again. "I was having a bit of a, um, moment, so I turned my phone off."

"I'll say," she huffs. "Will you explain to me what's going on? King hasn't been real clear on the details."

I turn the phone to speaker, setting it on the bed in front of me so I can press my hands to my cheeks. "In King's defense, I kinda blindsided him with it."

"He's acting like the whole world is ending." I can hear Savannah's eye roll. "And I get that he doesn't like surprises, but I don't see the big deal. He trusts Dom. To some degree, at least."

She doesn't see the big deal?

"I'm not sure..." I start, but she keeps talking.

"I mean, Dom can be a little scary, but he was nothing but nice to me that time he brought me to his place."

My mouth drops open.

"Not to mention hot." Savannah makes a humming sound.

"Wait." I shake my head. "You know who Dominic is?"

"*Dominic,*" she repeats. "I only met him that one time, so that

148

probably doesn't qualify as *knowing* him. But I get it now, why you had a different name in your phone. King would've lost his shit about you guys dating."

"Yeah…" I trail off.

She doesn't know.

Savannah has no idea that *I* had no idea who Dominic was. That I was tricked into this marriage for the sake of Dom having access to The Alliance. Whatever that means.

"King said you were pretty upset," Savannah says cautiously.

Does King know the full extent of it? Would he have put that together? I mean, he had to, right?

I pinch my eyes shut and think back through the interaction.

King was pissed that I married Dom. And he was pissed that Dom was demanding entry into The Alliance, which is when he made that comment about Dom *tricking me into bed.*

And King knew I was crying. He saw me.

But did he put it all together? Or does he think I was just upset over them not getting along?

Could King really think I've known who Dom was all along and that I've kept it a secret because I thought he'd be mad?

"Val?" Savannah says, probably concerned over my silence.

I could tell her.

I could tell her everything.

Then she'd go to King and demand he *free me.* And then King and The Alliance and Dominic and the Chicago mafia would go to war.

For what?

For me?

I'm not worth that.

"Sor—I mean, yeah, I was. Having both those guys yelling at each other was kinda a lot." I try for a light tone. "I overreacted to them overreacting."

"You sure you're okay?" Her sincerity almost breaks me.

"I'm sure."

Savannah says something that's muffled before she speaks back into the phone. "King is asking to talk to you."

My eyes widen as I stare down at the phone. "Uh, can you tell him that I'll call tomorrow night? It's been a long day, flying in from Vegas this morning and then driving all the way down here." It's hard to believe that's all happened today.

"Of course. I'll tell him." Savannah sighs. "I'm sure you'll be busy settling in, but I definitely want to hear more about *Dominic* soon." She makes a sound of disbelief. "I still can't believe you live in Chicago. But if nothing else, the holidays are coming up. So we'll see you then."

It's November. If she's talking about Christmas, that's still so far away. And a long time to spend with strangers.

I swallow. "For sure."

"Night, Mrs. Gonzalez," she teases, then hangs up the call.

Mrs. Gonzalez.

A fresh round of sorrow fills my heart.

Why'd it have to be like this?

"Why'd you lie?" Dom's voice damn near gives me a heart attack.

"Jesus!" I slap a hand to my chest and turn my head as Dom pushes off the doorway. "How long have you been there?"

"Long enough." He starts to undo his shirt buttons while toeing off his shoes. "Why didn't you tell her the truth?"

I set my phone on the nightstand and shift down the bed until I'm lying under the covers. "To what end?"

Dom cocks his head at me. "To have her go to bat for you with King. Have her demand I let you go home."

"And you'd just let that happen?"

Dom slowly shakes his head.

"Like I said." I roll away from him, giving him my back. "To what end?"

"Val—"

I cut him off. "Is there any chance you'll let me sleep in another room?"

"No." His answer is swift.

I nod against the pillow. It's what I expected. "Then please turn off the ceiling lights and shut the fuck up so I can sleep."

His steps are quiet, but I hear them as he circles around the foot of the bed toward me.

My eyes are still open, but I don't move my gaze from straight ahead.

Dom's hips are right in front of me, but then he turns and reaches for something on the nightstand. "There's a button here. Press it once to turn them on and off. Hold it down to adjust the brightness. There's also a gun in this drawer." I hear him tap the wood. "But you need my palm to unlock it. Because this used to be my side of the bed." *Used to be.* "And I'll *shut the fuck up* in a moment. But understand that you're the only person who can get away with talking to me like that. And only in private." He crouches before me, his chest completely bare. "I'm not sure what I'd do as punishment if you did it in public. But I'm pretty sure *you* wouldn't enjoy it."

I close my eyes, ignoring him.

"Get some sleep." Warm lips press against my forehead. "We have a big day tomorrow."

I hold as still as possible until I hear him rounding the bed again.

When I hear the bathroom door shut, I let the last tear of the night slip from my eye and soak into the pillow.

How was I so wrong about everything?

It's nearly comical. All my mom's lectures growing up. How men will only want to use me. How I'm too stupid to understand them. How I'll end up ruined and alone. I really should have paid attention.

Wallowing in regrets, listening for Dom to return to bed, I finally slip into the escape of sleep.

CHAPTER 21

I TAKE MY TIME GETTING READY FOR BED. I WON'T LET Valentine have her own room. She'll eventually accept her place here, but giving her distance now would do more harm than good.

It's that same reasoning that makes me step out of my closet in nothing but my boxers. I can't let her get used to me sleeping in clothes when this is what I like to wear.

By the time I open the bathroom door and reenter the bedroom, Val's breathing has evened out in sleep.

Good.

Right on time, my phone flashes with a notification, letting me know he's here.

I grab a handful of cash out of the nightstand nearest me, then make sure to shut the door quietly when I leave the bedroom.

I'm at the top of the stairs when my men let Doc in, but I wait until I'm stopped before him to speak. "Appreciate the quick delivery."

I called him when Valentine first went up to our room.

The man in his seventies lifts a shoulder. "It's all stuff I had on hand."

Having no pockets, still wearing only my boxers, I hand him over the stack of hundreds so I can take the items he has for me.

"These should look exactly like the ones she has." Doc places a stack of foil rectangles, each containing twenty-eight little pills in neat rows, in my hand. "Just make sure you pop out the right amount before you swap them for the current one."

I nod.

Doc digs into his satchel for the second item, withdrawing a capped syringe. "This is the other thing."

I take it from him, then turn and head back upstairs to my wife.

CHAPTER 22

Val

IT FEELS LIKE I WAKE IN THE SPAN OF ONE BREATH. I was sleeping the sleep of the dreamless, lost in the black nothing of unconsciousness. And now I'm here.

It was early when I went to bed, and now dawn is breaking beyond the windows.

While my eyes adjust, I hear someone else breathing.

So Dom did sleep in here last night.

Part of me wants to wake him up, just to disturb him. But the other part of me wants him to sleep for the rest of the morning.

I push myself up, and my finger throbs.

Must've slept funny.

Carefully, I climb out of bed and try to blink my vision clear as I get closer to the windows.

Whatever floor we're on is high. Like scarily high. But this view is beautiful.

The city is coming to life below us and just past the buildings.

I inhale and place my palms on the glass.

Lake Michigan is right there, glistening in the sunrise.

I could get used to waking up to this view.

The thought stops me short, and I shake my head.

And then I freeze.

What the...

My hands are still pressed against the window and... And...

I lift my left hand off the glass.

That can't be.

I reach out with my right hand and touch the tender skin of my left ring finger.

"How the hell...?"

This motherfucker.

I slowly turn and face the bed. Where Dom is lying awake, hands behind his head, staring at me.

I hold my hand out, fingers up, between us.

"Did you seriously tattoo my whole fucking finger?"

Where my wedding ring briefly was, is Dominic's name in black ink, circling the digit. Above that, where a band might be, is Dominic's name again. But it doesn't stop there. Above that, between the next set of knuckles, are two more *Dominics*, stacked one on top of the other.

I pull my hand closer to my face so I can read the last ring of letters when I realize it's different.

Between the last knuckle and the bottom of my fingernail are the words *Til Death*.

"I hate you." I don't raise my voice, but it still fills the room.

Dominic shakes his head once. "No, you don't."

"I do." I'm still looking at my finger.

"You want to. But you don't have hate in you, Angel."

I hold my hand back out, turning my narrowed eyes on Dom. "Seriously, Dominic. What the hell is this?"

"I asked you if you'd wear my ring, and you said no."

I wave my hand around. "Are you fucking insane?" This time I do shout. "You can't just tattoo me! And my *whole finger*? What is wrong with you?"

Dominic flips the covers off and climbs out of bed.

He strides toward me. "I asked you and you said no."

"Is that your argument?" My eyes widen. "If the question had been *will you wear my ring, or would you prefer I tattoo your whole-*

ass finger like a psycho, my answer would've been a little different."

"Your answer was honest."

"Dominic," I snap. "You cannot just tattoo me."

"You. Are. My. Wife." He punctuates each word with a step, stopping directly before me. "And people need to know that. If I can't trust you to wear a ring, I'll mark you myself for everyone to see."

My mouth opens and closes.

This man is unreal.

"You couldn't just put your name once?" I ask, knowing I'd still be pissed about that. But the whole finger...?

"Four." He leans closer. "One to replace every other dick you've touched."

I just blink at him.

Every dick I've touched?

When did I tell him how many men I've slept with?

"Vegas." Dom answers my silent question.

"When did..."

"After our wedding ceremony, when you were begging me to let you come, you were also answering any question I asked you. You really need to learn how to watch your drink."

"You are such a—" I bite off my sentence and shake my hand between us. "Four men! You did this because, at the age of twenty-five, I've been with a total of *four* men."

Dom crosses his arms. "They've touched what's mine."

"Yours?" I scoff. "You tricked me into this. Into all of this."

"Doesn't make you any less mine."

"And what about you?" I hiss, jabbing my pointer finger into his chest. "How many vaginas have you stuck your stupid cock in? I bet it's more than fucking four."

The side of his mouth tips up. "It's more than fucking four."

I clench my jaw. "I'm going to kill you."

Dominic takes a step back. "Many have tried."

I look back down at my hand.

It's sore.

And having my lying husband's name tattooed so many times on my body is tacky.

And it's absolutely the most insane thing I could possibly think of someone doing to someone else.

And I hate it.

I do.

I would never do something like this.

But—and I can hardly even believe I'm thinking this—I've always wanted a tattoo. I'm just too frugal. And I'm not decisive enough. And I never wanted to deal with the pain.

The neon red flag finally unfurls in the center of my brain.

"Wait..." I lift my gaze to my husband.

Dom stops halfway to the door, his back to me. "What?"

"How did you even do this? Did you drug me again?"

Dominic turns to face me. "I wasn't going to let you feel the pain."

My outraged retort withers in my throat.

What sort of answer is that?

I press my fingertips into my temples. "I can't believe I have to say this," I grumble. "You can't drug me again. That can't be healthy."

"I know what I'm doing."

Great. The man I married knows how to drug people. How comforting.

"And you can't tattoo me again," I tell him.

"I don't have any plans to do either."

My hands drop. "Dom, that's not an answer."

"I prefer you calling me Dominic."

"I prefer you when you aren't drugging me and scratching your name into my skin."

Dominic's jaw ticks, then he tries to change the topic. "I moved your clothes into the closet."

"Dom." I stomp my bare foot. "I don't want your name tattooed on my finger."

157

"Little late for that, Angel." He turns and heads for the door. "Go get ready. And put on something black."

"Dom—"

Before he steps through, he looks at me over his shoulder. "We're going to a funeral."

His words stop my tirade.

A funeral?

CHAPTER 23

I CLOSE MY EYES AS THE LINE OF MATCHING BLACK SUVs makes its way through morning Chicago traffic.

This isn't the time for me to worry about Valentine.

I don't have space right now to think about the way her face paled when I told her we were going to a funeral.

There's no point in asking her if she's okay.

She's not.

I inhale, filling my lungs.

This is a family affair, but when I step out of this vehicle, I'm the Boss.

I'm untouchable.

Invincible.

I'm out for blood.

I breathe until I feel the vehicle slow, then I open my eyes.

We're here.

Val is sitting in the back seat with me, staring up at the cathedral. Trembling.

I place my hand over hers on the seat between us, causing her to tense. "I know you don't want to be here, but you're coming in as my wife. Everyone knows who you are, so you won't need to introduce yourself. They know our marriage was quick, but they believe it was a whirlwind romance."

She turns her head, finally meeting my gaze. "So did I."

Her eyes have always been so alive. From the first time I ever saw her, one look at those golden-brown eyes and I could see she was full of life and energy.

But not today.

Today they're dull.

And if the heart inside my chest hadn't already been turned into a diamond through decades of pressure, the expression on her face would break it.

CHAPTER 24

Val

My hands are shaking so badly I don't even protest when Dom helps me out of the vehicle.

Anything but a funeral.

Literally anything but this.

My throat feels tight, and I have to focus on breathing as Dom interlocks his fingers with mine. The sore skin of my ring finger protests, but the slight ache gives me something to focus on.

I need anything else to focus on.

We start forward across the sidewalk.

Dominic is dressed in uninterrupted black. And the look on his face reminds me that I don't really know him at all. Because for the first time, I see what Savannah meant.

He looks a little scary.

We lift our feet at the same time and climb the steps leading to the massive front doors.

Men line the stairs, all looking like they're ready for a war.

My black ballet flats are silent on the concrete, and I'm glad I wore these shoes.

My belted long-sleeve shirt dress might be a bit short for a funeral, but it was the first black dress I could find. And the single nod Dominic gave me when I came down from our room told me it was suitable.

The doors are opened before us, and everything inside me goes cold.

I hate funerals.

I hate them so much.

My fingers squeeze Dominic's.

He might be my enemy in this battle I didn't know we were fighting, but he's also the closest thing I have to a friend here.

And if he makes me sit alone...

I tug on his hand.

Dom tips his face down to me. He doesn't say anything. And his intensity almost keeps me quiet. But my anxiety is nearing phobia levels.

"Will..." My lips tremble, and I press them together for a second. "Will you sit with me?"

When he doesn't answer me, my eyes fill with tears.

I blink and look anywhere but at him, trying to avoid the eyes of the men still surrounding us.

"Angel." His voice is soft. *The voice I used to know.* A thumb brushes across my cheek. "You'll always be seated at my side."

He cups the side of my face with his warm hand, holding me still as he presses his lips against my forehead.

I want to hate him.

"You can be sad in there. You can let people see your beautiful heart. Let them love you." Dom brushes another tear away. "But we're walking in with our shoulders back. Because those people in there need to believe in us. And we're stronger together."

I want to hate him so badly.

I straighten my shoulders and use my free hand to brush my hair back from my face.

When I look up to meet Dom's bright blue gaze, I see that familiarity I heard a moment ago.

It hurts to see it. A reminder of what I thought we were building.

But even with that hurt, it's still comforting. And I don't care how toxic it is right now. I need the comfort of *him*.

I need someone.

"Come, Wife. And meet your new family." The side of his mouth pulls into the smallest smile, just for me.

Then he pulls me with him into the church.

The dull murmuring of a large crowd trying to be quiet dulls even more as we start down the aisle.

Memories try to pull me under. Flashes of the worst moments of my life. But I walk alongside Dom, one step at a time.

I work to keep my free hand relaxed at my side.

There are so many people here. Hundreds.

It's like my dad's funeral.

A woman smiles at me when my eyes fall on hers.

I give her a small smile back, my throat tightening even more.

A stranger just smiled at me. This is nothing like my dad's funeral.

Dom dips his chin, acknowledging the people we pass. An older woman reaches out and touches his hand. I do my best to breathe while I make as much eye contact as I'm capable of. Each set of kind eyes twists that barb deeper into my heart.

We keep walking, passing pew after pew, all the way to the front of the church.

And that's when I finally look forward. At the large photo of a man younger than Dominic. His smiling face, framed in gold, signifying his death.

Oh god, I can't do this.

Dom lets go of my hand, but before I can scramble to grab it back, he's pressing his palm against my back, guiding me to the right, into the front row.

The pew is full, except for the first two spots, and the woman seated next to the open spots stands.

"Aunt Dina." Dominic holds out his hands, and she clasps them. "I want you to be the first to meet my wife."

What is he doing? Introductions now?

The woman, probably in her sixties, turns to me with red-rimmed eyes.

Oh, sweet Jesus, is this the dead man's mother?

The woman steps forward, and before I can react, she wraps me in a hug.

I freeze.

For one heartbeat, I freeze.

Then I feel her body trembling against mine, and I hug her back. Holding her tight.

Because this is a clinging hug. One without reservations. One that's more than a greeting. It's... real.

"I'm so sorry," I whisper as tears drip off my lashes. "I'm so sorry."

After a long moment, she pulls back, and I release my grip on her, only for her to place her hands on my cheeks. "Bless you, sweet girl." She kisses one of my cheeks, then the other.

Dom lays a hand on my shoulder, the movement enough to have the woman, his Aunt Dina, letting me go.

He waits until she's back in her seat. Then he turns us. So we're facing *everyone.*

Dominic doesn't say anything.

He doesn't have to.

A man in the row behind ours rises, his eyes on me.

The woman next to him comes to her feet.

Slowly, and then all at once, everyone stands.

They *all* stand.

And they're all looking at me.

I swallow. And look back.

Feeling the weight of the moment deep in my soul.

Dominic lowers his arm from my shoulders, sliding his hand down the length of my arm until his fingers are twined with mine.

I squeeze his fingers, hard, feeling like I might disintegrate if I don't have something to hold on to.

Then, with the entire room standing, Dom turns us back around and guides me into my seat.

Without him, I'd collapse onto the hard wooden bench. But, still clinging to his hand, I manage to sink down onto it.

There's a collective sound of creaking wood as the entire congregation sits after we do.

A moment later, a priest appears at the front of the church, but I don't catch a single word he says.

The emotions in this place...

The feelings in this place...

Still clutching Dom's hand with my left, I reach my right hand up to rub at my chest.

I've never experienced anything like this before. This sense of *family.*

Of acceptance.

There are sniffles. A few open cries. The sounds of babies. And still a sense of solemn peace.

This is so different from the other funerals I've been to.

And I don't want to think about those. But I can't stop myself.

"He is survived by his wife, Barbara, and their two children, King and Aspen."

I press against my chest harder.

My mother's fingers pinching me.

Siblings I didn't know I had glaring at me. Ignoring me.

I squeeze Dom's fingers.

My first true feelings of being unwanted.

I try to forget.

Sitting alone in a small chapel in Florida. My dry eyes staring at the silver urn on an unadorned stool at the front of the room.

Another tear escapes the corner of my eye.

Walking out into the sun, still alone. More alone than before.

How different would my life be if I'd had someone?

How different would I be if I hadn't felt so... so fucking alone when I needed people the very most?

How different would I be if I'd had someone to hug when my

parents died? How different would it feel to mourn *with* someone?

Grief swamps me. Sucks me under its wave as I let myself feel everything I missed.

And it feels awful.

It feels so lonely and cold. And endless.

Like it will be my forever.

I blindly reach across with my right hand until I'm gripping Dom's palm between mine.

I want to hate him.

He settles his left hand on top of our combined ones.

I want to hate him, but I can't.

His body leans into mine, and he presses his mouth to the top of my head.

A kiss.

A sign of affection.

It's exactly what I need, but it's still too much.

I want to crawl into his lap.

I want to hit him as hard as I can.

I want to scream at him. And I want to tell him everything.

I want to tell him about my mother's funeral. I want to tell him how horrible it was. How much it hurt. How alone I felt.

How alone I feel.

How I haven't been able to shake that feeling.

It's been six years... Six years of feeling lost.

Six years of hoping and wishing for someone to come in and save me from myself. Save me from the desperate blank feeling inside me.

But I can't focus on any of that now. Because the man at my side, the one holding my hands like no one has before, might be my husband, but he's also the head of the Chicago mafia. And the people filling this room are his family and his men, and I can't break down here.

I can't break down next to a mother grieving her son.

I can't do anything but cling to him.
I'll have to pick up my pieces later.

CHAPTER 25

Dom

THE PRIEST GESTURES FOR US TO RISE FOR THE FINAL prayer, and I reluctantly let go of my wife's hands long enough to extract the handkerchief from my pocket.

I hold it out for her, and she takes it while the room choruses an *amen.*

It's been a long time since I've believed in anyone's god. I've seen too much of the underside of humanity to believe in a greater plan, but I do believe in tradition. And in honoring the dead.

I slide a hand up Valentine's back. "Stay right here," I tell her quietly.

Stepping away, I take the priest's place as he disappears into the shadows.

Because I also believe in avenging the dead.

"Family." The word booms out of me.

"Family." The room echoes back to me.

"We are under attack." I pause, making sure everyone can hear every word. "Someone is coming after us. After our family." I point at my cousin's photo behind me. "And they will pay." A rumble of agreement rolls up the aisle. "They will pay with blood. Because they came after us, and we won't settle at an eye for an eye." I look around at the faces before me. "We take a soul for an

168

eye." I let the rage simmering under my skin heat. "And we're owed a lot of souls, because this is our fourth funeral in four months. We will have no more. Not one more of us dies at the hands of these cowards. We *will* find them. And when we do, we will bring war to their doorstep. And we will win." I let my eyes move to the golden ones staring back at me from the front row. "We will win because we have The Alliance. Because a good woman can change your life."

And I see it. I see her understand.

CHAPTER 26
Val

HOPE IS HEAVY.

And when the hope of so many people settles onto my shoulders with that one sentence, I feel like I might sink through the floor.

Dom holds my gaze, and the silence in the church is deafening.

There's no need for a response. There's no room in this world for applause.

Dominic just made his family a promise, and it all hinges on me.

The hope of all these people hinges on the fact that I willingly married this man and that our union will bring them The Alliance.

Another tear drips down my cheek.

He shouldn't have done this to me.

Dom shouldn't have put me in this situation.

I use his black handkerchief to soak up the next tear.

DG is embroidered in the corner, with thread the color of his eyes.

Dom is still staring at me. Watching me.

And since I can't bring myself to hate him. Not completely.

I do the only thing I can in this moment.

The only acceptable action in a room filled with so much emotion.

I lean in.

CHAPTER 27

Dom

SHE COMES TO ME.

Valentine squares her shoulders, and she comes to me.

And when I extend my hand and she places hers in mine, I feel the weight of all the expectations I carry lessen. I feel her share them.

I feel her join me. Not just in this moment. Not just for show. But she joins me in this fight.

And when she turns to the sea of faces, I witness their acceptance.

Their acceptance of her. Of my decision to join with The Alliance. Of my promise.

I squeeze her fingers in mine and nod.

Then, together, we walk down the aisle and away from the sadness.

CHAPTER 28

Val

I UNDERSTAND NOW.

I don't like it. I'm not okay with it. But I understand it.

It doesn't fix anything, but being able to put a reason behind it all... it helps.

If Dominic had been open with me, told me about his family, told me who he was, I would've talked to King. Because I wouldn't have known any better. And if I'd told King that Dominic Gonzalez wanted me to marry him so he could have The Alliance's help, King would have locked me away. He would've saved me from this situation. And in doing so, he would have doomed another one of Dom's cousins. Or uncles. Or... Dominic himself.

The handkerchief is already balled tight in my fist, but I grip it tighter.

My eyes don't focus as the city blurs past us as we head back home.

Home.

I stay quiet because I don't know the men in the front seat, and there are things I need to say to Dominic, but I don't know who can hear them.

Obviously, there are people in his life who know everything.

People who had to help him coordinate his plan. And I'm guessing the men who wander the condo with guns are part of that group, so I don't care if they see me angry or hurt or upset. But the people outside that circle, if they're exposed to my true emotions, their newly found hope will wither. And if that happens, what was the point of any of this?

If my loneliness can help save even one person, it's worth it.

It's more than I was doing with my life anyway.

The vehicle pulls to a stop in front of a massive building, and when Dom reaches for his door, I realize this must be the building we live in.

"Wait for me," Dominic commands, just as he did outside the church, then he exits the SUV.

And just like before, I wait.

Maybe I've watched too many movies, but I always thought someone else opened doors for the man in charge. But Dom takes care of himself.

He circles around, then pulls my door open, and I climb out.

Before he shuts the car door, he leans in and says something to the driver. Something about waiting.

I keep my lips pressed together as we walk into the building, flanked by four men in black suits.

A few people are passing through the lobby, and a man sits behind a desk next to the bank of elevators, but no one even raises their eyes to us. I'm not sure if it's because of wariness or if they're used to the spectacle, but either way, I'm happy not to have any more attention on me.

Dom leads us away from the elevators to cut in front of the desk.

As we pass it, the seated man stands. "Mr. Gonzalez."

Dominic pauses, grabbing my wrist, so I pause, too. "Phil, this is my wife. Make sure everyone knows."

The man looks at me and nods. If he's surprised, he doesn't show it. "Pleasure to meet you, Mrs. Gonzalez."

I'm proud of myself for not flinching at him calling me that. "Likewise."

Manners have me wanting to hold my hand out, but since he keeps his hands at his sides and Dom doesn't loosen his grip on my wrist, I don't bother.

"I'm sure Mr. Gonzalez has already told you, but if you need anything at all, just call down."

Dom has not told me that, and I don't know how to *call down*, but I tell him thank you all the same.

Conversation closed, Dom moves us down a hallway on the other side of the desk to a single elevator that's not visible to the rest of the lobby.

There's a palm reader in place of a call button, and when Dom presses his hand to it, the doors slide open, and we step in.

I expect the group of men to enter with us, but they turn their backs to the elevator and stand in place as the doors slide shut.

The ascension is quick, and before I can think of what to say to Dom, the car is slowing to a stop, and the doors are reopening.

There's a man—one of Dom's, I assume—in the hallway outside the door to the condo, but Dom still uses the palm reader to unlock it.

He doesn't open the door, though. He taps the corner of the screen, and a keypad displays. Dom types in a series of letters, faster than I can track.

I'm starting to turn my gaze away, not interested in security equipment, when Dom lifts my hand, the one he's still holding by my wrist.

"Press it flat to the glass."

I do as he says. I don't see or feel anything, but after a few seconds, a tiny symbol blinks green below my thumb.

"Good."

I take that as permission to drop my hand, and he taps in a few more commands, then reaches past me to open the door.

It's been less than twenty-four hours since I first stepped foot in Dominic's home, but it holds a familiarity that allows my shoulders to relax for the first time since he told me we were going to a funeral.

"Stay here," Dom says to me, placing his hand on my back before raising his voice. "Everyone out."

The two men I can see start toward us, and two more men I hadn't noticed move into the main room, with another man coming in through the glass door from outside.

"You three." Dom points to a trio. "You stay in the hallway outside the door. You." He points to another. "You're in the lobby. And you." He points to the last man. "You're in the parking garage. These are your positions when my wife is home. No one is in here with her. If she orders anything, you'll collect it from downstairs and hand it to her at the door. Not a fucking foot inside. Got it?" The men all nod. "You're here because I trust you to protect my woman. But if you step out of line, I'll kill you my-fucking-self."

The serious looks on their faces turn even more stony.

They clearly believe him.

As the men file out the door, a flutter of something close to affection tries to take flight in my belly. But then I remember that protecting me is just Dom protecting his connection to The Alliance.

My shoulders slump as the door clicks shut, and I step forward, dislodging Dom's touch.

"What's wrong?"

At Dom's question, I spin around, finally grabbing hold of the fury that's evaded me all day. "Where do you want me to start?"

His expression is curious. "Start with whatever just happened. A second ago."

Oh. That.

As swiftly as it came, my temper is dampened by emotions. "I... I don't know how to act around you."

He furrows his brows. "What do you mean?"

"Because I don't know what's real with you, Dom. I don't

know what's real and what's a lie, and it leaves me..." I lift my hands and let them drop back down. "Stranded."

"I never lied to you."

My exhale is full of tangible doubt. "I don't believe you."

"Fine." He steps closer. "I told you one lie."

"One," I repeat, already not believing him.

"Yeah, Shorty, one." Then he tips his head to the side. "Okay, two." He holds up a finger to count off, and to stop me from retorting. "One, I wasn't in Vegas when you asked if I was. But I was there by the time you landed, so that's hardly a lie."

"That's a lie, Dominic." I catch myself too late and use his full name, causing his lips to quirk.

"And two, there are direct flights from Denver to Chicago."

It takes me a second to understand that he's referring to our very first meeting in the Denver airport.

I cross my arms. "Tell me how you did it."

"Did what?"

"The whole airport thing. Did you somehow plan for my backpack breaking?" This must be what they mean when they say *morbid curiosity*. Because I want to know the answers. I feel like I need to know. Even though I'm sure the answers will only make me feel worse, not better.

"If I can't get a knife past the clowns at TSA, then I should save my enemies the trouble and just slit my own throat."

I wrap my arms tighter across my chest, not liking the visual of blood pouring down Dom's neck.

Then I take in the first part of what he said, and my arms drop. "You cut my strap." My tone is so put out it makes Dom smile. I jab a finger at his chest. "That was a perfectly good bag, and you ruined it."

"That bag was a piece of shit." He catches my finger in his grip. "And before you ask me a million more questions, let me just tell you how it went." He holds my fingertip against his body, and I have to tip my head back to keep my eyes on his. "I bumped into you, cut your shitty backpack, knowing that was the only way to get you to stick around long enough to talk. If your bag wasn't broken, you'd have tried to run away from me at the first opportunity. And you know it." *I do know it, but how did he?* "And it only took one phone call to a man I know at the airline to get your seat upgraded."

I bite my cheek. That sounds way too easy but absolutely plausible.

Then I think of everything that came after. The movie. Sharing earbuds. Dom falling asleep on my shoulder. The pod.

"Was having sex with me a part of the plan?" I ask the question before I can chicken out. I need to know this part, too.

"From the first moment I saw you, I wanted to fuck you." Dom shifts closer. "So yeah, getting inside that sweet cunt was a part of the plan. But fucking you in the airport? No, that was just a happy bonus."

I try to pull my hand away, but he doesn't let go.

I scoff. "You expect me to believe that I'm really your type?"

I didn't want to say that. Didn't mean to voice it.

But Dominic made me feel so good about myself. He made me feel sexy in a way I never had. Made it so I wasn't constantly worrying about what angle he was looking at me from. But ever since it all went to shit, I can't stop those insecurities from screaming at me.

And I need to know if that was all fake, too.

Dom drops his gaze to my toes and back up. "I've never had a problem with short girls."

"Short..." I shake my head. "I'm not talking about being short. I'm talking about fat girls. Big girls." I flare my hand that isn't still trapped in his grip out to the side in a *look at me* motion.

Dom's free hand darts out to capture mine, and I squeak in surprise. Always forgetting how fast he is.

"Shorty." He flattens both my hands against his chest and forces me to walk backward. "Look at yourself next to me. You're hardly *big*." My back bumps into the door. "And yeah, if you really want to know, you're my fucking type. I live in a hard, unyielding world. It's nice to come home to something soft." He uses his grip on me to lower one of my hands, sliding it down his stomach. "I already told you—from the first moment I saw you, I wanted to fuck you." My palm connects with something hard. "And if I thought you'd let me, I'd fuck you right now just to prove it."

With a mind of their own, my fingers flex around his length.

Dominic groans and lets go of my hand but immediately leans his weight against me, trapping my palm against his cock.

"That's why things were so fast that first time. It'd been a long time since I'd had someone." He groans as he rocks his hips into my hand.

"Dominic." I'm trying to chastise him, but it's not coming out right.

"Your comment earlier about your four versus my *not four* was fair. But I haven't been with anyone in nearly a year. So yeah, when I saw the opportunity to sink my dick into your sweet cunt, I grabbed it with both fucking hands."

He grips my sides, his big hands flexing against me.

"A year?" I don't understand what he's talking about. "W-when was the first moment you saw me?"

He's said it twice now. But I wasn't really listening. I assumed he meant when we met at the airport.

He tips his face down toward mine. "Last December. You were all dressed up for your work Christmas party, and I followed you from the L to your office building."

"You... You followed me?" I don't even know what part to be more stunned over. The fact that a dangerous mafia man was following me and I didn't know, or that he hasn't slept with another woman since then.

"Yeah, Val. I followed you, and you had no clue." Dom rocks against my hand one more time, then steps back with a groan. "We're going to work on your situational awareness."

I ball my hand into a fist, thankful he can't see the state of my underwear. "It seems the only person I really need to protect myself against is you." My mind is too scattered to deliver the words with the right amount of bite. Even as I think of him drugging me—twice.

Dom ignores me. "But you'll never do that again, so that's one less thing to worry about."

"What?" I ask, trying to remember what the hell he's even talking about. "Go to my Christmas party?"

"No, I'll go with you to your next Christmas party. I'm talking about taking the L. It's not safe. And speaking of safety." He continues like he isn't flipping my entire world upside down. "When I'm not home, the patio area is off-limits. No one can get up here from the outside, but until we get this current problem under control, snipers are a threat."

"Snipers?" My voice pitches.

Dom nods, then grabs my shoulders to face me toward the little black screen on this side of the front door. "The windows are all bulletproof and treated on the outside so no one can see in, so inside is safe." *That explains the lack of curtains in the bathroom.* "If you want to order food, just press here." He shows me where. "And dial *Desk*." He shows me how. "Phil, or whoever is working, will answer and take care of the ordering. And the guys I have outside will bring it up to you and knock on the door when it's ready. Then use this button to open the camera to see who's outside the door." He taps another icon, and the screen switches to a wide-angle view of the hallway, showing the three men posted at various spots against the wall. "Your palm print is in the system now, so if you need to open the door, just place your hand against here like you did outside, and the door will automatically unlock. Then when you close the door, put your palm back against the sensor, and everything will lock back up."

"No one will try to come in?" I think this talk is supposed to make me feel safer, but these extreme measures are stressing me out.

"You and me and Rob are the only three people with access to this door."

"Which one is Rob?"

"He's not up here. He's my second in command, and as much as I don't want to give anyone else access to our home, I—" Dom grips my shoulders again, this time making me face him. "I'm not reckless, Valentine. I will come home tonight. And I will try to come home every night. But if something happens to me, Rob is the one who will come and get you."

"Get me?" I croak as my mouth goes dry.

I can't even make myself hate Dominic, no matter how much he deserves it, so I definitely don't want him to die.

Dom holds me steady. "If the worst happens, and Rob and I go out together, I have contingencies in place to alert your brother. Then it's up to you to wait for him. I imagine it will only take him a handful of hours to arrive, but the pantry is stocked with enough food to last you six months. While you're here, you're safe. Nothing and no one can get to you."

"Okay." I try to process everything he's saying.

"Good." Dom nods. "Do you have any questions?"

Overwhelmed, I start to shake my head but stop. "You'll still let me leave, though, right? Like to go to my office." I lift my shoulder. "Stuff like that," I add, even though I don't really have anywhere to go except the office.

"You're not trapped here, Angel. You can go to the office when you need to. Just let me know ahead of time so I can arrange to have Rob take you." His hands flex on my shoulders. "But you can't just leave by yourself. That isn't me being a dick. That's to keep you safe."

I know enough about this world to know I'd rather be here than kidnapped by someone Dom deems an enemy.

I swallow. "When I emailed my boss yesterday about the move, I said I'd come in for the Wednesday morning staff meeting."

"That's fine," Dom says like I'm a kid asking to borrow the family car.

"Rob can't come up to the office with me," I add. It's going to be a big enough deal that I moved here on a whim. I can't possibly explain a round-the-clock bodyguard to my coworkers.

"He won't," Dom says, but I'm not sure he means it.

He stares into my eyes, and I feel like I'm looking at old Dominic again.

I shake my head. "For the record, I haven't forgiven you. I understand why you did what you did. But it was shitty, Dom. It's all super shitty. And you should have warned me about the funeral. You should have warned me about everything." All the feelings from earlier war inside me. "I don't deserve this."

"You don't." Dom slides his hands up from my shoulders until his thumbs are lightly pressing against the front of my neck. "You deserve better." He strokes his thumbs up, then down. "But you're mine now. And I'll always keep you safe. Someday you'll accept that."

He starts to drop his hands away but drags his thumbs down my body in the process.

I'm too slow to react, and his thumbs brush over my pebbled nipples through the fabric of my bra and dress, showing that he knows just how much I'm affected when his body is pressed against mine.

I move to shove his hands away, but he's already stepping back.

"Now quit distracting me." He puts his hand on the door handle. "I have work to do. I'll be late, so order dinner when you're hungry."

"And when you say work...?" I cross my arms back over my chest.

Dom's lips pull up. "I mean hunting."

CHAPTER 29
Val

I PACE PAST THE BED. AGAIN.

It's almost midnight.

Dom has been gone for ten hours, and I don't know if this is normal behavior for him or if I should be worried.

My hands ball into fists, making the tender skin on my left ring finger throb.

"This asshole," I hiss, shaking out my hand.

It finally sank in, around the time the armed guard in the hallway handed over my bag of takeout, that I'm really in it. Like, *really in it.*

I stare at the four *Dominic*s circling my finger, making a point to avoid looking at the *Til Death* below my nail.

I can't believe he did this to me.

Seriously, can't believe it.

And I can't believe I'm not more angry about it.

Really, I'm more embarrassed than anything, because, eventually, I'm going to be back out in public, and it looks so out of place on me that I'm sure every person I pass will stare at it.

Maybe if I get a sleeve tattoo and paint my nails black, it won't stand out so much.

After Dom left me here, I stood in the living room for a weird amount of time, then gave up trying to feel comfortable in the giant space and came back up to the bedroom.

I showered off the funeral. Then I got into my comfiest sweatpants, and because it looked soft, I pulled a Yale sweatshirt off one of Dom's hangers and put that on, too.

Then I sat on the bed with my laptop and caught up on work. And Dominic still wasn't home.

So then I sat on the overstuffed chair in the corner of the bedroom and googled Dominic Gonzalez.

Mostly photos of him at big city events. One article title speculated about his involvement in the Chicago mafia. But overall, there was surprisingly little.

So, of course, then I did a search for The Alliance.

Which led to a text from King asking why I'm looking them up online. Which then led to me slamming my laptop shut and turning my phone off.

And now, with nothing left to do, I'm pacing. Wondering if there's a way out of this.

I spin around and pace back across the room when a sound stops me.

Was that the front door?

I tiptoe toward the bedroom door and lean into the opening to listen.

Footsteps.

All I hear are footsteps echoing through that giant-ass main room. But how the hell am I supposed to know if it's Dom or someone else?

While you're here, you're safe.

I back away from the door.

The footsteps are on the stairs.

It has to be him.

I keep backing up, around the foot of the bed and over to the side I slept on last night.

Torn between looking for a weapon and faking sleep, I'm standing there, frozen, when Dominic appears in the doorway.

He stops when he spots me, and I let out a rough exhale.

"You scared me," I accuse.

He grins. "That mean you're happy to see me?"

I narrow my eyes. "I was worried it might be an axe murderer. So, sure, I'm glad it's you instead."

"Next time I'll..." Dom trails off, and I follow his line of sight to my chest. "Hmm, I like that."

I pluck at the fabric. "You like me covered in your baggy clothes?"

"I like you covered in my alma mater."

My eyes widen, and I look back down at the sweatshirt. "You went to Yale?"

He stalks around the bed toward me. "Yeah, all the good schools were full."

"I figured you stole it." I shuffle a step back. "I didn't know Ivy League offered gangster studies."

Dom barks out a laugh, and I hate it. Because I wish he did it more often. "Dammit, Valentine, I like you."

"I—Well... I don't like you." The heat of my words is lessened by my hurried climb onto the bed. The only form of escape left to me.

His chuckle lets me know my barb didn't hit. "You liked me once. You will again."

I huff and drag the blankets up to my chin. "Your side of the bed is over there." I nod my head in the other direction.

He sits on the mattress next to my hip. "Give me your finger."

I hold up my middle finger.

"Cute."

I keep my left hand under the blanket. "Why? You gonna try to fill in the millimeter of blank skin you left?"

Dom holds up a small jar I hadn't noticed in his grip.

Only the dim ceiling lights are on, but I recognize the white jar and blue lid. Since I've always been fascinated by tattoos, I've looked up all the prep and aftercare. And I believe that's an ointment used to keep your tattoo looking nice.

Not willing to let go of my defiance, even flat on my back, I keep my hand where it is. "Sorry to burst your bubble, but this tattoo isn't exactly something I *want*. So keeping it pretty isn't really a high priority."

"Two things."

"It's always two things with you," I mutter.

Dominic looks like he's trying not to smile, but he fails. "Two things," he repeats. "One, what's worse? Having a tattoo you don't want, or having a tattoo you don't want that also looks bad?" I don't give him an answer. "And two, I bet that dainty little finger of yours is sore. This will help." He shakes the jar.

"My fingers aren't dainty." I'm grumbling. I know I'm grumbling because I hate that he has a point.

He lifts a dark brow. "Have you already forgotten about that time we put our hands palm to palm? Your fingers are extremely dainty compared to mine."

He's talking about our first plane ride.

Because I don't want to discuss that, and because my finger does hurt, and because—fine, he's right—I don't want the tattoo to heal poorly and look even more dumb than it already does, I pull my hand out from under the blanket.

"I'm still mad," I tell him.

"I know."

"This wasn't okay, Dom."

His eyes narrow the slightest bit, but he doesn't reply as he unscrews the lid and swipes his fingertips across the surface of the substance.

"I can do it." My jaw clenches. I don't want him taking care of me.

Dom sets the jar on the nightstand. "I'm doing it."

"No," I start, but his hand darts out and grips my wrist, dragging my hand closer to him.

"Dominic, knock it off!" I try to shove him away with my right hand, but he's immovable.

"Just hold still, Shorty."

I try to slap him away again, but he deflects with his elbow and swipes the ointment across my skin.

I brace myself, but his touch is so light it doesn't hurt at all. It... feels good. Soothing.

Bastard. It would be better if this hurt. If I could be angry over him causing me pain.

Watching him carefully rub my finger is too much, so I close my eyes.

But that's a mistake, too, because now there's nothing to distract me from his touch. From the warmth of his hold on me.

My thighs press together under the blankets.

Up and down, his fingers slide over mine.

The irritated skin has already cooled, but my blood is heating, and I can't take any more.

"Okay." I pull my hand away and hope he doesn't notice how breathy I sound.

My eyes are still closed, and I wait for him to stand, to leave, but he doesn't.

There's movement. The sound of rustling clothes and the jar being... set back down on the nightstand?

I crack my eyes open.

And then they widen all the way.

"What...?" I sit up and shove at Dominic's arm. "What is that?"

His shirt is unbuttoned, and he runs his ointment-covered fingers across his neck one last time before he lets me push his arm down.

"Dominic!" I gasp.

"You were right, Angel. It's only fair."

I blink. And blink again.

"Just the one?" I ask, not able to help myself.

"But it's big." Dom smirks. "And size matters."

I lean closer, shaking my head while I stare at the giant name tattooed across the base of his neck.

My name.

Valentine. In big black letters.

Not able to stop myself, I reach out and trace the *V.*

It's the same font that was used on me.

"This doesn't make up for what you did," I whisper, even as I trace the *A* and the *L.*

"Of course not." His voice is quiet, too.

I hadn't even noticed he had a strip of bare skin left, but it fits perfectly.

When I get to the center line of the *E,* I trace it, then drag my finger across the rest of the letters.

"I still don't forgive you." My finger slides down the center of his chest, stopping on the skull.

"You shouldn't."

I drop my hand down onto my lap. "I'm going to go to sleep now."

"You probably should."

I don't actually expect him to leave me alone, so I'm surprised when he stands.

But he doesn't leave the room or get into bed. He grabs the jar off the nightstand, then backs up to the armchair in the corner of the room.

He sets the jar down on the armrest, then takes his shirt off the rest of the way.

And his belt.

And then he's undoing his pants and kicking them off when they hit the ground.

Boxers. He's left in nothing but boxers, and they're not doing anything to hide the fact that he's rock-hard beneath them.

"W-what are you doing?" I know I should lie down and face the other way, but I can't. I just can't turn away from him.

"There wasn't room to add *Til Death* next to your name. So I had to find somewhere else to put it."

Speechless, I stare as he pushes down the waistband of his boxers to his hips.

I don't even notice that the patch of hair trailing down from his belly button has been shaved. I can't possibly focus on that. Because there, right above Dom's cock—like directly above the base of his fucking cock—are the words *Til Death*.

Big block letters to match his *Valentine*.

A lewd, oversized version of the tiny *Til Death* on my fingertip.

"You're insane." I almost laugh at the absurdity of it all. Except I'm too turned on to laugh. I want to trace the letters on this one, too.

"More often than not," Dom admits as he drops into the chair. Lounging back, he dips his fingers in the ointment and rubs it over the fresh ink.

I want to be the one doing that.

His eyes stay on me as he rubs over the letters.

Not able to take it anymore, I drop onto my back and stare at the ceiling.

This is insane.

I keep staring.

For about five seconds. Then I turn my head to look back at Dominic.

And I have to bite my lip to trap the moan trying to come out of my throat because he's pushing his boxers lower.

CHAPTER 30

Dom

THE LOOK ON VALENTINE'S FACE MAKES EVERY SECOND I spent under the needle worth it.

Her eyes are locked on my lap, and when I pull the band of my boxers low enough for my dick to spring free, she sucks in an inhale. Like she was holding her breath, waiting to see it.

I know I haven't done enough to earn another taste of her sweetness. So I won't take it. Not yet. But after the last twenty-four hours, I need a fucking release.

And so does she.

My hand closes around the base of my dick. Squeezing.

"You're gonna stay right there, Valentine," I say when I see her glance to the other side of the room, as if she's thinking about making a break for it. "It's been a long day." I drag my hand up my length, squeezing even tighter just below the tip. "And if you run, I'm chasing."

Val makes a sound—somewhere between worry and excitement.

I grip my base with my other hand as I start to stroke. "Now, slide your hand down all that soft skin and touch yourself."

"Dominic..." She wants to protest. To tell me she's not turned on. But I can see it in her eyes. I can see it in the way she can't look away from my dick. I can see it in the rise and fall of her chest.

"You're wearing my fucking shirt. And you're going to touch yourself in it." I keep my strokes slow.

She hesitates.

"If you haven't come by the time I finish, I'm going to take care of you myself. So if you don't want me shoving my fingers in your pussy tonight, you're gonna do as I say."

She's torn. I know she is. Because she secretly wants me to touch her. She wants me to fuck her. She's just not ready to admit it yet.

"Do it now, Mama. Put your hand in your panties and tell me how wet you are."

My Valentine tips her head back and closes her eyes.

I'm about to tell her to keep watching me. But then she kicks off the blankets that were over her legs.

It's my turn to hold my breath as she pulls up the hem of my sweatshirt. She doesn't pull it off; she doesn't even pull it up enough to show me her amazing tits; she just pulls it up enough to expose the waistband of her pants.

Her outfit, head-to-toe thick cotton, shouldn't be sexy. But she's already squirming, and it doesn't matter what she's fucking wearing because I'm ready to blow just from looking at her.

Her fingers wiggle to slide under the band.

I can't see what's happening, but I can see the outline of her hand in her pants as it moves lower. And then her knees fall open.

"That's it," I groan. "Spread those legs. Give yourself room to work that little clit."

She whimpers. Fucking whimpers. And I sit up.

Her eyes are still closed, but the expression on her face is pure pleasure.

I slide forward so I'm sitting on the edge of the seat, my stance wide, as I keep stroking my cock.

"Tell me," I demand. "Tell me that you're wet."

She shakes her head.

"Tell me, or I'm checking for myself."

She pinches her eyes shut harder. "I'm wet, okay?"

"How wet?"

Her shoulders twist, and I think she's trying to reach lower. *Fuck, is she sliding a finger inside?*

"Soaking."

I groan. "That's my good wife. Soaked that slit just from looking at my dick."

"I hate you," she pants. And it makes me smile.

"You don't." I quicken my pace. "And you love this cock."

She shakes her head.

"Open your eyes, Valentine. Open your eyes and watch me."

She tries to hesitate, but she's just as primed as I am. And when her head rolls to the side, and her eyes land on my length, her mouth opens.

I want to stand and shove my dick between those lips.

I want to come all over her pretty face.

I want to suck her tattooed finger into my mouth while she swallows me whole.

"Hurry up and come," I growl.

My hand feels rough against my dick. The dry skin on skin is nearly painful. But I'm not using anything but Val's sweet juices to lube my dick ever again.

I tighten my grip even more.

I'm so close, and so is she.

Val's other hand slides under her shirt, and I can tell she's playing with her tits.

"Jesus," I groan at the same time a moan leaves my wife's lips.

Her eyes are still on my cock, and I start stroking faster.

I'm past the point of stopping. Beyond any sort of decency.

"Keep doing that, Angel. Pinch those pretty nipples. Make yourself come all over your fingers."

Her breathing hitches. And then her back is arching.

And I explode. The first rope of release hits my chest, and Val's eyes are locked on it as she tumbles over the edge. A keening sound rolls from her and straight through my balls as they pump out everything I have onto my hand and dick.

Val slams her eyes shut, and her body twitches as her hands still beneath her clothing.

And it's the most beautiful thing I've ever seen.

Even better than the first time. Better than Vegas.

Because this time, she knows who I really am.

She knows who I really am, and she still let go. And even if I didn't lay a finger on her, she still gave herself over to me.

With her eyes still closed, I stand and close the distance between us.

Because I'll keep my word. I won't touch her perfect pussy. But I didn't promise anything more.

I grip the wrist sticking out of her pants and pull her hand free.

Val makes a startled sound, and her eyes open, but her attempts to pull her hand away from me are weak.

And they don't work.

I put her three glistening fingers into my mouth. And groan.

Fuck, she tastes like home.

With my hold of her, I slowly drag her fingers out, sucking off every drop of flavor.

She grips my arm with her left hand, and the sight of my name inked on her skin makes me groan again.

When her fingers are free of my lips, I bend down, placing her hand on her stomach.

"I've done bad things, Valentine." I brush my lips over her pinkened cheek. "But I'll always be good to you."

CHAPTER 31

Val

THE WEIGHT ACROSS MY BACK AND HIP AND LEG SEEMS to get heavier.

My brain is still surfacing from sleep, but I recognize the feeling of Dominic sprawled across me.

Not sure if he's awake, I stay as still as possible to act like I'm still asleep.

I can't believe I let myself do that last night.

What was I thinking?

The weight shifts again, and something long and hard presses against my ass, followed by a deep masculine groan.

I'm turned away from Dom and his side of the bed, so I let my teeth sink into my bottom lip.

I don't like this.

I'm a fucking liar.

I crack my eyes, wanting to see if the sun is rising, but all I see is Dom's big hand in front of my face. His arm is draped all the way over me.

His chest expands against my back as he takes a deep inhale, and my hair ruffles when he lets it out.

Just get up already! I scream inside my head. I have to pee, but

I need him to get up first and leave because I need to have at least an hour of self-loathing before I face him today.

Dominic's hand slides out of view, and then he finally lifts himself off me. Mostly.

I start to question what he's going to do when something presses against the back of my head. "Morning, Angel."

I'm too stunned to react, thinking he's caught me awake. But then he climbs off the bed, and a moment later, the bathroom door shuts.

Did he do that thinking I was still asleep?
Why?

"Shit," I say to no one as I open one cupboard, then another, before I finally find the mugs.

Grabbing one, I'm surprised at the weight, but I don't have time to think about the black ceramic as I rush to fill it with coffee—that was thankfully already made and waiting on the warmer for me.

When Dominic got up, I snuck down the hall to a bathroom I'd spotted earlier to relieve myself. But not wanting to talk to him, I rushed back to bed and pretended to still be asleep until I heard him leave the condo.

I have no idea where he is. Maybe *the mafia* has an office somewhere. But my cowardice threw me behind schedule, so I've been rushing to get myself ready for the web call I have in—I check my phone—two minutes.

Careful not to spill, I cross the great room to the large dining table between the living room and stairs and set my coffee next to my laptop.

The sky is bright blue above the Chicago skyline, and even though I'm flustered and running late, I can't complain about the view.

I click on the link to the meeting and connect just as the clock flips over.

Five people are on the call, including Bri, the woman whose bachelorette party I blew off so I could get drugged and subsequently married to Dominic. Then there are the two people who make up our marketing team and one other designer—like myself. Our boss was supposed to be on this call, but he emailed saying he couldn't make it.

I'm not sad he's missing it. This call full of women is much preferable.

"Morning," I greet everyone, as I'm the last to join.

"Damn, Val!" Bri whistles and leans closer to her screen. "Is that your new place?"

I could kick myself for not remembering to blur my background. But it's too late now because everyone is leaning toward their screens to get a better look, even the marketing people I hardly know.

I can't even blame them. From my spot at the dining table, the camera shows off the massive ceilings, the high-end, stupidly large kitchen, and part of the open stairs leading up to the second level.

It looks exactly like a billionaire's penthouse.

Before I can think of something to say, Bri continues. "I heard you upped and moved to Chicago, but you didn't say anything about it over the weekend, so I wasn't sure if I should believe it."

Her tone is mostly stunned, but there's a tiny bit of hurt in there, too. And I decide that the only thing to do is tell the truth.

Well, a partial truth.

"Okay, so..." I take a sip of my coffee as all attention moves to me. "When I last saw you, I didn't know I was moving."

"That was Friday." Bri shakes her head. "It's Tuesday."

The other designer, who I've met before, laughs.

"Well, to be fair, I decided Saturday night." I take a bigger sip of coffee. "But that was only after I got married on Friday."

Bri's mouth drops open.

"Aw, congrats," someone from marketing says, but Bri drowns them out.

"Shut up!" she practically shouts. "Please tell me it was to that hot-as-fuck man who picked you up."

I grin despite myself. "That's him."

"You guys don't even get it," Bri tells the rest of the people on the call, fanning herself. "This man was... I don't even know how to describe him. Like movie star meets *just got out of prison*. And it *works*."

The way she says *works* makes me laugh, but I have to admit the description is pretty good.

"I want to see!" one of the marketing team says.

"Yeah, wedding pics, please." Bri nods.

I have to work to keep the smile on my face.

I don't remember anything about the service. Nothing more than slivers of seconds. And before I can think about what I'm saying, I admit, "I don't know if there are any photos."

"You don't..." Bri leans closer again. "Oh my god. Did you get drunk married?"

She's cackling before I can even respond. But my cheeks are starting to heat, so I put my hands against them to cool them down, and that must be all the answer anyone needs because now everyone is reacting.

Then I remember my damn inked finger and drop my hands out of view.

Thank god everyone was so distracted laughing at me that they didn't notice the freaking tattoos.

I'll have to do something to cover them up when I go into the office tomorrow.

"If that's what his place looks like, then it's gotta be the best drunk decision I've ever heard of," the marketing team chimes in. "And if he's hot on top of it... Jackpot."

"He's not bad to look at." I pick up my coffee with my right hand. "Should we start?" I ask, trying to prompt the point of the call.

"I have more questions," the other designer says as everyone else nods. "Where does he work? You clearly didn't meet him at our company. Even Mr. Ritz only lives in a three-bedroom condo." She refers to our boss, who makes us all call him Mr. Ritz instead of using his first name. "And I only know that because he never shuts the fuck up about it. Like it's some sort of flex and not him proving he could pay us more."

Since I started a few years ago, I've been working remotely, so I don't know the boss as well as everyone else, but I'm not surprised that the people who go into the office a lot aren't fans. The whole *Mr.* thing is a bit pretentious.

One of the marketing girls snorts. "Yeah, I almost wish he was on this call."

Her teammate lifts a hand. "Let's not go crazy."

"Yeah, fair." The first girl concedes. "Plus, he'd probably just think he's paying us too much and not that Val here hooked herself a sugar daddy." She taps her chin. "Does a sugar daddy have to be older? Is he older?"

I set aside all my twisted feelings around Dom and my situation and figure I might as well try to enjoy this bit of comradery. "He's forty-one, so a little older."

"How old are you?" Bri asks.

I roll my lips together before answering. "I'll be twenty-six this month."

There's a snicker. "Yeah, I'd say that counts as a sugar daddy. What does he do? CEO or something?"

"Well, he has his own company. But I don't know what his title is." I'm assuming he has to have some sort of company. Mafia shit or not, you can't just move through society with huge amounts of money and no explanation for it.

I can hear someone typing on their computer. "What's the company name? I want to look it up."

"Nosy much?" The other designer laughs.

"Look, Val is over there living my damn dream. Let me ask my questions."

I take a sip of my coffee. "I don't know."

"What'd you say?" Bri asks.

"I don't know the name of it." I sigh and set my coffee down. "Remember that whole drunken marriage thing? I didn't exactly plan this." I ignore the pang in my chest as I say that. It's not a lie. *I* didn't plan any of this. "We weren't strangers, but we're not connected on LinkedIn or anything like that."

As soon as I say it, I regret it because I know what the next question is going to be.

"What's his name? I'll look him up." The nosy marketing girl is already tapping her keyboard, and I know there's no way for me to avoid giving them a name.

A good woman can change your life.

Time for me to lean all the way in.

"I married Dominic Gonzalez."

The other designer has her coffee cup against her lips, taking a drink, and I watch as she jerks, sloshing dark liquid down her shirt.

The girl who was ready to search him on LinkedIn has her hands still hovering over the keyboard, not typing.

And Bri... Bri's mouth is all the way open.

"So..." I awkwardly break the silence.

"Wait." The second marketing girl glances around at everyone's expressions. "Why does everyone know who that is? Is he like a big-time Chicago guy or something? I just moved here."

Bri clears her throat. "Jesus Christ, I thought he looked familiar."

I lift my shoulders. "He's really nice."

I want to hit myself. *He's really nice.* What a dumb thing to say about a crime lord.

Keyboard clicks fill the audio.

"Oh damn, is that him? He *is* fine," second marketing girl says to herself. "Oh, here, he's head of the..." She trails off, and I want to press my hands to my cheeks so badly.

She thought she found his company name, as in *head of*

finance for, but I know what it says because I did a search for him just yesterday.

Dominic Gonzalez, suspected head of the Chicago mafia crime syndicate.

She starts to giggle.

A lot.

"Sorry." She slaps a hand over her mouth. "Sorry," she says again, muffled this time.

And then Bri starts to laugh. And nosy marketing girl starts.

And then the other designer, who is wiping her coffee-covered hands onto her already ruined shirt, snorts. "Fuck, Val. Why are you even on this call?"

The smile that had started to form on my face falters. "What do you mean?"

Does she not want to work with me now?

She rolls her eyes. "Do you have any idea how rich that man is?"

Bri gestures toward her computer screen. "Look where she's sitting. I'm pretty sure she knows."

I glance around the condo like maybe it's changed.

I hadn't really thought about it until this moment. But if I stay with Dominic, then they're right, I really don't need this job.

I lift a shoulder. "I like working."

It's not a lie. I do like my job. I wouldn't say I love it, but I'm good at it. And it's good to feel productive. And I've worked since I was fourteen. I don't know what I'd do with myself all day if I didn't have a job.

First marketing girl raises her hand. "Well, I don't like working. So if you're ever looking to turn your duo into a throuple, just let me know. I'd love a sugar daddy."

"I don't share." The words are out of my mouth before I can stop them.

"Damn." Bri drags the word out. "Sounding like a member of *the family* already."

CHAPTER 32

Dom

"HOW IS THERE NOTHING?" I TURN AWAY FROM THE screens Joey is manning and pace across the bare floor.

"If the dumbass hadn't forgotten his phone at home, this would be easier," Joey grumbles and turns to a different display.

"Well, his mistakes and troubles are over." I grit my teeth.

The hits have been spaced out nearly a month apart. And other than our men dying of lead poisoning, there's nothing connecting the crime scenes. They're not even using the same type of bullets.

We've been able to find the cars used for the first three, all stolen from random parking lots and all with tinted windows, so even when we find them on traffic cams, there's no way to identify who's inside.

But we can't find the getaway car for my cousin's hit.

Joey is the best man I know at finding things, so he'll come through. But the waiting is killing me.

Every place we've hit has been empty. We're always too late. And it's getting really fucking old.

I run my hand over my hair.

I need Valentine to rub my head again.

I need Valentine to look at me with a smile again.

My fingers tap against my side, and then I pull my phone out of my pocket.

> Me: You didn't eat enough yesterday. Groceries were delivered this morning, but order something for lunch. I'll be home in a couple hours.

I hit send, then wait to see if she replies.

She doesn't.

I deserve that.

My phone starts ringing.

I stupidly expect to see My Valentine on the screen.

It's not her. But I still smile because it's her big brother.

I let it ring while I walk across the mostly empty warehouse, away from Joey, to give myself some privacy.

"Hello, King."

"Dom."

It sounds like it's killing him to be civil. And it makes my smile even bigger.

"To what do I owe the pleasure?" I lean against the wall.

"Cut the shit. You took my sister because you need something. Now what is it?"

I click my tongue. "Now, now. I didn't *take* anything." *Mostly true.*

"Bullshit," he snaps. "There's something else fucking going on, and I want to know what it is."

"I don't know what you're talking about, brother." I keep my tone annoyingly casual. "But you're welcome to ask Val."

"She's not answering my calls."

"And what does that tell you?" I taunt him.

King sighs. "Just tell me what you need. And if we can help you, then we'll help you. And then you'll send Val back home."

My humor vanishes. "You'll help because it's what you're honor bound to do. And *Val* will stay right where she is."

"You're not keeping her against her will."

I scoff. "That's fucking rich, coming from you."

"You tricked her!" King shouts through the phone.

The barb hits.

Though I don't think he really understands *how*. How badly I tricked her. How I set a trap made specifically for her. How I planned it all and kept her in the dark.

"I did what I had to." I end the call.

I did what I had to.

CHAPTER 33

Val

> Big Guy: You didn't eat enough yesterday. Groceries were delivered this morning, but order something for lunch. I'll be home in a couple hours.

BIG GUY.

I read Dominic's text. And burst into tears.

This is the first time he's messaged me since he picked me up from that hotel in Vegas. And his name, or *not name*, in my phone is the perfect reminder of how he targeted me. The perfect reminder that it was all just some plan to get The Alliance in his pocket.

My heart doesn't care about his reasons. Because reasons don't make the betrayal any less painful.

I don't reply to his text. I suddenly have no appetite. But I do go into his contact and delete the name.

I stare at my phone for a long time. There are lots of options, lots of insults I could use. But I end up simply typing in Dom.

CHAPTER 34

Dom

With no sign of Val, I set the takeout bags on the kitchen island.

Heading to the stairs, I can see that all the doors on the lower level are open.

So she finally decided to tour the place.

There's not much to find.

The lower level has a large gym, a cigar room, two guest rooms, two bathrooms, and my office.

I head up the stairs, where, aside from the master suite, there's another office, a guest bedroom, laundry, and a full bathroom.

Again, all the doors are open, and noise is coming from the spare bedroom.

After crossing the distance, I stop in the doorway.

There's a dresser along the wall, and she has all the drawers open.

"Can I help you find something?" I lean against the doorjamb.

Valentine spins around with a bra in hand.

"Is this your fuck room?" The anger in her question surprises me. And the question itself makes me want to laugh.

But I don't let my features show any reaction. "Would that bother you?"

She throws the bra at me. "Yes."

I jump out of the way, not letting the bra touch me before it falls to the floor.

"Why would that bother you?" I ask and resettle against the wall.

Val stomps her little foot. "Are you serious? Why would it bother me to have my husband fucking other people?"

My husband.

I push off the wall and stalk toward her. "Say that again," I growl.

She steps back, bumping into the open dresser drawer. "What?"

"Call me your husband." I stop right in front of her.

Val shoves at my chest. "No."

"Say it. And I'll tell you whose room this is."

"Are you serious?" Her jaw clenches, but I know I have her.

I lean closer. "Deadly."

She glares right into my eyes. "My husband, explain whose stuff this is before I start throwing it off the balcony. I won't have some skank's stuff under my roof."

Her tone is acidic, and she's trying to be a brat, but I'm too focused on her words again.

My roof.

She's still trying to push me away, but while she's busy shoving, her walls are falling. Because *my husband* and *my roof…* She's starting to accept this, even if she doesn't realize it.

Instead of bringing it to her attention, I breathe in her scent and tell her the truth. "This is my mother's room."

As always, Val wears her emotions on her face, and I can see her surprise.

I point behind me. "That's my mother's bra you threw at me."

Her mouth forms an O.

"Yeah. Oh." The top buttons of my shirt are undone, and I flick the material aside, giving Valentine a clear view of her name. "Maybe I didn't make myself clear when I tattooed your name across my fucking throat. This"—I tap the letters—"is so everyone knows who I belong to."

I've never given someone this sort of claim over me, and it feels fantastic.

"And inking the last words of my vow to you above my fucking dick." I reach down and cup my hand over the front of my pants. "That's all for you, Angel. So when you're ready to wrap those lips around my cock and take me into your throat, you'll be eye level with my promise to you. Even on your knees, I'll still be yours."

CHAPTER 35
Val

I'M SO FUCKED.

CHAPTER 36

Dom

SHE'S SO CLOSE TO CRACKING AND LETTING ME BACK IN, and I fucking love it.

But I don't want to ruin it. I can't push too hard.

I take a step back. "If you can put that bra back, I don't really feel like picking up my mother's underwear. Then come downstairs. I brought food since you never ordered lunch."

Val doesn't say anything as I exit the room, and I consider it a victory.

It doesn't take her long to come downstairs and find me in the kitchen. But she's looking at the takeout containers on the counter, not meeting my eyes.

"Gyros and fries," I tell her as she nears the island. "They're both the same so grab either one."

Val pulls a stool out, but she's a little short for it, so she has to use the bar across the bottom to climb on.

I don't laugh.

"What do you want to drink?" I open the fridge. "I got root beer."

She finally looks up at me. "What kind?"

I pull one of the glass bottles out and show her the label of her favorite brand.

"How... Is this another thing you asked me on our wedding night?"

Her attitude is understandable, but it still pisses me off that it's her first assumption.

"No." I shut the refrigerator. "You mentioned it to me once on the phone." I twist the cap off and set it in front of her.

She's quiet for a long moment, and when she rolls her shoulders back, I think she's going to start eating. But she asks a question instead.

"Is there a room I can use for some privacy?"

My spine stiffens. "For what?"

"If you must know, I have a therapy appointment that starts in fifteen minutes, and I'd like some privacy for it."

"Oh." I don't even know what I was expecting, but it wasn't that.

She reads my reaction wrong and balls her hands into fists. "This is my monthly session, and I want to keep it. I need to talk to someone. And she's already told me that she'll be out of office for the month of December."

"Valentine—"

"I won't tell her anything about you, so you don't have to worry—"

She cut me off, so I return the favor. "Shorty." That shuts her up. "You can always talk to me." I can see her retort building, but I keep talking. "But of course you can have your therapy. If you'd told me sooner, we could've flown back so you could go in person."

"It's always been virtual," she murmurs, uncurling her fists. "You don't care?"

"If being fucked in the head wasn't part of my job requirement, I'd go myself." I grab the root beer she hasn't touched and take a sip. "You can use my office down here if you want, but the one upstairs is fair game. You can set up shop in there for work or therapy or whatever you want. And if you need anything else, like screens or a standing desk, just ask."

"Um, thank you." She slides off the stool. "I'll go set up, then."

She stacks one of the boxes of food on top of her laptop, then grabs the bottle of root beer I took a sip out of and heads upstairs.

When I hear the upstairs office door close, I walk down to my office and retrieve my own laptop.

Back in the kitchen, I sit where Val just was and launch my security system.

As I take the first bite of my gyro, the camera feed comes to life. And I watch as Valentine sits behind the desk, readying herself for therapy.

CHAPTER 37

Val

I PRESS THE LITTLE LEVER UNDER THE CHAIR, AND THE seat lowers until it's at a comfortable height.

The office is nice. I looked through it earlier, and the heavy dark-stained furniture is very Dominic. But the leather office chair is comfortable, and there's a place to plug my laptop in right on the desk, so it'll suit me just fine.

For a moment, I think about leaving my cold bottle right on the desktop, but the craftsmanship of the desk is beautiful, so I start opening drawers, looking for a coaster.

I don't find one, but I find a blank notebook, which will work.

After turning on my laptop, I click the link to join the web session.

There's still a couple of minutes before we'll start, and I glance past my computer to the office door. I'm tempted to go lock it, but I have to trust that Dominic won't just walk in during my session. Not to mention I can't imagine a locked door would do much if he really wanted to get in.

My screen shows my face looking back at me as I wait for the doctor to join.

I tighten my ponytail.

I shift in my seat.

I take another sip of root beer.

I'm always a little nervous before our appointments because therapy is never exactly fun, but today I feel extra stressed.

Probably because I know I have to tell her that I got married and moved to a new state since we last talked.

I shove my hands in my lap and remind myself that she won't judge me. She never has.

The scent from the lunch Dom brought home for me fills the office. I won't eat it while we talk, but I always feel wrung out after therapy, so my plan is to just sit here and eat it cold afterward —by myself.

I'm considering opening the container to sneak a fry when the screen changes, alerting me that the doctor is about to join.

"Good afternoon, Val." Doctor Amy smiles at me, her springy gray curls framing her face.

"Hello." I wave. Like a moron.

"How was your day today?" She starts the session as she always does.

As I've learned to do, I take my time before answering.

I think about waking up with Dom half on top of me. And about him kissing the back of my head while he thought I was sleeping.

I think about the work call with the girls this morning and all the laughs and smiles we had.

I think about how I felt when I thought Dom had a room set up for another woman. How it made me feel sick to think about him with someone else.

And then how relieved I felt when he said they were his mother's things.

And I think about him dodging the bra I threw at him because it was his mom's bra.

I smile. "It was good." I think about the delicious-smelling food waiting for me, because my new, definitely crazy, husband checked on me and wants to make sure I eat. And that he brought me a gyro and fries because he likes my softness and isn't trying to put me on a diet. "It was actually pretty good."

"You sound surprised by that."

I lift a shoulder. "The last few days have been not so good."

Doctor Amy makes a sound of understanding. "Want to talk about that?"

"I don't really know where to start," I admit.

"What were some of the feelings you had that made it not so good?"

The lightness of a moment ago drifts away, and I roll my lips together. "I've been... I had to go to a funeral yesterday." I swallow. "And I know my mom's funeral was six years ago, but recently, I've been having all those feelings again."

"Which feelings?"

"Like I don't belong anywhere." It comes out quiet.

"And did you feel that way yesterday, too?"

I shake my head. "No. Yesterday was... how it should be."

She tips her head. "What do you mean?"

"It was sad. Horribly sad. But..." I have to break off. "Someone hugged me." Tears I didn't even know were building drip down my cheeks. "And it-it just... I didn't even know her, but she hugged me, and I hugged her back, and it helped. Ya know? It was just a simple hug, and suddenly, I didn't feel so alone anymore. And it just... It makes me so mad. Because why couldn't I have had that?" I rub my hands across my cheeks. "I know we can't change the past, but I can't stop myself from wondering how my life would be different if I'd had that sort of... support."

The doctor nods. "Just because we can't change the past, doesn't mean we can't be mad at it."

"I know." I sniffle.

"And it's okay to daydream about a different life, so long as you're still giving yourself credit for what you've accomplished on your own."

I nod.

"But you said today was better?" she asks.

"Yeah. I, um, slept well last night." My cheeks are already coloring from crying, so I don't have to worry about blushing. Because I hate to admit that I sleep better with Dom at my side. Or draped across me.

And the orgasm probably didn't hurt.

CHAPTER 38

Dom

I START TO LOWER THE LID OF MY LAPTOP.

It's not often that my conscience springs to life, but watching Valentine cry while talking to her therapist about feeling like she doesn't belong is starting to make me feel guilty.

"... been working on finding sexual completion with a partner?"

I lift the lid back up.

Come again?

Val nods and presses her hands against her cheeks.

I fucking love it when she does that.

"Kind of."

"Kind of?" the doctor asks.

Yeah, Valentine, just kind of?

"Yes," my wife admits.

"Is this with the man you met on the plane?"

I lean closer. *She told her therapist about me?*

Val nods, dropping her hands.

"Has it happened every time?" the doctor asks.

Tell us, Angel. Have I made you come every time?

Val nods again.

The doctor keeps going. "What made the difference?"

Say my big dick.

"I think it's like you said," Val answers.

And what did the good doctor say?

"Trust?" the doc clarifies.

"Yes." Valentine's answer is a whisper. But I hear it in my soul.

"Trust makes a huge difference in learning to let go with a partner," the doctor says, like it's simple. Like trust between two people is something that happens every day. "Does this have anything to do with those tattoos I saw on your hand?"

"Yeah." Val huffs. "I got drunk and married the guy."

"Good."

I can't see the laptop screen, so I can't see the therapist. But I can hear her smile.

"Good?" Val presses her hands to her cheeks again. "It's been less than two months since we first met."

"Time isn't the defining factor of a relationship," the doctor counters. "And you just said you have trust."

I watch Val's expression slip. "I trusted him."

Trusted.

Past tense.

I lean even closer to the screen.

"Trust and love mean more than time."

My wife's lips part.

Is she going to admit she doesn't love me?

She hesitates.

Or is it possible that she might? Even after everything I've done.

"I..." Val starts.

The front door unlocking cuts through what Val's about to say, and I slam the laptop lid closed.

There's only one person it can be, but I still pull the gun from the holster at the small of my back as I stride across the room.

The door swings open, and Rob steps into the condo.

Rob is my second cousin, as well as my second in command. He's not quite as tall as I am, but he's spent more time in the gym than most people I know, so you know he's a formidable opponent before his first punch.

He makes it a few feet before he sees me. The gun in my hand halts him in place. "What happened?"

"My wife lives here now. You won't just let yourself in again."

He smirks. "Afraid I might see more than you want me to?"

"More than *you* want you to." I step closer. "Because if you ever see more than you should, your sight will be the first sense I take."

He eyes me. "Alright, Boss. From now on, I knock."

CHAPTER 39

Val

THE HEAVY BODY SPRAWLED ACROSS MY BACK GROANS as my alarm blares from the nightstand.

"Turn it off." The sleep-soaked voice scrapes across my nerves.

No one should sound so sexy the moment they wake up.

I reach out with my left hand to grab my phone, but I can't reach it.

I stretch, but Dominic's weight is pinning me in place.

Before I met Dom, when I'd go to sleep imagining a life where I had someone to share my bed, I'd picture myself cuddled cutely into the man's side. His arm would be around my shoulders. I'd sleep with my head on his shoulder and my mouth closed, not drooling on his chest at all.

But no.

My sleep habits haven't suddenly changed, so I'm still face down, probably snoring. And the mafia kingpin who drugged me into marriage doesn't pull me into his side. He doesn't spoon me with his arm around my waist. Nope. He starfishes his body over mine. Smashing me into the damn mattress.

And like everything else with Dom, I hate that I like it.

"Get off me," I growl.

"It's too early, Angel." He nuzzles his face into my hair.

219

I can't take it.

"Get. Off." I twist and wedge my arms under myself, then push up with all my might, only getting up to my elbows.

Dominic groans but finally rolls off me. "Why are you up?"

I crawl out of the bed and turn my alarm off. "I told you. I'm going into the office today."

"Right." He drapes his arm over his eyes to fend off the morning sunrays.

I keep my gaze averted as I hurry around the bed and into the bathroom, shutting and locking the door behind me.

I've taken to sleeping in pants and long sleeves to minimize the chance of sex. But Dominic sleeps in nothing but his damn boxers. And I don't need to start my day looking at our wedding vow inked above his dick.

Snatching my toothbrush off the counter, I accept that I'm in a bad mood.

Therapy always leaves me feeling a little wrung out. But yesterday was extra intense. And confusing. The discussion of trust and love really messed with my head.

Because I don't want to trust Dom, just like I don't want to like him. What he did to me was unforgivable. And it's not like he'll ever apologize. He told me he never does.

And looking back at all our conversations, with the privilege of hindsight, I see all the clues he dropped for me.

Little breadcrumbs for me to pick up and carry into his poisonous gingerbread house. The truth hidden behind sexy tattooed walls.

I brush my teeth a little harder.

He doesn't deserve to have this hold on me.

It's time for me to push back.

CHAPTER 40
Dom

V ALENTINE'S FOOTSTEPS SIGNAL HER APPROACH, AND I lower my coffee mug.

She's holding her laptop in one hand and the railing with the other as she walks down the stairs. Her eyes are busy watching where she's going, so I can drink her in.

And drink her in is exactly what I want to do.

She's wearing another pair of those high-ass wedge heels. This time in a bright red. And her skirt...

I use my free hand to adjust my dick.

I've seen her dresses, but this is different. It's shiny, like leather, and it's hugging her like it's fucking painted on.

It has to be stretchy—to allow her to walk. But it ends at her knees, and I want to shove it up to her hips so I can see if she's wearing anything underneath.

Her top is bright white. Some sort of flowy silk material that she's tucked into her skirt. And it's...

It's low.

It's cut really fucking low.

Or maybe it's just her big tits that make it seem that way.

Val takes the last step down, brushing her hair back from her face and straightening her clothes before she spots me.

I watch her do a second take at the large TV in the middle of the living room, probably wondering where it came from. So I hit the button to lower it back into the floor. I won't be able to concentrate on watching anything after she leaves.

"Sneaky." She nods to the disappearing television.

"Valentine, what are you wearing?" I stand from the couch.

She looks down. "What's wrong with it?"

There's a slight hesitancy in her tone that I don't like.

"Nothing's wrong with it, Wife. You just look like the secretary in the beginning of a porno."

She narrows her eyes at me.

Rob clears his throat from the kitchen, catching our attention.

Right.

I hold a hand out toward my second. "Val, this is Rob. He'll be driving you to and from work today."

Something in Valentine's stance tells me she's annoyed. But I'm not quite sure what about. There's no way she knows about me spying on her session yesterday. And I got called out to check a lead last night. She was asleep by the time I got home, so it's not like we had an argument.

She looks at Rob, then back at me. "At least you got me someone hot to look at."

I think my mouth might drop open.

Did she just call Rob hot?

My traitor of a second coughs to cover his laugh. "Thank you, ma'am."

"Please." Val walks toward Rob. "Call me Mistress."

This time Rob does laugh.

"The fuck he will," I snap, moving toward the kitchen. "If anyone calls you that, I'll slice out their tongues."

Val pauses at the island to slip her laptop into her backpack, then rolls her eyes at me. "Don't be so dramatic."

"Dramatic?" I repeat.

And then, as she's zipping up her bag, I see it.

"You want to play, Wife. We'll play." I cut the distance between us in a matter of strides.

She tries to back away from me, but I catch her around the waist, slamming her front to mine.

"What are you—"

I grab her left wrist and lift her hand. "No."

She tugs against my hold, causing her makeup-covered ring finger to wave in my face. "Dominic—"

"No, Valentine. I gave you a choice. And since you won't wear my ring, you *will* wear my name."

Her jaw clenches. "I have to go to the office."

"Yeah. And the people at your office will know who you belong to, just like the rest of the fucking world. Now wash it off."

I'm furious.

And impressed with her defiance.

And more than a little turned on.

Val's nostrils flare, and I'm excited for her answer before she even gives it.

"No."

I smirk. "Wrong answer."

Then I lift her.

"Dominic!" Her feet dangle a foot above the ground as I walk us around the island. "Put me down."

I ignore her.

"Dominic. Seriously—"

She cuts off when I slide her down my body. I know she can feel how hard I am. "Press my buttons, Wife, and you'll pay the consequences."

Before she can retort, I spin her around and press my hips against her ass, my feet on either side of her own, pinning her to the counter.

"I can do it." Her voice is breathy now.

"You had your chance." I keep one arm wrapped around her,

high enough that her breasts are resting on top of my forearm. With my other arm, I reach out and turn the water on.

I leave my fingers under the stream, waiting for the water to get warm, then I fill my palm with soap.

"Give it here."

Her ribcage expands under my hold, but on her exhale, she submits and places her hand in mine.

I release my hold of her waist so I can lather the soap, her hand between mine.

Then I carefully wash the makeup off. The stuff she used did a good job of covering the ink, but it washes away easily enough.

When it's clean, I turn the faucet to cool, then hold her finger under the stream. "You're going to irritate the skin using crap like that on a fresh tattoo. I can get the ointment if you want to put it on before you leave."

Val shakes her head, and her breath hitches.

I have one awful second to think that she might be crying, but then her ass shifts against me as she rubs her thighs together.

I lean against her a little harder.

She wants me.

I need to remind her how much.

CHAPTER 41
Val

MY REFLECTION STARES BACK AT ME IN THE ELEVATOR doors, and I want to button my shirt up to my neck.

I've been to the office before, and I knew today would be a bit much—because I knew the girls on the conference call yesterday would spill the beans about me marrying Dominic. And I knew the tattooed finger would become a big deal. But I didn't expect my boss to act so slimy.

Mr. Ritz has always been a little... too friendly. Pushing that line between being socially awkward and something you would report to HR. But today—

I run my hands down the sides of my skirt.

Maybe it was my fault for wearing something more formfitting than usual, but you'd think being recently married would put me in the *off-limits* category. I mean, every employee should be in that category for Mr. Ritz anyway, but his looks today were more like leers. And more than once, he stood too close to me, and I swear he looked down my shirt.

Rob is standing silently at my side, and I open my mouth to ask him if I should tell Dom about it.

But then I shut my mouth.

If I ask Rob, he'll tell Dom. And I'm not entirely certain Dominic wouldn't kill my boss.

In fact, I'm fairly certain Dominic would kill him.

And even though I'm beginning to believe that Mr. Ritz is a sleazeball, I'm not sure he deserves death.

The elevator opens, and I step out ahead of Rob.

I don't know if he's been told not to talk to me, but he was silent on the ride to and from work, so I keep up the trend.

All I want is to go upstairs, put on sweatpants, and scream into my pillow for a bit.

Since I get to the door first, I put my hand on the security screen and wait for the sound of it unlocking, then I walk through.

I make it four steps into the condo before I freeze at the same time Rob says "Oh shit" under his breath.

Because standing in my kitchen is a woman. Practically a girl since she looks younger than me. With long black hair, a crop top showing off a trim waist, and leggings so tight I'm surprised she can breathe.

I let my backpack slide off my shoulder.

Rob catches it before it can land on the ground, but I don't care.

"Who the fuck are you?" I snap.

My feet are killing me, but I'm not about to show weakness in front of this woman, so I keep my shoes on as I stride toward her.

She stops what she's doing, her eyes going wide as she watches me. "Um, I'm making dinner."

I refuse to think about how delicious it smells in here.

If Dominic thinks he can hire some sexy woman to make me jealous... Well, it's working.

"You're home." Dom's voice fills the great room, and my head snaps to the side to see him walking out from the lower hallway in nothing but workout shorts.

Sweat is dripping from his body. His chest is still rising and falling in a way that says he literally just stopped working out.

And he's letting this random woman see him like this. Practically naked.

"What are you doing?" I hiss.

He runs a hand over his head, and my belly clenches. Because I remember doing that.

"Just gonna go grab a shower," he says casually, then starts to jog up the stairs. When he reaches the top, he pauses. "Oh, I'm out of towels up here. Could one of you bring some up? I'll leave the door open."

Then he's gone. Disappeared down the hallway toward our bedroom, where he's going to leave the door open so *one of us* can bring it to him.

Bring it to the clear glass shower stall.

Fuck this man.

My hands flex.

Fuck him so much.

Spinning on my heel, I stomp into the kitchen.

The woman backs up quickly, trying to get away from me. But I'm not after her. She's just here as another one of Dom's pawns. Because he thinks we're playing games.

I jerk open drawers, one after another, until I finally find the one with the hand towels.

I pull one out, then continue on to the pantry that I found yesterday. It's a big, beautifully organized room, but I'm here for one thing.

Finding the appliance I need, I grab it off the shelf and storm out of the pantry.

"Uh, Val..." Rob says cautiously. "I can't let you kill him."

I huff as I shove the towel into the bread slot on the toaster. "I won't plug it in."

I think I hear the girl snicker, but I don't stop.

My thick shoes sound heavy on the steps, and I'm practically huffing by the time I reach the top.

How dare he.

At the end of the hall, our bedroom door is open.

How fucking dare he.

When I step inside, I find he's left the bathroom door wide open, just like he said he would.

My anger builds as I think about that other woman being the one to walk in here.

And by the time I enter the bathroom, I'm seething.

Dominic's naked form is somewhat hidden by the steam building behind the glass, but I can see enough.

And the view is mine alone.

No one else's.

"Here's your fucking towel," I snap, then throw the whole toaster over the top of the glass wall.

I make sure I don't hit him because I don't want to actually crack his head open, but the sound of metal meeting marble is satisfying as hell.

"What the—" Dom jumps away from the noise.

I turn and leave.

Message delivered.

Except booming laughter follows me. And it makes me more furious.

And when hot tears fill my eyes, I get even madder.

He's laughing. And I'm dying inside.

"Wife!" Dom shouts after me.

My inhale is choppy. "Fuck you!"

I have one foot out of the bedroom, wondering if Rob will take me if I ask to leave, when a large wet body collides with my back.

I'm so worked up the shock makes me scream.

"Oh, you'll fuck me, alright." Dom lifts me, just like he did this morning, and backs us into the bedroom.

"Get off me!"

I hear him kick the door shut. "No."

I struggle, but his arms are solid muscle, and his hold doesn't budge. "Put me down."

"You don't hate me." He walks us straight to the bed, then

throws me down. I land on my stomach, but before I can roll over, he's on top of me. His still-sopping-wet body presses into mine. "You want to." I try to push up, but he snags my wrists and holds them together in one of his large hands above my head. "But you can't. Because part of you loves me, Angel. Part of you fucking craves me."

It's hard to breathe. But not from the weight of his body. It's from the weight of his words.

"I don't love you." The emotion in my voice makes me question my own words.

I don't love him.

But I want to.

Teeth scrape against the side of my neck. "Not yet, Mama. But you will." His hips rock against my ass. "Now let me see how wet that hot little slit is for me."

He roughly slides his free hand down my side, over my hip, and down to the hem of my skirt.

That movement alone is enough.

I'm already ready for him.

The weight on my back disappears. Then he yanks the tight skirt up and over my hips, showing him the little black thong I wore all day.

"Fuck."

I try to push up again. But then his weight is back, and my hands are back above my head.

"Get off me," I pant.

"No." Dom is breathing just as heavily as I am. And I can feel his naked body against mine.

"I don't want to fuck you," I lie.

He chuckles against my hair as his hips lift.

He pulls aside my thong, and the head of his cock nudges against my slippery entry.

"That's fine," he groans. "I'll fuck you."

His hips thrust forward, and he buries his length inside me.

My mouth opens in a silent cry.

I'm so full.

So fucking full.

Feeling him inside me again is too much and not enough.

"Just take it." He slides his cock almost all the way out before shoving it back in. "Take me like the good little wife I know you are."

I turn my face into the mattress so he can't see it as I arch my back, letting him in farther.

"God." Dominic slams into me. "Tell me you love it. Tell me you love when my cock is buried inside you."

I shake my head.

Dom's exhale tickles over the back of my neck. "Your pussy is fucking dripping for me."

His hips never stop. And he's sliding in and out of me so easily because he's right. *I am fucking dripping for him.*

"I love it," I say into the mattress.

His length slides out of me, and I try to lift my ass to follow him, needing him.

Dom uses his grip on my wrists and a hand on my hip to flip me onto my back.

His eyes are blazing.

"Say it again." He tears my thong off, then shoves my legs apart.

I shake my head.

Dom leans over me, holding my hands back up over my head. His other hand is between us, lining his cock up with my entrance. "Say. It. Again." He fills me to the hilt.

"I love it," I cry. "I love your cock, you stupid bastard."

Dom falls onto me, crashing his mouth to mine.

He lets go of my hands, and my arms and legs instinctually wrap around him.

I missed this.

I missed *him*.

I pull at him, needing him closer, needing the taste of him.

He grips my side, then tugs at the material of my shirt.

"Off," Dom says into my mouth.

We both reach for my shirt. And I hear a tear as Dom rips it up over my head.

Dom slams as deep as he can go, a hand behind my back, undoing my bra.

He's too good at this.

Then I think of the woman downstairs, and I claw my fingernails down his back.

But he doesn't recoil. He groans.

And then my bra is gone, and Dom feeds my breast to himself.

He sucks the nipple into his mouth while his cock is dragging over the spot inside me.

I'm so close. So close to losing it completely. So close to losing myself to Dom.

He switches nipples. "Goddamn."

He sucks the other one into his mouth, and I'm getting wetter. I can hear it.

"Your sweet tits make me fucking salivate." A hand grips my jaw. "Open up, Angel. Open up and show me you'll take everything I give you."

My vision is fuzzy.

My nerves are on fire.

And my clit is begging for a touch. Just one touch, and I'll be done.

Dominic licks up my cheek, then places his mouth next to my ear. "Open your fucking mouth."

He widens his legs, pushing mine wider.

Then his cock slams into me so deep I feel the twinge in my stomach, and my mouth opens.

And he spits into it.

My eyelids flutter.

My back arches.

And I feel his claim everywhere.

I feel my submission to him like a chain unlocking around my neck.

The sound of him, the taste of him...

"Swallow." His growled command spears through me.

And I do it.

I take everything.

And when he rolls his hips, rubbing the base of his dick against my clit, I come.

I don't even make a sound.

I'm too overwhelmed.

My body shakes and trembles, and I hold Dom against me as tight as I can.

"That's it," he tells me as he slips his arms under me. "That's my girl."

And then he's hugging me.

Dominic Gonzalez hugs me back, just as tightly, as his body tenses and he fills me with his release.

He hugs me.

I squeeze him tighter, pretending the dampness on my lashes is from his wet hair and not tears slipping from my eyes. Because as Dominic clings to me, groaning, the last of my defenses shatter.

CHAPTER 42

Dom

I HOLD HER TO ME, NEEDING THIS JUST AS MUCH AS I think she does.

The loss of Valentine's affection was slowly killing me inside. I'd only had it for a short time, but its withdrawal was filling me with emptiness. A wife-sized hole inside my chest I didn't know was there before her.

And now that I have her back, now that I have her clinging to me, I don't want her to close up again.

I know nothing has really changed. I still haven't earned her complete trust back. But I will.

Val's face is pressed into the crook of my neck, her heavy breaths warming my skin.

"Hold me tight," I tell her.

She does. And she stays exactly how she is, arms and legs wrapped around me as I slide us off the side of the bed.

My cock is still buried inside her as I walk us into the bathroom.

The steps jostle our positions, and I slip free from her body right as I step into the shower.

Valentine squirms in my arms.

"Let it out, Angel." I flex my arms around her, and her body relaxes.

I'm tempted to walk us back over to the sinks so I can stand in front of the mirrors and watch our combined release drip from her puffy slit. But not now.

Another time.

I use my foot to kick the towel-stuffed toaster out of the shower, then pull the door shut.

Angling our bodies so the water hits my back first, I turn the handle, knowing just where to turn it for the perfect amount of heat.

When it's just right, I turn us around so the water is on Valentine's back. Then I turn another knob, and a sprayer on the other end of the shower comes to life.

The shower stall is long enough that the streams don't touch but close enough that a swirl of steam instantly surrounds us.

I pat her bare ass. "Lower your legs for me."

Val listens, letting her legs slide down my hips until they're hanging straight down.

I bend my knees until I feel her feet touch the floor, then her arms slip from around my neck.

Without meeting my eyes, Val turns to face the far showerhead and steps under it, soaking her hair.

My fingers itch to help her. To wash her.

It's an intimacy I've never experienced before, but I'm not sure Val is ready for that. And I can wait.

We move through the motions to the sound of falling water.

I finish before she does, but I leave my side running—to keep the steam thick—while I step out of the stall to fetch us towels.

I've dried off and pulled on a pair of workout pants and a T-shirt when Val turns the water off.

I'm waiting for her, towel spread in my arms, when she pushes the glass door open.

She narrows her eyes on the towel but still steps toward me, and I wrap the thick cotton around her.

Valentine silently wraps it around herself, and I hand her a second towel for her hair.

"Miranda is one of my many cousins," I tell her.

She slides her eyes up to meet mine. "Miranda?"

I nod. "I told her if she came over and made us a pan of her lasagna, I'd pay off her student loans."

"The woman downstairs is your cousin." She sounds like she's repeating it to herself.

"Yep." My eyes search hers.

"You asked your cousin to come over, dressed like that, to make us dinner, to... what? Make me jealous?"

My shoulders lift. "Basically. Though I didn't give her any direction on what to wear. She just always dresses like she's allergic to clothes."

"Dominic." She says my name the same way my mom does before scolding me for something.

I grip the top of the towel wrapped around her, my fingers sliding into her cleavage, and pull her closer. "That was payback for calling Rob hot." She scoffs, but I shake my head. "Turns out I'm a jealous bastard."

"You're an idiot."

I grin. "A little of that, too. But nonetheless, save your compliments for me."

Valentine does that thing where she lowers her chin, then looks up at me like she's stuck halfway through an eye roll. "You know you're hotter."

Warmth blooms inside me. "You should probably remind me more often."

Because she's here—and because I can—I pull her even closer and press my lips to hers.

I don't push for more. Just a kiss.

A simple kiss. One that only lasts for a second. But one that makes my heart thud a little harder behind my ribs.

Pulling back, I let her go. "Put something comfortable on. We'll watch a movie while we eat."

CHAPTER 43

Val

"WIFE."

Something touches my shoulder, so I pull the blankets higher.

There's a chuckle near my head. "Valentine, open your eyes for me."

I crack one open.

The sunrise is starting to break through the skyline outside the windows, but it's still early.

"Why?" I drag the blankets over my mouth, covering my morning breath from Dom, who is crouched right in front of me. Then I blink both eyes open. He's dressed in a suit. "What's going on?"

"I gotta go to California for a bit." I try to sit up, but Dominic keeps his hand on my shoulder, holding me in place. "Stay in bed."

"You're leaving?" Panic flares around my throat, making the words come out scratchy.

I grip the blanket tighter.

Last night was so... nice.

It was the first time since everything fell apart that I felt a tiny bit of hope that maybe we could come back from what happened. And now he's leaving.

His blue eyes lean in closer. "Just for a few days, Angel."

I don't reply. I don't know what to say.

He lifts the hand from my shoulder and strokes it over my hair. "We have a lead on someone who might have information on who's coming after me."

"And you have to go in person?" My question is muffled by the blanket.

Dominic nods. "But I'm leaving Rob here to keep an eye on you. I put his number in your phone. He lives a few floors down, so even when he's not in the hallway outside the door, he's nearby." He tucks my hair behind my ear. "I'd prefer you stay here. But you'll use him if you want to go to the office."

When I don't say anything, he pulls the blanket down from over my face.

"Tell me you won't go anywhere without Rob."

I yank the blankets back up over my mouth before I reply. "I won't go anywhere without Hot Rob."

Dominic narrows his eyes, then yanks the blankets out of my grasp and off my body.

I shriek.

And before I can reach for the blanket, Dom is shoving me onto my back and crawling on top of me.

"Dominic." I try to push him off while trying to cover my mouth with my other hand.

He shoves both my hands away, pinning me to the bed. "Why do you keep doing that?"

"Because I have morning breath!" I say, exasperated.

Dom shakes his head. "Angel, I don't really want to introduce you to the darker side of my life, but I will if it'll reassure you that I'll never be bothered by some morning breath."

I keep my lips together while I glare at him.

Dominic flexes his hips against me, and I can feel him getting harder.

"Now, this is your final warning. Every time you call Rob, or any other man, hot or attractive or anything else that you know I won't like, you're going to wake up with a new tattoo." He leans down until our noses are touching. "Don't test me."

"You're a beast." It's the best insult I can think of with his body against mine.

"Don't forget it." Dominic smiles. "Now give me a goodbye kiss."

CHAPTER 44

Val

Big Guy: Rob is coming to the door to drop off
food. I'm sure you'll forget to order dinner.

I BLINK AT MY PHONE.

Then blink again.

Big Guy.

My heart is stuck at a standstill between slowing and speeding.

Me: Why did you change your name back?

Delete.

Me: I don't want to call you Big Guy anymore.

Delete.

Me:

I set my phone down.

Dominic left this morning. He hasn't even been gone a full day, and yet he's still *here.*

Taking care of me.

I press my hand to my chest, then pick my phone up.

> Me: Good thing you aren't overbearing or anything.

Send.

> Big Guy: You have a lifetime to get used to it.

I set my phone back down.

I can't deal with this man anymore today.

> Big Guy: Good morning, Angel. Are you staying home today?

I BLINK, RUBBING THE SLEEP OUT OF MY EYES. THEN I see it's six a.m., meaning it's four where he is.

> Me: Yes. And why are you up so early?

Send.

> Big Guy: Up late but about to go to bed. Wish me sweet dreams.

I pretend not to smile.

> Me: Go to sleep.

Send.

> Big Guy: And a kiss.

I open the camera.

> Me: *sends photo of my middle finger with the sleepy city in the background*

> Big Guy: Rob told me you're going to the grocery store today. You can order delivery if you want.

I SHAKE MY HEAD AND FINISH MY WORK EMAIL BEFORE picking up my phone to reply.

> Me: Husband, I do not want to rot away in this condo every day, morning to night.

Send.

> Big Guy: So touchy. It's okay. I know you're grouchy because you miss me.

I set the phone back down.

I have work to do.

But my mind won't let me focus on the site I'm in the middle of building because the fucker is right.

I shove away from my desk and stomp all the way downstairs.

I just need coffee. I don't miss Dominic Gonzalez.

Big Guy: Valentine.

I REACH OUT AND PAUSE THE MOVIE.

Me: What?

Send.

My phone vibrates, showing Dominic calling. No...

I groan.

It's a video call.

I debate not answering for a long moment, but I know Dom enough to know he'll just keep calling.

Sighing, I hit answer.

"Angel." Dominic's tone is scolding.

"What?"

"Valentine, pick the phone up."

"I don't want to," I tell him.

I answered the call but left the phone lying on the bed next to me, camera aimed at the ceiling.

"Why not?" He sounds curious, not mad. And with all the security around here, it's not like he's afraid I'm in bed with a man.

"Because I'm not dressed for company."

He groans. "Are you naked?"

"What? No."

"Then show me your pretty face."

I grit my teeth. Charming Dominic is so obnoxious.

"Fine." I huff out a breath and pick up the phone.

I watch his handsome face as his eyes trail over mine.

This was supposed to be my night of pampering, but it's turned into a night of Dom.

"That the same mask you used on Halloween?" Dominic asks, and his question slices through my chest.

I started my period the day he left, and my hormones have

been all over the place. I'm a few days in, past the worst of it, but my heart still feels wrung out.

Before I realize it's happening, a tear tracks down my cheek, leaving a trail in the clay mask I'm wearing.

Dominic pulls his phone closer. "What's wrong?"

I shake my head and quickly dab at my cheek with a tissue so I don't melt my mask.

"Did something happen?"

I shake my head again.

"Val." His voice softens. "Talk to me."

More tears drip from my eyes, but I don't speak.

I try to blink through it, wanting to just hang up but knowing that won't make anything better.

Dominic's screen shifts as he starts walking. I can't see much of the background, but it looks like a warehouse.

His screen goes dark as he walks into a new room, then Dom flips a light on, and his image comes back to life.

I can hear him shut a door before he turns and leans against it.

"Shorty. Tell me what's going on." A command this time.

And I can't help myself.

"I miss you." The sentence is cracked with emotion.

The side of his mouth pulls up. "I'll be home in a few days."

I shake my head as I admit, "I miss the *you* from before."

The side of his mouth lowers. "What do you mean?"

"I want it to be like it was, Dom. I want—I want to feel special again. Like I did before. Like I did when I believed you wanted me." I press my palm against my chest. "Just *me*. Not the stupid Alliance."

"Angel."

"Just let me say it," I plead.

Dom slowly nods. "Okay."

I look down, away from the phone. "Those weeks after we met, when we were messaging... They were special to me. And I want to keep them, the memory of them. But it feels like they've been poisoned. Because every time I'm reminded about one of our conversations, I feel... I feel so fucking stupid." My breath hitches, and I give up on being careful and wipe away more tears. "Because each time, I was talking to someone I thought might fall in love with me. Someone I thought was so interested in me that he needed to hear from me every day." I inhale deeply. "You would always tell me to make your day better. And each time you did that, you made me feel useful. Needed." Another slow breath. "But when I sent you that picture of me wearing this face mask on Halloween, I was flirting. Or trying to. And all the while, you were sitting at home, stringing me along, so that someday you could trick me into marrying you." I finally raise my eyes back up to look at him. "And it hurts, Dominic. It hurts a lot."

"Val." His tone is so soft. "I'm..." He won't say he's sorry.

I save both of us from the silence that would surely follow. "The worst part is that I believe you." My shoulders sag. "You told me that you never lied about yourself in our conversations. And I believe you. But it was still fake. It was all just an illusion. And I'm having a hard time putting the two versions of you together in my head." The tears I thought were done drip from my lashes again. "And I hate myself for wanting to accept it. Because you don't deserve for me to accept it. But I deserve to be happy." I breathe and say it again. "I deserve to be happy."

Dom's blue eyes are locked on mine. Filled with... something.

"So." I sniffle. "I'm going to go wash my face, and then I'm going to finish watching this movie in bed. And I'm going to keep feeling sorry for myself until I fall asleep."

"What movie are you watching?" He almost whispers the question.

"*The Fugitive*," I whisper back.

"Valentine." His throat moves on a swallow. "I can make you happy."

I bite into my bottom lip. But I don't want to hear any more promises.

"Goodnight, Dom."

As I press the button to hang up the call, I hear a muffled pop. But I'm already touching the screen, and the call ends.

CHAPTER 45

Dom

ONE GUNSHOT REVERBERATES THROUGH THE BUILDING, followed immediately by several others.

Then silence.

I slide my phone into my pocket.

Tonight did not go as planned. And the shouts breaking out in the warehouse behind me prove the point.

I called Valentine because I wanted to see her face. Because these days away from her have been frustrating and stressful, and I've gotten used to her presence in my daily life.

But instead of making her smile, I made her cry. And not just a single tear. My wife was sitting there alone in our bed, *crying*.

"Fuck."

I turn around and jerk the door open.

My footsteps bounce off the rafters, and the arguing men quiet as I near them.

The large and growing pool of blood on the floor tells me our possible informant is dead.

I look over at Nick, the man I put in charge, but he points to another man, one of the locals we're using for the week.

"Explain," I demand.

The local bows his head. "He jumped out of the chair and grabbed Oz's gun out of his holster, so I shot him."

I glance at another local, Oz, then back to the first man. "He got Oz's gun." The man nods. "And then what?"

He finally looks at me. "What do you mean? Uh, sir."

"I mean." I step closer, avoiding the blood but putting the toe of my shoe against the dead man's shoulders. "His hands are tied behind his fucking back. He might've gotten a gun off one of you girl scouts, but he's not shooting up a building with his hands *tied behind his fucking back*!" Everyone flinches at my volume.

Oz shuffles his feet. "He, um, did get a shot off."

"Takes one wild shot behind his back, with his feet also fucking tied together, and you decided to fill him with holes. Did you assholes come from the police academy?" They shake their heads like I was asking a serious question. I pinch the bridge of my nose. "Give me your guns."

The two men start to pull their weapons free, and I hear the sound of my men aiming their guns at the locals.

I gesture to the other men from the local gang. "All of you."

One man squares his shoulders, making me turn toward him.

My steps are slow, but I close the distance between us. "I'm not disarming you so I can kill you. I'm disarming you because you fucking imbeciles don't deserve to carry weapons." I take another step closer, invading his space. "But I'm in a bit of a mood right now. My wife is at home, crying because she misses me, and I'm here, wasting my fucking time. So please, do something stupid and give me an excuse to add your blood to the collection on the floor before we leave your filthy city."

Anger blazes in the man's eyes, and I almost wish he'd take a swing at me. But if he did, I'd kill him. And cooperation with these dummies has been useful, so it's probably for the best that he lowers his gaze and hands me his gun.

I tuck it into the waistband of my pants, then direct a command to the gunless men. "Clean this up." Then to my men. "Get your shit. We're going to Phoenix."

Done with this night, I walk out of the building.

Inhaling the evening air, I push away the guilt that talking to Valentine caused and focus on the important part.

She was wearing my sweatshirt.

CHAPTER 46
Val

Me: Was that a gunshot?

DELETE.

Me: What happened?

Delete.

Me: Tell me you're alive.

Send.

Big Guy: I'm alive.

Big Guy: Get some sleep, Wife. We'll talk again tomorrow.

Me: You still alive?

Delete.

I roll over and scream into the pillow.

All night I tossed and turned. Dreams of witnessing Dominic getting riddled with bullets plagued my sleep. So now I'm tired and cranky and, worst of all, worried.

"Fuck you!" My shout is muffled. But it's not like it matters. There's no one here to hear me.

I flop back over and stare at the ceiling. I need a distraction.

With an idea in mind, I pick my phone back up.

> Me: Can I have some friends over tonight?

Send.

I make a face. I sound like I'm asking if I can go outside to play.

> Me: For dinner. I'll order something.

Send.

> Me: With my own money.

Send.

> Me: Even though I'm sure your stubborn ass will insist I charge your card or account or whatever you have set up with the front desk.

Send.

I force myself to roll out of bed so I stop sending more texts. And it's early enough that Dominic should still be asleep, so he probably won't reply for a while.

I'm halfway to the bathroom when he replies.

> Big Guy: Yes, your stubborn-ass husband will insist you use the payment I already have set up.

> Big Guy: And yes, you can have your friends over any time you want. But Rob has a standing order to toss any men who try to visit you off the roof, so make sure your friends don't bring anyone they don't want dead.

I stare at my phone.

> Me: Crazy much?

Send.

> Big Guy: You seem to bring it out in me.

> Big Guy: Have fun with your friends, Angel. We're about to board a plane for Arizona. Be a few more days yet.

A suspicion niggles in my mind.

> Me: Are you flying commercial?

Send.

> Big Guy: No. I usually don't.

> Big Guy: Most of the time I use flights to catch up on sleep. But I can't do that on a commercial plane because I don't know who's around. Who might want to kill me.

I hold my breath.

> Me: You slept on our first plane ride together.

Send.

Big Guy: I know. It was a first.

Big Guy: Something about you made me feel safe.

I press the phone to my chest and swallow.

Me: I know the feeling.

Send.

Big Guy: Did you have fun last night?

Me: I did. The bouquet of flowers was a nice touch.

SEND.

Big Guy: I can't have your friends thinking poorly of me.

Me: Pretty sure the eight hundred dollars of sushi you had delivered took care of that.

Send.

Big Guy: I'm glad you had a good night, Angel.

Big Guy: Did you enjoy your dinner?

I LOOK DOWN AT THE MOSTLY EMPTY PLATTERS ON THE coffee table.

> Me: I did. Thank you for ordering it.

Send.

> Big Guy: Next year I'll be home for Thanksgiving, and we can host some of my family if you'd like.

My eyes lock on the last bite of pumpkin pie.

I've never really cared about the holiday before, but the idea of celebrating it with Dominic twists something inside my chest.

> Me: Okay.

Send.

> Big Guy: How is it so fucking hot here?

> Me: Baby.

SEND

> Me: But feel free to bring some of that warm weather back home with you.

Send.
Home.
Fuck.

Big Guy: Heading into Mexico. Should just be one more night.

Me: Surprised they let you in and out of the country.

SEND.

Big Guy: Let me. Cute.

Me: How's Mexico?

SEND.

Big Guy: A waste of time. I'll be home tomorrow. Keep your calendar open. We're going to dinner.

CHAPTER 47

Val

"Ready?" Rob is standing next to the front door.

I blow out a breath and nod my head. "Ready as I'll ever be."

Rob chuckles, but my hands are shaking as I pull my jacket on over my dress.

It's just dinner with my husband, but he was gone for over a week, and I'm unbelievably nervous about seeing him again.

We've texted every day and have even talked on the phone, and not just the major meltdown I had that one night. So it's not like I haven't heard from him since he left. It's just...

I step into the elevator behind Rob and lean against the wall.

My ears pop as we descend, and privately, to myself, I can admit the biggest problem about today.

Today is my birthday.

I don't think Dominic knows. He hasn't said anything.

And I don't need him to. Honestly, I usually do everything I can to forget my birthday, so I certainly won't be bringing it up. But...

I glance down at my outfit and bite back a sigh.

Dom didn't tell me anything about the restaurant, but he's always dressed nicely, so I decided to try and match his vibe. And secretly, I dressed as though I'm going to a fancy birthday dinner. Because even if I'm the only one who knows, I can pretend that's what we're going out for. And I want to feel the part.

I'll never admit I had Dom in mind when I selected this navy-blue dress. It's a wrap dress, my favorite type, but the off-the-shoulder style is not my usual choice. My whole neck and chest are on display—accented with my small gold heart necklace and earrings—but the long sleeves make the dress feel modest. And instead of my usual wedges, I opted for knee-high brown boots—with a heel.

The boots are made of fake leather, which makes them comfortable and allows them to stretch over my calves.

I just did a high ponytail for my hair because not only could I not decide on a style, but curling my thick hair takes forever and I wasted all my time trying on every dress in the closet.

During our brief walk to the car waiting out front, I'm thankful I added my coat. The knee-length tan peacoat hides my dress completely, but it helps block out some of the chill.

They weren't lying when they named this the Windy City. I don't know if it's the lake or what, but the air seems bitter cold today.

From the back seat of the SUV, I watch as the city passes my window. It's not that late, but this time of year means the sun set hours ago. So it's up to the streetlights and glowing signs to light the world around us.

November twenty-ninth. Just another day.

The driver steers to the right and stops at the curb in front of a small restaurant.

The establishment's windows are tinted, so you can't see in, but a dark red awning over the door proclaims it as *Enzo's*.

It doesn't look like much from the outside, but some of the best places are like that.

Rob gets out of the vehicle and comes around to open my door.

I climb down and adjust the tie on my jacket when I notice

two men in black suits standing on either side of the restaurant's front door.

Dom put security outside the restaurant? Does he always do that when he goes out?

I take a deep breath.

Today is just another day. And this is just a dinner.

Rob stays behind me as we cross the sidewalk.

"Ma'am." One of the men greets me as he pulls the door open.

"Thank you," I tell him quietly, then step into the restaurant.

My nerves are already fried, so as soon as I'm inside, my gaze bounces around, searching for Dominic in the sea of people.

There are so many people.

Why are there so many people?

And why are they standing?

At once, they all turn to face me, calling out "Happy birthday!" with one singular voice shouting "Surprise!"

I freeze.

What?

I stare at the crowd before me.

Did they say...

The oxygen freezes in my lungs, halting my breath, while heat fills my eyes.

Did Dominic...?

I force my body to inhale. But it's choppy because there are balloons and flowers. And...

And...

"Happy birthday, Angel." Dominic cuts through the group of people looking at me expectantly.

My lips part, but I can't speak. Because if I speak, I'll sob. And there are so many people here.

It's a birthday party.

For me.

My husband's big body moves closer until he's all I can see.

He cups my cheeks with his palms. "Breathe, Shorty. It's just family here."

It's just family here.

I swallow.

And I swallow again.

He planned a birthday party for me.

"Shh." Dom's thumbs brush under my eyes, and I can feel the dampness. "Maybe we surprised you a little too much."

I sniffle and bite my lip.

His thumb brushes again. "Would you like a drink?"

I nod.

"Wine or something stronger?"

I nod again.

Dominic smiles at me. And it's so soft, so kind, it brings me that much closer to a complete meltdown.

His fingers flex on my cheek. "How about a margarita?"

A small scoff breaks free from my throat, and his smile grows.

"No? How about a shot of whiskey?"

I wet my lips. "Yes, please."

Dominic leans in closer. "How can I deny you when you say it so sweetly?"

He comes even closer, and I close my eyes, letting him press his lips to mine.

He lingers longer than he should—with his family watching. But I don't push him away.

I lean in.

And I press my lips harder to his.

My hands reach blindly for him, gripping the front of his suit jacket. And I let my hold on him ground me. Sink me back down to earth. Into the here and now.

Dom pulls back, heaving out a breath, and turns to stand next to me, facing the crowd. "I think we surprised her."

Everyone chuckles, and I drop my chin in embarrassment.

Dom's hand lands on the back of my neck, and he uses his thumb at the corner of my jaw to tip my head back up.

"Now, before you all crowd my wife for the rest of the night, she wants a shot of whiskey."

A cheer of mostly male voices goes up, and I can't help but smile as the wives of the cheering men roll their eyes.

An older man with white hair carries over a pair of full-to-the-brim shot glasses, the dark liquid never dripping over the rim.

He holds one out to me, and I take it.

"Thank you." I lift the small glass in thanks.

He starts to hold the second one out, but when Dom reaches for it, the man clinks the glass to mine, then takes the shot himself.

I glance up at Dom to see him glaring at the man. "If you were twenty years younger, I'd kick your ass."

The man grins. "If I were twenty years younger, I wouldn't have to get your wife drunk to flirt with her."

His answer startles a laugh out of me.

Dom narrows his eyes on me. "You think that's funny?"

Instead of answering him, I tip my shot back.

The burn is instant, and I put a hand over my mouth as I try not to cough.

"Everyone, grab a glass," Dominic shouts, and suddenly trays of whiskey shots are being handed around.

Dom grabs another one for me, then one for himself.

When everyone has one, he holds his in the air. Everybody follows suit. I keep mine at chest level. If I try to hold it higher, I'll shake all the alcohol straight out of the glass.

I brace myself for his speech, scrambling to build up my walls so I don't break down in front of everyone. But he keeps it short. And that's almost worse.

"To Valentine," Dominic says in his commanding voice.

"To Valentine," the room repeats back.

Heat fills my chest.

Never have I ever felt like this before.

Dom downs his shot.

And I do the same, chasing the building heat with fire.

Dominic's arm stays around my shoulders as the first person approaches.

And the second.

And fifth.

And then I lose count. Shaking hands, saying hello, thanking them for the birthday wishes.

After what must be half an hour, maybe more, Dominic is pulled from my side.

My panic at being left on my own doesn't have time to settle in before someone I recognize approaches. Her dark hair is loose, and her black dress is so tight and short she looks ready for the club.

"Hi." Her smile is shy and a little guilty. But she offers me a short glass filled with ice, an amber liquid, an orange slice, and a tiny plastic sword stabbing through three maraschino cherries.

She has an identical drink in her other hand, so I gladly take the one before me.

"Hello." At least this new embarrassment isn't written all over my face, seeing as how my cheeks have been red since I walked in.

"Sorry," we say at the same time.

"Me first." She grins. "I should've put it together sooner, but after you stormed upstairs with the toaster, Rob explained that Dom was using me to piss you off." She snorts. "I'm sorry you were upset, but your payback was freaking hilarious."

"Seriously, you have nothing to apologize for," I try to tell her, but she shakes her head.

"No, I do. It was dumb of me not to think about it. When he offered to pay off the rest of my student loans in exchange for lasagna, I figured he was just trying to make up a way for me to *earn it*." She does air quotes when she says "earn it."

"Which I know sounds ridiculous, because seventy thousand for a pan of noodles is insane. But it's nothing to him." She shrugs her shoulders. "And my parents only stopped paying for my college because they wanted me to use my first degree and didn't think I needed to get my master's. Which is dumb because they always told me school was important." She places her hand on her forehead. "Oh my god, sorry, I'm rambling. The whole point is that I should've seen through the ruse."

Her energy is so fun and happy I have to laugh. "Well, I hope he held up his end of the bargain, because that lasagna was delicious."

"Thank you." She beams. "I can't wait to tell my mom that. I'm Miranda, by the way." She offers me her hand.

I shake it. "Valentine."

"Duh." She laughs, then takes a sip of her drink.

Wanting the courage, I try my own and hum with appreciation.

"Good?" Miranda asks.

"Really good." I take another drink.

She shrugs. "Since Dom started you out with a whiskey shot, I figured an old-fashioned would be a safe choice for my bribe."

"Bribe?"

"A friendship bribe." She says it like it's just a silly gesture. But it's not. It's more appreciated than she could ever know.

"Well, it worked." I try to keep my tone light. "So, um, what did you get your master's in?"

"Art therapy."

My brows raise. "That sounds cool."

"It is."

We continue to drink as Miranda tells me all about art therapy and what she plans to do with her degrees. And for a bit, I'm able to forget how overwhelmed I am.

The old-fashioned disappears, and a server shows up to take my empty glass as I swallow the last bit.

"Another?" they ask with a dip of their head.

I shake mine. "Not yet, thank you."

With my hands free, I undo the belt of my jacket and start to pull it off. The alcohol and the packed restaurant have made me a little too warm.

Miranda whistles. "Love the dress."

"Thanks. Dominic always reminds me of blue." I lift a shoulder, not sure why I admitted that.

"Such a good wife." Dom's voice sounds from right behind me, startling me. "You should always dress with me in mind." Not waiting for me to reply to his absurd statement, Dominic takes the coat from my hands and passes it off to someone else. "Glad to see you two are friends now," he says to us, but his eyes are on me.

"I like her," I tell Dom, then turn to Miranda. "My sister-in-law is a painter. I don't know if you want to know more people in the art world, but I'd be happy to introduce you sometime."

Her eyes widen. "Really? Are you talking about Savannah Oates? Or I guess it's Vass now. I'd love to meet her."

My mouth opens.

She knows about Savannah?

Miranda must see something in my expression because her face falls. "Oh shit, sorry. Was that weird? I don't mean it in a creepy way or anything. It's just, well..." She shrugs her shoulders. "She did marry King, co-leader of The Alliance. So obviously, I was going to look her up online. And her work is top shit."

"Miranda." Dominic sighs. "You're making it weird."

I reach up and gently smack his chest with the back of my hand. "No, she's not."

Miranda lets out a sort of startled sound, and I follow her eyes to where Dominic caught my hand against his body.

The way Miranda is looking at us makes me wonder if I shouldn't have done that.

Should I not have hit the head Boss?

A few of the closest conversations have quieted.

My eyes widen, and I look up at Dom. "I'm sorry. I was just... playing around."

I don't know why my voice cracks at the end, but everyone has been so nice to me. I don't want to be the one who ruins tonight.

"Shorty." The side of Dominic's mouth pulls up, and I swear he knows to use that nickname whenever I'm starting to spiral. "I like you playing around. Alright?"

"Alright," I whisper, fighting away the panic.

He lifts my hand and presses a kiss to the inside of my wrist as his eyes trail down the length of my body, taking in all the bare skin.

"You look amazing tonight."

"Aww!" Miranda's voice cuts through the moment.

I bite down on my smile.

Dom shakes his head, then lets out a loud whistle.

All voices stop, and all heads turn toward my husband.

His chin lifts. "Let's eat."

CHAPTER 48

Dom

VALENTINE LOWERS HERSELF INTO THE CHAIR I'VE pulled out for her, and I take the spot next to her.

There's no assigned seating, but our table is spoken for. Two of my uncles and my aunt Dina, who hugged Val at the funeral, are already seated, but I wait for my mom to settle in across from Val before I start introductions.

I start with the uncles, and then I watch Valentine squeeze her hands together in her lap when I introduce her to my aunt. So by the time I get to my mom, I place my hand over Val's on her thigh, hoping to help calm her down.

"And last but never least, this is my mother." Val tenses beside me. "Mother, meet my wife, Valentine."

My mom presses her hands to her chest, one on top of the other, over her heart. "It's so nice to meet you. I—" She shakes her head and starts pushing back from the table. "No, this won't do."

"Mom, what are you doing?" I sigh.

Val tenses and turns to me. "Is she leaving?"

Her question shoots sadness into my heart. "No, Angel." I tip my head toward where my mom is now circling the table. "She's coming to accost you."

Val turns her head just in time to catch my mom opening her arms, clearly expecting my new wife to hug her.

Unaware of Val's obvious distress, Mom grabs Val's shoulders and pulls her up and out of her chair.

Val goes willingly, and I give them three solid seconds before I stand and place a hand on my mom's arm. "Mother, you have the rest of your life to smother Valentine with your affection. Can we have dinner now before everyone gets completely drunk?"

Mom lets her go. "Fine, fine."

As Mom hurries around to her seat, I keep my hand on the back of Val's neck and guide her back into her chair. "She can be kind of a lot."

Val glances at me. "Must be genetic."

I grin, glad she's teasing me. Even though there's still too much emotion in her eyes.

Emotion that has been there since she first set foot in the restaurant.

She was so stunned I wondered if maybe a party was the wrong idea. Maybe she doesn't like surprises or doesn't like to celebrate her birthday. But the expression on her face was more than simple shock. It was disbelief. Like she couldn't wrap her mind around the fact that people were gathered for her. And I don't understand that.

I was trying to do something nice, not knock her off balance.

"Now, if you don't want to call me Mom yet—"

"Mom." I widen my eyes at her, hoping she'll drop it.

She just waves me off and keeps talking to Val. "You can call me Bibi."

My mom doesn't even spare me another look, just starts pointing around the table, explaining who is sibling to who.

Picking up my drink, I relax into my chair.

I've done my research on Valentine Gandy. I know she grew up with a single mother. I know she shares a dad with King. I know, based on birth dates and the fact that their dad was married

265

to King's mom when he died, that Valentine must have been the product of an affair.

I know that even though she's much younger than they are, Val still spends time with King and Aspen. And I know she knows enough about The Alliance to accept having her own bodyguard.

But I also know her mom passed away when she was nineteen.

So I don't know how Val might feel about my mom basically asking her to call her Mom.

But she seems to take it in stride, nodding along and making sounds of understanding as Mom explains the entire family tree.

Servers swarm through the room, setting family-style platters of pasta on the table before us and refilling all our drinks.

The food steadily disappears, and Mom hasn't quit talking to Val. But as time passes, I can feel my wife finally start to relax.

CHAPTER 49

Val

A DISH OF TIRAMISU IS SET IN FRONT OF ME, AND MY mouth waters, even though my stomach has been twisted in knots all night.

My fingers close around the spoon, but before I can scoop up some of the sweet dessert, another utensil clinks against a glass elsewhere in the room.

I've seen plenty of movies about weddings, so I assume someone is going to shout for me and Dominic to kiss, but instead of one voice, the entire restaurant breaks out singing the "Happy Birthday" song.

And my throat closes.

They've done too much already.

Wanting to hide but unable to look away, my eyes rove around the room, seeing all the smiling faces as they sing to me.

To me.

How is this real?

The final verse is sung, and then a man finishes with "*and many more*" in the deepest bass voice I've ever heard.

I don't know what to say.

Or do.

So I just keep the tight smile plastered to my face as I try to think of what a normal person would do in this situation.

But as soon as they're done, everyone breaks out into applause before turning back to their desserts.

The large body next to me shifts. "Happy birthday." Dom's voice settles across my skin as he sets a gift in front of me.

It's wrapped in white and yellow polka-dot paper and is the size of a book.

I glance at him, and he dips his chin. "Open it."

As soon as I pick it up, I can tell it's a picture frame.

I look back up at Dom, and his expression is... hesitant.

My hands are unsteady as I start to rip the paper.

The back of the frame is exposed first. And I wait until the paper is completely off before I flip it over.

And...

And...

My heart squeezes so hard a tear slips from the corner of my eye.

It's us. Standing together in front of a Vegas altar. We're both dressed all in black, and I have Dominic's suit jacket draped around my shoulders.

I'm pressed into his side, but we're turned toward each other. And the look on my face...

I release the frame with one hand so I can press my fingertips to my lips, hoping to stop them from moving.

The look on my face as I gaze up at Dominic is pure adoration.

He's brushing his knuckles over my cheek, and I'm gripping his arm like I want him to stay right there, like that, forever.

And the look on his face...

I press my fingers harder against my lips.

His look is one of sadness.

If you didn't know him, you might think it was affection. But I've seen Dominic's expressions, and the one in the photo, the one he was feeling on our wedding night, was sadness.

My hand starts to shake too much, and I have to set the frame down.

Bibi says something, and I see Dominic hand her the photo.

How are there even photos?

Why would he give that to me?

And why did he look so sad?

"If we're doing gifts now." Dominic's mom pulls a tiny gift box out of her purse and sets it on the table in front of me. "I know you two decided to do tattoos. But I want you to have this." She nudges it a little closer to me.

Half-numb, I reach out and pick up the box.

I untie the red ribbon, then slide the lid off, and the tiny amount of composure I have left cracks down the middle.

Sitting alone at the bottom of the box is a ring.

I take it out with numb fingers.

The thick band is polished gold with swirling engravings twisting around the thin row of diamonds circling the ring. And in the center of the band is a large, sparkling diamond.

It's stunning.

Beautiful.

It's the vintage version of the ring I threw onto the highway. Different, but too similar to be a coincidence.

"It belonged to my mother. And now it belongs to you," Bibi says, like it's as easy as that. *Here, take this amazing and priceless heirloom.* "I know you kids nowadays like to do your own thing, so no pressure if it's not your style," she continues, being so nice and making me feel like an asshole. "But maybe you could use it for special occasions."

"It's perfect." I hold it up a little, and the light catches the gorgeous diamond as the ring trembles in my grip. "I love it. Thank you," I practically whisper.

"I'm so glad," Bibi exclaims, and Dom's aunt makes a cooing sound.

I move to put it on but realize it won't fit on my ring finger, so I slip it onto my pinkie. "I'll have to get it resized, if that's okay."

Bibi is tiny, so if this last belonged to her, it's no surprise it's too small for me.

"Of course." She flutters her hands. "If I'd been thinking, I would've done that for you." Then she turns her gaze to Dom, narrowing her eyes. "Or if *someone* had told me *before* you got married, I could've had it ready for you then."

I almost wince, thinking about how horrible it would've been to have thrown this ring out the window. And I'm eternally grateful that Dom didn't tell his mom ahead of time.

"Either way, it's yours now," she tells me. "And you can keep it until your daughter gets married."

Her statement is so casual, but it shatters my abused heart into a thousand pieces.

My daughter.

My head tips down as I squeeze my eyes shut.

I would love nothing more than to have a daughter.

My chest tightens almost painfully, and I have to open my mouth to pull in a breath.

Calm down, Val.

You need to calm down.

"Speaking of..." Bibi taps the picture frame still in front of her. "Will someone please tell me about the ceremony? I've always been curious about how it works in Vegas."

Oh god, please don't ask me that.

A buzzing noise builds inside my skull until I can't hear anything else.

I need separation from this situation.

I need distance.

My chair scrapes across the floor as I push away from the table.

"Excuse me," I try to say, not sure if I manage.

When I stand, I sway, the shots and the old-fashioned and whatever was served with dinner all catching up to me.

A large hand, which I know is covered in ink similar to my own, presses against my lower back, steadying me.

"Val," he says quietly, but I don't look back. I can't.

"I'll be right back," I tell him.

I don't know if he hears me, but I hurry away from his touch.

I head toward the little hallway in the back corner that I spotted earlier, hoping it has the escape I need.

And on my way, I pass another cluster of brightly colored balloons tethered to the wall, reminding me that everyone is here for me.

Dominic's whole family is here for me.

Not *his* family, *our* family. Because we're married now.

Just breathe.

One of the tables is full of men, and as I walk past, they all raise their glasses and cheer.

They're having fun. They're happy to be here.

And it's the final straw.

I manage to turn down the hall before the first sob breaks free.

CHAPTER 50

Dom

"I'M SORRY." MY MOM WRINGS HER HANDS. "IS IT something I said?"

I watch the corner where Valentine disappeared. "No, you're good, Mom. She's just had a stressful week, and I'm afraid this all might be a little overwhelming for her." None of that is a lie. "Just stay here and keep everyone occupied. I'll go check on her."

I reach across the table and pat my mom's hands.

Her smile is a little wobbly. "I really like her."

I smile at my mother's approval. "I really like her, too."

I slide back my chair, then follow Valentine's path away from the table.

My uncles cheer for me just as loudly as they did when Val passed them.

I almost keep walking but then stop and snatch a shot of something brown out of my closest uncle's hand.

Before he can protest, I tip the shot back and swallow it down, then hold the empty out to his table. "To marriage."

They all laugh and tip back their own.

I'm far from drunk, but the extra booze will hopefully help ease my guilt.

I don't know why I thought Val would like that photo of us

from the wedding. I know it's a *bad moment* in her memory, but I...

I drag a hand down my face.

I thought I could change that. Thought showing her how content she was in the moment would change that. But in reality, what I did was hand her a photo of a memory she can't remember because she had been drugged by me.

And then my mom's ring. Followed by her asking about the ceremony...

I'm thinking this whole night was bad planning on my part.

I depress the handle and enter the women's restroom.

Similar to the men's, the room is small. Just two stalls and two sinks.

My cousin's wife is at one of the sinks, washing her hands, and when she spots me, she hurries to turn off the water.

I don't know her well. And she must be a little scared of me because she doesn't so much as touch her hand to a towel to dry off before scurrying past me and out the door.

The farthest stall is closed, the other unoccupied.

And my wife's soft cries fill the room.

Because I don't want to traumatize her more, I bend down and look under the door. But her feet aren't in front of the toilet. They're facing the wall.

I pull the knife out of my pocket, flick it open, and use the blade to unlock the stall door.

Slipping the knife back in my pocket, I push the door open.

The hinges squeak, and Val spins around.

Her hands are over her mouth, and tears are streaming down her face, but it's her hunched shoulders that break my heart.

I step into the stall and close the door behind me. "Angel—"

But before I can get out more, she closes the distance between us and throws her arms around my neck.

I don't question it. I just wrap my arms around her in return. And when she tightens her grip, I tighten mine, hoisting her into the air.

I hate seeing her cry. Hate knowing I've caused it. But a part of me relishes in her coming to me. In her reaching for me.

I hold her tighter.

She's so warm. So soft.

So mine.

And then she rocks my world completely.

"Thank you," she says against my neck. "Thank you, Dominic."

Did she really just thank me?

I boost her higher, and she wraps her legs around my waist, her loose skirt bunching at her hips.

"What are you thanking me for, Valentine?" I rub my thumb in a circle on her spine.

I feel her sniff. "This is my first birthday party. And... And you even have balloons."

I slide my hands down to grip her by the ass so I can lean back a little to hear her better. "Your first surprise party, you mean?"

She sniffles again, then shakes her head.

My brows furrow in confusion. "You've never had a birthday party?"

"No," she whispers.

"How is that possible?"

Val finally meets my eyes. "No one ever wanted to give me one." She lifts her shoulders.

"What about your family?"

Val presses her lips together as she shakes her head again.

I swallow against the uncomfortable feeling closing around my throat. "Why?"

"Because no one ever cared, Dominic." She heaves out a breath. "I never had anyone." More tears drip down her cheeks. "And even if you did this for—"

"I did this for you, Valentine." I can't let her finish that sentence. Can't fucking bear to hear her say it. "I did this for you. Because I do care."

Her lungs hitch.

She's ripping my fucking heart out.

Her eyes search mine, looking for something, and I wish I knew what it was so I could make sure to give it to her.

"I do care, Angel." I try to make her believe me.

Another tear rolls down her cheek before she leans closer. "Show me."

Val slams her mouth against mine.

It's desperate.

Searching.

And I think I need this as much as she does.

I raise a hand to cup the back of her head before I shove her against the wall.

Val's tongue laps against my lips, and I open for her, angling my head and meeting her lash for lash.

"Hurry," she whines into my mouth.

"I'll show you just how much I fucking need you. Anytime you want." I press my hips into her, pinning her against the wall so I can yank her skirt out of the way. "You just need to ask."

Val moans and her hips tilt, searching for that friction.

"I've been away from this sweet pussy for too long." I boost her higher, above my belt, so I can undo my pants.

"Please, Dominic."

"Are you ready for me?" I have no right to ask her that. I've hardly even fucking touched her. But I know her body and how she's always fucking primed. "Is that juicy slit dripping for me?"

She doesn't answer my question, just drags her nails up the back of my neck and over my head.

My eyes roll back. "Do that again."

She does, and I have to focus to free my dick from my pants.

Val rolls her hips with a whine.

"It's okay, Angel. Just pull those panties out of the way, and I'll stuff you full of this dick."

She shifts, leaving one arm around my neck and reaching down between us with the other.

My cock is there, bumping against the damp cotton, so when she pulls it to the side, I don't give her even a second to prepare.

Thrusting my hips, I sink every inch of my length into my wife.

Before she can scream over the intrusion, I seal my lips to hers again, catching her sounds and swallowing them down.

She's everywhere. Her legs around me. Her arm around me. Her breath filling my ears. Her scent surrounding me. Her emotions, her sadness, her gratitude, her heartbreak... It's all a part of me now.

And I'm never letting her go.

"You have me," I tell her as I claim her body. "You'll always have me." I promise her by pressing my mouth back to hers.

Wetness touches my lips, and I can taste the saltiness of her tears.

I pull my hips back, my cock sliding through her wetness, then shove back in.

"You're mine now, remember?" Her pussy squeezes me with each movement of my cock, and I can hardly form words anymore. She's so goddamn hot for it. Hot for me.

"I remember," she breathes.

"That's right, Wife. You're mine." My fingers dig into her ass as I slam her body against mine. "And as mine, you're going to do as I say."

Val nods, breaking our kiss to gasp for air.

I tip my head down and press a soft kiss against the side of her neck. "Then be my good wife and come for me. Rub that little clit and milk me fucking dry."

She slides her hand back down between us, and I can feel the tips of her fingers against the top of my dick.

I slow my movements, keeping them steady as I feel her response.

When her breathing starts to change and her pussy starts to clench, I pull back so only the tip is inside her. And I hold still.

"That's it," I murmur against her cheek, letting her exhalations fill my ear. "You're so close."

"I-I am."

"Be my pretty birthday girl and come all over this dick."

Valentine tips her head forward, and she bites my suit jacket as her channel clamps down around me.

I pull out just a little more so her entrance is spasming around the head of my cock.

And when her moan reverberates from her body into mine, I slam all the way in

Claiming her.

Spilling into her as deep as I can go.

CHAPTER 51
Val

M Y   B O D Y   I S   S T I L L   T R E M B L I N G   W H E N   D O M   L O W E R S   M E to my feet.

"Jesus, Val." He presses his lips to my forehead. "You're fucking perfect."

I don't know how to reply to that or really to any of my behavior today, so I don't try.

Because I'm standing here, clenching my thighs together, trying not to make a total mess of myself since I just had sex with my super-hot, super-strong husband in a public bathroom at *my* birthday party.

Dom tucks himself back into his pants and straightens his clothes. "I'll step out so you can get cleaned up. And then we'll walk back to our table, you'll eat your dessert, and then we can go home. Sound good?"

I nod my head, biting my lip.

Dom exits the restroom, and as soon as that door shuts, I shuffle over the toilet.

Once I'm standing in front of the mirror, I accept there's no way to fix the fact that it looks like I've been crying. I don't have any sort of makeup with me, let alone on me, so I dampen a paper towel with cold water and press it to my face for a few seconds.

When nothing else can be done, I pull open the bathroom door and stop short when I find Dominic leaning against the wall next to it.

I know he said we'd walk back to the table, but I guess I hadn't realized he meant he'd wait for me.

"Ready?" He straightens.

I blow out a breath. "Sorry I ruined the party."

Dom lowers his brow as he moves to face me. "Don't apologize. And you didn't ruin anything. Why would you even think that?"

I gesture at my face and aim for a *duh* expression. "Everyone is here for me, and I look like I've been crying, because I *have been* crying."

The side of Dom's mouth pulls up in that stupid smile I love so much. "Shorty, your face is flushed." He trails a fingertip down my cheek. "Your eyes are bright." He traces across my bottom lip. "You don't look like you've been crying. You look like you've been well fucked."

He startles a laugh out of me. "Dom!"

"What?"

"I don't want your entire family thinking we had sex in the bathroom."

He grins. "We did have sex in the bathroom."

"Dom."

"Valentine, I hate to break it to you, but my mom knows I'm not a virgin anymore. She's known since she accidentally walked in on me and Stacy having sex on the couch when I was in high school."

I narrow my eyes. "Who the fuck is Stacy?"

Dominic leans down until we're eye to eye. "A name I made up just to make you jealous. Now come with me so I can watch you eat your fucking dessert."

Watch me?

Dom grabs my hand, lifts it into the crook of his arm, and then guides me back into the main dining room.

No one stops talking.

No one stares.

Even the table of guys that cheered me earlier keep their conversation steady and their eyes on each other.

I don't know if they all really don't care about our little disappearance or if they were told to act this way after I left. But either way, I appreciate it.

When we reach our table, Bibi smiles and pours me a cup of coffee to have with my dessert, pointing out that it's decaf.

Bibi starts talking about some Christmas market that the family will be going to soon, and I do my best to tune it out. I can't add my Christmas baggage to tonight's tension. That's too much.

As if he can sense my building stress, Dominic leans closer.

I put the spoon in my mouth, expecting him to tell me to relax when he says something completely different.

"For the record, I wouldn't mind watching you drip out the cum I filled you with. I stepped out of the bathroom because I figured you'd prefer the privacy." His voice rumbles low so only I can hear him, and I nearly choke on my mouthful of cream.

A finger trails down the side of my neck. "You just let me know if you want me to stay and watch next time."

I force myself to swallow, then hold the cloth napkin over my mouth. "Jesus, Dominic."

He hands me my coffee. "Just being honest, Wife."

"You're a menace," I scoff.

But when he grips my chair and pulls me closer to him, I let myself rest against his side.

CHAPTER 52
Val

I TAKE AS LONG AS I CAN TO GET READY FOR BED. BUT when I can't delay anymore, I turn off the bathroom light and step into the bedroom.

Our bedroom.

I know Dominic is going to ask me about tonight—why I reacted the way I did.

And I'm going to tell him.

Because I'm sick of pretending that I don't want to stay here. That I don't want to stay with him.

And I know what he did isn't okay. And I know how he did it was shitty. But the more of his family I meet, the more I accept it.

I'd do just about anything to protect his mom, and I only met her tonight.

So if we're going to do this, I need him to know the truth about my family. All of it.

And there's a part of me that's terrified. Because what happens when I explain to him that I'm not that close to King?

Will he regret choosing me as the linchpin?

CHAPTER 53

THE CEILING LIGHTS ARE STILL ON, SO I WATCH VAL walk around the bed and notice her thick sweatpants and my Yale sweatshirt.

I'm starting to recognize this as her comfort outfit, and as much as I wish she didn't need it, I can't help but feel pride that my wardrobe is a part of it.

Instead of lying on her side, like she does when she's ready to fall asleep, she lies on her back.

I roll onto my side, facing her profile.

Her eyes are open, but she's staring at nothing.

Something twists inside me, and I move closer until her shoulder is against my chest.

"Want to tell me?" I ask quietly.

She bites her lip even as she nods her head. "It's a lot."

"We have time."

Val pulls the blankets up to her chin, and I slip my arm under the covers. She only tenses for a moment when I rest my hand on her stomach. She's so soft. I want to be touching her always.

"I'm... I'm just gonna start at the beginning."

I nod against my pillow. "I want to know everything about you, Valentine."

I watch as her throat works.

She opens and closes her mouth. "Hold on." She leans away from me, reaching out to turn off the ceiling lights.

There's still ambient light from the city, but darkness settles around us.

Val lies back, and I put my hand back where it was, feeling her body rise and fall with breaths.

"I don't know how much you know from your, um, research." She exhales. "So you can tell me to skip stuff."

"I don't really want to talk about the background check I ran on you," I admit, knowing I need to give her something in exchange for what she's about to give me. "I know you have a different mom from King and Aspen. And that you grew up in a different house. But I want to know how it's possible that you've never had a birthday party."

The blankets shift, and one of her hands starts to settle on top of mine on her stomach, but I lift my hand a little, and she slips hers underneath, trapping it between my palm and her body.

I close my fingers around hers.

She's quiet for a long moment. And I give her the time.

"I really loved my dad." She takes another deep breath. "He would bring me presents on my birthday. They were always great kid gifts. Toys, stuffed animals... And there were a few times when he'd bring cupcakes, too. But there was never a party. My mom... sucked. She only ever pretended to be kind when my dad was around. When he wasn't..." I can feel her shrug. "She was mean."

Her mom was mean to her?

Rage starts to creep in on the edge of my vision. My mom is my rock. She's always been there for me. For everything. To imagine growing up in a world where she was cruel to me... I can't.

"Did she hurt you?" I ask as calmly as I'm able.

Valentine shrugs again. "Nothing bad."

I squeeze her fingers. That's a terrible answer.

"She liked to pinch," Val tells me. "But she wielded her words with much more precision."

"Angel..." I don't even know what to say.

"When I was like eight, I found a book about pregnancy and birth. It was really simple. A children's book with illustrations. But it talked about how a baby needs nine months in their mother's stomach before they can come out. I'd always been told that I was a Valentine's Day baby, which is what I was named after, so I pulled the calendar off my wall and counted back from my birthday. And when it didn't match up, I made the mistake of asking my mom about it." She huffs out a derisive laugh. "She told me I was stupid and I didn't know what I was talking about."

Val slides her other hand on top of mine, sandwiching my hand between hers.

"I was a stupid kid, though. Because I always believed her. I believed her when she told me I came out late, rather than her conceiving later in February, because she wasn't with my dad on Valentine's Day. Because he was probably with his actual wife. And I believed her when she told me my dad was too busy and too important to live at home with us. I didn't know seeing your dad only six times a year wasn't normal."

"You weren't stupid."

She clutches her fingers around mine. "The first funeral I ever attended was my father's. I was nine. And I couldn't figure out why we had to sit in the back." She swallows. "Dom, I was so confused."

I move even closer.

"There were so many people there. It was like..." She sniffs. "It was like your cousin's funeral. Really nice like that. Lots of people. But my mom... I cried so much when she told me he'd died, but she only ever seemed angry about it. I didn't see her cry once over him, and the more I cried, the angrier she got. I remember her pinching me during the service. Mad that I was being so emotional."

"Fuck," I whisper, wanting to wrap child Valentine in my arms and protect her.

"That was before the priest mentioned my dad was survived by his wife and kids, which he referred to by name."

"Fuck." It comes out louder this time.

"Pretty much." She sighs. "It broke my little heart. Because he was the only person that ever told me he loved me. And... it was a lie."

"He might've been a cheating asshole, but there's no way he couldn't love you," I say, meaning it, before I realize how true the words really are.

Who wouldn't love this woman?

Her stomach trembles with a choppy breath. "When the service was over, and the family walked out first, King's mom glared at me like I was the worst thing she'd ever seen. I can't even really blame her now, but at the time... It was bad. Made me feel really bad. And Aspen had the same look on her face."

"It wasn't your fucking fault," I grit out.

"I know. But I was living proof."

"What about King? You said you were nine. He's twenty years older, right? He surely wouldn't have blamed a kid for his dad's infidelity."

"I wasn't brave enough to watch him walk past."

Wasn't brave enough. It's like every sentence she speaks rips another piece of my soul.

I focus on her hands around mine. "What happened after? How'd you end up becoming close with them?"

"I'm not," she whispers as her fingers tighten their grip on mine. "After the funeral, my mom got worse. She was a user. Different drugs. Different people. Whatever she could use to pretend life wasn't real. We moved apartments a lot, but when I turned fifteen, King showed up at our front door."

"Was that the first time you'd seen him since the funeral?"

"Yeah," Val confirms. "And he was there to tell me that my

dad had left me in his will. And that I'd be attending a private high school and that it was all paid for."

"Those aren't the actions of a man who doesn't care," I tell her quietly, hating that she thinks neither of her parents loved her.

"You're probably right," she concedes without conviction, and I have to wonder how intimidating a thirty-five-year-old King Vass would have been to a fifteen-year-old Valentine. "But it just made my life worse. Because my mom resented me even more."

"How?" I seriously can't understand this bitch.

"Because my mom got herself pregnant with me thinking she'd be set for life. And she kinda was. He paid her rent and gave her an allowance for food and stuff my whole life. Until he died and the money dried up, and my mom was still stuck *feeding another greedy mouth*." The way she says the last line tells me she's heard it said before. "So when King came to tell us about the tuition, my mom lost it. Demanding that she should get that money. And how come King couldn't just write her a check for the total amount of the tuition and let me go to public school. He obviously didn't do that. And even though he was nice to me, I could feel how much he hated my mom. He scared me."

"Did you go to the school?"

"I did. And eventually, my mom just got used to it. Or forgot about it. But she mostly left me to my own devices. Until I turned eighteen."

I almost don't even want to ask. I know the answer isn't going to be a birthday party. "What happened when you turned eighteen?"

"King came back and told me that my college was paid for, too." My eyes have fully adjusted, so I watch as Val blinks toward the ceiling. "He also told me my dad had left me seventy-five thousand dollars in a trust. That I'd get twenty-five thousand when I turned nineteen, twenty-five thousand when I turned twenty-one, and twenty-five thousand when I turned twenty-five. I know that might not sound like a lot to you, but for me... it was life changing."

"It is a lot. And smart of him to spread it out."

Val huffs. "Funny, my mom didn't agree. She wanted seventy-five in a check written to her, right then and there. King told her it didn't work that way. And that the money belonged to me, not her, and she had no say or access to it. He told me that he set up an account for me at a bank my mom wasn't a customer of, and since I was over eighteen, she couldn't access it."

"Smart man."

"He was nice to me." Sadness fills her voice. "He gave me his phone number and told me to tell him when I got into college and that he'd arrange the tuition payments, just like he'd done for high school. And he did."

"You say that, but why does it feel like he *wasn't* nice to you?"

Val shakes her head. "He was. I think he knew how shitty my mom was and felt bad for me. We weren't, like, friends or anything, but he never seemed bothered by my existence."

I grind my teeth. "Angel."

"I just mean that he didn't actively hate me. Like our moms did."

I close my eyes. "Jesus."

This poor fucking girl. Not being actively hated is her gauge for niceness.

Val had nothing to do with her shitty parents' actions, and yet all the adults that should've been protecting her put the blame on her tiny shoulders.

"I got into a college in the Twin Cities and found an on-campus job for the summer that would allow me to move into a dorm early."

I slide my eyes open to look at her profile. "My smart girl."

"It felt really good to finally feel safe."

Fucking fuck me.

Needing her closer, I push my hand through her grip and hook my arm around her waist.

Valentine rolls to face me, and I pull her into my body, slipping my other arm between her and the mattress.

Her hands are between our chests, her little fists pressing against my bare skin over my heart.

I want to rip her childhood apart.

But I can't, so I just tuck her head under my chin and wrap both arms around her in a hug, keeping her where she is. "You'll always be safe with me," I promise her.

"I know," she breathes. And her acceptance settles inside me.

"Did she leave you alone once you moved?" I have a sense of dread for what must still be coming.

"Mostly. The month after I moved out, she met a guy and followed him to Florida. I think she lived with him for a while because I didn't hear from her for a few months." Tension builds in Val's shoulders. "King reached out at the start of the school year. He'd seen I'd taken a summer course while I was working. Told me I did a good job. And then reminded me that I'd be getting my first payout in a couple months. As though I could forget." She scoffs. "He told me not to spend it all at once. And when I told him I was thinking about getting a car, he said to send what I was looking at to him first. It felt a little overbearing at the time, since no one had ever been that involved before, but I was grateful to have someone to help me. It's not like I knew what I was doing."

"Did you buy a car?" I try to picture what nineteen-year-old Valentine would buy. Something practical, I'm sure.

But Val shakes her head. "My mom called me on my birthday and asked me to come visit her in Florida." A rumble of anger vibrates my chest, and Val flattens her hand against me. "I thought the worst, too, at first. But she never mentioned the money. And I wanted... It was so dumb, but I just wanted to believe she wasn't awful. So I told her when the semester was over, I'd visit."

I hug her a little harder, my own throat starting to itch.

"That was the first thing I spent any of the money on. A plane ticket to see my mom."

Val is quiet for a long moment.

"What happened?" I ask against her hair.

"We got into a huge fight. The guy she'd followed down there ditched her, and she said she needed some money to get by. And I told her no. I told her no because I was hurt. I wanted her to want me around, but she only asked me to visit because she wanted my money."

I press my lips to the top of Val's head; the theme of being tricked and used isn't lost on me. "You didn't owe her anything, Valentine. You did the right thing."

"She called me all sorts of names, but that was the first time I ever shouted back." Her body starts to tremble. "I packed up my bag to go, didn't even care that I'd be wasting money on a hotel if I left, but then she convinced me to stay. Said she'd drop it and that we could go out for breakfast in the morning. So I stayed."

It falls together. Before she tells me, it all falls together.

Her mom died when she was nineteen.

I curl my fingers into her sides. "Valentine."

"She killed herself that night." The tears finally fill her voice.

"Angel." I kiss her head again.

"It was a shitty little one-bedroom apartment. And she told me I could have her bedroom and she'd sleep on the couch." Her fingertips press into me. "I figured she'd just drink until she passed out, so I locked myself in her room and cried myself to sleep. When I got up in the morning, I found her sitting at the little dining table. Slumped in her seat. With an empty bottle of vodka and an empty bottle of painkillers prescribed to someone else."

I can't imagine. I cannot fucking imagine.

"Was she already gone?" I have to ask.

Val nods against me. "I didn't realize at first. I thought she was asleep. But when I touched her shoulder... She was stiff."

"Jesus Christ." I stare over the top of Val's head. I know exactly what happens to dead bodies, so I know exactly what teenage Val would've seen. "Did she leave a note?"

"Not in the way you mean."

I close my eyes. "What did she leave?"

"Her stack of bills."

"I fucking hate her," I snap.

And I swear Val laughs a little.

"I'm serious." I hook my leg over Val's thigh. The hug doesn't feel like enough. "If she wasn't already dead, I'd kill her myself. You didn't deserve that. Tell me you knew that you didn't deserve that."

Her hand flexes against my chest. It's all she can do with how tight I'm holding her.

"A part of me knew it. I knew she was miserable, and no matter what I did, she'd always be miserable. But it was still hard, ya know? Because she set those there for me to find." I feel her shake her head. "I'd been used to being on my own, but once she died... I really was."

"I hate her," I repeat.

Val's exhale tickles my chest hair. "The second funeral I ever went to was my mom's. And it turns out everyone else that knew her hated her, too. Because it was just me and the priest. Or, well, funeral director, I think."

"You had a funeral?" I furrow my brows. "Should've just fed her to the alligators."

Valentine snorts. "First, gross. Second, I was a stupid nineteen-year-old. I thought you had to have a funeral."

"You planned it?" I can't hide the shock in my voice. But I don't know why I'm surprised. Like she said, there was no one else in her mom's life that would've done it.

"Unintentionally. I called 9-1-1 when I found her, and the ball just kinda started rolling on its own. Her body was brought to a funeral home. The director called me and asked what I wanted to do with the remains and if I wanted to do the service in their hall. I just kept answering questions, and before I knew it, there was a funeral." I make a mental note to look up this funeral director because if he's still alive, I'm putting him in his own incinerator. "And then her landlord was demanding payment for rent she was behind on and that I deal with moving all her stuff out." I add *landlord* to my list.

"You paid for all that, didn't you?"

"It was the second thing I spent my money on," she admits, and I curse again. "I was worried I'd get in trouble with King over spending it on my mom. But he never said anything, so I figured he didn't know."

"Wait." I pull back a little. "What do you mean?"

She leans her head back to look up at me. "What do you mean what do I mean?"

"You said you were at the funeral alone. Why wasn't King there?"

Val tries to lift a shoulder, but I'm holding her too tightly. "Why would he be? I didn't expect him and Aspen to actually come when I invited them. Their family didn't exactly like my mom."

"So fucking what? He's your brother!"

She shakes her head. "No, Dominic, it's okay."

"It's not fucking okay. Don't make excuses for him. You told him your mom fucking died, and he left you to deal with her suicide alone." I'm mad. I'm so fucking mad. My sweet, precious little Valentine didn't have a single person to count on.

"Dom." Her tone is soft as she tries to comfort me. "It wasn't like that. I don't even think he knew how she died."

"You didn't tell him when you told him about the funeral?"

"Well." She dips her chin so she's back to looking at my chest. "I left a message."

"Say that again," I growl.

"I only had his office number. I left a message with his assistant."

"And he never called you back." I don't ask it. She, at nineteen, left a message for her brother telling him her final living parent had died, and he never even called her back.

He's going to pay for that.

"Don't be mad at him." She tries to defend her piece-of-shit brother.

"None of that is okay, Valentine." I don't care if he has the power of the free world at his back. I'm going to hurt him.

"It's in the past. We're okay now."

"If you were okay, tonight wouldn't have been your first birthday party." I stroke a hand up her back. "What happened after the funeral?"

"I came home and went back to school. And that next summer, King invited me over to have dinner with him and Aspen."

"And you went?"

"I went."

"Why?" I can't imagine letting all that go.

"Because I wanted a family."

My eyes close.

I fucking hate them all.

Valentine deserves a life full of gold, and all she got was ashes.

"Ask me about the third funeral I went to," she whispers.

"I don't want to," I say truthfully.

Val moves her arm from between us so she can wrap it around my waist, hugging me back. "The third funeral I ever went to was for your cousin."

I breathe through the ache behind my eyes.

And I hate myself the same way I hate King.

That funeral was the day she woke up with a tattooed finger.

It was the day after I revealed my plan to join The Alliance and destroyed her heart.

It was one more horrible fucking experience for her to go through alone.

And I was the one who did it to her.

I remember the way she paled when I told her we were going to a funeral. And the urge to apologize, for the first time in twenty years, grips at my throat.

But then Val continues. "It was everything I've always dreamed a family could be. Could mean." She presses her forehead against my sternum, and I slide my hand up to grip the back of her neck. "I was terrified to go."

"Val—"

She cuts me off. "I want to thank you for letting me be a part of that. It doesn't change the other funerals I've been to, but it proved to me that it doesn't always have to be like it was."

This fucking woman.

"It will never be like it was. Not for you," I promise her. "We grieve together."

"I know." Her lips press against my skin. "I like your family."

Her muscles loosen under my hold. "They're your family now, too," I say quietly because I think she's falling asleep as we talk.

"Only if you keep me."

I barely hear her.

"I'll keep you forever."

Her tired fingers grip my sides. "But now you know."

"Know what?" We're both whispering now.

"That I'm not valuable."

I'm not valuable.

Her words hit me with such force I can't breathe.

I hate the people who made her feel this way.

I curl around her, trying to protect her from her own past, her own awful emotions.

She's so fucking valuable.

She thinks because King is a shitty-ass brother to her that I'll just... what? Return her? That I suddenly wouldn't want her anymore?

I press my nose into her hair and inhale her scent.

Of course that's what she thinks. Every member of her family has either betrayed her, ignored her, or left her.

I inhale again.

Not me.

Never again.

"You're worth more than everything I have," I tell her a moment too late, as her body relaxes fully into sleep.

I stay that way, holding my wife, for the next hour as I stare into the distance.

I fill my lungs with her.

I don't shy away from the story she told; I replay it. I do my best to understand how she's felt all these years. I listen to what she said she wanted.

And then I contemplate if there's anything that's *too far* when it comes to making sure I can keep her.

There isn't.

So if my wife wants a family, I'm going to give her one.

Carefully, I extricate myself from the bed and silently move into the bathroom. I shut the door to block the light, then go into the closet and open the safe I have hidden in the back wall.

I don't hesitate. I just reach in and take out the three rectangular sheets of pills.

This is how I keep her.

And how I give her everything she craves.

I open the drawer where I know she keeps hers and replace the two backup sheets with two from my hand, and then I pick up the one she's currently using and pop out a matching number of pills on the last sheet from my safe.

I let the water run, washing away the evidence, while I make sure to put the last packet down exactly how I found it.

Then, with a feeling of rightness filling my chest, I put Val's real birth control pills into the safe. And lock it.

CHAPTER 54

Val

"Oh hey, I keep forgetting to ask you!" Bri stops me before I hang up our call. "Are you coming tonight?"

"Uh, coming to what?"

"The Christmas party."

I shift my position, crossing my feet where they are on my desk. "What Christmas party?"

Bri put this call on our work calendars, and I thought maybe we had a project that overlapped, but she just wanted to fill me in on some gossip about a guy from another branch who's going through a messy divorce.

She groans into the phone. "Did you seriously not get an invite to the company party?"

"No, but maybe they only sent it to locals this year, and I just became a local."

"No, it's because Tosh in HR is a lazy bitch."

I snort out a laugh. "I'll take your word for it."

"Alright, well, it starts tonight at eight. It's a whole building thing again, so it's still in the atrium on the fourth floor. But I've heard there's a decent buffet this year."

"Oh, a buffet," I say sarcastically.

"Yes, you rich twat, a buffet. The thing we peasants flock to because we like free food."

"You're not a peasant." I laugh.

She ignores me. "Speaking of your life being better than mine, bring that handsome-as-fuck husband with you."

I shake my head, having seen the photos she sent me from her elopement last week. "Don't act like your new hubby isn't attractive." He really is. Just in a boy-next-door kind of way, not a tatted-gangster kind of way.

Movement at my open door startles me, and I let out a little scream.

Standing against my doorframe, Dom glares at me, arms crossed and eyes narrowed. "Who are you calling attractive?"

Bri says something to me at the same time, but I miss it.

"You scared the shit out of me," I tell him, dropping my feet off the desk to ground myself.

"Is that him?" Bri's excited voice cuts through my sudden adrenaline.

"Yes," I tell her, keeping my eyes on Dom. "It's my overbearing husband."

He lifts a brow.

"Tell him thank you for the sushi." Bri swoons.

I roll my eyes because I picture her batting her eyes as she says it. "No. And don't try to flirt with my man, or I won't bring him with."

She snickers, and I can see Dom fighting against the urge to smirk.

I don't really want to go to a stupid work party tonight. But I haven't left the house since my birthday party, and it's been almost a week. Plus, Dom has been... different. So maybe it'll be good for both of us.

He hasn't been *different bad*. Arguably, he's been even more caring. Constantly feeding me. Gifting me things I don't need nearly every day. But he hasn't touched me *like that*.

I don't know if he thinks I'm too emotionally fragile or what the deal is, but maybe a fun night out can solve the problem.

And I'm not going to overthink wanting Dom to touch me. He's my husband. I'm his wife. And I'm trying to be all-in.

"Are you free tonight?" I ask Dominic, the phone still against my ear.

"Oh please, oh please..." Bri chants.

"For what and when?"

"God, even his voice is hot," Bri groans.

"Shut up." I laugh into the phone, then rotate it away from my mouth. "Apparently my company Christmas party is tonight. I know it's last minute since everyone forgot to tell me. I can go alone if you aren't free." I add that last sentence to push him.

And it works.

"I'll meet you there."

Bri squeals, and I know Dom can hear it because the side of his mouth finally pulls up.

CHAPTER 55

Dom

"So..." Rob starts as the four of us step into the elevator in Val's office building. "What's the plan?"

I situate myself so I'll be the first one out when the doors open on the fourth floor.

"The plan is that we're going to a fucking Christmas party."

We're all on edge. Someone did a drive-by shooting at a storage facility I own on the edge of the city. No one was hurt. And I don't have anything of value there. But it's the principle. And it's fucking juvenile. And we're all getting real sick of not having a target for our anger.

"Okay, but do you want us to pretend we work here? Or are we watching Val?" Rob lifts his hands when I glare at him. "We'll just prowl the room. Got it."

The other two men I brought wisely stay silent.

My fingers itch to punch something, but instead, I button my jacket and smooth out the charcoal-gray suit over my crisp white shirt.

I know Val likes being able to see the outline of my tattoos. And even though she's testing my patience by not responding to my last text—when I messaged to say I'd be a little late—I want her attention on me. So I dressed with her in mind.

The elevator doors slide open, and we're assailed with festive music that grates on my already raw nerves.

I should've said no to this.

I also should've asked more questions because there are a lot of people here. I know the Chicago branch of her company has less than twenty people, so this must be a multi-company party.

My men fan out, and I step into the throng.

We're a handful of stories up on a mezzanine floor with one side entirely open to the twenty-story atrium looking out over the river. A bar's been set up over to my right. And to my left is a DJ stand blasting Christmas music.

This is too many corporate douchebags for the mood I'm in.

I exhale.

I'm gonna get my wife another job. She shouldn't be wasting her time and talent around these morons.

I stop halfway through the crowd and let my gaze move over the people, searching for the only one I want to talk to.

And then I see her.

She's across the space, near the railing overlooking the atrium, and her side is to me, showing me her profile.

But I know it's her.

I'll always know it's her.

Target in sight, I move through the crowd quickly.

Having her so close fills me with a mix of relief and tension.

Relief that she's here, and I can see she's okay. Tension because there are so many other people here, too. And unless we're alone in a room together, I'll always be worried about her safety.

People move across my path, blocking her from my view, then revealing bits and pieces of her person.

When I register the splash of yellow, my steps slow.

Because just yards away from me is my beautiful wife. And she's wearing the same exact outfit she was wearing in the airport when we first met.

I glance down at her feet and feel myself smile.

So not exactly the same. Tonight she's wearing a pair of her wedge heels rather than tennis shoes. But it's the same brightly colored wrap dress that doesn't look at all like something you'd wear to a Christmas party. The same simple jewelry. The same ponytail.

But my newfound calmness slips away when I notice her posture. It's all off.

Her back is ramrod straight. And she's clutching her drink in front of her body, her elbows pressed hard against her sides.

It's a defensive posture.

And my wife should never be in a defensive fucking posture.

I close the distance between me and my Valentine in four steps.

Her eyes catch mine a second before I'm at her side, and satisfaction fills my chest when I see her relax at my presence.

My fucking Valentine.

I reach out and grip the back of her neck, feeling her relax even more.

"Dominic," she sighs.

"Angel." I hold her still as I lean in and press my lips to hers. It's chaste...ish.

I pull back enough to look her in the eyes, the gold flecks of her irises glinting at me under the party lights. "You good?"

She gives me a little nod, rolling her lips together.

"Why didn't you reply to my text?" I ask.

Her eyes dart to look past me, but I flex my fingers against her soft skin, keeping her attention on me.

Her throat works under my thumb. "I left my phone in my purse upstairs, in the office."

"You'll keep it on you from now on," I tell her.

"Yes, Dom." The exhale of her words dances across my lips.

My eyes slowly close, and as they open, I turn to face the man standing in front of my wife.

I didn't miss him when I was approaching.

I didn't miss the fact that he's the one making my woman feel uncomfortable.

And standing to my full height, I'm tempted to slap his fucking face.

"Who are you?" My tone is dangerous, even though I already know who this is.

He holds out his hand, his inferior suit bunching on his weak frame. "I'm Mr. Ritz."

My right hand is gripping the back of Valentine's neck, and I'm not letting go of her to touch him.

"Ricky." I greet him using his first name. And the side of my mouth lifts the smallest amount when he visibly starts. "I've read a lot about you."

He sort of chuckles, like I'm joking or making a play on words. But I'm not doing either.

If he thinks I'd let my wife work in an office with a man I haven't thoroughly vetted, he's dead wrong.

While Ricky stands there uncomfortably, I take Val's drink out of her hands and bring it to my lips.

It looks like a whiskey and Coke, and after today, I could use a couple.

The sweetness hits my nose before the flavor coats my tongue, and a full smile pulls across my mouth as I swallow.

I look down at my wife. "Root beer?"

Her eyes are on my smile. "I didn't want to drink without you here."

I slide my hand up the length of her neck, then back down. "Well, I'm here now." I let her see me looking at her dress. "How long do we need to stay?"

A real smile finally reaches her features. "I need to introduce you to Bri."

"The girl from Vegas?"

Val's eyes move up to meet mine. "Yeah. Did I tell you her name already?"

I tip my head from side to side, then go with the truth. "I saw her name on your group text."

"Group text...?"

"You were a little sleepy, so I replied for you."

She narrows her eyes as she remembers. How they'd told her to check in if she was going to be banging me all weekend. And how I was the one who actually replied to that text since Val was literally unconscious.

My shoulder lifts in a half shrug. "Didn't want them worrying."

Val's mouth quirks to the side. "I'm not sure if I should thank you or slap you."

I flex my fingers on her neck. "I'll let you do both."

Val rolls her eyes. And I feel the victory of it in my soul. Because I just referred to our wedding night, and she rolled her eyes. She didn't clam up. She didn't cry. She rolled her beautiful eyes at me like it was silly and not a nightmare.

"Go get your friend." I press a kiss to her forehead, then let her go.

Val turns away from her boss to leave while I turn back toward him, amazed he just stood here the whole time like a fucking idiot.

But before I acknowledge him again, I make eye contact with Rob across the room, then raise two fingers and make two different gestures. The first tells him to follow Val. The second tells my other men to converge on my location.

When I look at Ricky Ritz, his eyes are darting between my face and my hand, probably wondering what I just put in motion.

I stay silent, just fucking praying that he'll give me an excuse.

It takes him three seconds.

"You've really, uh, left your mark on her, huh?" He lifts his left hand and wiggles his ring finger.

I take a step toward him, and he takes a step back.

"Do you know who I am?" I ask, my voice calm as I take another step.

"Y-yeah." He takes another retreating step.

I keep advancing.

"But do you really know who I am?"

The man glances around as he continues to stumble back.

When he doesn't answer, I take a quicker step, closing more distance between us. "Answer me."

"I-I know who you are." His eyes are wide now.

Val's boss takes another step back, only stopping when he bumps into the railing, the last barrier between us and the lobby four floors below.

I step closer still, putting my body only inches from his. "Then you must know that looking at *my wife* is a bad fucking idea."

"I didn't—I-I wasn't," he stammers.

"You were." I take the final step, which presses my chest to his. "And I don't like it."

"S-sorry. Sorry." He tries to hold his hands up in supplication, but he has to hold his arms out to the side because there isn't room between us.

I lean forward, forcing him to lean back.

His arms windmill once before he grips the railing by his hips.

My fingers press against the metal in my pocket, but that's all I allow of myself.

I look past him, over his shoulder and down the four stories to the marble-floored lobby below.

"I don't like you, Ricky." I move my eyes back to his and lean in a little farther. Our bodies are flush, my bulk working to both push him back but also hold him in place.

"I'm sorry," he pleads.

"I don't want your apology," I growl.

"W-what do you want?" His hands grapple with the railing, his palms probably slick with sweat.

"I want your brains splattered on that floor." I nod to the drop behind him.

His hands jerk up from the railing to grab at my jacket.

But my men are at my side. And they each take a hold of one of his arms, shoving them back down.

They do it smoothly. Quickly. But I know people are watching.

And I don't give a single fuck who sees. Because this man made my wife feel uncomfortable.

"Here's what's gonna happen," I tell him, leaning just a little farther into him, arching his back out over nothing. "You're going to quit this job. Tonight."

"But—"

I snap my teeth together, inches from his face, and he shuts the fuck up.

"You're going to quit tonight," I repeat, slower this time. "And while you're quitting, I'm going to take my wife home, and we're going to have a chat. And if I find out that you've ever laid a finger on her or made a comment to her about anything other than work, I'm going to smash your ribs through your heart." Ricky's body is trembling against mine, the proper amount of fear finally setting in. "Do you have any questions?"

He shakes his head.

"Do you believe I'm a man of my word?"

He nods.

"Good." I slowly straighten up, and my men let go of his arms. "Now get the fuck out of here so people can enjoy their party."

I step back, and Ricky Ritz hugs his arms around himself as he leans forward, away from the railing.

I lower my face to his. "Now."

He opens his mouth, but instead of replying, he darts away through the crowd.

CHAPTER 56

Val

"Um, actually, I don't think I want to meet him. I'm going to go find us some dessert," Bri's husband mutters before stepping away from us.

"Chicken!" Bri calls after him.

I want to laugh at their exchange, but I'm too busy trying to keep my tongue in my mouth.

I didn't know I was attracted to over-the-top, brutish behavior, but it turns out I am.

I really am.

I have to press my thighs together under my dress as my boss scurries away from Dominic.

Whatever was said between them was clearly enough to scare Mr. Ritz half to death. Obviously, I can't work for him anymore after this. Maybe he can pretend nothing happened, but all I'll see if I look at him are Dominic's broad shoulders and the way it made me feel all hot inside.

As Dominic says something to two men who are clearly his, I glance at the people around them.

Dom never raised his voice. And the movements between him and Mr. Ritz were subtle, but the interaction didn't go unnoticed.

But no one is shouting. And no one even has their phones out to record the incident.

No one cares.

Or maybe no one here wants to do anything to cross Dominic Gonzalez.

More than one set of eyes turn my way, and they're looking at me because I'm his.

And he's mine.

It only takes a second after Dom stops talking to his men before he finds my gaze.

And just like that, I'm over this party. I want to go home and be alone together.

Dominic's chest expands, and my eyes drop to look at his chest through his white button-down shirt. I wonder if I can convince him to step into the shower fully dressed. Just so I can see the material cling to his inked body.

My eyes lower as he moves closer.

And I picture how his *Til Death* tattoo must look underneath his clothing while he walks like that. His hips twisting with each step. The movement pulling his skin tight over his muscles.

And then I think about the designs that trail down his legs.

My mouth starts to water, and I lift my root beer, taking a sip in an attempt to quench my new thirst.

I know what I want for Christmas. And it's a calendar full of nude photos of Dominic. Hard and ready and for my eyes only.

Bri snaps me out of my daydream when she smooths out the skirt of her red dress next to me, a much more appropriate color for tonight than my yellow. Except Dominic is looking at me like he wants to consume me, so I'm feeling like I made the right choice in wearing this.

He stops before me, and I can't stop my smile. "Everything okay over there?"

Dom inclines his chin. "Of course. Though it does seem as though you'll be getting a new boss."

"Oh?"

"Something about him quitting tonight and never coming back." Dom's mouth pulls to the side, and he gives a small shake of his head. "Never can tell with people, can you?"

I raise my brows and similarly shake my head. "So weird."

His eyes stay on mine. "You look perfect."

This man.

I twist from side to side, letting the skirt dance around my knees. "This old thing?"

Dom's lids lower, and I'm suddenly afraid he might just sling me over his shoulder and carry me out of here like a warrior with his prize.

I hold my hand out toward Bri, who has been silently standing at my side. "Dominic, this is Bri. My friend." I tack on that last part and hope it sounds sincere. Because I really do consider Bri a friend now, and I want Dom to know that she's not just some work acquaintance. "Bri, this is Dom."

"Pleasure to meet you." Dom holds out his large hand, and Bri takes it. "Any friend of Valentine's is a friend of mine."

When I look over at Bri, I expect her to be beaming, but the look on her face is so serious.

"Thank you." And her voice is just as serious.

Dom nods his head, then lets her hand go, and I realize serious is probably the right tone. I think Dominic just offered her the protection of the mafia, and she accepted it.

"I hear congratulations are in order as well," Dom says to Bri, even as he holds his arm out for me, and I tuck myself into his side. "Is your new husband here?"

Bri smiles this time. "He is. But I think he got a little too intimidated because he's trying to hide over by the Christmas tree."

Dom huffs a little laugh and tips his head. "Looks like my man found him anyway."

We all turn just in time to see Rob patting Bri's husband on the back, startling him so much he drops the cupcake he was trying to take a bite of.

"Did you want to hit up the buffet before we go?" Dom squeezes my side.

I narrow my eyes up at him. "How much of our conversation were you eavesdropping on today?"

He looks down at me with zero guilt in his expression. "Learn to pay attention to your surroundings and you'd know the answer to that."

Bri tries to cover her laugh with a cough.

"For your information, we ate when we got here," I tell him.

"Good." Dominic turns to Bri. "It was nice to meet you." Then, without another word to anyone, he guides me toward the elevators.

The doors open right as we get there, and the two men who were holding my boss's arms at the railing are waiting inside. One of them holds my jacket and purse.

Well, that's convenient.

Rob steps into the elevator behind us, and the five of us ride down to the main level together while I pull my jacket on and take my purse from the man I don't know.

Just as the cab slows to a stop, four phones sound with notifications. Mine is the only one that stays silent.

Dominic pulls his phone out of his pocket, and I look up, watching his expression harden.

There's no use asking if something is wrong.

Something is.

Dom slides his phone into his pocket and circles an arm around my shoulders while the elevator doors slide open. "We're bringing Mrs. Gonzalez home. Then we're going to the shop."

Dom has never called me that before. Not like this. And it scares me.

Rob steps out first, his head moving back and forth as he moves through the lobby.

Then it's Dom, with me at his side. And the other two men behind us.

I hug my purse to my front and move with them, their long strides making me walk faster than I'm used to.

Rob steps through the front doors and onto the sidewalk first.

I'm not sure where we're going since the parking ramp is on the other side of the building, but then I see a large black SUV idling at the curb in front of the building, with two matte black cars in front of it and two more behind.

A man jumps out of the SUV, circling around to meet us.

"We're going to the condo first," Dom tells the man, who simply nods once, then jogs to the car directly in front of the SUV.

I continue to let Dominic guide me forward, only pausing for him to open the rear door of the large vehicle.

I climb in, and when Dominic starts to get in behind me, I scoot over to the middle of the bench seat.

Rob gets in on the other side of me, and the two men I don't know take the front.

"Seat belt, Angel." Dom's voice is soft, and I don't realize I'm shaking until I try and fail to comply.

Dominic turns toward me, reaching across my body to close his fingers over mine.

His hands are steady as he helps me.

The click fills the car, and I see a strobe of light out the windshield, which I think is our driver flashing his brights. Then the caravan pulls away from the curb.

"Did you come here with all these guys?" I try to keep my voice quiet as I ask Dominic.

He literally just got that text a moment before we exited the building. There's no way they'd have been able to get here this quickly if something just happened.

"Yeah, Shorty." Dom places his hand on my knee.

I want to ask more, like why he's traveling in a five-car lineup, but the tension in the vehicle is so thick I swear I could reach up and touch it. So I stay quiet.

We maneuver through the streets in a row, and I feel bad that all these guys are driving to our place just to drop me off when they clearly have somewhere else they need to be.

But I have a feeling that offering to take an Uber home wouldn't go over well.

And honestly, if something bad is happening, I'm glad I'm surrounded by big, scary men.

We start to slow, and I look up to see we're approaching our building.

I unbuckle, but Dom doesn't open the door right away when we stop.

He waits. And I watch as four men, the passengers from each of the other four vehicles, line up between us and the front door of the building. Facing away from each other, their backs creating a hallway of sorts.

"With me." Dominic must direct the command at Rob because I hear his door open at the same time Dom opens his.

I'm careful to keep the skirt of my dress down as I slide off the seat. And when my feet touch the ground, Dom takes my hand, and we walk across the wide sidewalk.

It's late enough that there aren't a ton of pedestrians around, but there are definitely some. And they're watching. But Dom's men ignore them, so I do, too.

I know we're making quite the scene, but if it keeps me from dying from some invisible threat, I'm okay with it.

Rob follows Dom and me inside, but the other four men stay where they are.

Phil is seated behind the front desk when we walk past, but everything feels too serious to break the silence, so I just raise my hand as we pass.

When Rob follows us onto the elevator, my paranoia creeps up another notch. Dom must be really worried if he's having someone come all the way to the door with us.

The ride up is silent, and when the doors open, Rob presses the button that will keep them that way.

With Dominic's palm on the small of my back, I walk toward

our door. And since I'm closest, I place my hand on the reader next to the door, but Dom reaches out to open it after it unlocks.

I step inside, then turn to face Dominic. "Be careful," I tell him, and at the same time he says, "Stay inside."

Dom grips my chin and lowers his face to mine. "Be a good wife and stay inside. I'll be fine." He presses his lips to mine.

Then he's gone, the door locking behind him.

CHAPTER 57

When I step back into our home, fury is still boiling under my skin. Another business was hit, and this time someone got hurt.

With the lights off, I cross the great room.

But I don't go upstairs, I go down the lower hall to my gym.

Because they didn't kill my man. But they drew blood.

We'll track them down soon.

And we'll take our revenge.

But we don't have them right now.

And I'm too angry to be gentle.

CHAPTER 58

Val

MY BARE FEET ARE SILENT ON THE STAIRS.

I've waited.

I waited for an hour after I heard Dominic come home. But he didn't come to bed. He didn't come upstairs at all.

He's alone—I'm certain of that much—which means he's unhurt.

I keep my hand on the railing until I reach the main floor.

I know I'm still naive compared to Aspen—and probably all the women in Dominic's family. Hell, I googled *what is the mafia* just weeks ago. But I know enough to know it's dangerous. And even though my first day here was spent attending a funeral, I don't think I really understood it.

Tonight, I understood.

I've felt sick to my stomach with worry since Dom left me here—alone. And I need to see him. Knowing he's back isn't enough. I need to see him.

I feel like I'm doing something wrong as I walk down the dark hallway, but this is my home, too. And I'm not trying to spy. I'm just trying to find my husband.

Light comes from behind the cracked-open door that leads to the gym.

I pause outside it, listening to the rhythmic sound coming from inside.

Placing my palm on the door, I hesitate for only a moment, then push it open.

And catch my breath.

Dominic is in the center of the room, pounding his fists into a large punching bag suspended from the ceiling.

Only half the lights are on, casting shadows across the floor, but it's the man himself that holds my gaze. Because he's magnificent.

His suit coat is lying on the floor, as if tossed aside while Dominic strode through the room. And his white shirt is still on but unbuttoned, the open sides moving with him as his body shifts and turns with each punch.

And his body.

Jesus.

His shirt is soaked through with sweat, making the white material transparent over his back and arms, showing me every ripple of muscle. Every inch of inked skin.

And I want him.

I want him so bad that I start across the room.

Dominic is facing away from me, but in front of us is the wall of windows, and with the darkness outside and lights on inside, it's become a mirror, alerting Dom to my approach.

He drops his arms to his sides while his chest heaves.

He doesn't turn to face me, just stares at my reflection in the glass.

My yellow dress swishes with my steps, my loose hair lying across my shoulders.

And I don't say anything.

I just circle around the punching bag until I'm standing in front of him.

He's quiet. Just breathing heavily. But I can see it in my husband's eyes. He's tired. And angry.

And I want to give him something.

I step closer and press my hands to his body, parting his already open shirt so I can take in his strong chest, his muscular stomach.

I slide my hands lower.

When I reach his belt, Dom's hands move, grasping my wrists.

And that's when I see the blood.

It's his own. His own split knuckles from slamming his bare fists into tough leather over and over again for an hour.

And my heart clenches for him.

This man carries the weight of so many people on his back.

I know I can never carry that burden for him. But maybe I can help ease it.

With my mouth.

He doesn't remove his hands, but he doesn't stop me either as I undo his belt.

And he doesn't stop me when I unbutton his pants or when I pull the zipper down.

And he lets go of my wrists when I sink to my knees, allowing me to drag his pants and boxers down with me.

My fingers graze over his newest tattoo in the process, and I stare at the base of his already swollen cock. Which is still growing.

I wet my lips, and his length bobs in reaction.

He's sweaty. Still breathing heavily. His dick is inches from my face. And I'm so turned on I'm going to start dripping onto the floor.

I pull at the material pooling around Dominic's bare feet, and he lifts one foot, then the other, so I can push it away.

Looking down at me, Dominic peels his shirt off his shoulders, tossing that aside as well.

Neck to ankles, his tattoos make him look like a mythical soldier. A man made solely for battle. A protector.

A man made for me.

I shift up onto my knees so my mouth is level with his hips. But before I close the distance between us, I reach down and untie my dress, unwrapping the sunshine material until it's hanging open at my sides. Exposing my front to Dominic and the fact that I have nothing on underneath.

His next exhale is audible. And before he can stop me, or decide he wants something else, I lean forward and wrap my lips around the head of his cock.

We both moan.

And wetness floods my center.

I grab the base of his dick at the same moment he digs his hands into my hair.

His hold is tight, and it's like he's trying to stop me from taking him deeper. But I want this. I want to do this for him.

I stick my tongue out, licking the underside of his length, tasting as much as I can as I lean against his hold.

I need more.

Dominic lets out another guttural groan, but instead of pulling my head back, he drags me forward, letting me—making me—take him deeper.

I suck. And lick. And make sounds as I swallow as much of him as I can.

His tip bumps against the back of my throat, and my body reacts, my muscles contracting in revolt.

But instead of feeling sick over gagging on his cock, I feel... sexy.

Proud that I'm trying.

His hold on my hair loosens, letting me pull away and pick my own pace.

I try again, my hand still on the base of his cock, holding him steady as I slide my lips down his smooth, thick dick.

I blink when he hits that spot again. Tears form as a bodily reaction, nothing else.

And I stare at his vow, stare at his promise, as I take him just a tiny bit deeper.

My nipples are aching to be touched. And my pussy is begging to be filled. But right now, with Dominic's cock in my mouth, I feel more settled than I have in a long time.

He's mine.

Til Death.

And I'm his.

I pull back, sucking on his tip, swallowing the beads of precum that leak from his cock and inhaling the scent of his cologne mixed with his sweat.

I want this life.

My free hand reaches up to cup his heavy balls, and I lean in, taking him to the back of my throat and pushing through—just another inch.

CHAPTER 59

Dom

Valentine gags around my cock, and I can't take it anymore.

I need to thrust. Need to pound myself into her hole. Any one of them will do. But I can't throat fuck her.

Not yet.

Not when I need to fill that unprotected pussy with my cum.

I jerk my hips back, dislodging myself from her mouth.

But I don't let her get up. I drop down to meet her on the floor, shoving her onto her back.

Val's legs automatically spread, and the shine of her slickness coats her thighs.

This is the first time she's come to me for sex. And she's come to me soaking wet.

I grip her knees and shove them even wider.

My bloodied hands are a contrast to the soft, pale skin of her inner thighs. Further proof of my corruption of her life.

Val's head lifts from the floor, and I know she's looking at my hands, too.

"Can you teach me to like it?" Her whispered words snap my gaze up to meet hers. "The pain."

Slowly, I shake my head as I slide my hands higher up her thighs. "I'll never hurt you, Angel."

My hands slip up her hips, up her sides.

I rub my thumbs over her nipples as I shift myself between her spread legs.

I slide my hands up her chest. "I'll never hurt you."

I move one hand to beside her head as I lean forward, the tip of my cock against her entrance.

With my other hand, I circle the front of her neck. "But I'll choke you a little. If that's what you want."

Val's eyes widen, and her lips part, and I feel her nod before I see it.

And then I squeeze, knowing exactly where to press.

Val's eyes flutter shut.

My sweet wife.

My kind, caring woman.

I will never hurt her.

I will never teach her to love pain.

But I will teach her to love me.

Her body shifts under me.

Her hips try to lift to take me inside her.

But I don't let her. I just squeeze a little harder.

Her eyes open. And her hands reach up to grab at my arm.

But she doesn't push me away. She clings to me.

She looks up at me with those beautiful eyes, and her body twitches. Once.

I'm leaking all over her slit. So ready to fucking burst. But I need her with me. I need her as feral as I feel.

And when her fingers dig into my arm and she twitches a second time, I tighten my hold the tiniest bit.

Her back arches, and I release my hold on her neck as I slam my entire length inside her.

Val's orgasm is instant.

An implosion.

Her limbs wrap around me, clutching me.

And I'm lost.

I'm surrounded by her heat, and I'm fucking lost to it.

I rut her into the floor.

Slamming my hips into hers as she whines and whimpers beneath me.

Feeling her channel grip to keep me inside her each time I withdraw.

Feeling her breath on my neck with each thrust forward.

She's everything.

She's perfect.

I pull free from her body, and gripping her by her hips, I flip her onto her stomach.

I don't give her time to catch her breath.

I rip the dress from her shoulders, yank her hips up, and shove into her from behind.

Her orgasm is still trembling through her body, but it's not enough.

Reaching forward, I grip the front of her neck again and pull her back until she's upright on her knees before me. And we both stare forward at our reflection.

Her body jiggles and bounces each time my hips slam forward into her ass. And it's the best fucking thing I've ever seen.

My woman at my mercy. Baring herself to me. Asking me to take her.

I tighten my hold on her neck again, starting tighter than I did last time. Because this time, I'm close.

I'm so close to filling her with my seed, and I need her to milk it out of me.

I place my mouth at her ear and slide my other hand down her belly to her slick clit.

"I'm going to come inside you, Valentine. I'm going to come so deep inside you it'll be dripping out for days." I rub my fingers in circles around her bundle of nerves. "But I need you to come first. So grab those titties for me. Show me what you like."

She doesn't even hesitate. Val's hands fly up to her chest, and her fingers pinch and pull at her nipples.

Her pussy starts to clench around me.

I try to control my movements, sliding in and out.

But then her eyes start to roll back. And I press harder against her clit. And she comes.

I release her throat, and the sound of her ragged inhale is the last push I need before my balls squeeze and I'm unloading deep inside her.

"Valentine," I groan as I fill her with my release. "God, you're so fucking good. So fucking good at doing what you're told."

For the final pulse of my cock, I shove myself as far in as I can get, the thrust tipping us forward.

In our reflection, I watch as Val doesn't even try to brace her fall. But I hook an arm around her waist, putting my other out in time to connect with the floor in a single-arm push-up.

Still buried inside my wife's pussy, I press her hips down with my own, then lower us the rest of the way.

I'm crushing her.

I know I am.

But I need a moment.

Focusing on my breath, I take my first controlled inhale since I started punching that bag an hour ago.

I take another deep inhale and acknowledge what Valentine did for me, what I couldn't do for myself.

She centered me.

By willingly giving herself to me, she brought me back.

Steadier than I was, I shift my weight off Val, slipping free from her heat and dropping onto my back beside her with a groan.

"Are you okay?" Val pushes up onto her elbows to look at me.

I know she's asking about more than my pounding heart.

"Yeah, Angel." I reach out and drag her up and over me, her bare-naked body against mine.

"Dom!"

She tries to roll off, but I hold her in place.

Her struggle is short lived before she relaxes against me, letting her legs part, dropping her knees on either side of my thighs.

"I'm a mess," she mumbles against my neck.

I pat her on the ass, knowing she's talking about the stickiness between her thighs. "Yeah, but you're my mess."

She shakes her head, and I imagine her rolling her eyes at me.

"Thank you," I tell her, patting her ass once more.

"You're welcome." Her fingertip traces over the letters of her name across my neck. "For what?"

I wrap my arms around her, not wanting her to get cold as the air settles around us.

I close my eyes as I answer her. "For just being you."

Her fingers still against my skin.

I stroke a palm up her spine. "I haven't forgotten."

"Haven't forgotten what?" she asks me.

"That I don't deserve your affection." I flatten my hands against her back, wanting to touch as much of her as possible. "But I appreciate you giving it to me all the same."

Her back expands with a big breath, and I expect her to push away, but she doesn't. "What you did was shitty. But it's hardly the worst thing that's happened to me."

I clench my jaw and hold her a little tighter.

I don't like being compared to all the horrible things from her past, even if I deserve it. And I hate that me drugging her and tricking her into marriage isn't the worst thing she's been through.

Val surprises me when she continues. "Doing something shitty doesn't mean you don't deserve affection, Dominic."

Too stunned to say anything, I lie still while her finger starts to trace the *V* of Valentine again.

"I've always wanted a tattoo," Valentine admits quietly.

I open my eyes and look down at the top of her head. "Yeah?"

"Yeah." She traces the next letter. "I told myself a hundred times that I'd do it. But I always backed out before I could even make the appointment."

"Why's that?"

Her fingertip goes back to the *V*. "I was afraid of the pain."

Can you teach me to like it?

I'll never teach her to like pain because I'll never allow her to feel enough of it to become used to it.

"What did you want to get?" I ask, assuming it wasn't a man's name four times around her finger.

She sighs. "I could never decide. I'd go back and forth between something pretty or something tough."

"Tough?"

She shifts so she can tap her finger to the center of my chest. "Like a skull."

I grin at the ceiling, picturing my sweet Valentine with a skull tattoo.

"Well, if you want another one, just let me know. I'll knock you out again so you don't have to feel it, then do whatever design you want."

Her head pops up, and she looks at me with wide eyes. "Wait. Did *you* do it? Like the actual tattooing part?"

I lift a brow. "You really think I was gonna let someone else touch you?"

She huffs out a laugh, dropping her head back down. "You really are a man of many talents."

"Well, I'd love to demonstrate my talents again, but you need to sleep and we both need to shower." I pat her ass again, soaking up the lightness of hearing her laugh, as small as it was.

Val groans as she sits up, showing me all her glorious nakedness. "I won't argue about being tired. But I have a feeling most people won't be working too hard tomorrow, seeing as it's the Friday right after the party. Not to mention the *no boss* thing."

I grip her soft sides. "If you hear from him, you tell me."

"I will."

I feel myself smile. "I kinda like compliant Valentine."

She darts her hand down to flick my nipple.

"Hey!" My hands slap up to cover them from further assault, and Val takes advantage of my occupied hands by jumping up and hurrying away.

I should chase her. Or do something.

But I just lie naked, lifting my head so I can watch every glorious inch of her as she disappears from the room with a laugh.

CHAPTER 60

Val

"WHAT IS THIS PLACE?" I GRIP DOMINIC'S HAND IN MY mittened one and look around at all the food stands, displays of merchandise, and decorations. *So many decorations.*

"It's the Christmas market." Dom lifts his hand to wave back to someone.

"Well, yeah. I mean, I know that's what you said on the drive over." I can't stop looking around. "But I didn't know it was like this."

"You like it?"

I nod, noticing a whole bunch of people in line to get—I squint my eyes—apple cider mini donuts. "Holy shit. We need that."

Dom chuckles, seeing where my eyes are focused. "The food is the reason I come. That and my mom would throw a fit if I didn't."

"Your mom is here?!" I nearly choke on my gasp.

Dominic looks down at me, a brow raised. "I know I told you that. Are you alright?"

Am I alright?

No. No, I'm not alright.

I nod my head again anyway.

325

Dom squeezes my hand, his fingers bare, apparently unaffected by the evening chill. "We've got a bunch of family here that will want to see you, but if you ever feel too crowded by them, just point to something you like, and everyone will fall over themselves to buy it for you."

I look up at Dominic, letting him see my incredulous expression. "I'm not doing that."

He smirks. "Figured as much. But that's okay. I transferred some money into your account."

I stop, making him stop with me. "You what?"

He tugs on my hand, forcing me to keep walking into the market. "I haven't had time to get you your own credit card yet, but I will."

"Dom, that's not the problem."

"Then what's the problem, Shorty?"

My sigh is loud. "You don't need to give me money. I have my own credit cards." I lift my purse, shaking it for good measure. "With my own money."

"Valentine, you're my wife. I'll give you whatever the fuck I want."

Eyeing him, I let go of his hand so I can slip my phone out of my purse.

I feel like he probably did tell me that his family would be here, and maybe he mentioned his mom, but I was too stressed out to pay attention.

It's not that I hate Christmas. I don't.

Or rather, I don't want to. But my brain won't let go of bad memories long enough for me to enjoy the holiday in the present.

And I made such a shitty first impression on his mom at my birthday party... I almost cringe thinking of it.

Nearly breaking into tears at the table... Fucking her son in the bathroom... I'm sure she thinks I'm real classy. So I really can't have another mental breakdown in front of her. And that's what Christmas does to me, so this should be a ton of fucking fun.

I swallow down a self-pitying groan.

As my phone opens my banking app, I rub my fingers together inside my mitten, secretly loving the feeling of having a ring to wear again. Dom surprised me with it this morning, having brought it to a jeweler so now it's resized to fit me perfectly.

My phone screen changes, the app opens, and I nearly throw up.

"Dominic!" I yank on his hand.

"What?" He halts, looking around before looking down at me.

I hold up my phone for him to see the same bank balance I see.

And then he rolls his eyes.

This motherfucker rolls his eyes at me like I'm the one being absurd.

I lift my phone higher so it's even with his eyes. "You gave me eighty thousand dollars."

He finally stops walking and turns to face me. "Yeah, Valentine, I gave you some money."

"Some?" I nearly screech.

"Yeah. Some." He snatches my phone out of my hand, drops it into his pocket, and grabs my hand again to start walking. "I told you; I'll get you a card soon, then you can spend whatever you want. But this will hold you over until then."

"Hold me over," I repeat slowly. "This is more than most people make in a year, you... you... crazy man."

"You're welcome to spend it or hoard it however you want."

"It's..." I can't even think of the right words to explain how insane this amount is. "Why eighty? Why not, like, two?"

"If you want two hundred grand, just say so. I just chose eighty because it was more than the seventy-five your dad gave you."

My mouth opens, and I have to hurry to keep up as my arm stretches out between us.

"There is so much wrong with what you just said." I shake my head. "First off, I meant two, as in two thousand. Which would be more than I'd spend on... anything. And second, you're not in a competition with my dead father."

"First." His tone is mocking. "I'll probably spend two thousand tonight. And second, your dad is still ahead of me with the tuition he paid for. But I'll even that out soon enough."

"I don't even know what to say to you."

Dom's hand flexes around mine. "You could just say *thank you, husband. How would you like another amazing blow job, husband?*"

"Dominic!" I hiss, spotting his mom approaching us.

He laughs. "You're too damn cute."

My face scrunches up as I try to decide if I want Dom to think of me as cute.

"My favorite newlyweds." Bibi greets us with her arms open, awaiting hugs.

Wanting to get the awkwardness out of the way, I step ahead of Dom and take the first hug. "It's nice to see you again."

She pulls back and grips my upper arms. "Aww, look how cute you are!"

Dominic snorts, but I ignore him.

I didn't realize just how vast this market was going to be, but Dominic told me it was outdoors and to dress warm. So I did, with dark-wash stretchy jeans tucked into leather ankle boots, a sweater under my tan peacoat, and a bright white knit hat that matches my mittens.

Bibi moves to hug Dominic, and I melt a little watching him bend down to wrap his mother in a big hug.

He's in his usual all-black everything, the long black wool coat his only concession to the cold December air. His hand and neck tattoos are the only ones visible, and they play against his pretty blue irises.

I already know every woman here is going to gawk at him. Case in point, a tall stunner is walking past, a man at her side, but her eyes are all over Dominic. And I want to strangle her with her scarf.

Deep breath, Val.

I can't believe we're already halfway through December. It seems like my life got flipped upside down just yesterday, but it's been weeks.

I don't think I've exactly forgiven Dominic, and I'll probably still have insecurities about him for a while. But I've spent enough time with him now to see that the man I *met* in the airport, the one I texted with for over a month, the one who made me feel good about myself... It's him. He's the same man I thought I knew. I just didn't know everything.

"Come on, let's go get your wife something to drink. Then we can start shopping," Bibi says over her shoulder as she starts to stroll down the gravel aisle.

"You heard the lady." Dom places his hand on my back, and we follow her.

The market takes up a large open space that must be some sort of park, as we're not far from the lake. But it feels like the size of a city block, and there are so many people here I'd call it packed. Lines at all the food stalls, crowds in front of the merchandise stalls, people standing shoulder to shoulder along the outskirts while they sip steaming drinks.

It feels like too many people.

I tug on Dom's jacket, making him bend down to hear me.

"Is it safe to be here?" I ask. "With, well, whoever is out there?"

I don't know the details about who is killing Dominic's men. And honestly, I don't really want to know. But every night since that Christmas party, and the amazing sex I had with Dom in the gym, I've gone to bed alone because he's been staying out late, looking for the ones responsible. I usually wake up a little bit when he comes to bed in the middle of the night and drapes himself over me, but when my alarm goes off in the morning, he's gone again.

I was surprised when he came home earlier this evening and

told me we were going out. And now that I'm looking at these crowds, I'm even more surprised.

Dom slides his hand up my back and around my shoulders. "I know there are a lot of people here. But a hundred of them are mine."

"A hundred?"

He nods. "Half of them are around the perimeter, and half are walking through the crowd."

I'm tempted to ask him if they know who they're looking for. But I don't.

I SHAKE MY HEAD. "I CANNOT EAT ANOTHER BITE."

Bibi laughs. "Okay, fine. We'll just hop in line and meet you back here."

She gestures to the pretzel stand a few stalls down before she and one of Dom's aunties wander that way.

Between the donuts, mulled wine, bratwurst, stollen, and hot chocolate, I don't know where the tiny woman plans to put another bite.

A stand with brightly painted wooden bowls is just on the other side of the aisle, so I step over to it while I wait for the ladies to get their food.

The colors on all the pieces are amazing, but my fingers trace over the surface of one bowl that's been painted to look like intertwined stained-glass stars.

I pick it up, turning it around slowly, taking in the blues and golds.

There is literally no reason I need this hand-painted serving bowl, but I still flip it over to check the price written on the sticker on the bottom.

I nearly put it back, the price being higher than I'd usually allow myself to spend on something like this, but then I remember the eighty thousand dollars that just got added to my bank account and decide *fuck it.*

"I'd like this one, please," I tell the woman behind the display, handing her the bowl and my debit card.

Dominic broke off from us a little while ago to wander with one of his uncles. He didn't really give a reason why they couldn't just walk with us, but his mom's need to stop and look at every single ornament probably had something to do with it.

The woman wraps the bowl in brown paper, then slides it into a plain white bag.

I thank her and tuck my card back into my wallet, then hold the bag in one hand and my purse in the other.

My feet turn me the wrong way at first, and I only notice when I don't see the pretzel stand, so I stop and turn back the other way. Except when I spot the pretzels, I don't see Bibi.

Excusing myself as I bump into someone, I walk past the stand. But they aren't there.

I spin around.

Maybe they went to find me.

But I didn't see them walking over here.

I take a few steps.

What if I'm going the wrong way?

I stop.

They didn't leave.

I say it to myself again.

They didn't leave.

I spin around again. I can't see them.

Stay calm. It's okay.

Facing away from the pretzel stand, I start to walk.

The market is only so big.

They couldn't have gone far.

Dominic is here somewhere.

Dominic has a hundred men here.

Except I don't recognize anyone.

I try to walk quicker, but it's still so crowded.

Breathe.

I stop again, and someone bumps into me from behind.

"Sorry," I mumble as I open my little purse.

I'll just text Dom, tell him to find me.

But I don't see my phone.

I yank my mittens off and tuck them under my arm. With bare hands, I dig through the contents of my purse, but I can already see that there's no phone.

I close my eyes as I try to think of where I left it. Then I remember Dominic taking it out of my hand when I was looking at the money he sent.

I don't have a phone.

I'm separated, and I don't have a phone.

Panic slithers through my brittle defenses, and I spin around again.

Where is everyone?

Angling my body, I weave through more people until I get to one of the intersections, where the paths of Christmas fun spread out in all four directions.

There are so many people, but none of them are familiar.

It's okay. You're just lost. Not left.

My chest starts to hurt.

Where is Dominic?

My vision starts to get blurry, and I blink.

Just breathe.

I try to. I try to pull in an even breath. But...

I try again.

Panic is winning.

I need to find Dominic.

I whirl around again, deciding to pick a new direction. But I'm too distracted, and my foot catches on something, stopping its motion while the rest of my body continues forward.

I trip over the front wheel of a baby stroller. And there's enough time for me to let out a little shriek as my hands stretch out, and I catch myself on the rough gravel with my palms.

The sting of sharp rocks meeting skin is instant and causes me to lose my battle against the tears.

"Oh my god, are you okay?" A woman crouches down next to me. "I'm so sorry." She apologizes, even though we both know I was at fault.

She grabs my arm, helping me up. "Are you alright?"

I nod, using the backs of my hands to wipe at my cheeks. "I'm okay."

The words sound anything but, but I don't have it in me to explain that my crying has nothing to do with falling. So I hurry away.

It only takes a few steps to notice that my knee is aching. I must've landed on that hard, too.

I wipe at my cheeks again and blink. But still, none of the faces around me are familiar.

My lower lip trembles with the urge to yell Dominic's name. If I focused on taking a breath, I could probably yell it pretty loud.

But what if I yell for him and he doesn't come?

He didn't leave me.

Dominic is here; he didn't leave me.

But no matter how many times I tell myself that, I can't drop the disgusting worry that maybe he did.

I stumble a few more steps.

What if he left me?

There's a part of my brain that knows I'm fine. A part that knows this is just a trauma response. More shit I need more therapy for.

But the other part of my brain is in charge right now. And that part is spiraling.

I suck in another jagged breath.

I can't see the faces around me anymore. My vision is too fuzzy.

If they were people I knew, they'd say something. They'd get Dom.

But even with all these people, no one recognizes me.

What if everyone left?

I spot a break in the crowd ahead and push through it.

I keep going, not turning, until I find the edge of the market.

No one stops me.

No one calls my name.

I cut through the final flow of people and find an unoccupied bench on the outside of the last aisle. I lower myself onto it slowly because my knee is really starting to hurt. Once I'm seated, I set my purse in my lap, then—careful not to bump my injured palms —I pull the bowl I just bought out of its bag.

When I fell, I felt the bowl get smashed between my elbow and the ground, and I need to check to make sure I didn't break it.

Peeling the paper away, I ignore the ache in my elbow and bite down on my lip. Hard. Because the top edge of the bowl is chipped—a piece of the shiny paint missing, revealing a jagged half-moon of dullness.

My thumb rubs over the spot as a tear drips off my cheek and splashes onto the curved surface of the bowl.

This is only a moment.

I will be happy in another moment.

I try to do the *three rule* thing my therapist taught me.

I try to look for three things. I try to hear three things. I try to focus on three things in my body.

But all I see are the broken parts.

Because everything breaks on Christmas.

CHAPTER 61

Val

"ANGEL." DOMINIC'S SOFT VOICE TOUCHES ME A moment before his hands land on the sides of my calves.

He's crouched in front of me so we're eye level.

I sniff before I look up at him. "Hi."

Dom reaches up, brushing his thumb across my cheek. "What happened?"

"I got separated." I sniff again.

"Don't cry, Valentine." He swipes another tear away.

I shift, and the stuff in my lap crinkles. "I broke the bowl."

He looks down, noticing the dish I'm still holding.

"We'll fix it." Dom lifts his hands and settles them over mine so we're holding the bowl together. But the position pushes my palms against the wood and causes me to wince.

Dominic jerks his hands back so fast it's like I burned him.

"Sorry." I apologize, even though I know I shouldn't. But I don't like making him feel bad.

He takes the bowl from my grip and sets it on the bench next to me. Then he gently grabs my wrists and turns my hands palm up, revealing the angry scrapes and the couple spots of blood.

"Who did this?" Dominic's voice is so level. It sounds so controlled.

But I don't think it is.

"No one."

"Valentine." He lets go of one hand to grip my chin, forcing me to look at him. "Who touched you?"

I try to shake my head, but I can't with his hold on me. "It wasn't—"

Dominic leans in closer to me, and his eyes reveal the fakeness of his calm exterior. "If someone hurts you, I will kill them. Do not attempt to stop me."

His words lace up around me, tightening and forcing away the last of my lingering panic.

"I fell," I whisper.

He shifts closer. His abdomen pushes against my knees, and my leg gives a little jerk.

Dominic immediately leans away, his hands moving to my thighs as he looks down at the tear in my jeans on my right knee.

"Did someone push you?"

"No." Another whispered admission. "I tripped over a stroller."

He looks back up at me, careful to avoid my knee. "Are you okay?"

I nod. A few more tears break free at his tender tone.

"Why are you crying, Wife?" He slides his hands up my legs until he's gripping me under my jacket, holding my hips.

"I—" I lower my eyes to my lap. "I thought maybe you left me."

"Left you?"

I press my fingertips onto my thighs, wishing I had something to hold.

"I thought..." I stop to take a breath. "I was buying that bowl" —I gesture to it—"while your mom went to get a pretzel, but when I tried to find her after, she was gone. And then I couldn't find her. And I tried to find you." My voice hitches, and I feel so stupid, but I can't help it. "You said there were so many of your people here, but I couldn't spot anyone." His thumbs rub circles on my hips. "I thought you left me."

"Angel." Dom shifts closer, carefully nudging my hurt knee aside. "I'm not going to leave you."

My shoulders lift in the smallest shrug. "I know."

"Valentine." He waits for my gaze to meet his. "I'd choose you. You know that, right?"

I move my head from side to side, not understanding him.

Dom cups my cheek with his warm palm. "If there was no Alliance—never was—I'd still choose you."

Those words...

My eyes close, then open, and he's still there. Still before me.

"You make me feel special," I tell him, my voice so full of emotion it spills between us.

He glides his thumb across my cheek. "Good."

Someone carrying a bag of jingle bells walks past, the noise high and light. And I inhale, needing to tell him this one last thing. "My mom killed herself on Christmas Day."

CHAPTER 62

Dom

I RISE, SCOOPING VALENTINE INTO MY ARMS, THEN I SIT on the bench where she just was.

"You should've told me," I say with my lips against her soft hat. "We didn't need to come here. You should've told me."

"I want to like Christmas." Her words are so quiet they make me hold her tighter.

My wife... The shit she's been through. All by herself.

"You'll never be alone, Angel. Not on holidays. Not ever," I swear to her.

"I'm okay," she says with her head against my chest.

"We'll get the bowl fixed," I promise.

"It's okay."

I pull a pair of dirty white mittens out of my pocket and hand them to her. "And we'll get these cleaned."

She lifts her hands to take them, and I'm not sure if she even realized she dropped them.

When I found her mittens on the gravel, my first instinct was to burn the whole market to the ground. But then I spotted her, the white of her hat calling to me.

It's my fault.

This is all my fault.

I didn't realize I'd kept her phone until it was too late.

I didn't put together the dates of her story on my own. I should have. Her nineteenth birthday. Waiting to visit until classes were done. I should've figured it out. And I should've known her bitch of a mother would choose fucking Christmas Day.

I should have done better.

I owe Valentine better.

Val tries to sit up, but I keep her secured to me.

"I really am okay." She gently puts her mitten-covered hand against my chest. "It was just a stupid panic attack."

"There's nothing stupid about it." I kiss the top of her head. "I'll do better."

"No, Dom, this isn't something you did."

"I'll do better," I tell her again. "And we'll make our own traditions."

I feel her exhale. "Okay."

"Uh, Boss." A male voice cuts into our space.

I lift my head to find Ben standing a few feet away from us. "What?"

His eyes don't drop below mine, making sure he doesn't look at my wife. *Good man.* "We have a location."

I sit up straighter. "Local?"

He nods. "Rob is getting the cars ready. Told me to come get you."

Val presses against my chest to sit up, and I finally let her.

"I'll be right there," I tell Ben, dismissing him.

Her eyes are full of worry as she blinks up at me. "The bad guys?"

Jesus, this woman.

The edge of my mouth quirks. "Yeah, Shorty. I gotta go get the bad guys." She said it as though I'm not also a bad guy. But I'm not an idiot, so I'm not going to remind her that I'm one, too. "I'll have a group of my men bring you home. Same rules as always." I know she doesn't need the reminder, but I want to say it anyway.

"Okay," Val agrees, and when I loosen my arms, she climbs off my lap.

I carefully take her hand in mine, and we walk around the edge of the market toward my row of waiting vehicles.

Guiding her to the middle of three SUVs, I turn her to face me. "An older man and his wife will be waiting in the hallway outside the apartment for you. He's my doctor, and he's going to look at your hands and your knee and whatever other part of you is hurt." She opens her mouth, but I shake my head. "This is happening. And I trust him, but his wife will be in the room with you, too. Don't ever be alone with any man that isn't me." I gently grip her face in my hands. "They won't survive my jealousy."

"I won't." She glances past my shoulder to the dozens of men gathering around us. "You'll come home?"

Home.

"Yeah, Angel, I'll come home." I kiss the tip of her nose. "Now, be my good wife and get in the vehicle."

She surprises me by gripping the lapels of my jacket and pulling me to her as she lifts onto her toes, pressing her lips to mine.

I let my eyes close for one second as I soak in her essence before I pull back. "Good wife, indeed."

Valentine bites down on her lip, then climbs into the back seat.

I wait until she's buckled herself in, then I close the door.

The driver starts to walk past me, but I grab him by the collar, pulling him so we're face-to-face. "If there is so much as a scratch on her, you'll pay with your life."

He nods. "Yes, Boss."

I let him go. "When she's secure, double the usual security team. We haven't had a lead on these guys in weeks. If this is a setup, I want you ready."

He nods again, then circles around to the driver's door and climbs in.

THE HOUSE IS IN A SHITTY PART OF A SHITTY SUBURB and looks just like the flophouse it is.

Neighbors in a place like this mind their own fucking business. Which is perfect, because we're about to do some business.

No cars are in the driveway, but one of my men checked the detached garage, and the vehicle inside matches the one we're looking for.

The yards are all surrounded by tall but rickety fencing, so it doesn't take much for my guys to silently remove a few boards, letting us walk into the target backyard.

I left my jacket in the car—for dexterity—but there wasn't time to change into tactical gear. So I'm walking through knee-high dead grass in my fucking suit.

But we don't need tactical because there are twenty of us and only two of them.

Twenty is overkill, but half of them will stay outside as backup and cover. And the ten of us entering will break off, half through the front door and half through the back door.

Our second-best lockpick goes around to the front, and I step up to the back.

It's been a while since I've gotten to use this particular skill, but no one does it better. And in a matter of seconds, I have the deadbolt sliding free.

Staying radio silent, the men surrounding the house signal to each other when both doors are unlocked.

And we enter as one.

Adrenaline and anger flare through my system. And I inhale it, filling my lungs with the power I feel as the first man through the door.

Our guns are drawn, silencers on—our goal is to keep this quiet.

The back door opens into the kitchen. It's small. The lights are off, but a glow comes from the living room off to my right, and it's enough to show me there's no place for a man to hide in here.

The TV is on, playing a football game, and the noise is enough to cover the small sounds our shoes make on the linoleum floor. But the front door leads directly into the living room, so my five turn the other way, down the short hall, letting the front crew take care of the man in the living room.

Half a shout reaches us, but it's muffled before it finishes. And with the game on, it just sounds like someone yelling at the TV, not someone getting grabbed by five men dressed in black.

There are two open doors—dark bedrooms beyond—and one closed door with light and steam coming through the gap between the floor and the bottom of the cheap door.

My mouth pulls into a grin.

He's in the shower.

I move my gun into my left hand and slip my right hand into my pocket.

Threading my fingers through the perfectly sized holes, I slide my brass knuckles into place.

It's been too long.

Careful not to click the metal against the door handle, I turn the knob slowly and push the door open even slower, eliciting no sound.

Two of my men break off to check the bedrooms, and another stays in the hallway, but Rob follows me into the tiny bathroom.

The shower is small. A corner stall with a wavy yellow-tinged fake glass door.

Perfect.

My fist flexes, my grip tightening around the thick black metal.

And then I move.

In two strides, I'm at the shower. The man behind the cloudy door turns, putting his back to the spray, and he sees me, sees the movement.

But it's too late.

Using my momentum, I throw my fist forward through the thin door, sending shards of plastic in every direction.

My punch carries on, my body turning with it, until my reinforced knuckles meet with the man's chest.

My forward motion was slowed by the door, so I don't hit him with my full force, but it's enough to stun him, to take him out of the fight before it even starts.

Rob reaches past me into the shower and yanks the target forward by the arm, causing the naked man to stumble through the broken doorframe.

Shower guy is still trying to catch his breath from the hit to his solar plexus, so he's not screaming, but he does try to take a swing at Rob.

Except I'm behind him now. And with an open hand, I shove his head to the side. Hard. Into the mirrored medicine cabinet.

The whole thing caves in, shattered glass cutting into the flesh of his face.

He does scream now. But it's too late. No one is coming to save him.

CHAPTER 63

Val

I LET THE STEAM SWIRL AROUND ME AS I STAND UNDER the powerful shower spray, washing away the feelings from earlier and hoping Dominic is being safe.

CHAPTER 64

Dom

WITH MY RIGHT HAND IN A FIST, I TAP THE UNDERSIDE of my wedding ring on the raised metal.

The metallic clink marks my approach as I take the final step into the shitty house's basement.

It's unfinished. Just a bare concrete floor with empty shelves along one side of the room. And just like the neighborhood, it's perfect for our needs.

My pace is slow as I near the man from the shower.

I stop two feet in front of him. "Who sent you?"

The man arches his head back like he might try to spit on me, but the arm around his neck tightens.

Hard to spit when you can't breathe.

Instead of dealing with ropes and tape and shit like that, we just use manpower.

One of my guys stands behind the captive, his arm around the man's neck and his other hand on the back of the man's head. Quickest way to subdue the captive as needed. Then I have two more men, one on either side of the captive. Their arms are hooked around the man's elbows, immobilizing his arms, and their feet are on either side of his, keeping the man standing exactly where we put him.

I turn my head to look at the man from the living room, three more of my men holding him in the same way.

Rob is behind me, and two more guys flank the bottom of the stairs. No one is getting out of this basement unless I want them to.

I run my tongue over my teeth, debating if I should start with the living room guy instead, but I decide to stick with the shower guy.

Neither of them looks like much. But killers for hire rarely do. Just some normal-looking white dudes with brown hair. No discernible ethnicity. Nondescript clothes.

And thankfully, one of the guys grabbed a pair of shorts from somewhere, making shower man put them on so we don't have to stare at his dick during the entire interrogation.

I roll my shoulders out once. "You're going to tell us who hired you. And then you're going to die. The only unknown is how much it's gonna hurt. And that depends entirely on you."

The arm around his neck loosens enough for him to talk.

The man gasps a few times, catching his breath. And I allow him this.

For a moment.

"Who sent you? What's the mission?"

He tries to smile, but the slices across his cheek make it hard. "You're the mission, tough guy."

I incline my head. "Well, here I am. Though I don't think this is a real *mission accomplished* moment for you."

He shrugs. "Maybe not. But we took a few of you with us, though. Didn't we?"

My gun is back in my holster, so I use my empty left hand to slap him across the face.

A slap is both painful and degrading. And satisfying as fuck for me.

"You've got a lot to pay for. And we'll get to that. But I want to know who sent you." My voice is even, almost friendly. But it's a lie. Because even if he didn't pull the trigger, he's involved. And he'll die for that.

He glares at me, pissed at being caught and trying his best not to be scared about dying.

"Why are *you* here? You a hire?" I know he is. I just want him to tell me.

He tries to shrug. "If I tell you I was paid to do this, you gonna let me go?"

I shake my head. "Just want to know how much information you have inside that skull of yours. And hires typically don't have all that much to spill."

"Yeah, well, I do what I have to do. Not all of us can just marry some fat bitch and become part of The Alliance."

Some fat bitch.

My fingers tighten around my brass knuckles as visions of my beautiful Valentine fill my mind.

And this man... This man is here, on a mission to kill people close to me, and he just brought up my wife.

My Angel.

Red seeps across my vision.

"Let him go," I command.

And they do.

All at once, my three men drop their hold on the man and step back.

I wait. Half a heartbeat, I wait.

Then the man lunges at me. But I meet him halfway.

My left arm deflects his wild swing as I twist my hips, throwing my weight into my right fist as it connects with his side.

His ribs flex under the hit.

The man is fit, but I'm stronger, and I weigh more. So when we go down, I'm on top.

His back smashes into the hard floor, stunning him.

I lift myself onto all fours, like I'm crawling over him. My left hand is planted on the concrete next to his head, bracing my weight, and my knees are on either side of his hips, with my right hand pulled back.

He has enough time to widen his eyes and start to lift his hands in defense before my metal-covered fist slams into his chest, hitting where the ribs and sternum meet, right above his heart.

The man without a name grunts and tries to hit me.

But I hit him again, my fist thudding against his chest.

And I hit him again.

The shock of the collision reverberates up my arm. But all I can feel is anger.

Rage.

I punch him again.

Fury.

He's trying to push me away. But I slam my fist right back down, right into that same spot.

A tendril of panic crawls up my spine. Because this man knows about my wife. He knows about my Valentine.

And no one will ever touch her.

I arch my shoulder back and bring my fist down with all my might, feeling the first crack.

Untamed violence consumes me. And I strike him.

Again and again, I slam my knuckles over his heart, relishing in the crunches that reach my ears.

His knees hit my back. He thrashes. He tries to stop me.

But he can't. Won't. Because he's two hits away from his last breath.

I let the fear of failure fuel my next hit, and his ribs finally snap away from his sternum.

I don't look anywhere else. I just stare at the man below me.

Then I lift my fist for the final time. And I think of my sweet Angel, think of my need to keep her safe, as I hit him once more—as hard as I can.

The give is instant.

With the ribs no longer connected to the center of his chest, they bend with the hit. The jagged edge where they broke away from his sternum causes the skin stretched across to rip open. But I keep pushing. I keep shoving my fist into his chest. Not stopping until the sharp edges of his ribs pierce into the pumping organ below.

Breathing heavily, I pull my fist away and lean back until I'm kneeling upright over his corpse.

I always wondered if I could do that.

I tip my head to the side and watch as deep red arterial blood pools in the crevice over his heart and the organ squeezes one final time.

The sound of someone vomiting cuts through the silence.

Some of the men make sounds of disapproval as they drag the second man back a step, away from his regurgitated dinner splattered on the floor.

I sigh, and placing my hand below the blood-filled wound, I push myself up and away from the corpse.

I open and close my fist around the soiled brass knuckles, loosening my fingers, as I step up to Living Room Guy. "Guess you're the one that will do the talking."

CHAPTER 65
Living Room Guy

JESUS FUCKING CHRIST.

Dominic Fucking Gonzalez stares at me with his cold blue eyes.

I try to step back, to flinch away. But these fuckers don't budge.

Dom steps closer, and I have to fight not to puke again.

He...

I fight off a gag.

He just fucking punched his way through Hendry's chest.

And he did it without making a fucking sound.

"I'll tell you!" I cry out before he can come any closer. "Our-our handler is a dude who goes by the name Casey. His number always changes, but he'll text my phone tomorrow to check in."

Dom nods once and flexes his hand around the bloody brass knuckles. "I'm assuming there's some sort of confirmation code so he knows it's you."

I keep my eyes on his hand. "Keep me alive, and I'll type it in myself."

The mafia kingpin makes a humming sound like he's considering it. "Seems like a hassle."

My legs start to shake.

"I have something else." My voice gets more frantic with each word as he takes a step closer.

"What's that?" Dom asks me.

I force my gaze up to meet his. "Whoever hired us, they wanted you to think someone else was behind it."

"Who?"

"Someone named Hans," I tell him. I don't know what that name is supposed to mean, but Dom lifts a brow.

"They want me to believe that some human trafficking asshole is hiring thugs to kill me?"

"I don't know, man!" I try to convince him. "I've never even heard that name before."

"What were your instructions exactly?" he asks me.

He's so calm, so chill. It's even scarier than if he were screaming in my face.

"I-if." I have to swallow. "If we were caught, we were supposed to tell you that Hans hired us."

He keeps staring at me like I'm some sort of science experiment. "And why didn't you?"

"Because I want to live, man!" I shout.

Dom steps closer until our faces are only a foot apart. "And what makes you think I'd let you live?"

He jerks his chin up, and hands grip my head.

Then—

CHAPTER 66
Dom

THE MAN'S NECK MAKES AN AUDIBLE SNAP.

All three of my men let go, and the newest dead man falls to the floor.

There is no room for mercy in The Alliance.

And I am The Alliance now.

THE ROOM IS DARK WHEN I ENTER. VALENTINE'S FORM is still with sleep under the blankets. I want to go straight to her, but I need to wash away the ugliness of my night.

So I do.

The scent of her shower products lingers in the bathroom, confirming she did this same thing before getting into bed.

On my way back here, I read the message from Doc. He reported that she suffered no more than a few scrapes and bruises. He cleaned and checked her palms for debris and recommended salve and a couple of bandages. He also told me that she wanted to shower and said she'd treat them herself afterward.

As I step under the scorching spray, I find I can't be angry with her decision. I understand the need to rinse off a bad day. And even though the doctor and his wife could've waited downstairs for her to shower and then treat her hands after, I don't think I would have been okay with my Angel being naked while someone else was in the condo without me around.

I lather a palmful of my body wash, then vigorously rub it over my chest and up and down my arms. And again, scrubbing at my torso and legs. I take an oversized squeeze of Valentine's face wash, and I breathe in the clean scent as I roughly clean my face.

I've never felt so rattled during a killing. There have been too many dead men at my feet for me to even count anymore. But tonight. It was different. That man...

I close my eyes and put my face directly under the water.

Hearing that man talk about Valentine that way, it split me. It divided the two sides of me. The man. And the murderer. And without the tether, the violence inside me was completely unleashed.

Even Rob stayed an extra step away from me when we left that basement.

But I don't regret what I did.

The dead men will never tell anyone how they died. But my men will talk among themselves. Word will get around. And then people will understand. They'll finally understand just how off-fucking-limits my wife is. That even the smallest slight against her will result in me crushing their hearts inside their chests.

I open my mouth and let it fill with water.

After swishing it around, I spit it out, washing away the metallic taste that's been lingering at the back of my throat. Then I turn off the water.

When I see the empty towel hook next to the shower, I have a ridiculous urge to laugh, remembering how Val threw that damn toaster at me.

My wet feet slap across the floor as I fetch a towel.

Not wanting to waste another moment, I dry off as quickly as I can, tug on a pair of clean boxers, and step into the bedroom.

Val hasn't moved positions; she's still sprawled out on her stomach—head turned away from me, her far leg bent, her foot at the edge of the bed.

My need to be close to her overwhelms my need for stealth.

I climb onto the bed, crawling over until I reach her, then I lower my weight, letting my body pin hers to the mattress. I revel in the softness of her perfect ass pressing into my groin and nuzzle my face against the back of her head. But I need more, so I bend my leg, putting it on top of hers, my thigh against the back of her leg, my chest against her back, and my arm on top of her arm in front of our faces.

I line up as much of our bodies as I can.

But it's not close enough.

I stretch my leg past hers, hooking my foot around her ankle and pulling her leg back.

I grab the wrist of her outstretched arm and slide it across the bed toward our bodies so her arm is bent and her hand is near her face.

I curl around her, locking her to me with my limbs.

And I put my mouth against her hair, breathing her directly into my body.

Val lets out a sleepy groan. And I hold her tighter.

I need her.

I need to keep her safe.

I need to keep her happy.

I need to keep her with me.

Always.

CHAPTER 67
Val

I TAKE A SIP OF MY COFFEE BEFORE SETTING THE MUG down on the vanity next to my sink.

Dominic waking me up with coffee was where the good part of this morning started and ended.

I pick the mug back up and take an even larger sip.

I think about the little bomb Dom dropped after handing me the mug... that I could have done without.

Spending the night with King, Savannah, and Aspen in a secluded cabin doesn't sound like a good idea. In fact, it sounds like a really, really bad idea. Add in King's crazy friend Nero and his wife, Payton, and it becomes a terrible idea. A horrible idea. An *I can't believe anyone thinks this will be relaxing* idea.

I know we're all supposed to be one big happy Alliance now, but the truth is I have no idea if Dominic has even talked to King since *that day*. Well, other than King apparently calling Dom last night to invite us to Colorado. And I don't know if King ever realized just how in the dark I was about everything. And I don't know how Dom and Nero will get along, but I know Nero is crazy protective of his wife... So ultimately, it's a lot of big, over-the-top personalities and the women they're obsessive with, all jammed into one cabin.

What could go wrong?

Considering the invite is about as last minute as you can get, I don't think they were actually planning to invite us.

I grimace at myself in the mirror.

It's probably because I've been avoiding Savannah's calls—texting her hours after I watch my phone ring and never calling her back.

I groan as I tug the towel from my hair. I'm gonna need more than a cup of coffee to prepare for the grilling she's gonna give me tonight.

I take my time moisturizing and brushing through my hair. Dom said I had two hours to get ready, and that was an hour ago. So I should still have plenty of time to finish my hair and makeup and pack.

We're taking a private jet to Denver, and while that just confirms that our whole first meeting was a setup, I'm looking forward to not flying commercial. Not that I need to pack that much for a single night. But this way, I don't have to mess around with travel-size things, and I can put it all in one bag.

Pulling open the cabinet beside me, I pause.

Last night I was a little out of it after my shower, and I didn't use the antibiotic cream on my palms like the doctor told me to.

He was really nice, and so was his wife, but I didn't want to be with strangers, so I rushed through his exam and had them leave.

Sighing, I pull out the large zippered leather bag the doctor's wife gave me before they left, which I just shoved into the cupboard without opening. It's worn and looks like a vintage doctor's bag.

I half watched Doc put some extra bandages and the tube of cream into the bag, but his wife told me she had already filled it with the usual first aid items, so I should keep it handy because I might find them useful.

Heavier than I expected it to be, I set the bag on the counter with a thud and unzip it.

The antibiotic cream is right on top, so I pull that out first, followed by two bandages, and set them aside. Then I shuffle through the rest of the contents, just so I know what's in here.

More bandages—of every size—a thermometer, a bottle of rubbing alcohol, a bottle of iodine, a little bag with what looks like medical tweezers, a box of tampons—interesting—packets of blood-clotting powder—yikes—what looks like a sewing kit for stitches—extra yikes—a bottle of prescription painkillers and another bottle of antibiotics with my name on it—guess that could come in handy—and... I pull the last item all the way out. A pregnancy test?

I stare at the box for a long moment.

Why would that be in a first aid kit?

My eyes move back over to the prescription pill bottles. Maybe there are certain drugs you can't take while you're pregnant, so you'd want to test first?

I'm sliding the box back into the bag when a thought hits me.

I jam the box into place and pull open the drawer at my hip.

There, right on top, are my birth control pills.

I take them every morning. I try to take them at the same time. I'm not always exact, but it's always before noon.

My hands are starting to tremble as I lift the packet out of the drawer. I haven't had my dose for today yet, so I carefully push the pill through the thin foil on the back of the packet.

I place it in my mouth, but my mouth is suddenly too dry to swallow the tiny pill, so I have to grab my coffee in order to swallow it.

But my eyes can't make sense of what I'm looking at. Because according to the pill I just took, I'm three days late.

My period is never late.

A wave of nausea hits me, but I shove it away.

That's just my imagination. My mind playing with me.

I'm not pregnant.

I cannot be pregnant.

I put the pills back in the drawer and slam it shut.

Then pull it back open.

I need to pack those.

I pick the packet back up and set it on the counter while the pregnancy test mocks me from inside the leather bag.

Should I take it?

I stand frozen, staring.

What would I even do if I was pregnant?

Would I keep it?

I look down at my body wrapped in a towel.

Could I really bring a child into this world? Have a child with Dominic Gonzalez, a man who runs the freaking mafia?

My hands shake as I press them to my stomach.

I've wanted a family of my own so much, for as long as I can remember. I've even researched how much it would cost to go to a sperm bank and just knock myself up.

I don't know that I would've ever done it. But I was convinced I'd never fall in love with someone.

Fall in love.

Something twists around my heart, but I can't place the feeling.

It's almost... hollow.

Because I think I am falling in love with Dominic. I think I might already be there. But I don't think he feels the same way, and the thought of unrequited love is too much to bear.

And having a baby with someone who doesn't love me back...

I look back up at the pregnancy test.

It's only been three days.

I've been under a lot of stress.

I haven't missed any of my pills.

My eyes move to the packet of pills.

Did I remember to take it in Vegas?

I mean, I was drugged for a night, but I'm on the right day. So unless he found my pills and threw away the one for the morning after our wedding, I must've taken it. Plus, I've had my period since then.

I snatch my phone off the counter and do a quick search on

the effectiveness of birth control pills and what it means when you're three days late.

The answers I find aren't answer enough.

The pill is between ninety-three and ninety-nine percent effective. And considering I'm not always taking it at the exact same time, I think that means I'm at the lower end of that. Meaning there's a seven percent chance of pregnancy every time I've had sex with Dominic. Which isn't helped by the fact that we've never used condoms. Not even that first time in the airport. And I don't think we've ever even talked about it.

I set my phone down.

The internet also tells me that being three days late could be a baby or stress or absolutely any other thing.

I pick up my coffee mug.

Is that why Dominic didn't put on a condom in the airport? Because he planned to marry me all along?

We've obviously never talked about kids. We aren't there. We aren't anywhere near there. Our relationship was built on lies and deception. And I already half hate myself for how easily I've just pushed that all aside simply because I want to make this work. Because I want to be with Dominic.

I start to take a sip of my coffee, then realize what I'm doing and bend over to spit it into the sink.

If I'm pregnant, I don't think I can drink caffeine.

"Something wrong with your coffee?" Dominic's voice startles me so much I scream. He chuckles and takes the mug from my hand, then lifts it to his nose to sniff it. "I had two cups already, and it tasted fine to me."

Mortified at being caught, I say the first thing I can think of. "There was a hair in it."

Dom raises a brow. "Do you want me to get you a fresh mug?"

I shake my head, hoping the color in my cheeks can be played off from him scaring me and not from me freaking out about the possibility of being fucking pregnant.

Looking at him, I admit to myself that the idea isn't as terrifying as it should be. And not just because he looks incredibly handsome in his black pants and white shirt. And not because his eyes are the prettiest thing I've ever seen. And not because of my name inked across his neck.

It's just him.

He's a good man.

A good husband.

"Do you want—" My inner voice starts speaking, about to ask him if he wants kids, but I cut myself off. "Are we exchanging Christmas presents?"

He narrows his eyes slightly, like he knows I was going to say something else. "You don't have to get me anything, Shorty."

I banish all thoughts of babies from my mind. "Are you getting me something?"

His mouth pulls into a smirk. "I'm not telling you what your present is."

"So you did get me something?" *Other than pregnant.*

I shake my head. I need to stop thinking about this.

I'm not fucking pregnant. I'm just late.

"Finish getting ready. You sure you don't want more?" Dom gestures to my mug in his hand.

"I'm sure," I murmur, noticing a line of discoloration across the top of Dominic's fingers that looks like a bruise.

He sees me looking but doesn't say anything about it, just dips his chin and tells me, "One hour."

I watch him walk out of the bathroom, waiting until the door clicks shut behind him before I turn back to the counter.

One hour is not enough time to deal with all this, so I zip up the doctor's bag and shove it back into the cupboard. I need to finish getting ready.

And I'm not pregnant.

CHAPTER 68

Dom

I MOVE DOWN THE STAIRS AHEAD OF VALENTINE, THEN offer her a hand down from the plane.

I know she doesn't love flying, but she's been acting extra stressed out all day. And when she wobbles a little on the last step, I grip her hand tighter.

"You alright?" True concern tinges my voice.

Val nods her head.

"Valentine."

She sighs. "I'm a little nervous."

I place a hand on her back, guiding her toward the big SUV that Rob is already loading our bags into. "No one knows we're here. And even if they did, they won't be able to track us to the cabin," I tell her, assuming she's talking about the guys who are trying to kill me.

"Oh, um, it's not that." She blinks up at me. "But now that you've mentioned it..."

I slide my hand down and pat her ass. Then I palm her ass because it's too delicious not to, especially in these stretchy jeans that look like they're painted on her.

We reach the Suburban, and I guide her to climb into the back seat, then follow her in.

Once Rob starts driving, I turn to Val. "What are you nervous about?"

She blows out a breath. "Just seeing everyone, I guess."

My brows furrow. "What do you mean?"

Val lifts a shoulder before she finally turns her head to look at me. "I just don't want it to be awkward. Ya know?"

I shake my head. "I don't know."

She tugs at the bottom of her off-white sweater, making me wish I'd insisted she put her jacket back on before we got out of the plane. It's not as cold here as it is back home, but I don't want her to be uncomfortable.

"You know about our..." She lifts one hand to make a circular gesture. "Parental history. And I know that was all in the past, but I've worked really hard to make them like me."

I clench my jaw. "Them?"

"King and Aspen," she clarifies calmly, like she isn't igniting my anger all over again. "I just don't want them to be... I dunno. Mad at me. Or disappointed."

"What the fuck would they have to be mad or disappointed about? They can be mad at me, but that's for *me* to handle. You've done nothing wrong, Angel." I work to keep my tone even.

Val looks away from me. "I didn't fight back."

I unbuckle my seat belt and slide across the seat until I'm next to her.

When she doesn't look at me, I grab her chin and lift her face to mine. With her eyes on mine, I tell her the truth. "There was no fighting me, Valentine. You're mine. There is nothing you could have done to make that not true." Her jaw muscles move as she swallows. "Tell me."

"I'm yours."

I pull in a deep inhale through my nose, filling my lungs.

I was looking for *I understand*, but *I'm yours* is so much better.

"Say that again," I demand.

She stares me in the eyes and tells me, "I'm yours."

My lips are on hers.

I tighten my grip on her chin and slide the fingers of my other hand through her hair to hold the back of her head, guiding her to tilt to the side so I can deepen the kiss.

Val doesn't just let me, she participates. She grabs at me, pulls me to her.

I slide closer, tempted to undo her seat belt and pull her into my lap. But I won't compromise her safety.

Then she scrapes her nails up the back of my head, and a shiver skitters down my arms.

Breaking our kiss, I drop my face to her shoulder. "Do that again."

Instead of scraping her nails over my scalp, she lightly rubs her palm over my short hair.

I slip my arms around her in a hug, and her body shudders.

"I like your hair," she whispers.

I squeeze her. "I like your hair, too."

"Thanks." Her palm makes another pass over my head. "I used to not like it, but I do now."

I slide my hand up her back to play with the ends of her thick, shiny hair. "Why wouldn't you like it?" I turn my head a little so my lips are nearly against her neck.

"Promise you won't get mad?"

I start to pull back, but she scrapes her nails over my head again. "I promise," I lie. "Now tell me."

She's back to using her palm on my head. "After my dad's funeral, when I saw King and Aspen for the first time, I started to hate it." I have to force my body not to react, not to tense. "It wasn't their fault. I just had always loved that I had my dad's hair, but that day..." She shrugs, lifting my head with the movement. "I started sneaking my mom's leftover hair dye. I'd always get in trouble for it since it's not like she didn't notice my hair was a darker color. But when I was old enough to get a job, I'd buy the boxes myself and dye it at home."

"Because you didn't want to look like them?"

I can feel her nod. "Pretty much. Every time I saw my natural hair color, I was just reminded that my dad had other kids he'd never told me about."

"When did you stop dying it?" I ask, keeping my anger bottled inside.

"A couple years ago. I had a hairdresser convince me to go back to my natural color. He said it was too pretty to cover up."

I press my lips to her exposed neck. "I feel that way about every inch of you."

"Dominic," she chastises quietly, probably embarrassed about Rob hearing.

But I'm not embarrassed about how much she turns me on.

I kiss her neck again, then pull away. "How much longer?" I ask Rob.

"Another forty, Boss."

"Good," I reply as I slide down onto my side until my head is in Val's soft lap and my feet are wedged against the door. "Just enough time for a nap." I reach up and grab Val's hand. "Keep scratching my head, Shorty."

My eyes lower. Enough time for a nap. And to let my rage simmer.

CHAPTER 69

Val

I'M NOT SURE IF DOMINIC REALLY FELL ASLEEP OR NOT, but he didn't stir until Rob turned down a driveway leading toward a beautiful log cabin somewhere in the Rocky Mountains.

And it's not until I see the giant house that I remember.

Dom catches me smiling as he sits up. "What's that for?"

"I just realized what this place is."

He glances out the windshield to look at the house. "You been here before?"

"No. But I think this is the place Savannah spent thirty thousand dollars bidding on at a silent auction because she was mad at King."

Dominic smirks as he rolls out his shoulders. "I knew I liked her."

I purse my lips as we roll to a stop, forgetting that I never asked about the time he met Savannah. "I feel like I need the rest of that story."

"Another time," Dom says before opening his door.

I climb out, ignoring the chill and carrying my jacket in my arms as I circle around to meet Dom at the back of the vehicle, where he's pulling out our two overnight bags.

I expect Rob to join us, but when Dom closes the back door, Rob drives away.

"Where's he going?" I ask as Dom lifts both bags.

"Another rental not far from here."

I'm curious about why he couldn't just stay here. There's got to be more than enough rooms, but Dom's already striding toward the front door.

I hurry after him, hugging my jacket for warmth.

He gets to the door a step ahead of me, and I try to move around him so I can knock, but he sets the bags down at his sides and knocks himself, not letting me past.

"Dom, what are you—" My question is cut off by the door opening.

Dominic is blocking my view, but over Dom's shoulder, I can see the man's hair color that matches my own.

King opens the door wide, stepping back to let us in. "Come in."

Dom steps forward, not grabbing the bags. "Fuck you."

And then Dominic Gonzalez punches King Vass in the face.

CHAPTER 70

Dom

THE FEEL OF MY BARE KNUCKLES HITTING KING'S CHEEK is so fucking satisfying I don't even care that it hurts my already bruised hand.

I think Val shouts my name, but I'm too preoccupied with channeling my fury at her brother.

King swings for my head, and I deflect it so it only grazes off my ear, but I miss the punch aimed at my ribcage.

It connects, but I turn with the hit, and I use my shoulder to ram into King's chest.

We go down, flipping an armchair in the process, but King manages to twist so we land on our sides rather than landing with me on top of him.

"What the fuck is your problem?" he snaps as he catches my chin with his elbow just as I land a jab in his side.

He rolls away, and I get to my feet at the same time.

"You're my problem," I growl. "You call yourself a fucking brother?"

"Dominic!" Valentine tries to come between me and King, but I catch her around the waist and push her back behind me.

King lowers his brows as he tries to see Val behind me.

I use my free hand to point at him, and he slaps it away, stepping up into my face.

"Ask me where Valentine was when her mom died," I grit out.

My words stop King in his tracks.

"Dom," Val says quietly, and I feel her lean her forehead against the center of my back.

"He deserves to know," I tell her with my eyes still on King. "Now fucking ask me."

As we face off, I start to register the other people in the room. The woman near King's side. Another woman, across the room. And a couple off to my right.

But I don't care about them. Not yet.

"Where was Val when her mom died?" the woman, Savannah, asks from King's side.

I turn my gaze to King's wife and tell her, "Val was at her apartment in Florida."

The blond woman's eyes widen, and I bring mine back up to meet King's. "Now ask me *how* her mom died."

I can see his jaw working. "Val." He looks at me but asks her, "How did your mom die?"

My fingers squeeze into a fist. For a man with his resources, finding this out would take him mere moments. But he doesn't know because he didn't care.

And from the emotion brewing behind his eyes, I think he's starting to understand that.

Val's forehead lifts from my back so we can all hear her when she answers. "Suicide."

Savannah's indrawn breath is audible. "While you were there?"

I continue to stare at King. "Ask me what she left for Val to find next to her corpse." I don't give him time to ask. "A pile of bills. Because Val stood up to her and wouldn't let her have your dad's filthy money." I take a step closer to him. "Now ask me what fucking day it was."

King drops his gaze from mine as he shakes his head. "Christmas Day."

So he remembers that much.

"No." Savannah practically cries the word.

"Now tell me why my Valentine had to sit through that funeral all alone." Standing here, in front of my wife's family, I feel the full weight of what she went through. To have these people so close but so uninvolved had to be the worst kind of loneliness. "No fucking answer, huh?"

A small hand gently grabs my wrist.

I unclench my fist, and Val slides her hand down, her fingers entwining with mine. "It's okay, Dominic."

And here she is, trying to comfort me over what happened to her.

"I'm sorry." King stares at our hands gripped together and shakes his head again. "It's not okay, Val. I'm so sorry."

It's not a gloating sort of satisfaction that fills me hearing the mighty King apologize to my wife; it's a different feeling. A warmer one. The satisfaction of giving someone something they need. Because even if Val fooled herself into thinking she was over it, she wasn't. She needed to hear him say it.

"King..." Val starts, like she's going to tell him *it's okay* again.

King lifts his head to look at her. "Your husband is an asshole, but he's right. I wasn't the brother you deserved back then. There's no excuse."

Savannah sniffs, wiping at her cheeks.

I let my glare lift over King's shoulder, catching Aspen's eye. She looks sufficiently pale, clearly understanding she was just as shitty of a sibling.

I watch her straighten her shoulders. "I'm sorry, too."

Val lifts the hand not holding mine and wipes away a tear. "Thanks, Aspen."

King's eyes zero in on Val's tattooed finger before they snap up to mine.

In answer, I undo the top button of my shirt and let the material part so he can read Valentine's name across my neck.

The woman to my right, still standing off to the side with Nero, makes a humming sound of approval.

Savannah reaches for Val. "Can I hug you now?"

I reluctantly let go of my wife's hand when she moves to meet Savannah.

"So, who is this guy?" the female voice I've never heard before asks.

Before Nero can answer, I turn to Payton, who I've only seen in pictures, and hold out my hand.

"I'm Dominic." She places her palm in mine, even as I hear her psychotic husband growl. "But feel free to call me Daddy."

The man at her side darts forward and shoves me back, breaking my hold on his wife's hand.

I automatically step back, but he's quick and already sweeping my feet out from under me.

I start to fall. But I'm quick, too, and I snag his collar, dragging him down with me.

Only I'm not quick enough to dodge the punch he aims at my jaw.

His wife, who started laughing after I said *daddy*, jumps forward and starts tugging on Nero's shoulder, trying to stop him from beating on me.

And since I'm not going to accidentally hit a woman, especially not Nero's woman, I force myself to stop fighting back.

Nero stares down at me with his devilish black eyes, but he also relaxes. "If you ever hurt my wife, I'll skin you."

I lift a brow. "Is that all? If you ever hurt my wife, I'll dangle you over a hungry bear. Let him rip off pieces to eat until no number of tourniquets or amount of adrenaline would wake you back up."

Nero makes an impressed face. "Decent idea."

Payton reaches out a hand and tugs on Nero's dark hair. "Can you two talk torture techniques standing up, please?"

Nero presses his fists into my chest, putting his full weight onto me while he pushes himself up.

I flex against his heaviness so he doesn't crush me, but to get him back, I kick the heel of his foot as he steps over my legs, making him trip.

Nero spins around, ready to fucking pummel me again, but King puts his arm out between us. "You're even now," he says to Nero, then lowers his hand to help me up.

I lift my head to see Val hugging Aspen, both of them wiping their eyes, then take King's offered hand.

Back on my feet, I follow King when he tips his head toward the kitchen.

Nero steps up close behind me. "I kinda like you, Dom."

I smirk at him over my shoulder. "Feeling's kinda mutual."

He slaps a hand, hard, in the center of my back. "It'd be a shame to have to kill you."

He moves to step around me, so I get him with a backhand to the gut. "Feeling's still mutual."

King rolls his eyes at us before pulling open the fridge, and I feel my mouth pull into a grin.

I said my piece, and while I'm not happy about seeing Valentine cry, I think this will give her some closure for that chapter of her life. And she needs that so she can start looking forward to our future.

King turns back around with three beer bottles in hand. It's not one I know, but I'm not picky. Before I remove the cap, I press the cool glass to my jawline, where Nero's hit connected.

Nero eyes me. "You deserved that."

I remember the rabid look on his face before he shoved me and smirk. "Worth it."

He huffs and snags the beer King holds out for him.

King stares at me as he lifts his own bottle to his cheek, where I first hit him. "It was a cheap shot," he tells me, like there's any excuse for letting yourself get caught off guard.

"Maybe. But Val said some shit on the way over here that

reminded me I owed you a punch to the fucking face." I flex my fingers, releasing the stiffness. "And if you make me think about it too much, I'll want to do it again."

King watches me for a long moment, then drops his eyes to the ink on my neck. "She really tell you all that? Or did you dig it up?"

I lower the bottle from my jaw. "She told me. We talk. A lot."

He nods once. "I'm glad she did. I'm surprised. But I'm glad." King leans back against the counter. "I know I owe her more than one shitty apology, but I'll take care of it."

I eye him, then lower my beer and twist off the top. "Good."

As much as I'm still pissed, I believe him. And it'll be up to Valentine to decide whether she forgives him.

Nero moves to lean against the counter next to King. "So how about you finally clue us in on what's going on? Why do you suddenly need the help of The Alliance?"

This is the whole reason this all started, so I tell them.

I explain how each man has been hit. How someone is targeting my family without leaving behind any calling cards. How the cowards are coming onto my turf, and how I'm going to make them pay.

"I can handle Chicago," I tell them. "But when we find the man behind this, I'm going to need backup. Because it's not a local. I'm not sure if the person behind this is even in this fucking country. But we're close. And when I get a name, I'm going to wipe them from the face of the earth."

Nero takes a pull of beer. "Sounds fun."

"I'll admit, I'm looking forward to it."

"How close are you to finding them?" King asks me.

In answer, my phone dings with an incoming text.

I slide my phone out of my pocket and look at the text from the unknown number.

"Just got closer."

Living Room Guy told me his handler's name. I knew there'd be no contact for him in the phone, but this text is him.

Unknown: Check in

I open the message and click to add an attachment.

Me: *sends photo of the dead man with his chest caved in*

Me: You had my attention, Casey.

Me: And now I have yours.

I open a different chat and make sure my men back home saw that he messaged.

Rather than worrying about the hitters' phones being traced, I just had them cloned to this untraceable one. There's no guarantee we'll find Casey through this text, but we're already halfway to nailing down his location.

I move back to the chat with Casey, but he hasn't replied. And I doubt he will.

Hopefully he's too busy shitting himself.

"What's that?" Nero asks, suddenly at my side, pointing to the photo I sent.

"A dead guy."

"No shit, dumbass. Let me see." He holds out his hand, and I set the phone in it.

Nero sets his beer on the kitchen island so he can use both hands to zoom in on the photo.

Then he holds the phone closer to his face.

"Need a minute to borrow King's bifocals?" I snort.

"Fuck off." Nero's face is still close to the phone screen. "You're a year older than I am."

"Sure." I take a long drink of my beer. "But clearly my vision is better."

"I don't wear bifocals," King mutters, but it's lacking heat because they're now both bent over my phone, looking at the corpse of Shower Guy.

King straightens to look at me. "What did you hit him with?"

"Yeah." Nero moves the photo from side to side, still zoomed in, like he's looking for clues on the floor. "There's no blood under him, just in that hole." He points to the spot just left of the man's sternum. "So it's not like you used a bazooka on him. That would've gone through."

"Sometimes you just gotta stick with the classics," I tell them, then slide the brass knuckles out of my pocket.

King's brows raise. "Seriously? Who even has brass knuckles anymore?"

Nero reaches out and takes them from me, sliding them onto his own hand, then looking back down at the photo. "So you put these on, then wallop the dude in the sternum until what, the ribs crack off and into his heart?"

"Someone knows his biology."

Nero clenches his fist around the knuckles. "I know how to kill people."

"What a surprise," I deadpan.

Nero grunts. "Can I keep these?"

"Fuck no." I open and close my hand in a *gimme* gesture. "Your slender little fingers don't even fill it out properly."

King snorts.

"Slender?" Nero rears back, offended. "Just because I don't have big-ass sausage fingers doesn't mean mine are slender. You fat fuck."

King laughs this time.

I just shake my head. "Jealousy is an ugly color on you, Nero."

I'm far from fat, and Nero is far from little, but I'm the thickest guy here.

Nero grumbles something under his breath as he pulls the brass knuckles off his fingers and slaps them into my hand.

I've worked with these guys a few times before, but it's never had the comradery feeling like this. They may still be mad about me finagling my way into The Alliance, but they seem to be treating me as though I'm one of them.

Sliding the metal into my pocket, I type out a quick text to

Rob, then drop my phone in the other pocket and lean against the large island.

"Hey, Angel," I call across the room to Valentine, but all four women turn their heads my way. "You want a drink?" If no one else is gonna offer my lady a beverage, I'll do it.

Her mouth opens, then closes, like she's not sure.

"Come on." Savannah herds the little group toward the kitchen.

My eyes stay on Val as she approaches me. And my chest swells when she comes right to my side, standing next to me.

I run my palm over her hair, loving that she left it down. "What'd you like?" I hold up my beer. "Not sure what they have, but this is pretty good."

"Umm…" Val leans into me while Savannah opens the fridge.

Savannah starts naming options. "There's beer, chardonnay, Bailey's. I know there's some red open somewhere." She leans back to look past King to see what's on the counter. "I think there's some bourbon."

"Any chance you have ginger ale?" Val asks quietly. "That plane ride was kinda bumpy, and I'm not sure my stomach has recovered yet."

The side of my mouth pulls down. It's always a little rough landing by the mountains, but I didn't think it was that bad.

"You should've told me," I say quietly.

Val lifts a shoulder. "It's not that bad. But alcohol just doesn't sound good quite yet."

"Found some in the pantry," Payton chimes in from across the kitchen, green can in hand. "If you don't mind drinking it on ice."

"That'd be great, thanks," Val replies.

I rub my hand up and down her spine. "You need something else, too? Pills or something?" I offer, though I'm not sure what you take for a stomachache.

My wife looks up at me, biting her lip and shaking her head.

"Just let me know," I tell her before I press a kiss to the top of her head.

Savannah is standing across from us, grinning.

"What?" Val asks.

"Nothing. Just enjoying how cute you two are together."

"Oh my god, shut up." Val shakes her head.

"Will not." Savannah takes the glass of wine Payton hands her. "And if you don't want to talk about him calling you *Angel*, then let's talk about those tattoos."

Val crosses her arms, and my urge to smile withers a little. I'm not sure I want to talk about that either.

I chance a look at King and find his narrowed eyes on me.

Pretty sure telling them I drugged Valentine and tattooed her against her will is not going to end well for me.

The sound of a vehicle pulling up to the house breaks our stare off.

"Who—" King starts, but I cut him off.

"It's for me." I step away from the island and stride toward the door.

Of course, King and Nero follow.

I open the front door, and we wait as Rob climbs out of the SUV.

"Who's that?" Nero asks as he tries to slip his hand into my pocket to grab my brass knuckles.

I knock his hand away. "Rob, my second. Now quit trying to grab my nuts."

King gives us a look.

When neither of them steps back, I'm forced to be the one to move if I want to let Rob into the house. But then Nero and King slide so they're shoulder to shoulder, blocking Rob anyway.

I sigh. "Would you just let him in?"

"You're not staying," King tells Rob.

Rob gives him a bored look. "Not planning on it."

"What's in your pockets?" Nero asks him.

"Get your own fucking brass knuckles, man." I shake my head. "They aren't that hard to find."

Nero, god of the underworld, frowns in disappointment before he finally moves.

Rob lifts a brow at me in a *what the fuck* sort of way. And I shake my head in a *these two are fucking weird* way.

It's not really necessary for Rob to come inside, but it's cold out. And I want to prove a point.

If I'm in The Alliance, so are my men.

"Got 'em?" I ask, holding out my hand.

Rob nods and takes a velvet bag out of his coat pocket.

Ever curious, the women head our way with their drinks in hand.

"Who are you?" Aspen is the first to speak, and her tone is definitely interested.

King points a finger at his sister. "No."

She ignores him, stepping past King to hold her hand out. "I'm Aspen."

Rob gives her one of his bright smiles as he takes her hand. "I know. I'm Rob."

"And I killed her last husband," King adds. "At her request."

Aspen lifts a shoulder, hand still in Rob's. "It's true."

"Hot." Rob's smile doesn't fade as he lifts Aspen's hand to his mouth and kisses the back of it.

King steps forward. "No. Get the fuck out. This is family only." He grabs Aspen's arm and pulls it out of Rob's grip.

I click my tongue. "Sorry, Robbie. You heard him—family only."

Rob snorts. "Have a nice group hug later." Then he turns his gaze to King's sister. "Sweet dreams, Aspen."

King crowds Rob back out through the door, slamming it behind him.

"You're so ridiculous." Aspen shakes her head.

"You two making eyes at each other is ridiculous."

"Okay, grandpa." She takes a sip of her wine.

"What's in the bag?" Val asks, having made her way back to my side.

"Gifts." I gesture with my open hand. "Ladies, if you will."
They all look at me a little funny, then finally, Savannah, Aspen, and Payton stand next to each other in front of me. "You, too," I tell Val, and she joins the row.

I can already see Nero grinding his teeth, and I can't wait to give his wife something worth more than a car.

"Hands out, please," I request.

"There aren't worms in there or something like that, right?" Payton asks.

"Worms?" Savannah makes a face. "Ew."

"Not sure what your Christmases are usually like but..." I shake the bag, and the sound is faint, but clearly the items inside are hard. "Not worms."

Valentine holds her hand out first, and the others follow.

"That's my girl." I wink at her, enjoying the way her cheeks turn pink.

I decide there's no point in asking them to close their eyes, so I reach in and pull out the first of four identical items.

I lay the first diamond tennis bracelet in Savannah's hand. Then in Aspen's. Then in Payton's. And last, I hold out the final bracelet for Valentine, gripping the open ends, and clasp it around her wrist.

"Dominic," Val breathes, staring down at the glittering stones.

"Are those really real?" Nero is leaning over Payton's shoulder, looking at the bracelet as his wife holds it up to catch the light.

My face scrunches. "Dude."

"Just asking," he says, like I'm the one in the wrong.

"What is this for?" Savannah asks as she touches the diamonds.

"It's tradition," I tell her as I pull Val back into my side. "All the women in my family have them. And now, through Val, you're all part of my family." I gesture to the four women.

My wife. Nero's wife. King's wife. King's sister.

The women of The Alliance.

"Not sure how to feel about you buying my wife jewelry,"

King mumbles, but Savannah thanks me before making him help her put it on.

Val steps over to help Aspen, and Nero looks ready to slit my throat while he fastens the bracelet on his wife's wrist.

When Valentine turns back to me, and I see she's blinking, I hold my arms out.

She walks into my body, wrapping her arms around me in a hug.

"Thanks, Big Guy. That was really nice."

Hearing her use that name, I squeeze her tighter against me.

"You're welcome, Shorty." I rest my cheek against the top of her head.

Her hands grab hold of the back of my shirt. "I'm sorry about the ring."

Her voice is quiet, so I match it. "What ring?" I know she's still wearing the one my mom gave her. And even though I love seeing it on her, I kind of hate how it covers up one of the *Dominic*s circling her finger.

She leans back so she can look up at me. "The one I, well, threw out the window."

I smirk. "Oh, that one."

Val grimaces and nods. "I'm not sure I'd do it differently, but it was really pretty. And I do feel a little bad."

"There's a reason I didn't ask my mom for the family ring," I tell her honestly.

She lifts a brow, and I'm glad to see she's not on the verge of crying anymore. "You knew I'd throw it out of a moving vehicle?"

"Maybe not that exactly. But I did figure the chances were high you'd do something to it. After... Ya know."

Thankfully the light expression stays on her face. "You did deserve it."

I smirk at her. "A little bit."

She slides her hands down and around until she grabs my hips, holding herself steady as she looks up at me. "Since you're so clever, tell me that wasn't a real diamond in that ring."

"What's with everyone asking about them being real?" I look past Val and find everyone staring at us, clearly listening to every word we've said. "The diamonds are real, alright." I tell the room. "They're mine. And they're fucking good."

Val reaches up and slaps her hand against my chest. "That was huge!" When I grin, she smacks me again. Lightly. "The diamond, idiot."

"Yeah, well, toss it or not, I'm not going to give my wife a fake diamond when I'm a fucking diamond importer."

King hums and nods. "Good investment."

The money guy approves, so that's good, I guess.

Nero still has his chin on his wife's shoulder, reaching around to hold her arm up while he continues to inspect the bracelet. "You ever added diamonds to a pair of knuckles?"

"Jesus Christ, man." I shake my head. "Do you want me to order you a fucking set?"

Nero looks up. "Yeah."

I almost laugh. "You want it fucking sparkly?"

"Bet they break skin nicely."

I take a moment to consider it and have to agree.

CHAPTER 71

Val

"HE'S OVERWORKING IT." DOMINIC SHAKES HIS HEAD and takes another sip of beer.

"How do you know that? Have you seen this episode before?" King asks Dom from his spot on the couch between Savannah and Aspen.

Dom gestures to the television. "First, I have *not* seen this episode. Second, any half-rate baker can see he's about to over-work that dough. It's gonna be like rubber when he's done."

I can't stop my snicker over how disgusted Dominic sounds.

My laugh makes the arm he has around my waist tighten.

After what turned out to be a rather pleasant dinner, we moved to the living room to watch a marathon of *Second Bite* holiday episodes.

I think we were all surprised when Aspen, of all people, demanded that we watch the televised baking competition. But apparently, it's her favorite show. She claims it helps her relax.

"How do you know this shit?" King can't seem to let this go. And the way his jaw goes tight every time he looks this way, it doesn't seem like he can let go of me sitting on Dominic's lap either.

381

"I know it because I'm not a caveman," Dom replies. "How do you not know this shit?"

Nero shoves a handful of popcorn into his mouth, looking back and forth between the guys before he tips his head to Dom. "Kitchen is fully stocked if you want to prove yourself, Chicago. Make me some cookies."

"Nah." Dom runs a hand up my arm. "I'm good where I am."

I settle back even farther and rest my head against Dominic's shoulder.

I've never seen Dominic bake. I don't think I've even seen him cook beyond heating up leftovers. But every time I've been around his mom, she's brought up something or another about baking. So I'm guessing he gets his expertise from her.

The contestant Dominic was talking about is now shaking his head, and when the good-looking male host comes over to ask what's wrong, the guy says he has to start his dough over because he ruined it.

"Told ya," Dominic says to no one in particular before he lowers his head to talk just to me. "You feeling okay?"

I nod and shift my arms until I'm hugging the arm he has around me.

I feel a little bad about making him, and everyone else, think I wasn't feeling well.

But it's not like it was a total lie. Ever since I saw that damn pregnancy test this morning and realized I was late, I can't get it out of my head that I might be. And on the slight possibility that I am, I can't drink.

And then, on top of that, I feel like maybe I'm crazy because there's a part of me—a rather large part of me—that's excited at the prospect.

But what sort of lunatic would be excited about having a baby with a guy she practically just met, who lied and tricked her into a marriage?

My mind clings to the word tricked, and I wonder...

Then I brush away the thought.

It's not like Dom would have a way to screw up my pills. Unless he's been feeding me antibiotics without my knowledge. But I don't know how he'd manage that. Plus, he promised not to drug me again. And that seems like it would count as drugging.

I take a deep, slow breath.

There's no point in stressing about babies and what-ifs tonight. Tonight is for relaxation.

Dom shifts around me. "Want to go to bed?"

I shake my head. "Not yet. I'm comfortable."

Dom accepts this and settles back to watch the baking drama unfold.

When we first got here and Dom punched King, I about had a heart attack.

I know them both well enough that I was certain neither would back down until the other was dead. And then when Dominic started talking and I realized he was attacking King because of me—*for me*—the tears just started.

Because no one has ever stood up for me like that.

And hearing King apologize. And then Aspen. And seeing Savannah's tears...

I didn't know how much I needed that.

I thought the past was something that I just had to get over, that I was stuck dealing with. But Dominic... He's only known me, truly known me, for a couple of months. And in ten minutes, and with a few punches, he was able to lift a lifetime of weight off my shoulders.

It shouldn't have worked. And having those simple apologies shouldn't have made such a difference to me. But they did. Because I could tell they meant it. And I could see the self-loathing written all over King's face when Dominic laid it out.

I know they never meant to hurt me. I can't even imagine what it was like for them, finding out you have some much younger half sister, a product of an affair. So really, the fact that we're friendly at all is probably a miracle.

I nuzzle my cheek against Dom.

This man.

He's done plenty wrong. But he's also done so much right. He's made such a difference in my life already.

And ready or not, I think I'm in love with him.

I squeeze his arm tighter, and the movement causes my new diamond bracelet to catch in the light.

A freaking diamond importer. Why am I not even surprised?

I reach up and touch my tiny heart earrings.

"You know..." I tip my head back so I can look at my husband. "I could use some earrings to match my new bracelet."

SOMETHING JOSTLES ME, AND I GROAN.

The body against mine vibrates. "Keep sleeping, Angel. I'm just bringing us to bed."

I feel myself being lifted into the air and blink my eyes open. "Dominic?"

I don't know why I say his name. There's no one else that would hold me like this, carrying me like a bride through the dark living room.

"Yeah, it's me, Valentine."

"I love when you say my full name."

"I love saying it." Lips press against my forehead.

"I can walk," I mumble.

"I know you can." Dominic's words rumble through me. "But I want to hold you."

So I let him.

And it's the last thing I remember.

CHAPTER 72
Dom

NERO HOLDS HIS HAND OUT TO SHAKE. IT'S AN OLIVE branch. An acceptance.

And I want it.

But I also love fucking with him.

So I take it but then use my hold to pull him into a hug.

Nero stiffens.

"Thanks for inviting us," I say, patting his back.

He tries to shove me off. "King invited you, not me."

Payton steps up next to us, and I start to let him go. "Alright, alright, ya big baby. Gotta hug your wife goodbye, anyway."

Nero tries to get a jab to my kidney, but I'm expecting it, so I manage to get out of the way just in time.

I tsk. "Hit me and you won't get your blinged-out knuckles." Nero's jaw works. "And don't worry, I'll order it in a lady's size so it fits."

"I take it back." He stares at me with his black eyes. "I don't like you."

His little wife elbows him in the side, and he drapes his arm over her shoulder.

King approaches, Savannah already tucked under his arm. "Appreciate you making the trip."

385

"It was our pleasure."

Valentine finishes tying the belt on her jacket, having already done her goodbye hugs. "If you guys want to shell out a fortune to rent this place again, we'll gladly come back." She smiles. "And maybe next time I'll stay awake for it."

Savannah grins. "I'm sure we can arrange something." Then she turns her smile on me. "Thank you again for the beautiful bracelet."

Payton gives her thanks as well.

Val bites her lip. "I feel bad leaving without saying goodbye to Aspen."

Savannah snorts. "Serves her right for getting up to go on a run or whatever the hell she's doing."

Valentine nods, but I can tell she doesn't want to leave without seeing her sister.

I hear Rob pulling up the driveway, so I glance out the window next to the door, watching him drive through the fresh coating of snow. And then I grin.

"I'm guessing it wasn't a run." I swing the front door open, and we all watch Aspen climb out of the passenger seat in the same clothes as last night.

Val slaps her hand over her mouth, but it's too late to cover the gasp.

"What the fuck?" King booms.

Rob wisely stays in the driver's seat.

"That's our cue, Mama." I press a hand to Val's back to get her going, then pick up our bags.

"Mama?" King mutters. "What the fuck is wrong with everyone this morning?"

He says more, but we're out of earshot.

Val takes a few hurried steps so she can give Aspen a quick hug as I catch up.

"Enjoy your day," I tell Aspen, and she rolls her eyes at me before striding up to the house.

Valentine's smile is so full of humor when she looks back at me that I have to kiss her.

There's no other choice.

Taking a few long steps, I drop the bags and catch her around the waist.

I dip her back, then capture her mouth with mine.

Val melts into me. Not resisting at all.

And I love it.

Her mouth opens, and I slide my tongue against hers.

I love the way she tastes.

She lets out a small moan, and it makes me regret not sleeping with my cock buried inside her all night.

I love her.

My eyes slowly open.

I love her.

I slide the hand not at her back up around her throat.

I fucking love this woman.

Everything about her.

Every goddamn inch.

Every curve.

Every tear and every whimper.

I love her.

Something cold hits the back of my neck, and I jolt upright.

Looking back, I see King scooping up another handful of snow.

Val sees him and lets out a girly squeal, then darts toward the vehicle.

I walk backward toward the car, and when the second snowball flies for me, I backhand it out of the air, then hold up my middle finger to King and climb into the back seat next to my wife.

But before I can pull her in for another kiss, my phone starts to ring.

And when I answer it, the plans change.

After we drop Val off in Chicago, I'm going to Costa Rica. Because that's where Casey is.

CHAPTER 73

Val

My lips still tingle from Dominic's goodbye kiss as I walk up the stairs toward our bedroom.

I hate that he's gone again. But at least I can do this next part with privacy.

Just breathe.

My feet take me through the bedroom, into the bathroom.

I've already decided that I'm going to do this. Because I need to know. So I don't hesitate. I walk straight to the cabinet next to my sink and open it, taking out the leather bag.

My fingers shake a little as I unzip the top and pull out the slender box.

It's just a moment. One moment in time.

"You can do this," I say, trying to convince myself that I'm not terrified.

I read the instructions on the side of the box. Then I read them three more times.

I've never had to take an at-home test before. I've never had so much as a pregnancy scare before. But now... Well, now I can't imagine having done this before today. Like some of the other broke girls I went to college with, taking these tests in their early twenties. I don't know how they survived the stress. At least I'm more financially secure than I ever could have dreamed of. And I'm with someone I'm pretty sure I'm in love with. And he comes with a big family that would certainly be involved in our child's life.

But even with all that, I'm still terrified.

And even though I want a family more than anything, I don't know if having the baby is the right choice.

It's too soon.

This life is too dangerous.

People are actively trying to kill my husband.

We need round-the-clock security.

And yet...

I rip the box open and take out one of the two sealed tests within.

Reading the box one more time, I set it down and tear open the packaging around the testing stick.

It looks just like it does on TV. Exactly like the picture on the box.

"Just pee on the stick for five seconds. Set the stick on the counter. Wait."

Worried I might accidentally pee on my hand, I decide I don't want to have to deal with pulling my pants back up, so I shove them and my underwear off. Then I walk to the little toilet room with nothing but my shirt on and leave the door open.

I purposefully didn't go to the bathroom after we landed, and now I really have to pee, so even though I'm freaking out, I sit with my legs spread wide and immediately start to go.

And I pee on the stick.

Five seconds feels like forever. But I can't really stop going once I start, so now I'm just sitting here, holding the peed-on test in front of me while I finish.

It's going to be fine.

It will all be fine.

I repeat that mantra to myself as I fumble with the toilet paper one handed and then walk bare assed back to the sink.

I'm careful to set the test away from the edge of the counter so I don't accidentally bump it, then wash my hands. Twice. Then I set my phone alarm for the correct amount of time, according to the test box, and go into the closet.

Dressed in my comfort outfit—sweatpants and Dom's Yale sweatshirt—I pace into the bedroom.

These are the longest minutes I've ever lived. But I can't just stand there and watch the test. I have to wait it out.

I'm turning, ready to pace the other way, when my eye catches on something glittering in the sun.

Is that...?

My breath catches as I move toward the chair in the corner of the room. Because sitting on the seat is the bowl. My bowl. The one I bought at the Christmas market.

It takes me two tries to swallow as I lift it into my hands.

Using my fingertip, I trace the upper lip of the brightly painted bowl, spinning it slowly, feeling the perfectly smooth surface all the way around.

I bite down on my lower lip to keep it from trembling.

The chipped part, the piece I broke when I fell, has been filled. With hundreds of tiny diamonds. And sealed with something clear and smooth. So when you close your eyes, you can't even tell where it is.

I hug the bowl to my chest.

Dominic fixed it for me.

He fixed what was broken and made it better.

I am so fucking in love with this man.

When my phone timer goes off, I set the bowl back where I found it and slowly walk back into the bathroom.

Standing two steps away from the counter, I press my palms to my cheeks.

My stomach is rolling.

My heart is thudding.
And I don't even know what answer I'm hoping for anymore.
I can do this.
I can do anything.
I step closer and look at the test.

CHAPTER 74
Dom

Me: Landed. Make sure you order dinner. And don't leave for anything.

Angel: I won't.

Angel: I mean I won't leave.

Angel: I will order dinner.

Angel: I already did.

Angel: Glad you made it.

Angel: Please be safe.

I SMILE TO MYSELF.

Me: Never change, Valentine.

Me: Morning, Shorty. I won't have great service today. I'll send another number for you to save. It's satellite.

Me: *sends new contact number*

Me: I'll still be able to check my phone occasionally, but call that number if you need something urgent.

Angel: Okay. My work is closed until New Year's, so I'll just be here eating takeout and watching TV. Don't worry about me.

Me: If I can't reach out and touch you, I'll worry about you.

Me: Tell me something good.

Angel: I ordered groceries this morning and have been baking Christmas cookies.

A PAINED SCREAM RIPS THROUGH THE AIR AS I SMILE down at my phone.

Me: I think I need proof of this.

Angel: *sends photo of sink full of dirty mixing bowls*

Me: I want your pretty face in the picture, Angel.

Angel: *sends selfie with her hair up in a bun and a bit of flour on her cheek*

I save the photo to my phone, then save it as my background image.

Me: I'm looking forward to eating your cookie.

Angel: I want you to know how hard I'm rolling my eyes.

I roll onto my back and groan. The mattress in this place is shit.

As I'm reaching for my phone, it buzzes with an incoming text.

> Angel: I miss you.

Warmth floods my heart, and I hold the phone against my chest, letting my eyes close.

I'm ready to go home and be done with this.

> Me: I miss you, too.

> Angel: Happy Christmas Eve.

> Me: I'll be home tomorrow morning. You'll never spend Christmas Day alone again.

> Me: Angel, we're running a little late. I'm sending a car to pick you up so you can meet me at the airport. It's about an hour from home, but it'll put us on the right side of town to head to my mom's house.

My fingers drum on the armrest.

I don't want to go to my mom's for our family Christmas. I want to go straight home and bury myself inside my wife.

But this holiday has only ever been bad for her, and I need to change that.

She never mentioned her early childhood, before her father died. But based on everything she's told me about her mom, I can't imagine she did a real great job of playing Santa to little Valentine.

My Valentine.

I'm going to throw the biggest fucking Valentine's Day party she's ever seen.

And if she's not pregnant by then, I'm going to stuff her so full she'll have fucking twins.

> Angel: Who will all be there?
>
> Angel: I only have one present for your mom.
>
> Angel: And it's not wrapped because your stupid bachelor ass doesn't have wrapping paper.
>
> Angel: And I don't even know if she'll like it.

I grin at her name-calling.

> Me: Valentine.
>
> Me: She just wants us. Leave the gift at home.
>
> Angel: I can't show up empty-handed.
>
> Me: We'll have her over. Now go get dressed. I want you ready with a kiss for me when I land.

CHAPTER 75

Val

I DRUM MY FINGERS ON THE CENTER CONSOLE.

Dominic was supposed to land ten minutes ago, but this snow is slowing him down. And from this spot, parked with the back of the SUV to the back of the airplane hangar, I can't see anything.

Well, other than the two men standing outside the vehicle with visible holsters at their sides.

They both drove me here, but when they parked, they got out and told me to get in the passenger seat. Apparently Dom will be driving us to his mom's house. Guess it figures that all these guys have families they'd like to be with, too.

I fiddle with the edges of my oversized red flannel button-down.

This is my Christmas outfit.

It's not fancy, but I wore it last year when I left the house to go get takeout, and I want to wear it this year and fill it with good memories.

It's stupid.

They're just clothes.

But looking at my light-wash jeans, I second-guess every item I'm wearing.

Dom is going to step off that plane in an all-black suit. And next to him, I'll look like a country bumpkin in my jeans, leather ankle boots, black turtleneck sweater, and my oversized, unbuttoned flannel shirt. My ring and bracelet are the only expensive things on my body.

I close my eyes and inhale slowly.

Last night, I was digging through the boxes I have yet to unpack in our closet, and I came across the suit jacket I kept after my first meeting with Dom. It was no longer bundled up like a baby, and it's been too long, so it didn't smell like him anymore, but I still brought it to bed and slept with it like a security blanket.

I miss him.

I picture Dominic.

Not his fancy clothes. Not his aura of intimidation.

I just picture him. The man. My husband.

His short hair that feels so soft under my palm.

His bright blue eyes that see more than I want them to but exactly what I need them to.

His strong body, capable of so much damage but so unwilling to inflict it on me.

I picture him.

And our future together.

The family we could have one day.

I picture him with me. Years from now.

I picture us. And I smile.

Because he's the future I want. And the future I need.

Grasping the calmness I've been searching for since Dominic left, I open my eyes.

And I see him.

He's striding toward me, the fat snowflakes softening the intensity of his gaze.

And just like that, my body is on fire.

Dom says something to dismiss the men, and they walk away, but my eyes stay on him as he comes around to my door.

He pulls it open. But he doesn't pull me out. He doesn't even undo my seat belt. He just climbs into the vehicle. There is nowhere near enough space for his bulk, but he crams in anyway. Covering my body with his. Gripping my neck in one hand. Grabbing my hip with the other. Slamming his lips against mine.

One of his legs is still outside the car, but it feels like he's touching me everywhere. It feels like he's inside me.

And then his tongue is there, demanding entrance, and I let him in.

I suck him in and moan for more.

He rocks against my leg, and I can feel his hard length straining for more.

"Dominic," I gasp.

"Angel." He kisses me again. "My Valentine." Another kiss. "Wife."

My lips smile against his. "Welcome home, Husband."

He smiles back. "Merry Christmas."

"It's starting to feel like it." I shift my leg.

Dom groans and pulls back. "I want nothing more than to fuck you in the back seat. But I promised myself we'd have a family holiday."

His words hit me right in the center of the chest. "I would like that."

He presses his forehead against mine for one long breath before he climbs back out.

"Alright. Then let's go have a family holiday." His tone is salty, and I can't help my laugh when he slams the door and circles around the hood.

The engine has been running this whole time, keeping the heat on. So Dom just buckles his seat belt, then puts it in drive, and we pull away from the little airport.

"This isn't the same airport we used when we went to Colorado." I point out the obvious as we turn out of the main gates onto the quiet street.

"We keep our locations random, not using the same airport two times in a row. But it's just a precaution. All my flights and planes are registered under real names that have nothing to do with me."

There's a blacked-out SUV that matches ours right in front of us and a pair of those all-black cars about a hundred yards ahead of them.

"Are these guys going to your mom's too?" I gesture out the windshield. "I thought it was just us?"

The airfield stretches out on our right, on my side. And on Dom's side is some sort of industrial complex. Large, low buildings that look unoccupied for the holiday. We must've been the only people at the airport because the roads are empty.

"They'll drive with us there, then break off."

I've gotten so used to having someone drive us around that it feels weird to be alone in a vehicle with Dominic. And I hate that it makes me feel a little nervous to not have extra security on hand. Apparently I've gotten too used to the chauffeured, bodyguard lifestyle.

The brake lights of the two cars illuminate in the snow as they approach a stop sign.

I almost snicker at them stopping. Bunch of law-breaking gangsters stopping for street signs when no one is around.

To hide my smile, I look out my window.

The ground drops down about ten feet into a ditch, and I can see the top curve of a large culvert running beneath the road.

I'm suddenly reminded of a time when I was a kid; I wandered into a small one next to a park, and a toad jumped onto my foot.

It scared the crap out of me, but it's a fun memory. A happy one.

I want more of those.

Bracing myself to talk to Dominic, telling myself to be brave, I turn to my husband.

And our world explodes.

CHAPTER 76

Dom

EVERYTHING ROLLS.

Upside down. Right side up. Upside down.

The crunching glass and bending metal sound quiet. Too quiet. Muted compared to the explosion that went off under the road.

The vehicle stops, the passenger side crunching against the ground a dozen yards away from where we started.

I don't wait.

Don't check for wounds.

I just grip the handle above my driver-side door with my left hand and undo my seat belt with my right while bracing my knee against the center console so I don't crash down on top of Val.

"Valentine!" I shout.

My voice echoes in the small space, and I have to blink to clear my vision.

She's slumped against her door, the muddy ground of the drainage ditch pressed against her window.

Keeping hold of the handle, I swing my legs free and stretch down until I'm standing on her doorframe, my back to the windshield, covering my wife.

"Val!" I shout louder, panic infusing my voice.

And then she moves.

Her hand lifts.

"I-I'm okay," she croaks, but I hear it.

She's not okay.

Only, there's no time to do this right.

"Come on, Angel." It's hard to maneuver in a vehicle tipped on its side, but I manage to crouch down and undo the belt that saved her life. "We gotta move."

My hands reach her shoulders just as the automatic gunfire starts.

The sound of heavy metal slamming into the underside of our SUV peppers the air.

Valentine scrambles up, and I stay crouched over her as she climbs between the seats toward the back.

A round hits the windshield. Followed by a dozen more.

I had enough time to see the vehicle in front of us get totally fucked up in the explosion before we rolled off the road. They're out of the game. And I have no idea what condition the other two cars are in.

And if you don't know, you have to assume they're out.

So it's just me.

Just me and my fucking wife.

I keep my hands on Valentine as I help her climb through the wreckage past the second row of seats.

The windshield spiderwebs behind us.

Bulletproof glass is only good for so many rounds.

It's meant to get you through the shit, not to hunker down in the middle of it.

More gunfire.

I listen for a half a heartbeat. It's not automatic, but a different caliber.

My men.

The return fire will keep the enemy on the front side of our location.

"Right here." I push Valentine into the corner between the

back of the rear seat and the passenger side wall that's against the ground.

She drops down, sitting with her back to the seat.

I kneel in front of her. "I need you to stay right here." Her eyes are wild. Full of tears. "Tell me you will stay right here."

She's nodding, even as she begs me, "Don't go."

I grip her face and kiss her. Hard.

"Call your brother and don't fucking move." I press my phone into her hands and move to the floor of the car, which is vertical on the opposite wall of our confined space.

The trap door is a little bent, but I tear it off, revealing my weapons.

The gun in my holster won't do it against multiple combatants. But this will give us a chance.

CHAPTER 77

Val

DOMINIC PULLS A LONG BLACK GUN FROM THE HIDDEN floor well, followed by a rifle and several clips.

With a pile of weapons and ammo ready, he kicks open the back door, the edge of the large hatch scraping against the ground.

I want to yell for him to stop.

To come back.

But then he's crawling through the opening to the outside. Where the bullets are.

He's crouched just beyond the interior, staying low, keeping his head down.

His eyes flick to mine, then he moves over, out of my view, to the back corner of the downed SUV.

And he unleashes. The sound of bullets leaving his barrel is almost deafening.

I can't lose him.

My fingers fumble with the phone. I don't even remember when I started to cry, but my vision is blurry as I look at the screen, which unlocks with my facial recognition.

I have to try twice before I click on the phone icon.

And I have to try three times to hit the letter K to find KV.

Dominic reaches through the open back to grab a new clip.

I press King's name just as Dom opens fire again.

At the same time, I hear new gunfire from somewhere else outside. And the vehicle I'm sitting in rocks with it.

I press the phone hard against my ear and cover the other ear with my other hand.

"What is happening?" King's voice vibrates against my eardrum; I didn't hear him answer.

"K-King."

"Val!" His voice is more startled than I've ever heard it.

"We need help," I cry. "P-please help."

"Val, where are you?"

I look around. "I don't know. Some a-airport." My breaths are coming shorter. "I don't know."

"It's okay. Val, it's going to be okay." King doesn't sound okay. "I'm tracking your phone now. You called me on Dom's but is your phone there, too?"

I nod because I can't form the right words.

"Fuck," Dom grunts, and he rolls back into the car through the open back door. "We have to move." He grabs the clips that are left and slides them into his pockets. "Can you carry this for me, Shorty?"

He holds out the rifle, and I take it, sliding the phone, King still connected, into my pocket.

"Stay right behind me." Dom brings his face close to mine and grabs my neck, his grip tight, owning. "I love you. Stay right fucking behind me."

He's telling me now?!

A sob traps my response in my throat.

I love you, too.

I want to scream it. But I can hardly breathe.

Dom lets go of me and crawls back through the opening.

I quickly yank off my flannel, not wanting to be a bright red target, and crawl after Dom, rifle in hand.

The noise is even louder out here.

Dom stays crouched, and I stay behind him, right fucking behind him, as he moves around the roof of our SUV.

He must be aiming us toward the half-caved-in culvert.

It's the only place to go.

CHAPTER 78

Dom

IF WE DON'T GET TO THOSE CONCRETE TUNNELS, WE'RE going to die.

And Valentine isn't dying.

Not today. Not fucking today.

Lifting the barrel, I squeeze off another round of shots, keeping the edge of the road above us clear.

We have the low ground.

We have limited ammo.

We have fewer people.

We have—

I turn my head back to Valentine to tell her we're going to sprint the thirty-foot distance, hoping that the other end of the culvert is sealed off from the explosion. But it's not Valentine I see. It's the man rounding the back of the vehicle behind us.

My arm darts around her, and I spin us.

Val's eyes widen up at me, but she's out of the way.

And it's my body that takes the bullet.

I feel it rip through my back. Feel what has to be my rib cracking as it comes to a stop against my bone. At the exact height of Val.

This motherfucker just tried to take my wife out with a head shot.

I push Val to the ground and spin again, unleashing on the man who shot me.

Another bullet hits me. Somewhere in the chest. I feel the instant effect it has on my strength. And it hurts.

But not as much as it should.

I keep the trigger depressed until my clip clicks empty and the man's chest is nothing but mist.

I stagger.

I'm standing too high.

I try to crouch back down, lowering my head out of view from the road. But my muscles don't respond correctly, and my body collapses. First down to my knees, then down onto my hip.

There's a scream.

Val?

I try to turn to see her but just end up slumped, sitting against the roof of the vehicle at my back.

"No, no, no, no." Val is in front of me.

She's crying.

I need to focus.

She's trying to press her hands against me, trying to stop the bleeding.

I grab her wrists. "Valentine." My voice is fucked up, sounds off, but I keep going. "Look at me."

Her eyes are so pretty.

So damn full of life.

"Angel. You need to live."

She shakes her head. "You can't give up."

I hold her hands against the center of my chest.

My vision is starting to blur.

This isn't good.

"I'm sorry."

Val lets out a sob. "You never apologize."

She's the best thing that's ever happened to me.

A coldness starts to creep up my spine, the burning bullet wound in my back going numb.

I knew my time would come.

But not this soon.

I didn't want it to be this soon.

"I'm sorry, Angel. Not for taking you. Never for that." My blink is slow. "For leaving you."

She's against me now. On my lap. Getting as close as she can. "You can't leave me! You promised!"

"I know, Mama." My eyes start to close. I don't want them to. But I can't hold them open anymore. "I know. I'm sorry."

CHAPTER 79
Val

"Dominic!" His hands let go of mine, dropping to his sides. "You can't be sorry," I cry. "You can't go!" I sob. "You need to stay with me." I press one hand to his bleeding chest and one hand to my stomach. "You need to stay with us!"

Dom's head lolls to the side as more blood seeps from his chest, between my fingers.

And the loss rips through my mind.

He's not gone.

He can't be gone.

Not today.

He can't die today, of all days.

A fresh round of gunfire blasts from up the road, where I last saw the cars.

I reach into my front pocket and pull out the black handkerchief with blue lettering and put it between my palm and his body. I don't know why I grabbed this today. I just wanted to have it with me.

Another sob breaks free.

We've come so far.

I press the handkerchief harder against him.

And he's not going to make it.

Without a miracle, he won't make it.

None of us will.

My pocket vibrates.

I'm still practically in Dom's lap, but I reach down and pull it out. King's name on the screen.

He must've hung up and called back.

I answer the call, but I can't stop crying.

"Nine minutes," King tells me. "Val, my men will be there in nine minutes."

The gunfire up the road slows, one side having overwhelmed the other.

And I know what that means.

I know it's not my side that won.

"W-we won't last nine minutes." I admit the awful truth.

"Can you run?"

I focus on King's steady voice and look over my shoulder at the deserted airfield. "No. There's nowhere to go."

And I can't leave Dominic.

Not while his heart still beats.

And not after it stops.

"Do you have a weapon?"

I look down at the gun next to me. "There's a rifle."

"Use it," King commands.

King taught me how to shoot two summers ago. And I was good, but I haven't practiced.

"It's been too long," I choke.

"You know what you're doing, Val. You know how to do this."

"I don't know if I can!"

"You have to!" This time he shouts.

And I know he's right. This is my only chance. Our only chance.

I reach for the gun with my free hand. "If-if I don't make it..."

"Val."

"If I don't make it." Tears stream down my cheeks. "I just need someone to know—"

But I can't say it.

I can't say the words out loud.

Because if I don't make it, neither will they.

"Val," King says, focusing me. "Right now, you aim at everything that moves."

"Okay." My voice is cracking. "Okay. I'm putting the phone down now. Thank you, King."

"Thank me later. Now go kill the bastards who dare to fucking shoot at you. You *are* The Alliance, Val. Show them why."

I set the phone on the ground next to Dominic's thigh and move toward the front end of the SUV.

My eyes close for one breath.

Lean in.

I fill my lungs.

My hands lift the rifle, and I rest the stock against my shoulder.

I pull the bolt back just enough to see that there's a round already in the chamber.

Them or us.

It's them or it's us.

I twist around the front of the vehicle.

A man crests the top of the street, his figure silhouetted with the fluffy snow fall.

I squeeze the trigger.

His face disappears.

Them or fucking us.

Movement to my right draws my barrel.

I exhale and squeeze again. Twice.

Blood sprays from his chest.

One more head.

One more bullet.

Another man down.

I roll back behind the vehicle and stay low as I rush back around, past Dominic and past the dead bad guy, until I'm at the back doors.

A pair of men appear above me, but their attention is on the front of the SUV.

Where I was.

I squeeze the trigger.

The first man falls. Half his neck gone.

The second man drops, but not before I get off one more shot.

I run back around, not daring to stop and check on Dominic.

He's alive.

He has to be alive.

I peek my head around the front of the vehicle and see the pair of men too late.

There's a barrage of gunfire, and I pull back, but not before a round hits the barrel of my gun, jerking it to the side and out of my grip.

It falls to the ground, past the front bumper. Out of my reach.

That last shred of hope I'm clinging to frays.

I can't reach the rifle.

Scrambling, I crawl back to Dominic.

It's been one minute. Maybe two. Not nine.

King's men won't get here in time.

"Just hang on," I whisper to my handsome husband as I shove my hands into his pockets. "Just hang on, okay?"

Except the only clips I can find are for the rifle, and his weapon is out of ammo.

I reach around to Dom's back and find the handgun tucked into his holster.

It won't win against the men coming toward us with assault rifles.

But it might buy us a few more seconds.

A few more seconds together.

I reach up and put just the barrel of the gun over the top of the vehicle and squeeze the trigger.

I space them out, angling the gun a little between each shot. Just enough to keep their heads down, even as they return fire.

But then my gun clicks empty.

And all the gunfire stops.

Because I'm out.

And they know it.

I sink down onto my knees.

I failed us.

The falling snow suddenly thickens, and the blanket of silence is overwhelming.

I shuffle to Dominic's side.

I want to sit in his lap, want to hug him and turn my back on everything. But I can't do that to him.

I'm going to face this.

He's dying because he was protecting me.

It's my turn now.

Picking up the last item from his pocket, I thread my fingers through the heavy metal.

Squeezing my right hand into a fist, I kneel next to my husband and press my left palm against the hole in his chest. And I wait.

Three things I see.

The lowering sun glittering through the snowfall.

Dominic's blood on my hands.

The empty rifle lying in the snow.

Three things I hear.

Ringing in my ears.

King's voice shouting through the phone, somewhere on the ground.

Approaching footsteps.

Three body parts.

My heart cracking in my chest.

My baby, barely formed, in my belly.

And my soul, in the center of my being, wailing over our lost chance at happiness.

"I'm sorry, too, Dominic," I whisper. "I'm so sorry I couldn't save us." I bend to the side and press a soft kiss to his cheek. "And I'm sorry I never told you how much I love you."

A man rounds the front of the bullet-riddled vehicle.

And I straighten, still touching Dominic, still gripping the brass knuckles.

The man's mouth pulls up on the side as he lifts the barrel of his gun.

Our lives are about to end, and he thinks it's amusing.

I lean against Dom.

Together.

And then chaos erupts around me.

More gunfire than before.

The sound is deafening.

So many weapons unloading all at once.

The man in front of me vanishes, his body ripping apart before my eyes.

The noise is so loud.

It's so incredibly loud.

I brace.

Waiting for the pain.

But nothing hits me.

Nothing hits Dom.

I turn my head, craning to see where the shots are coming from.

And I see it.

I see *them*.

A row of people. A whole fucking row of people, walking shoulder to shoulder out of the snow with their weapons raised, aimed over my head.

They keep walking.

Keep walking and keep shooting. And I don't know where they came from.

They materialized from the field, dressed in all-white tactical gear.

And...

I notice the formfitting snow suits. Notice the curves.

They're women.

My mouth drops open.

There are like twenty fucking women raining down hell on the people attacking us.

Maybe more than that.

Their thick knitted face masks hide their facial features. But they're women.

I know they are.

They keep walking nearer.

And they keep shooting.

Reloading as they move.

I can't even tell if anyone is even shooting back at them.

The line moves closer until they're near enough for me to see their eyes through their masks. Then their line parts, and they walk around us and our downed vehicle, never sparing me a look.

But then one person breaks off from the line. And they move toward me. Toward us. Their gun lowered toward the ground.

My shaking fist drops.

As they stop before me, the person pulls their face mask off.

And this one is not a woman. I was too awed to notice how large his build is in comparison to the rest of them.

His dark eyes are kind and calm, so when he tips his head toward Dom, I nod, and he crouches down on the other side of my husband's outstretched legs.

The man pulls a clear bag out of his jacket pocket, and I recognize it as a collection of first aid supplies.

I stay at Dominic's side, keeping my hand in place as I give the man room.

"Let me see." The man finally breaks the silence, and I pull my hand away from Dom's chest. Hesitant to stop pressing on the wound, but more hesitant not to take the help.

The stranger reaches forward and rips Dominic's shirt open, then dumps the contents of the bag onto Dominic's lap.

As he's bent over, tearing open a package, I notice the man has long hair. It's pulled back into a bun, the golden strands partially covered by the collar of his white jacket.

"Who are you?" I whisper.

The man doesn't look up. "Later."

I hear my name, muffled, coming from somewhere, and I realize that all the gunfire has stopped, so I can hear King shouting from Dom's phone again.

Glancing around, I find it next to me on the ground.

One final shot rips through the air.

Okay, now *it's over.*

The man wipes a little cloth over Dom's bullet wound, then follows it with some kind of gauze bandage.

I expect him to press it against the bullet hole, but then he starts jamming it *into* the bullet hole.

"What are you doing?!" I half shriek.

"This is how it's done." He doesn't spare time explaining to me. And I have to trust him.

What other choice do I have?

He shoves more of the gauze into the hole, then wads up the rest of it and presses it against the wound.

"Hold it here."

I do as he says and press down with both hands. The oversized brass knuckles still around the fingers of my right hand.

King's voice sounds from the ground again, and the man reaches across Dom's body and picks up the phone.

He reads the screen before hanging up the call.

But I don't care about the phone call.

Because under my palms, Dom's chest moves.

He's alive.

New tears stream from my eyes.

I want to fall forward onto Dominic.

I want to hug him as hard as I can.

But I don't want to hurt him. And I have a job to do.

The man drops the phone back onto the ground. "Was Dom hit anywhere else?"

"H-his back, I think." I don't know who this stranger is. And I don't care that he knows who Dominic is. I just care that he's helping.

"Keep your hands where they are," he says, then pulls Dom's shoulders forward.

I brace Dom's weight as he leans unconsciously into me, his head hanging down.

The man pulls something out of his pocket and flicks his wrist, flipping open an angry-looking blade.

In seconds, he's sliced through Dom's suit coat and shirt so he can find the entry wound on Dom's back.

Split down the front and back, Dom's destroyed clothing slides down his arms, pooling around his hands.

I hate that his bare skin is exposed to the snow. I don't want him to be cold.

The man grabs another packet of gauze, and I can't see what he's doing, but I think it's the same thing he did to his front, something to stop the bleeding.

I look down, and Dom's slumped body is blocking my view of his chest, but I know what's there.

Too much blood.

Even if his heart is still beating... he's lost too much blood.

The man eases Dom back against the car just as the faint sound of sirens filters through the air.

"We took the liberty of calling an ambulance." His voice is somehow soft and gravelly at the same time.

That tiny, frayed strand of hope twists around itself, making it stronger.

"Thank you." I hold the stranger's gaze. "I can never repay you for this."

The man stands to his full tall height. "Just remember me. That's all I ask."

I don't understand what he means, but I answer with the truth. "I'll never forget you. We're in your debt."

He almost smiles, but then he pulls the white mask back down over his face and jogs around the back of the SUV just as the ambulance lights appear in my vision.

And then he's gone.

And we're the only ones left alive.

"Help is here," I tell Dominic. "We're going to be okay."

But the ambulance stops down at the end of the road, on the far side of the cars. And I realize they can't see us. And there is so much carnage, they won't know where to look.

And Dominic is so pale.

I lean in and press my forehead to his. "You need to lie down, okay?"

Even with the stranger's help, we don't have time.

And I need to get the medics' attention.

Taking my hand off the bundle of gauze, I grip Dominic's shoulders and pull him, tugging, until I get him turned enough so I can lay him on his back. I don't know if this is the right call, but my instincts tell me to do it.

"I'll be right back." I push off the ground, my legs half-numb underneath me. "I'll be right back."

Then, hoping all the bad guys are truly dead, I run away from Dominic. I run away from the cover, out into the open.

Waving my hands in the air, I scream.

I scream for help.

Beg them to see me.

And then they do.

And when two men get out of the ambulance and start to run across the distance, stepping around bodies strewn on the road, I turn and run back to Dominic.

And when they reach us, when the road fills with more men —King's men—I break.

I collapse on the ground next to my husband and break.

CHAPTER 80
Dom

Fuuuuuck.

Every muscle in my body aches.

I try to roll over, hating sleeping on my back, but I can't even lift my arm.

A garbled sound comes out of my throat. My mouth feels too dry.

"Keep it down," a masculine voice says quietly beside me.

I force my eyes to open. The room is dim, but bright enough that I can see the golden-flecked eyes staring down at me.

They're familiar but the wrong ones.

"Where?" I croak.

"You're in the hospital," King tells me, like I'm a fucking moron.

"Where is Val?" My words are barely audible, so I hope he can hear me call him an idiot in my mind.

He tips his head toward me. "She's finally asleep."

Then I feel it. The warm body against my side.

I make my head turn. And there she is. On my left side, her face pressed against my shoulder. Her hair pulled back. Her eyes closed in sleep.

My top half is bare, so everywhere she touches is skin. There's a thin blanket from my waist down, but her thighs are flush against the side of my leg. Like she tried to touch as much of me as possible.

I lift my right arm to reach across and touch her and have to bite down on the groan that tries to break free at the movement.

King's big hand presses my shoulder back down. "Stay still. You got out of surgery like an hour ago."

I don't have the strength to fight against his hold, so I settle for staring at Valentine's beautiful face. "Is she okay?"

"She's fine."

"What time is it?"

"Four a.m.," King tells me. "The hit was about twelve hours ago."

"I'll live?" I ask, assuming that I will but wanting to be sure.

"Seems like it. Just a nicked artery and two cracked ribs—one for each bullet." King shakes his head. "Only took a few stitches and a bathtub full of new blood, but you should be fine."

"And my men?" My gaze follows the slope of Val's nose. Another question I already know the answer to.

"Gone."

My eyes close.

I told my family no one else would die. And now I'm a liar.

There was only one man in each of the vehicles, but that's three more deaths on my back.

"But the crew that hit you..." King pauses. "They're all dead. All fucking twenty-four of them."

My eyes open. *Twenty-four men.* "How?" *How are we even alive at all?*

"Well, from what I heard on the phone, Val took out a handful."

My head jerks back to look at King, making my neck muscles strain. "She did what?"

King sits back in the uncomfortable visitor's chair. "She's a bit

420

of a sharpshooter. Taught her myself." He looks way too smug. "Finally know something about her that you don't. Feels kinda nice."

"Fucker."

"As for the rest..." King shrugs. "No clue who the fuck showed up, but someone did."

"What—" My throat is so scratchy I can't finish the sentence, and I tip my head toward my water on the side table.

We don't make eye contact as King holds up the cup with the long, bendy straw while I carefully take a sip.

"Thanks," I say as I drop my head back against the pillow.

"Don't mention it. Please."

I almost smile at King's dry tone. "So who saved our asses if it wasn't you?"

"We don't know. Val said a man had his crosshairs on her when an army of women appeared out of nowhere and mowed down the entire enemy force."

I blink at him. "Women?"

King gives me a slow nod. "And one man."

I blink again. "Who in the fuck are you talking about?"

"Like I said, not a fucking clue. But the guy apparently field dressed you and saved your stupid ass, and now you owe him a life debt."

I let my eyes close. "Great."

"But we know who's after you."

My head nods. "I know, too."

"And what are we going to do about it?" King asks me.

We.

"We're going to delete them from the history books."

"When?"

I let my lungs fill. "Three days."

"What do you need me to do?"

"I need a plane full of men who are good with their hands."

"We going to them?"

I nod. "We're going to Colombia."

Using the last of my energy, I ignore all my protesting body parts and roll onto my side, wrapping my arm and leg over Valentine, holding her close.

CHAPTER 81

Val

"What else do you need?" I ask Dominic as I pick up the tray with our empty breakfast dishes off the nightstand.

He pats his palm against his bare chest while reclined on the bed. "I need you to finally do as you're told and sit on my face."

I don't smile.

I won't.

I can't encourage this behavior.

"Dominic Gonzalez, you aren't even supposed to be home. It's only been three days since you almost died."

He rubs his fingertips along the black letters spelling my name across his throat.

He's been doing that a lot since we came home from the hospital yesterday.

"Angel, I'm not asking you to suffocate me all the way to death. I just need to taste what's mine." He starts to sit up. "Or you can just lay back and let me fuck you."

I point a finger at him. "You are impossible."

"Impossible to resist."

Snorting, I turn away from him and walk out the door. "Watch me."

"Always a pleasure," he calls after me.

The only good thing about Dominic recovering from surgery is that his diet is currently made up of oatmeal, soup, and crackers, which happens to be the same sort of food that I'm able to eat.

The morning sickness isn't awful, but it's there.

I shift the tray so I can hold it with one hand against my side as I hold the railing with the other hand and make my way downstairs.

King and Savannah flew down while Dom was in emergency surgery and insisted that I get looked over by a doctor as well.

I didn't argue because I knew it would be pointless. Savannah also insisted on staying in the exam room with me, so when the doctor asked if there was a chance I was pregnant and I told him yes, she had to slap a hand over her mouth to keep in her shout. I wasn't sure what emotion she was trying to keep in, but when she lowered her hand, showing me the smile underneath, we both broke down into tears.

And then the doctor tested for himself.

We're still waiting on the official blood test, but the pee test was another positive.

Luckily King didn't ask why we'd both been crying when we came back out. And I made Savannah promise not to tell him until after I'd told Dom.

And I've been meaning to tell him.

I really have.

But I need him to be better first. Because I'm pretty sure he's going to be the most overbearing baby daddy imaginable once he finds out.

I'm setting the wooden tray down next to the kitchen sink when there's a knock on the front door.

"Uh..." I say to the empty room.

We're not expecting anyone to show up at the door.

I stand in the middle of the kitchen, unsure what to do, when Dom's voice echoes down from upstairs. "You can answer it."

"Okay!" I shout back. "Stay in bed."

My feet pad against the floor as I cross the room in my leggings and oversized sweater.

Even though Dominic told me to open the door, I still check the security screen.

I pull the door open. "Hey!" I greet King and Savannah.

Then my eyes widen as Aspen, Payton, and Nero all file into the condo as well.

I smile. "What's going on?"

My smile fades when I see the serious expression on King's face.

"What's going on?" I ask again, my tone dropping.

"The girls are gonna stay here with you," King replies, and I notice the overnight bags in his and Nero's hands.

"And where are you going to be?" I look back and forth between him and Nero.

"We're taking a few boys south. With your husband," Nero answers.

"What?" I look back to King. "You can't take Dominic anywhere. He just got out of the hospital!"

"That's what I said." Savannah crosses her arms.

"And I'll tell Val exactly what I told you." King crosses his arms in return. "This is Dom's call."

"But he can't. It's..." I spin away and hurry across the great room.

He would've told me if he was leaving.

I rush up the stairs, angry with myself.

Of course he wouldn't tell me.

I'm breathing heavily when I step into our bedroom.

And standing before me, buttoning the last button of his black shirt, is Dominic.

"Where are you going?" My voice cracks before I even finish the sentence.

He steps closer to me. "Colombia."

"But you're still hurt. You're supposed to rest." I stretch my arms out toward the bed.

"I'll be careful." His tone is so calm. So steady. And it makes me so mad because I'm panicking.

"Dominic, you c-can't go. Not now. Not with—" I press a hand to my stomach.

He reaches out and cups the side of my face. "I'll come back to you, my Valentine." His thumb strokes my cheek. "The woman I love."

I lift my free hand and press it over his heart as emotion swamps me. He hasn't said it to me since that first time. And I haven't said it to him at all.

"I love you, too." I feel his heartbeat beneath my palm. "So much."

His eyes close, and I watch him inhale as he listens to my words.

Dom opens those beautiful blue eyes and bends down, stopping with his lips an inch away from mine. "Say that again."

Lean in.

I blink, loosening another set of tears. "I'm pregnant."

The room is so quiet I can hear his puffed exhale.

Dom brings his other hand up to hold the other side of my face. "Say that again." Emotion chokes his voice.

"I love you. And we're going to have a baby."

Dom opens his mouth, but he closes it and tips his forehead to mine. "You're the good woman who changed my life."

"Dominic." I say his name like a prayer.

"I'll come back to both of you. I promise."

Both of us.

Just like that.

His acceptance is everything I've ever wanted.

And the thought of losing him now makes fear wrap around my heart. "But you can't go."

His big hands flex against my cheeks. "I have to."

"W-why can't you just make them go?" I plead, not caring that I'm throwing my brother into harm's way.

"Because this is about me. And I won't let it hurt anyone else I love." He pulls back to look me in the eye. "I will come back, Valentine. Because you are my everything."

More tears spill. "But—"

"Will it help if you're mad at me?" he asks, the side of his mouth pulling up the slightest bit.

"I don't want to be mad at you." I sniff.

"Even better." Holding my face still, Dom kisses me softly on the lips. "I'm glad you're pregnant." He lowers one of his hands, sliding it down my body until it's pressing against my belly. "It probably happened the night of your office Christmas party."

"Why that night?" I ask him, not sure how thinking of our sex in the gym would make me mad.

Dom slides the hand on my cheek down until he's holding my neck. "Because that was the first time we made love after I switched out your birth control pills with fakes."

His words take a moment to sink in.

"You..." I blink up at him. "Why would you do that?"

His hand tightens, just a little, around my throat. "Because I wanted to keep you, Angel. And that's exactly what I'm going to do."

Dom leans in for one more kiss. One more press of his lips to mine.

"I'll be home tomorrow," he promises.

And then he's gone.

CHAPTER 82

Dom

THERE'S SOMETHING CALMING ABOUT THE SOUND OF weapons being cleaned. The soft sounds of cloth on blades. The click of bullets filling a clip.

And there's something satisfying about knowing that everyone here is going to spill blood for me. For my family.

I stand, stepping out of my aisle, and move to the front of the plane.

King and Nero are in the front rows beside me, but they stay seated.

"You all know where we're going." I start talking, and everyone stops moving. "You all know the plan." I move my eyes over the guys in front of me, a collection of Gonzalez mafia men and original members of The Alliance. "We're hitting the compound at sunset. Earlier than anyone would expect. And that means they'll have visuals, which is why we're going to be silent. We're going to kill them before they even know they're under attack." I look down at my brother-in-law. "Sorry, King, that means no rocket launchers."

A few men laugh, and King looks at me like he's wondering how I know about that.

I turn back to the men and feel the weight of the blades

attached to my hip. "You have your assignments. And the timing. And we're going to finish this without another casualty on our side. They've taken enough from me. And now I'm going to take everything from them." I nod once, deciding to tell everyone here the *why* of it. "The man at the center of this is my uncle. My grandfather, Daniel Gonzalez, was a low-level man for the Colombian cartel when he was sent to Chicago for a job. But instead of doing that job, he met my grandmother. And, as he always said, a good woman can change your life. So he stayed. He abandoned his position, his shitty family back home, and he stayed. And if my grandma was half the woman my Valentine is, then I understand him completely." A few heads nod, and I know they're the ones with good women in their lives. "But my grandfather had a brother. And when he decided to stay in Chicago, his brother was murdered as a message." I lift a shoulder. "All signs point to his brother being a piece of shit anyway, so I'm not gonna cry over it. But he'd already had a son. Another male in the Gonzalez line. And he grew up to be another piece of shit. A cousin to my own amazing father, but he never cut it. Never made rank in the cartel. And never mattered enough for anyone to end him." My fists clench at my sides. "I met him a decade ago when he invited me to his home. I went. I kept my eyes open. And I told him to go fuck himself when he offered me a partnership that would give me nothing and him everything."

The plane starts to descend, and I spread my feet apart, bracing against the change.

"He said I'd regret it. And the only thing I regret is not killing him right then and there. Because after that, he found money. And now he's using that money to come after me. Some last-ditch attempt to make a name for himself. But he didn't even come after me himself. He hired mercs." Grumbling sounds from the men before me. They know how dishonorable that is. "And I'm pissed. I'm pissed that I didn't put it together sooner. Pissed that I'd written him off. Pissed that my men have paid the ultimate price for my uncle's grab at glory. And I'm pissed that he tried to kill my fucking wife." My jaw flexes and I roll my shoulders back. "And that's why I'll be the one who kills him. Everyone else is fair game. Everyone on that compound works for him and knows the risk. There are no women. No children. It's just a circle jerk of assholes. So they all die. And we all walk out."

King rises to stand beside me. "You heard the man. We all walk out."

Nero stands on my other side and cracks his neck from side to side. "The Alliance just got bigger. And meaner. Let's give the world a little demo."

As the tires beneath us hit the ground, I grin. "Welcome to South America, boys."

"ABOUT FUCKING TIME." MY UNCLE SLIDES HIS WINE glass toward the edge of the table without even looking up from his food. "You trying to kill me with dehydration?"

"That's not how I'm going to kill you."

His head jerks up at my voice.

The room is lit by a gaudy chandelier hanging above the long, heavy wooden table. It's an old-school dining room, closed off from the rest of the house, and set for one.

But it happens to have three entry points. And I took the doorway straight across from my uncle. So I'm the one in his line of sight.

And when he looks at me, I know exactly what he sees.

A man dressed all in black. Tactical vest. Holstered silenced gun. Long-bladed knives strapped to each thigh. Blood dripping from the tips onto the tile floor.

His mouth moves, but nothing comes out.

When I step closer, he tries to lunge for the gun he's carelessly left on the table in front of his plate.

But he doesn't see Nero standing directly behind his chair.

And when my uncle leans forward, Nero swings his arm down in an arc, fingers clenched around his own straight blade, tip down. When his hand reaches the bottom of its trajectory, and Nero's hand swings back toward him, the tip of the knife pierces through my uncle's shoulder, under the clavicle, and slides all the way through until it embeds in the wooden backrest of my uncle's chair.

The pinned man screams.

And I sigh. "No point in screaming, old man. Everyone is dead."

He tries to jerk forward, still going for the gun, but the knife holds him in place.

King steps into the glow of the light from the side entrance. "Nicely done," he tells Nero, nodding to the blade, his own bloody knives at his sides.

Nero smirks. "Learned that trick from you."

"W-what do you want?" my uncle grits between clenched teeth.

"What do I want?" I cock my head. "I should think that's obvious. I want you dead."

"You ungrateful—" he starts.

But I close the distance between us, slamming my palm into the butt of the knife in his shoulder, shoving it deeper.

"You want to talk about ungrateful?" I use my right hand to draw one of my blades free. "I was willing to let you live out your pathetic life down here, unbothered. But not anymore."

I grip the knife in his shoulder with my left hand and jerk it free. It takes effort, especially since I just pushed it deeper, but the singing in my ribs reminds me how close this man came to ruining everything I have.

Sensing what I'm going to do, Nero grabs the back of my uncle's chair and yanks it back from the table, giving us space.

"Gonzalez means Chicago now. You're done." I toss the knife I just pulled out of his shoulder onto his lap.

He curses at me, and Nero cuffs him on the back of the head.

"Pick it up," I snap at my uncle.

His eyes flare, and I can see he's going to be a bitter fuck right until the end.

He grabs the knife and stands, blood soaking through his shirt. "You think you can just walk in here and kill me?"

"Yes."

Instead of coming at me, he lunges toward the gun like the coward he is.

But I lunge, too. And I get there first, my upswing catching him in the chin. The V shape of the jawbone allows my knife to go in smooth, like cutting through cake. And our joining momentum means that the sharp point of my blade easily pierces through the roof of his mouth, sliding up into his brain.

The knife falls from his grip, and his hands weakly grab for me.

"Say hello to your father for me." My bicep flexes, and I shove the knife higher, twisting as I do.

The last of his life flickers from his eyes.

And it's over.

I shove him away as I release my grip, leaving the blade inside his head as he falls to the floor.

Reaching across the table, I pick up his unused napkin and clean some of the blood off my hands.

Nero makes a sound close to a snicker. "Circle jerk of assholes."

King snickers, too.

I roll my eyes. "I can't believe you idiots run The fucking Alliance."

"You went to pretty long lengths to join us." Nero lifts his left hand, flexing his fingers around his stained red diamond-encrusted brass knuckles. "Guess that makes you an idiot, too."

I roll my shoulders and press my hand to the ache in my chest, feeling the strain in my sutures. But I think of Valentine waiting for me at home. I think of her and the baby she's growing in her belly, and smile. "No regrets."

CHAPTER 83

Val

THE SUN IS RISING, FILLING THE PENTHOUSE WITH A soft orange glow, as I climb down the stairs and find the girls in the kitchen.

Aspen is seated at the island next to Savannah while Payton fiddles with the coffee maker.

"Morning." I greet them as I pull out a stool next to Aspen.

"Can't sleep either?" she asks me.

I shake my head. "I know they do stuff like this all the time, but I don't know how you get used to it."

"You don't. Not really," Payton answers, having been married longer than any of us. "Want coffee?"

I shake my head. "No, thanks." I can hear the disappointment in my voice.

"You sure?" Payton asks, probably having heard the same thing.

"I'm sure," I sigh.

"Oh, that's right, you can't," Savannah says casually, but my eyes still widen.

Aspen slowly turns to face me. "What does she mean *you can't?*"

I lean over the counter to look past Aspen at Savannah, who has slapped a hand over her mouth.

"Sorry," she says, her apology muffled by her palm.

"Are you pregnant?" Aspen looks so shocked it almost makes me laugh.

It's too early to really be telling people, but since the cat seems to be out of the bag, I shrug. "Yeah."

Aspen shoves at my shoulder. "And you told Savannah but not me?"

"I didn't mean to!" I defend. "She was with me when the doctor was checking me over. And when he asked if there was a chance I was... I had to tell him the truth."

Savannah grins. "Does this mean I can finally tell King? The secret has been killing me."

I shrug. "Might as well."

"How did this even happen?" Aspen asks.

Savannah snorts. "Well, when a man puts his penis inside you..."

Aspen spins around to shove at Savannah. "Clearly I'm not the one who needs *the birds and the bees* talk."

Savannah lets out a snicker. "Fair point."

"For the record, I don't need the talk either," I tell them, then decide that if I want this group to be my family, I want to be open with them. "Right before the guys left yesterday, I told Dominic I'm pregnant."

Savannah gasps, leaning against the counter to see me. "What did he say?"

"He told me he was happy." I bite my lip. "And he told me he changed out my birth control pills with fakes a few weeks ago."

Aspen shoves my shoulder again. "What?! Why?!"

I try not to smile at her outraged reaction. "Because he wanted to keep me."

Aspen's jaw drops just as Payton lets out an *aww* from the other side of the counter.

Aspen swings her head around to face Payton. "You think that's sweet?"

Payton doesn't look at all embarrassed when she nods her head. "It is."

Aspen guffaws. "It's psychotic."

I huff out a laugh. "You think *that's* psychotic," I mumble before I can think better of it.

Everyone turns to face me, so I hold up my ring finger, the black ink on display. "After I threw my ring out the car window, Dominic drugged me and tattooed his name on me. One time for every man I've been with."

"I knew you wouldn't have done that on your own." Savannah slaps her hand down on the counter. "I've heard finger tattoos fucking hurt."

Instead of the anger I expect to see on Aspen's face, she looks impressed. "Okay, that's kinda hot."

I laugh. "You're just as crazy as the rest of us."

Aspen shrugs and picks up her coffee.

"Wait." Payton tilts her head. "Why did you throw your ring out the window?"

I purse my lips. "Oh, right." This one I don't think I should tell them. "Well..."

Before I'm forced to think of a lie, I hear the front door unlock, and I'm off the stool, hurrying across the floor before the door opens.

"Dominic!" His name comes out as a cry, and my vision is blurring. Because he's here. He's here, and I'm so relieved.

Dominic doesn't even hold the door open for anyone else, just strides through, crashing his body against mine.

"My Angel," he murmurs against my hair as I bury my face in his chest. "My love." His hand strokes down my loose hair. "My Valentine."

"I was so worried." I hug him tighter.

"I'm fine." He kisses the top of my head. "We're all fine." He kisses my forehead. "But I'm tired, Angel. Take me to bed."

Remembering that he's still injured, I pull away.

But Dom doesn't let me get far as he twines his fingers with mine.

As he leads me toward the stairs, I glance around, seeing King and Savannah embraced in the kitchen and Payton sitting on Nero's lap in the living room. As we take the first step up, I see Aspen walking out the front door. With Rob.

But I put them out of my mind because we're at the top of the stairs.

And then we're at the bedroom. And Dominic pushes me through the door and slams it shut behind us.

"Clothes off," he demands as he starts to undress himself.

I do as he says, dropping my shirt on the floor next to his.

I have a flicker of a moment to realize he's in different clothes than he was when he left yesterday and that he must've found a place to shower and change. But then he's shoving his pants down his hips, and I no longer care what he was wearing.

Because he's naked. And he's mine.

The bright white bandage on his chest reminds me how close I came to losing him. And when he turns to climb onto the bed, the white bandage on his back reminds me that he took those bullets to save me.

He risked his life to protect mine.

And that's what matters.

Not how we started.

Not his motivations.

Not any of what happened before.

What matters is what happens now.

What happens next.

Dom settles onto his back. "Climb on top of me, Mama."

I drag my panties off, then move to the foot of the bed to comply.

Except I don't crawl all the way over him. I stop, kneeling between his thighs.

My hand grips the base of his already hard cock. "I know I

should be mad at you. About the pills." I drag my hand up his length, then back down. "But I'm not."

His gaze is hooded as he looks down at me. "Why's that?"

I lower my mouth until it's right over his swollen head. "Because I want to keep you, too, Big Guy. And I've decided to *lean in*." Then I close my lips around him, taking him as deep as I can.

Dominic arches his back with a groan.

I slide back up, licking along the underside of his length. "But if you ever scare me like that again, I'm not having sex with you for a month." I threaten him, then suck him back into my mouth.

He reaches down and gathers my hair away from my face so he can watch me work his length in and out of my mouth.

"Never, Angel. Never again," he promises.

I take him even deeper, and my throat constricts at the intrusion.

He tugs gently on my hair. "Jesus, that's enough. Get the fuck up here so I can fill that sweet pussy."

I let him pop free from my mouth, but before I move, I lower my head and lick across the words inked right above his dick.

"That's right, Mama. Til fucking Death." He drags me up his body. "Now sit on my dick and show me how wet sucking my cock made you."

His hands are still in my hair, and he pulls my mouth down to his, pushing his tongue into my mouth as I lower onto his length, the whole of him sliding into me smoothly, because he's right. I'm so fucking wet.

"God damn," he groans against my lips. "God fucking damn." His hips thrust up to meet mine.

I clench around him.

"Talk to me, Angel. Tell me how you feel," he commands.

"Full," I tell him. Then I push back so I'm sitting up, bracing my hands on his flexing abdomen. I widen my legs, taking him a little deeper. "So full."

He grips my hips, rocking me over him. "That's right, my love. I'm gonna fill you up every fucking day."

He slides one of his hands over my belly. It's already soft. Already round. But he's looking at me like it's perfect. Like I'm all he's ever wanted.

"We're gonna do it like this." His hand makes a gentle circle as his other hand grips my hip tight. "You're gonna bounce on top of me once a week so I can watch this amazing body change. Watch you grow." He slides his hand up to pluck at a nipple. "Gonna watch these glorious tits get even bigger. And you're gonna give me a taste. Aren't you?"

A shudder rolls through my body at the thought of him doing that. At the thought of him sucking on my breasts.

"Jesus." He thrusts his hips. "You like that, don't you? We're gonna have to go back to that little room at the airport. Do it right this time."

"Dominic," I groan. That shouldn't turn me on. But I squeeze around him.

"Fucking perfect." He slides the hand on my hip to the spot between us. The spot I need him most.

As he rubs his fingers across my slippery clit, I groan.

He slides his other hand up to my neck. "Open your mouth, Angel. Stick that pretty tongue out."

I do as he says.

"I won't choke you again. Not until you bring our beautiful baby into the world." His hand flexes, then he slides it higher, sliding his thumb into my mouth. "But I'll fuck you any way you want. I'll fill this sweet mouth. I'll fill every inch of you."

He works his thumb between my legs faster. Harder.

I'm so close. So close to combustion.

My hips rock in an uneven motion. His cock hits me so deep, his fingers rubbing just right.

"Come for me, Valentine. Show me who this body belongs to."

I hollow my cheeks around his finger, sucking him into my mouth as I tip over the edge.

My pussy convulses around his length, and Dom pulls his thumb free so he can grip my hips with both hands and hold me down against him as he explodes inside me.

Every muscle in his body tenses as his cock pulses, filling me with his release.

When I can't take any more, I collapse forward onto him.

Dominic's arms wrap around me. "I don't even remember who I was before I loved you, Mrs. Gonzalez."

I rub my palm over the top of his head. "I don't remember either. I don't want to."

"It doesn't matter." His hold tightens. "Nothing before us matters."

The warmth of happiness and family settles around me.

"My forever," I tell him.

"My always," he agrees.

Epilogue – Dom

I lean back against the cushioned seat, putting my arm behind Valentine, as King hands the stack of menus to the server.

"I can't believe we're leaving tomorrow." Savannah sighs.

"I know," Payton agrees from her seat across from Savannah. "It was fun to spend New Year's down here. We should make Chicago a tradition."

Nero grunts, and I don't know if it's in agreement or annoyance, but I've seen them together enough over the last few days to know he'll do whatever she wants.

Val takes a sip of her root beer and leans into my side.

Since it is our last night all together, we decided to do a dinner out. And when Val requested Thai food, I knew this would be the perfect place.

We're near the back of the dining room, in a large U-shaped booth, with me and Val along the back. Usually, I wouldn't let myself be trapped like this, but with Nero and King on the two outer spots, I'm not worried. Those dickheads can handle whatever might happen.

A different server, this one wearing a full suit, stops at the end of our table, straight across from me, and sets a tray of spring rolls down.

"A gift." His head is tipped down, and his voice is low.

I sit up straighter.

Something is off.

Then the man lifts his head, looking straight at me. "Evening."

"The fuck—" I start to get up, forgetting that I have nowhere to go.

King and Nero snap their gazes to our *server*.

They both start to move, but Hans uses his empty hand to pull his jacket back, showing his other hand tucked under the fabric, holding a live grenade.

A mother fucking grenade.

He takes a small step back, wisely putting himself out of Nero's reach.

I move my arm from behind Val to in front of her. Blocking as much of her as I can from this monster. "What do you want?"

His eyes meet mine. "Just a quick chat."

"Could've called," Nero growls.

Hans shakes his head, his long hair shifting against his shoulders. "This is more of a face-to-face thing."

Val's indrawn breath pulls Hans's gaze to her.

"Don't fucking look at her," I snap.

But it's not Hans who speaks next. It's Valentine.

"It's you," she breathes, then turns to me. "It's him."

"Him who?" King asks, and I notice him trying to inch out of the booth.

Hans holds his jacket open farther, for only our table to see, showing us three more grenades hanging from inside his shirt.

King stills his movement.

"That's the man who saved us." Val tugs on my arm.

All eyes turn to her.

She doesn't look scared of him at all. Doesn't look the least bit nervous that he's covered in explosives.

"What are you talking about?" I ask her.

She points to Hans. "That's the man who treated your bullet wounds. He's the one who saved our lives."

Now all eyes turn to Hans.

He dips his chin to my wife. "It was my pleasure."

"What do you want?" I grit out. If this is true, and I know it is, I owe this man.

And I don't want to owe this man.

"Like I said, I just want a chat." His stance is casual. "It's come to my attention that you're all under the false assumption that I do bad things." He tips his head. "Okay, well, I do some bad things, but only to bad people. I'm not the man you're looking for."

"No?" I ask, because he's right. We all do believe that he's the man behind the new human trafficking ring. Because his name always comes up. "Then who the fuck are you?"

"I'm no one." He takes a step back. "Just a man seeking vengeance."

He takes another step back, lowering his jacket to hide his collection of grenades before he turns and disappears through the kitchen.

Silence reigns over the table until Savannah breaks it. "Uh, who the hell was that?"

I relax against the seat, putting my arm back around Valentine's shoulders. "Apparently, no one." Then I point to the plate of spring rolls Hans left on the table. "Someone pass that here. My wife is eating for two, and I mean to feed her."

HANS

ALLIANCE BOOK FOUR

About the Author

Like all her books, S.J. Tilly resides in the glorious state of Minnesota, where she was born and raised. To avoid the freezing cold winters, S.J. enjoys burying her head in books, whether to read them or write them or listen to them.

When she's not busy writing her contemporary smut, she can be found lounging with her husband and their herd of rescue boxers. And when the weather permits, she loves putting her compost to use in the garden, pretending to know what she's doing. The neighbors may not like the flowery mayhem of her yard but the bees sure do. And really, that's more important.

To stay up to date on all things Tilly, make sure to follow her on her socials, and interact whenever you feel like it!

Don't forget to sign up for the newsletter https://sjtilly.com/newsletter

Links to everything on her website www.sjtilly.com

Acknowledgments

As always, I gotta start out by thanking my mom for all of her help as my alpha reader and beta reader, help with edits, constant support, constant *are you writing yet* message, and overall awesomeness. I appreciate everything you do. And I really appreciate being able to still shock you.

Thank you to Kerissa, the best PA a chaos-brained girl could ask for. The best beta reader. And the best damn friend. You are such a good girl.

Thank you, G. Marie (go check out her books), for being all-in on the dark romance train with me.

Thank you, Ali, for your undying support and love and for the outstanding number of times you've already read Dom.

Thank you, Elaine and S.L., for all the sprints and encouragement.

Thank you, Mr. Tilly, for making me so many dinners and listening to me tell you every detail of this, and every other, book. And thank you for your help in formatting and sticker design and anything else that has to do with computers.

Thank you, Lori, my absolutely amazing cover designer. Every book is just as amazing as the last.

Thank you, Wander Photography, your photos are so goddamn hot.

Thank you to my editors, Jeanine and Beth, for making me look smarter than I am.

Thank you, Nikki, for your kickass palettes and even more amazing friendship.

Thank you to the rest of my family for always recommending my smutty books to your friends.

Huge thank you to my ARC team. You guys are the freaking best, and with every release, I get more and more blown away with the love and support you give me.

Thank you, Sam and The Smuthood, for being so wonderful and supportive.

Thank you to all the other mafia romance authors that I binged in years past. I didn't plan to write dark romance, or The Alliance Series, but now that I'm here...

Thank you, Mikayla, for being a force of nature and for enjoying my book mail so much.

Extra special thank you to all of my BeanBaggers. Having a safe space to go online that's filled with nothing but love and excitement means the world to me.

Thank you to all my friends on Bookstagram, BookTok, and Facebook. With each book, I make new friends, and this list is now too long to name everyone individually. But I hope you know who you are, and I appreciate you and your content so much.

My brain is basically mush at this point, so for those I forgot to name, allow me to apologize.

Last, thank you to Nero and King. You guys made The Alliance real. And fucking wonderful.

And if you've read all the way to this sentence, thank you for your dedication. If you aren't already following me online, the time is now. Links for everything on my website, sjtilly.com, and make sure to sign up for my newsletter to get cover reveals and blurbs a day before everyone else!

Books By This Author

Alliance Series

Dark Mafia Romance

NERO

Payton

Running away from home at 17 wasn't easy. Let's face it though, nothing before, or in the ten years since, has ever been easy for me.

And I'm doing okay. Sorta. I just need to keep scraping by, living under the radar. Staying out of people's way, off people's minds.

So when a man walks through my open patio door, stepping boldly into my home and my life, I should be scared. Frightened. Terrified.

But I must be more broken than I realized, because I'm none of those things.

I'm intrigued.

And I'm wondering if the way to take control of my life is by giving in to him.

Nero

The first time I took a man's life, I knew there'd be no going back. No normal existence in the cards for me.

So instead of walking away, I climbed a mountain of bodies and created my own destiny. By forming The Alliance.

And I was fine with that. Content enough to carry on.

Until I stepped through those open doors and into her life.

I should've walked away. Should've gone right back out the door I came through. But I didn't.

And now her life is in danger.

But that's the thing about being a bad man. I'll happily paint the streets red to protect what's mine.

And Payton is mine. Whether she knows it or not.

KING

Okay, so, my bad for assuming the guy I was going on a date with *wasn't* married. And my bad for taking him to a friend's house for dinner, only to find out my friend is also friends with *his* wife. Because, in fact, he *is* married. And she happens to be at my friend's house because her husband was *busy working*.

Confused? So am I.

Unsurprisingly, my date's

wife is super angry about finding out that her husband is a cheating asshole.

Girl, I get it.

Then, to make matters

more convoluted, there is the man sitting next to my date's wife. A man named

King, who is apparently her brother, and who lives up to his name.

And since my *date*

is a two-timing prick, I'm not going to feel bad about drooling over King,

especially since I'll never see him again.

Or at least I don't plan to.

I plan to take an Uber to

the cheater's apartment to get my car keys.

I plan for it to be quick.

And if I had to list a

thousand possible outcomes... witnessing my date's murder, being kidnapped by his killer, and then being forced to marry the super attractive but clearly deranged crime lord, would not have been on my Bingo card.

But alas, here I am.

DOM

VAL

When I was nine, I went to my first funeral. Along with accepting my father's death, I had to accept new and awful truths I wasn't prepared for.

When I was nineteen, I went to my mother's funeral. We weren't close, but with her gone, I became more alone than ever before.

Sure, I have a half brother who runs The Alliance. And yeah, he's given me his protection — in the form of a bodyguard and chauffeur. But I don't have anyone that really knows me. No one to really love me.

Until I meet him. The man in the airport.

And when one chance meeting turns into something hotter, something more serious, I let myself believe that maybe he's the one. Maybe this man is the one who will finally save me from my loneliness. The one to give me the family I've always craved.

DOM

The Mafia is in my blood. It's what I do.

So when that blood is spilled and one funeral turns into three, drastic measures need to be taken.

And when this battle turns into a war, I'm going to need more men. More power.

I'm going to need The Alliance.

And I'll become a member. By any means necessary.

Sin Series

Romantic Suspense

Mr. Sin

I should have run the other way. Paid my tab and gone back to my room. But he was there. And he was... everything. I figured what's the harm in letting passion rule my decisions for one night? So what if he looks like the Devil in a suit. I'd be leaving in the morning. Flying home, back to my pleasant but predictable life. I'd never see him again.

Except I do. In the last place I expected. And now everything I've worked so hard for is in jeopardy.

We can't stop what we've started, but this is bigger than the two of us.

And when his past comes back to haunt him, love might not be enough to save me.

Sin Too

Beth

It started with tragedy.

And secrets.

Hidden truths that refused to stay buried have come out to chase me. Now I'm on the run, living under a blanket of constant fear, pretending to be someone I'm not. And if I'm not really me, how am I supposed to know what's real?

Angelo

Watch the girl.

It was supposed to be a simple assignment. But like everything else in this family, there's nothing simple about it. Not my task. Not her fake name. And not my feelings for her.

But Beth is mine now.

So when the monsters from her past come out to play, they'll have to get through me first.

Miss Sin

I'm so sick of watching the world spin by. Of letting people think I'm plain and boring, too afraid to just be myself.

Then I see *him*.

John.

He's strength and fury, and unapologetic.

He's everything I want. And everything I wish I was.

He won't want me, but that doesn't matter. The sight of him is all the inspiration I need to finally shatter this glass house I've built around myself.

Only he does want me. And when our worlds collide, details we can't see become tangled, twisting together, ensnaring us in an invisible trap.

When it all goes wrong, I don't know if I'll be able to break free of the chains binding us, or if I'll suffocate in the process.

Sleet Series

Hockey Romantic Comedy

Sleet Kitten

There are a few things that life doesn't prepare you for. Like what to do when a super-hot guy catches you sneaking around in his basement. Or what to do when a mysterious package shows up with tickets to a hockey game, because apparently, he's a professional athlete. Or how to handle it when you get to the game and realize he's freaking famous since half of the 20,000 people in the stands are wearing his jersey.

I thought I was a well-adjusted adult, reasonably prepared for life. But one date with Jackson Wilder, a viral video, and a "I didn't know she was your mom" incident, and I'm suddenly questioning everything I thought I knew.

But he's fun. And great. And I think I might be falling for him. But I don't know if he's falling for me too, or if he's as much of a player off the ice as on.

Sleet Sugar

My friends have convinced me. No more hockey players.

With a dad who is the head coach for the Minnesota Sleet, it seemed like an easy decision.

My friends have also convinced me that the best way to boost my fragile self-esteem is through a one-night stand.

A dating app. A hotel bar. A sexy-as-hell man, who's sweet, and funny, and did I mention, sexy-as-hell... I fortified my courage and invited myself up to his room.

Assumptions. There's a rule about them.

I assumed he was passing through town. I assumed he was a businessman, or maybe an investor, or accountant, or literally anything other than a professional hockey player. I assumed I'd never see him again.

I assumed wrong.

Sleet Banshee

Mother-freaking hockey players. My friends found their happily-ever-afters with a couple of sweet, doting, over-the-top in-love athletes. They got nicknames like *Kitten* and *Sugar*. But me? I got stuck with a dickhead who riles me up on purpose and calls me *Banshee*. Yeah, he might have a voice made specifically for wet dreams. And he might have a body and face carved by the gods. And he might have a level of Alpha-hole that gets me all hot and bothered.

But when he presses my buttons, he presses ALL of my buttons. And I'm not the type of girl who takes things sitting down. And I only got caught on my knees that one time. In the museum.

But when one of my decisions gets one of my friends hurt... I can't stop blaming myself. And him.

Except he can't take a hint. And I can't keep my panties on.

Darling Series

Contemporary Small Town Romance

Smoky Darling

Elouise

I fell in love with Beckett when I was seven.

He broke my heart when I was fifteen.

When I was eighteen, I promised myself I'd forget about him.

And I did. For a dozen years.

But now he's back home. Here. In Darling Lake. And I don't know if I should give in to the temptation swirling between us or run the other way.

Beckett

She had a crush on me when she was a kid. But she was my brother's best friend's little sister. I didn't see her like that. And even if I had, she was too young. Our age difference was too great.

But now I'm back home. And she's here. And she's all the way grown up.

It wouldn't have worked back then. But I'll be damned if I won't get a taste of her now.

Latte Darling

I have a nice life—living in my hometown, owning the coffee shop I've worked at since I was 16.

It's comfortable.

On paper.

But I'm tired of doing everything by myself. Tired of being in charge of every decision in my life.

I want someone to lean on. Someone to spend time with. Sit with. Hug.

And I really don't want to go to my best friend's wedding alone.

So, I signed up for a dating app and agreed to meet with the first guy that messaged me.

And now here I am, at the bar.

Only it's not my date that just sat down in the chair across from me. It's his dad.

And holy hell, he's the definition of Silver Fox. If a Silver Fox can be thick as a house, have piercing blue eyes and tattoos from his neck down to his fingertips.

He's giving me Big Bad Wolf vibes. Only instead of running, I'm blushing. And he looks like he might just want to eat me whole.

Tilly World Holiday Novellas

Second Bite

When a holiday baking competition goes incredibly wrong. Or right...

Michael -

I'm starting to think I've been doing this for too long. The screaming fans. The constant media attention. The fat paychecks. None of it brings me the happiness I yearn for.

Yet here I am. Another year. Another holiday special. Another Christmas spent alone in a hotel room.

But then the lights go up. And I see *her.*

Alice -

It's an honor to be a contestant, I know that. But right now, it feels a little like punishment. Because any second, Chef Michael Kesso, the man I've been in love with for years, the man who doesn't even know I exist, is going to walk onto the set, and it will be a miracle if I don't pass out at the sight of him.

But the time for doubts is over. Because Second Bite is about to start - "in three... two... one..."

Made in the USA
Coppell, TX
22 January 2024

27913293R10262